LADY OF THE STAR WIND

VERONICA SCOTT

Cover Art by Fiona Jayde

To my daughters Valerie and Elizabeth, my best friend Daniel and my brother David for all their encouragement and support through the years

ACKNOWLEDGMENTS

Julie C and the E-book Formatting Fairies!

Joyce L

LADY OF THE STAR WIND

BY
VERONICA SCOTT

CHAPTER ONE

Anything could happen on the wide-open world of Freemarket. Mark Denaltieri *could* fulfill his employer's expectations and rescue Princess Alessandra from her kidnapper. Not that it would be a long-term rescue, since he was also being paid to deliver her into the hands of people she hated. A real "out of the supernova into the black hole" situation. He'd walk away with more credits in his account than most people accumulated in a lifetime.

And Alessandra would be lost to him.

Again.

Was that the outcome he truly desired? Despite his cool head's best arguments, his sentimental heart pushed him to accomplish a genuine rescue of his former lover, setting her free.

The great house across the street from his hiding place blazed with lights, as it did every night. Alessandra's kidnapper kept late hours. Surveying the mansion and its occupants from all angles, in many guises, had chewed up the better part of two weeks. One of his bribes got him a temp job as a deliveryman's helper, and he'd gone inside the house. He'd also been on the grounds at night, testing the defenses indicated on plans obtained through another bribe. Grand Duke Portuc apparently had untested faith in standard household safeguards, bolstered by expensive bodyguards. Accustomed to defeating the defense perimeters of alien races, Mark anticipated no trouble disarming a low-end commercial system.

In the whole time he'd spent setting up for tonight's extraction, he'd seen the Imperial Princess Alessandra Alishia Zhivanov once.

The brief glance had seared like a blaster burn to the heart. Seeing her had shaken his self-control more than he'd expected. What had happened to locking emotion and memory safely away? She'd matured into a beautiful woman, but he'd seen traces of the girl to whom he'd once sworn eternal devotion. That was the crack in his mental armor.

Frequenting low-end bars, he'd eavesdropped on servants' gossip, confirming she stayed a virtual prisoner in her room, under heavy guard.

As Mark reviewed his plans a final time, his attention was drawn to a flurry of unusual activity on the quiet, dead-end street. Cruising lights off, five hulking black groundcars glided to the Portuc house. The convoy parked, the last vehicle in line swinging to block off the street.

Tzerde. Mark swore under his breath. Why tonight, of all nights, did the household's routine have to change? He debated whether to stand down, maybe reschedule to tomorrow. Freemarket's moons would still be thin crescents shedding scant light.

Guardsmen, wearing a crowned-lion-and-snake household crest he recognized, even after all these years in exile, disembarked from the groundcars.

Barent Kliin. Even as Mark thought the name, the man himself stepped from the third car in the cavalcade. Memories rushed into his mind's eye. Gritting his teeth, he shoved the images into the recesses of his mind. That life ended a long time ago. He didn't need the distraction.

Attitude disdainful, Kliin eyed the house for a moment. Making no effort to keep his voice down, the Outlier noble said, "Trust Portuc to rent something grandiose like this." As his companion nodded sycophantic agreement, Barent tugged at the black glove on one hand. "Let's get this errand done."

The squad of guards deployed along the street with military precision. The Kliin contingent had been supplemented by an assortment of the local for-hire talent, easily distinguished by their motley garb and sloppy movements. Five Kliin ascended the stairs behind Barent and his lieutenant.

Seeing Kliin convinced Mark he'd run out of time. The extraction had to be done tonight. Kliin wasn't here on a social call, and his presence at the house where Alessandra was held was unlikely to be coincidence. Slipping from his perch, Mark slunk through the underbrush to a spot halfway down the street, behind the last man on the perimeter. It was a moment's work to choke the guard into unconsciousness and drag him out of sight. Mark donned his victim's coat and night-vision helmet. He took a moment to hide his service blaster at his back, where the coat hid it nicely. Buckling on the man's weapons belt with its less than impressive civilian blaster took another few seconds before he stepped onto the street, marching toward the house as if under some urgent order.

He passed two Kliin guardsmen with no problem, striding past the car blocking the street, happy to hear the motor idling. The driver, a local, was taking it easy, leaning back in his seat, listening to music, and watching a miniature hologram do a striptease.

Visor lowered, Mark climbed the stairs to the house unchallenged. Saluting crisply, he passed the two men posted outside the door and entered the ornately decorated foyer. Voices filtered from the dining room, located across the entry.

Crossing to the dining room doors, he stood at parade rest, facing the entry, eavesdropping.

Over the years, countless dialects and alien languages had been hypno implanted in his brain for clandestine missions, but he'd never forgotten Outlier, his mother tongue. Listening to the ebb and flow of the argument, he had no trouble following the nuances, nor identifying the speakers, despite not having heard their voices for two decades.

Staring at his distorted reflection in the gleaming parquet flooring, he assessed and discarded contingency plans.

"I told you, Alessandra's impossible to deal with." Portuc's voice hadn't lost the grating whine capable of setting Mark's teeth on edge. "She's a piece of work, astonishingly like her grandmother. The girl always seemed docile, but she's worse than a gorbeed shrew."

Barent's voice was smooth. "I appreciated your skill in luring Alessandra away from the safety of Throne Planet. Bringing her to Freemarket was inspired planning on your part. My compliments. But I don't need *you* any longer."

"What are you talking about?" Confusion and the first faint stirrings of fear quavered in Portuc's voice.

Mark grinned behind the visor. Everyone knew you couldn't trust the Kliin. It was practically an axiom in the Outlier Empire, had been for centuries. What outcome had Portuc expected when he got tangled in a Kliin plot?

"I'm not here to pay you off for bringing me the princess," Barent said, his voice a lazy drawl. "I'm here to rescue her and take revenge on her kidnappers."

"I don't understand."

"I'm going to kill the bastards, dear boy, execute them summarily for the crime of kidnapping an imperial granddaughter. I slaughter you and a few of your household guards to give the story a tinge of veracity, take Alessandra home to Throne Planet, the empress rewards me with her granddaughter's hand and substantial dowry, then I ascend the throne with my reluctant bride—" Barent's voice broke off. Mark had a mental picture of the man shrugging.

He'd heard enough. Barent might toy with poor Portuc a few moments longer, but the duke's fate was sealed. Alessandra's was to be equally grim if Mark didn't take immediate action. Hand to his earpiece, as if listening to new orders, he crossed to the sweeping staircase, ignoring the men he passed. The empress would accept whatever outcome transpired. If Mark brought the errant princess back to her, Ekatereen would pay him and continue to use her granddaughter as a pawn to control the various factions. If Barent succeeded, the empress would acknowledge his guile and accept him as a worthy heir to her throne.

No one cared what happened to Alessandra.

Especially not Mark.

Of course not.

Even as he had the thought, he knew he was lying to himself.

Her quarters were on the third floor. Two Kliin soldiers had disposed of Portuc's hapless men, as evidenced by the bodies piled farther down the hall, and now guarded her door. The men watched him climb the last steps without any visible sense of misgiving. In his stolen uniform and helmet, Mark blended into their company. Not pausing for a second in his easygoing approach, he reached casually under the folds of his coat, thumbed the setting on his concealed weapon to stun, and shot the pair between one step and another. The men crumpled to the carpet without a sound.

Mark stepped over the bodies. He burned through the lock with a low setting on the blaster, then tried the door. It wouldn't budge.

She'd barricaded herself in. Clever, but ultimately futile.

Holstering the weapon first, Mark put his shoulder to the stubborn panel and shoved.

A moment later he entered the room, moving around the heavy piece of furniture positioned as a pitiful last defense.

Alessandra stood, straight and imperious, across the chamber from him, her face set in grim lines but showing no fear. Her luminous blue eyes were wide, and she was breathing rapidly, but she faced him with open defiance. A maid cowered behind her.

"You." Pointing at the servant with his free hand, Mark gestured toward the door. "Out. This house is about to become a death trap, and the men downstairs won't leave any witnesses. I advise you to run."

Hunching over to make herself less of a target, the woman edged along the wall until she passed Mark and bolted into the corridor.

Mark stared at the princess, Seeing her again after all these years was like a hallucination. The changes in her face—older, a few lines, but still beautiful by any standard—fascinated him. Annoyed, he realized just being in the same room with her dangerously distracted him from the job.

"You can tell your master I won't agree to anything," Alessandra said in Outlier, voice cold but tremulous.

"I'm not one of Kliin's boys." Mark removed the helmet, setting it on the bureau amidst a clutter of jewelry and trinkets. Catching a whiff of her delicious perfume, the same she'd always worn for him, Mark felt a moment of vertigo. "I'm here to get you out."

Eyebrows raised, apparently puzzled by his words, she studied his face.

Mark moved forward. As if engaged in some macabre dance, she stepped back, one step and then another as he advanced, until her shoulders hit the wall with a thump.

"Sandy, damn it, it's me, Mark Denaltieri." Unaccustomed emotions battering at him, he regretted ever agreeing to this venture. Some things were best left permanently in the past.

Eyes narrowed, lips thin, she glared at him. "What kind of a fool does Barent Kliin think I am? Or is this some new plot of my grandmother's?" She grabbed a vase from the table beside her and threw it at him. "Mark is *dead.*"

Dodging the missile, he retreated to the door, cracking it open a sliver. "Your aim is as bad as ever, I see." He heard the rumble of voices from the floor below. Barent evidently wasn't done toying with poor, deluded Portuc. Over his shoulder, Mark said, "Who the seven hells ever called you Sandy besides me?"

When he eased the door shut and turned, she'd sunk onto the sofa under the windows, slumped on the cream and blue floral cushions. She wiped away tears.

Crossing to the couch, he stood in front of her. Taking fierce control of his own emotions, he pitched his voice lower and injected more calm into his tones. "Your Highness, this isn't a plot or a trick. I'm Mark."

She shook her head in pained denial, closing her eyes as if to avoid the sight of him. Tears coursed over her cheeks. "My grandmother had him tortured and killed. I saw the records. You're *not* him, and I'm not going anywhere with you."

"Tortured, yes. Killed, no." He blew a gusty breath. "It's a long story. We haven't got time for explanations. Barent Kliin is downstairs, about to murder

Portuc. His plans for you aren't much better. Will you trust me to get you out of here in one piece? Once I have you somewhere safe, you can make your own decision about what to do next. Word of a *bogatyr*. Sworn on my family's honor."

Cheeks red, dark blue eyes flooded with tears, she stared at him, seeming lost in grief. "I knew, even when Portuc claimed to have found him, it had to be a lie. Grandmother never would have let Mark Denaltieri live. I wanted it to be true so badly."

Mark knelt, placing one hand over hers. "We have to get out of here. Now."

"Prove who you are, or I go nowhere." Hand fisted, she shoved his shoulder. "I'll scream and bring them running. I'd rather trust Barent than an impostor."

Had he changed that much in twenty years? He'd never been able to forget her face, why didn't she know his? Maybe she was blocking the memories. Or maybe he hadn't mattered as much to her as he'd believed. Either way, he was committed to this action, no time for doubt. "If I convince you I'm Mark, will you let me get you out of here?"

She nodded. "But you can't prove such a thing."

Impatient, he threw off the heavy Kliin overcoat and yanked the left side of his blue tunic free of the pants, revealing his abdomen. "We met when I took a force knife meant for you, in the Spring of a year long ago."

Fingers trembling, she touched the long, white scar running parallel to his ribs, near his heart. Even when he'd been severely injured in the Special Forces, requiring time in the rejuve resonator, he'd demanded the medtechs leave the scar. It represented the last pitiful link to his past. Proof he had indeed been someone else, with a far different destiny than the one forced upon him. Now he shivered, flinching from even the lightest touch of her hand. Too many memories. He endured the contact for a moment before pulling away and jerking the tunic into place as he stood. "You have a birthmark shaped like a heart in a very intimate place, Your Highness. If you require further proof."

"I'd wandered off from a family picnic in the gardens at Nemalpaue." Alessandra stared at him, eyes wide. "You'd recently been assigned to the house guards as a cadet, and you were lost, confused by your first time in the imperial gardens—"

"We were in the gardens at Tsiolovad, and you were reading a book by yourself," he said, temper growing short as she continued to test his claim. "I was in the wrong place at the right time. In time to see the assassins entering the garden. I'd no chance of getting help, so, being young and stupid, I tried to take them on all by myself."

"No, you were so brave, displayed amazing courage through the entire fight." Staring at him, she massaged her temples as if to soothe a massive headache. Unexpectedly, she grabbed his chin, tilting his head until the lamp on the wall bathed his entire face in merciless light. Leaning forward, she peered into his eyes, then released him and fell against the cushions a moment later with a gasp. "It is you—that tiny fleck of gold in your left eye always fascinated me. I've never seen anything like it in anyone else's eyes."

He walked to the bureau and donned the helmet, visor retracted. "We have to go. Trust me, don't trust me, believe me or not, but if we don't leave this room right now, you're going to be Barent Kliin's prize. I'm not waiting around to go over old times in the cadets with him. Are you coming?"

"All right." Her measured tone gave nothing away of her inner thoughts. "We can put aside the need for explanations temporarily. I always trusted you. You were the only one I could rely on."

"Still am, at least to get you out of here. Trust me tonight."

Moving like a coiled spring, she stood, kicking her tangled skirt out of the way. "There's something I can't leave behind."

"You don't have time to pack."

Sandy ignored him, going to the closet and rummaging in the deep drawers under the hanging dresses, while Mark's meager store of patience evaporated. She backed out of the storage space holding a medium-sized, caramel leather bag. The satchel appeared to be quite heavy, but she slid the strap onto her left shoulder with a practiced move and walked across the room to join him. "I'm ready now. What do you have in mind—a stroll out the front door?"

He stood aside. "No, we'd run right into Kliin and his hired thugs. We're going over the roof."

She stopped, eyebrows raised, hand to her mouth. "The roof? Are you mad?"

"Let me see your shoes."

She slid one high-heeled foot out from under the hem of the clinging turquoise skirt.

"Anything more practical in the overstocked warehouse you called a closet?"

She shook her head but kicked off the offending shoes.

"Barefoot?" Mark sighed but wasn't about to argue. After he reconnoitered, he motioned for her to precede him into the hall. No sign of the maid, no sign of any alarm having been given. He told her to wait while he dragged the two unconscious men into the room, then closed the door behind him. Visualizing one of the alternate escape routes he'd identified when studying the plans, he led her deeper into the recesses of the house until they reached a staircase.

Every other riser creaked. Concerned the noise might draw unwanted attention, he urged Sandy to climb faster. When she reached the top floor of the house, he moved into the lead, going to a hidden door at the far end of the corridor. Burning through the lock with his blaster, Mark yanked the door open and pulled down a ladder. "Up here, quickly."

Sandy clambered to the attic. He made quicker work of the ascent than she had, pulling the old-fashioned ladder closed behind him.

"I-I heard a scream." She fidgeted with the strap of her bag.

Taking her elbow to escort her to the window, he felt tension vibrating through her. "Kliin probably got tired of toying with poor old Portuc and shot him. We're running out of time. He'll be scouring the house for you next."

The window was sealed and set with security alarm sensors. Holstering the blaster, he got out a small toolkit. He went to work on the window while she watched with great interest.

"What are you doing?"

"Something illegal on all the civilized worlds." He kept his focus on the task. "These tools are standard issue for the Sectors Special Forces."

Leaning on the wall beside the window, she eyed him. "You were in their military?"

"Twenty years. Ah, there we have it." He slid the window out of its frame. Stepping through the opening, he offered her his hand. "Come on, this part of the roof is flat."

"Then what?" Gamely, she climbed through the opening after him.

"Follow my lead."

He traversed the roof, staying close to the center, drawing her behind him, until their progress came to a halt at the rear wall. Sandy took one horrified glance and hunched closer to the ornamental fretwork running the length of the house in the center. "I don't like heights, in case you've forgotten. It's three stories to the ground. How are we supposed to manage the descent?"

"No problem. Antigrav pads." He took them from a pocket of his borrowed coat and slipped the military devices onto the soles of his boots. Self-activating with a faint hum, the antigrav cast a blue glare. He rose a couple of feet into the air, gesturing to her. "I'll have to carry you."

Sandy glanced over her shoulder at the window she'd climbed through. "Maybe this isn't such a good idea. We can talk to Kliin."

"He's not in the mood to listen." Mark scooped her into his arms and stepped off the roof, floating to the ground faster than he'd expected—the pads were old, military surplus, and not rated for a double load, but the best he could get on the black market. She kept her eyes shut and her head tucked into his shoulder.

Rather unceremoniously, he deposited her on the manicured grass a moment later.

Shouting erupted inside the house. A glaring floodlight came to life above them. He shot it out and grabbed her by the hand, taking off at a dead run across the garden, toward the perimeter fence of the small estate. Forcing her to go first through a hole he'd precut about a week ago, he followed right on her heels, pushing her behind a large bush. "Wait here."

"Where are you going?" She sneezed as a cloud of sparkling pollen from the ornamental plant drifted in the slight evening breeze.

"I've got to retrieve the rest of my gear. I'll just be a second."

Hoping she'd obey orders and stay hidden, Mark ducked and ran before she could ask any further questions. Working his way through the extensive hedge, he paused at the edge of the street. Then he stepped onto the pavement, sauntering to the idling groundcar. The local merc continued to listen to mind-numbing music, tapping his hand on the control panel with the beat. Mark stunned him with one efficient, silenced shot. Opening the door carefully to keep the body from toppling out, Mark shoved the man into the passenger side.

"I'll be right back," Mark assured his victim cheerfully, in case anyone farther down the line of idling vehicles was paying attention, which he doubted. The nearby mercenaries were staring at the house, debating amongst themselves how much carnage was occurring inside. Retrieving his battered, green-and-black kitbag from concealment in the hedge, he heaved the equipment into the rear seat, before jogging to where Sandy crouched.

"Let's get out of here, Your Highness. Our luck has held too long already." He walked to the passenger side of the groundcar and pulled the unconscious man out, dropping him on the lawn.

Stepping over the guard, she slid into the front seat, clutching her bag.

"You there!" A shout from the vicinity of the house challenged him for the first time on this escapade. "What do you think you're doing? Where's Ivor?"

Mark got behind the manual controls as fast as he could, throwing his stolen ride into motion before he'd even shut the door. He yanked the vehicle in a tight circle, servo motors whining, and took off toward the center of town at high speed. There wasn't much traffic to impede them at this late hour, even on Freemarket.

Sandy peered at the vidscreen. "Got four cars coming after us. Can't you go faster?"

"Yeah. Hang on!"

He shifted into overdrive and tore through the streets, dodging slower traffic in his way. He'd memorized a variety of escape routes during his first week on the planet.

Sirens wailed in the distance.

"Local cops. Damn, I hoped the police would stay out of this like they usually do. Kliin must have paid them one hell of a lot of money to be at his beck and call. We're going to have to ditch the car and make a run for it." He took his attention off the road for a moment to assess how Sandy was holding up as the groundcar slewed from side to side in his violent maneuvers.

She screamed a warning, but even Mark's reflexes weren't fast enough to avoid a collision with the cargo hauler pulling into his lane. The groundcar rammed the side of the truck, safety mechanisms deploying instantly and retracting.

"Damn door is stuck." Mark exerted his full strength, pushing the lock to release. "Are you all right?"

Ignoring his question, she shoved her hair out of her eyes. "The sirens are coming closer. Get us out of here!"

"I'm doing all I can." He could hear the banshee wail of their approaching enemies. "Grab my kitbag from the back."

She twisted in the seat to get both hands on the straps of his bag, dragging it over the divider into her lap.

"Where the seven hells did you learn to drive, pal?" demanded the truck driver as he burst from his vehicle. Cursing, the man yanked the door open, freeing them.

Mark half fell from the car, dodging under the trucker's arm and coming up behind him, striking at the vulnerable spot on the man's neck. The citizen collapsed, half in and half out of the car. Mark shoved him to the pavement and reached in to grab first his bag, then Alessandra's outstretched hands.

"Now what?" Leaning on the car, she scanned their surroundings for an escape route.

Mark pivoted on his boot heel, getting his bearings. "The independent market-place is this way. We can try to lose Barent and the local boys he's hired in there. It's a maze. The vendors don't much like cops, which might work in our favor since we're fugitives."

Taking the lead, he ran down the alley away from the wrecked car and the cargo hauler. Even at this late hour, the marketplace overflowed with diners and shoppers. Mark slowed to a walk, keeping a tight grip on her hand. They walked past a whole row of jewelry merchants, ignoring the shouted offers from the eager vendors, then took a sharp right turn into an aisle of hanging baskets. He glanced behind and ducked under the nearest display, drawing Sandy after him, seeking a shortcut deeper into the convoluted arrangement of stalls and merchandise.

Fending off a rack of leather belts as she snuck under it, Sandy said, "Do you know where you're going?"

"I always have multiple escape routes. We get to the other side, we can steal another groundcar from the parking structure. Are you okay?"

"My feet hurt and I twisted my ankle when we crashed, but I can keep up, don't worry."

As he swerved under a row of baskets to cut into the next aisle, Mark stopped Sandy before she could take another step. "Cop."

Head tilted, talking into a com, the local policeman maintained an unblinking surveillance of the marketplace.

"Searching for us?" she asked, bending over to rub her bruised ankle.

"Probably—and now he's seen us." The man's stance had shifted. He was talking fast into his com link and coming in their direction. Taking her elbow, Mark pulled her across the narrow space and into the next shop. Reaching out, he snagged a rack of leather purses and bags and toppled it across the entryway.

Dodging the proprietor and his wide-eyed customers, they bolted out the rear door. Their pursuer shouted at them to stop. People flowed into the aisle behind them, blocking the lawman's progress with their arms full of merchandise.

"The locals don't know who the seven hells we are, but being on the run is enough to get us help, like I hoped." Mark dodged a refreshment cart and cut through an open-air dining area, a surprising number of the tables occupied at this hour. He stopped for a moment next to the food services, so Sandy could catch her breath while safely surrounded by a milling crowd of customers shouting orders for delicacies and drinks.

She straightened, adjusting the bag's strap on her shoulder. "There's another cop."

Needing only a swift glance in the direction she indicated, Mark realized the situation was worsening. "And he's got friends—Kliin's mercenaries." There were five uniformed men surrounding the local policeman.

He drew her behind the line of cooks at the nearest open-air grill, crouching among the bins and barrels of fish on ice and crustaceans crawling in barrels of salty water as the Kliin guards ran past, accompanied by three policemen. The men slicing and dicing vegetables and stirring vats of savory stew ignored the byplay, continuing their preparation without missing a beat. Mark breathed a silent prayer to the Lords of Space, thanking them for the indifference of the Freemarket citizenry.

"We'll never get out of this predicament," she said, breath catching on a sob. "There's nowhere we can go. The police are all over the market."

"The parking garage is probably locked down too." He couldn't believe he'd failed. This job meant more to him than anything he'd ever done for the Sectors. So how had he let it go so wrong so fast? Preoccupied, trying to think of other options for escape, he didn't notice the small being approaching until it stopped in front of him.

Assessing the sentient's pointed face and triangular, gray-furred ears, the wide yellow-flecked eyes, he wasn't sure what he was dealing with. Nothing he'd encountered previously. Waving his blaster, Mark tried to shoo the being away for its own good. Not intimidated, the newcomer clutched his sleeve with four curved claws. "Come with me—I know what you need, but you must make haste."

Instinctively trying to yank his arm away, Mark couldn't free himself from the creature's grip. "Who the hell are you?"

"Come, come, there is no time, traveler." Tugging harder on him and reaching with its other hand for Alessandra's skirt, the creature sidled a few steps. "You must hurry."

He exchanged glances with Sandy. Eyebrows raised, she rolled her shoulders in resignation. "I don't think we have any choices, do you?"

"Not now, no," Mark agreed. "Out of options here. All right, what do you have in mind, friend?"

"Come, come, come!"

The being's vocabulary seemed to be pretty limited. Still maintaining its hold on Mark, releasing Sandy's skirt as if it didn't care for the feel of the silky material, the sentient backed away. It escorted them along the line of stalls, keeping low and stealthy. Mark reached for Sandy's free hand to make sure they didn't get separated on this strange jaunt. A hue and cry erupted behind them.

Their odd guide led the way, weaving and dodging through the crowded aisles until the two humans were hard-pressed to match the pace.

Mark checked their six, stumbling over refuse on the path. Around a corner, through a narrow passageway, past a blur of staring citizens, doubling back occasionally, they ran. All at once their guide darted sideways, into a dark purple tent, and stopped. The sudden change in direction, followed by the unexpected halt, took Mark and Sandy by surprise. She tripped on his heel, bringing them both down in a heap, tangled with their guide. Mark lay on the carpeted floor, watching in astonishment as six cops sprinted past the tent's open portal, never even glancing inside.

"What the seven hells?" Mark realized the strange being he'd fallen on top of was gone, vanished as if it had never been.

Rising, Mark reached to help Sandy regain her feet, relieving her of the heavy bag. She staggered as soon as she put her weight on the ankle she'd twisted escaping the wrecked groundcar.

"Welcome," said someone from deep within the recesses of the tent.

Still supporting Sandy, trying to shield her from whoever approached from behind them, Mark turned.

A veiled woman, dressed head to toe in shimmering lavender, stood a few feet away, as if guarding the entrance to a second, larger room.

"I'm sorry we're intruding," Sandy said between panting breaths. "The little— the sentient thought you could help us."

"The Nelafinari are never wrong in their assessment of Travelers," their hostess answered, giving the last word a special emphasis.

Mark couldn't decide if he and Sandy were in more danger from their pursuers outside or from this uncanny new player.

A second group of Kliin's mercenaries and local police ran by, two men stopping to stare into the tent where Mark stood. Cursing under his breath, he shoved Sandy behind him and aimed his blaster at the nearest adversary.

"Do not." A jarringly slender, seven-fingered hand reached out to grasp the barrel of the M27 and push it down. "The men you fear cannot see us. We're outside their existence. For now." In a heartbeat, the woman in lavender stood where she'd started, on the threshold of the other room. "I advise you to accept what is and move on. Our time is short."

"Mark!" Sandy's voice quavered on a note of pure terror as she grabbed his arm, pulling him to face the entrance.

Barent Kliin stood in the alley, glaring at the merchandise displays.

Mark took one step toward the exit. Barent would make a valuable hostage, exactly what he needed to buy their way out of the dead-end trap the marketplace had become.

"Leave and you can never return to this spot," said their mysterious hostess. "This chance comes but once to a Traveler such as yourself."

Sandy tugged at his arm, drawing him a step or two farther into the tent and interfering with his aim at Barent. "I think we need to listen to her. Maybe she can help. She's protecting us right now. That's worth something."

Their unusual hostess laughed, and the sound trilled like birdsong, changing from second to second. "I'm Lajollae, Keeper of the Globes of Amarkana."

"Which doesn't mean anything to me," he said, holstering his blaster as Barent strode out of his line of sight, going deeper into the marketplace.

Lajollae extended her arms, hands cupped in front of her at waist height. She held an iridescent bubble about a foot in diameter, which had materialized in the blink of an eye. A second bubble fought to come into existence, pulling itself out of the first. Tiny flecks of gold floated in the second bubble.

One golden mote separated from the rest and drifted through the skin of its own bubble and across empty space to sink inside the lower bubble. A moment later, another particle began the same journey.

"We have until the top bubble empties into the lower," Lajollae said. "Then I'll be gone from this place and time, your opportunity gone with me."

"Opportunity?" Mark tried to focus on the vaguely sensible part of her declaration. "To do what exactly?"

"To Travel—come." She beckoned for them to follow her into the tent's second chamber.

Mark and Sandy exchanged another wary glance.

"What have we got to lose?" She bent to retrieve her bag.

"I've got it," Mark told her, suiting action to the words. "All right, let's go see what this Lajollae is peddling. Stay behind me."

The princess trailing him, Mark followed the strange being into her other room, giving the floating bubbles a wide berth. He attempted to calculate how many of the golden motes might have already descended, but focusing on the glittering shards was hard, making measurement impossible.

Seeing the dimensions of the inner chamber, he was positive this tent couldn't have been in the part of the market they'd been running through just moments ago.

Lajollae was intent on him, her lavender face unnaturally long. Even the diamond-shaped pupils of her eyes were lavender. "I'm the servant of Ones who came before, setting me to follow my appointed rounds through their domain, to provide the amusement of Travel. My mistresses are gone eons ago, to an existence you could never fathom, young race that you are. But I was left carelessly discarded, with no choice but to keep to my route. You aren't what the globes were created for, true." She shook her head, as if recalling a great tragedy. "But if the Nelafinari bring you to me, then I can serve—you're marked as ones who can choose."

"The-the Nelafinari? The little fellow who guided us here?" Sandy had apparently identified at least one tangible fact to anchor herself in all this unreal discussion.

Lajollae pointed, and Mark swung around to find two of the small beings now kneeling at either side of the tent's entrance. "They know my need, know I must send Travelers on their way. So the pack hunts."

Mark didn't like the idea of being prey, but the Nelafinari had saved them from immediate capture and, no doubt, his painful and prolonged death at the hands of Barent Kliin.

"We waste time." Lajollae sounded uneasy. "You must choose to Travel or to stay."

"You keep talking about traveling. How do you propose to help us get away from the men pursuing us? Do you have a groundcar or some kind of ship here?" Mark wondered if the tent included a third chamber, a garage maybe.

One of the Nelafinari growled deep in its throat, baring impressive fangs.

"Behold the Globes of Amarkana." She yanked at a corner of what Mark had assumed to be the tent's rear wall. The shimmering panel fell away, revealing a tree taller than Mark fashioned entirely from crystal. Jagged, sharp branches of clear glass, patterned with leaves incised deep into the surface, jutted from a thick trunk at odd angles. At the tip of each branch hung a perfect golden ball, ethereal bubbles made of solid material. The globes were translucent, empty at first glance, but then Mark saw faint spirals of white smoke in some, flickering lightning in others, flames in a few. Several appeared to contain misty rain droplets suspended as if captured in midair…the branches stirred with a faint chiming sound.

"The time is nearly gone." Lajollae's voice broke into their fascination.

He checked the floating timer. Sure enough, the upper bubble was almost empty of the sparkling contents, sagging in upon itself. "What do we do?"

"Pick the globe meant for you," Lajollae said. "You'll know which one is your destiny."

"What if we pick differently?" Sandy clutched at his sleeve. "I can't lose you again!"

Lajollae shook her head. "You can each choose your own destination, or one may decide for both."

Mark and Sandy exchanged glances. "We stick together," he said, clenching his jaw.

"Agreed, this mad escapade we're on is because I trusted you," Sandy said, releasing his sleeve with a smile that didn't reach her eyes. "So I trust you to decide for us."

Mark took a step toward the globes, studying them, trying to decide which to pick, not sure what would happen next—there was no retreat, no other way to end this.

He kept going back to one particular globe, high on the tree, dangling precariously on its crystal branch. Nothing differentiated this bubble from all the rest, but it drew him nonetheless.

When he stretched to touch the globe, it fell into his hand.

"You've chosen, now breathe the air of the destination you've selected," Lajollae said in a harsh whisper. "Make haste, for your time is over—I'm leaving this place for my next station."

Mark stared at the surprisingly heavy globe in his hand, not sure what she wanted him to do. Breathe the air? Was that what the shimmering glass encapsulated—air from somewhere else? How could air win them freedom from Kliin's pursuit?

Mark knelt, the gesture feeling somehow appropriate at this moment. He let the globe roll from his fingertips onto the carpet. Rising, he positioned his heavy boot on top of the orb and glanced at Lajollae. Features difficult to discern in the blinding aura now surrounding her, she nodded. Mark drew Sandy into his arms. Closing her eyes, leaning against him, she locked her hands behind his back, over his spine. Angry shouting grew closer, Kliin calling the princess's name. Mark raised his foot and brought it down in one violent motion, shattering the globe.

Heat and a rush of spice-scented air swirled around them. Mark felt as if he'd been picked up by a whirlwind. He was afraid to open his eyes as the air filled with grit, scraping across every inch of exposed flesh. Tightening his arms around Sandy, he buried his face in her soft, fragrant hair. From the sensations, he'd have said they were flying through the air, yet a solid footing remained under his boots.

Worries flooded Mark's mind. Had Lajollae been trying to save them, or had she sent them into the path of some worse fate?

Too late for regrets.

CHAPTER TWO

The first time Mark opened his eyes, the world continued to swirl around him, so he blinked hard, hoping to quell the vertigo. His head ached like he'd been on a three-day bender with cheap rotgut, his left shoulder throbbed like someone had stuck a jagged knife into it, and his stomach was on fire with cramping pain. Closing his eyes against the mad whirl of the vertigo, he tried to curl into the smallest ball of sheer misery possible.

Murmuring reassurance in a soft, feminine voice, the medic treating him tugged at his right shoulder.

Mark half opened his eyes to see the woman, preparing to tell her with a blistering string of profanity to let him die in peace. But even through the dizziness and nausea, he was startled to see Sandy, not a Sectors medic. Pressing an inject to his bicep, she said, "I hope when you regain consciousness next time, these symptoms have worn off. I don't think you were as good a candidate for Traveling as Lajollae thought."

Vague memories surfacing, he said, "What happened? All I remember is breaking the globe and then a whole lot of hot wind—like being in a sandstorm."

"Exactly," she said, pushing him to recline. "Now rest."

Before he could continue the conversation, the injection she'd given him took effect, and the world lost focus as he spiraled into unconsciousness.

As Mark passed out under the influence of the medication, he sighed and rolled onto his side. Sandy studied his face, noting that he appeared younger now that he wasn't consciously worrying about their safety. She pushed the glossy brown hair out of his eyes. "Hardly regulation, soldier," she murmured.

Pulling the stolen Kliin coat serving as a blanket higher on his body, she watched him for a moment, assessing his condition. When he continued to sleep, snoring a bit, she slid off the dais, or bed, or whatever the piece of furniture might be, and took his blaster from the spot she'd arbitrarily designated as the foot. "It'll be hours before you wake again and we can compare notes," she said to his sleeping form. "I'm not going to sit here and watch you breathe. Time to find out where we've landed and what we're facing."

His blaster was surprisingly substantial in her hand. The weapon had a dull finish, nothing to attract the eye, and seemed fairly simple to operate, although she'd never fired one and had no true idea of the process. Did blasters have safety mechanisms? She studied the buttons on the grip for a moment. "Not testing this in here," she said out loud, mostly to dispel the eerie quiet.

She had no pockets in her evening gown, no belt, so she carried the blaster as she walked from the chamber where she'd dragged Mark. After they'd arrived it became clear how severely incapacitated he'd was as a result of their traveling. He'd been able to stagger most of the way, leaning on her, although she'd had to speak sharply to get him to cooperate.

She retraced their steps now and studied the arrival point, not planning to go too near. Who knew how Lajollae's magic or technology worked? Sandy didn't intend to travel again and certainly not without Mark. A circular platform denoted the arrival spot, dark black stone veined with iridescent accents. Opal maybe. What interested her right now was the pedestal set into the stone floor next to it. The column was plain black stone, but the top had been carved into the representation of a three-horned animal with a long, graceful face and huge eyes. Two necklaces hung from the outermost horns. When they'd arrived, the place had been cold, pitch black. Mark had been suffering convulsions, and she'd been terrified. Rubbing her arm as she relived those moments, Sandy shivered, although the ambient temperature now hovered in the comfortable range. Trying to locate her bag or his by touch after landing, she'd brushed against the necklaces, and like magic, the lights had come on and the room had warmed.

Thankful for small mercies in a mad adventure, she'd prioritized Mark's situation, but now the necklaces drew her. Not liking the utter silence, she spoke aloud. "Keys maybe?"

The chain on the one closer to her was a simple set of gold links from which hung a translucent, lavender rectangle incised with tiny characters completely unfamiliar to her. There were cutouts in the stone at irregular intervals. The pendant suspended from the other necklace was black, flecked with gold, but identical in shape. With one hand she lifted the lavender necklace off the hook, pausing for a long moment to see if anything happened.

Lights flickered on in the hallway and she heard a sound as if machinery was whirring into life. Gripping the blaster, she set off to explore the place. Realizing she couldn't afford to have both hands full if she had to defend herself, she bent her head to loop the necklace over her hair. Working one-handed was awkward, and the key tangled in her messy chignon, but eventually she got the chain settled properly, pendant dangling between her breasts.

A single short corridor extended from their point of entry. There were two closed doors on the right-hand side, and two open entrances on the left, beyond the bedroom where Mark lay oblivious, snoring. The room next to the bedroom struck her as possibly being a bathroom, with an odd fixture in the far corner and a sunken area like a tub in the opposite corner, although she couldn't find a way to draw water. Some basins at waist height might have been sinks. Deciding not to experiment further, she went to the next open room, pleasantly surprised to find a massive table, made from stone like everything else here. There were thirty ovals and squares of lighter stone, ranging in color from blue to green, set into the far wall. "Controls maybe? Or storage cabinets?" Sandy waved the key at the closest one, but nothing happened.

Frustrated, she walked into the hall. Why had she and Mark been so quick to trust Lajollae? *Maybe I could have negotiated with Barent. If Mark didn't kill him first.* Her stomach rumbled, and she decided to check his kitbag for something to eat.

Sure enough, there were energy bars in one side pocket. Wandering to the bedroom, she sat on the side of the bed, munching on the relatively tasteless item. She derived comfort from proximity to Mark, even if he was unconscious. Being virtually alone unsettled her. An Imperial Princess of the Outlier Empire was surrounded by guards, courtiers, servants, all of whom were supposed to carry out her slightest wish. Give their lives for hers. Even at Portuc's house on Freemarket, there'd been a maid. His personal guards had watched over her wherever Portuc escorted her, ineffectual though the men might have been. The constant surveillance chafed, but at least someone was always there if needed. Sandy took a deep breath. Here, there was only her. Even Mark, indomitable as he was, had to rely on her at the moment.

No longer hungry, she folded the remaining third of the bar into its packaging. Fingering the key, she eyed the hallway. Taking a moment to check Mark's pulse and respiration, she grabbed the blaster and forced herself to walk to the hall and face the other doors. A humming noise attracted her attention, because the whole place had been so silent from the moment she'd arrived. Realizing the sound emanated from behind the door at the end of the hall, she felt hopeful as she walked to it. No indentation or other sign provided an indication where the key necklace might fit. Berating herself for expecting anything so simplistic to work, she waved the key at the door, pressed the lavender to various spots on the slab, and finally retreated in frustration. Hands on her hips, she resisted the urge to kick the offending door.

All right then, time to explore the remaining doors, if doors they actually were, on the right side of the hall. She waved the key at the first, not really expecting any result, and jumped sideways, blaster raised, as the portal slid noiselessly aside. Inky blackness loomed on the other side of the threshold. Tiptoeing, she crept to the edge of the door and stuck one foot inside. Lights sprang to life, startling her again. The illumination revealed a capacious space, completely empty. Squinting, she saw another door at the far end. After a moment, she stepped into the room and retreated in the same breath because a flicker of the disorientation she'd endured when she'd Traveled whirled through her body.

One step at a time, Sandy retreated from the door, which closed when she'd moved two feet down the hall. Hand to her forehead, she leaned against the wall, trying to control her breathing and quell the panic response induced by the sensation of Traveling. Trembling, leaning on the wall to counteract her vertigo, she made her way to the bedroom and sat next to Mark for some time, blaster in her lap. *Maybe solo exploration isn't the best idea.* Yet the one door she hadn't tried was enticing. Finally, she rose and walked into the hall, straight to the door.

He woke with a gasp.

Having learned his lesson the last time, Mark had no intention of opening his eyes too soon. He rolled onto his back, assessing how he felt, trying to remember what the seven hells had happened. Memory answered him with the kick of an adrenaline rush. Forgetting caution, he opened his eyes at the same time he moved to a sitting position, staring at his unfamiliar surroundings. A mild wave of residual vertigo chased itself through his head, passing in a moment. He pushed aside the coat lying across his body.

He was in the center of a large chamber, opening onto a hall. The ceiling soared twelve feet above him, a translucent white surface crisscrossed with thin bands of black. The room had been cut from living rock, veined in greens, yellows, and browns of semiprecious mineral polished to a high gloss. Here and there along the walls he saw seams and other indentations whose geometric regularity indicated deliberate placement by sentients, not natural processes. He sat in the middle of a large, three-stepped dais. It wasn't rock, having molded itself to his body like a supremely comfortable mattress, but he couldn't identify what the material could be.

No sign of Sandy, which sent his adrenaline spiking higher.

He swung his feet over the edge of the bed, reaching for the boots flung on the floor. A slight noise distracted him, and boot in hand, he stared at the princess, standing there like an illusion. Incongruous in her beautiful turquoise silk and lace dress, leaning against the wall, she smiled at him. Meeting his gaze, she padded barefoot toward the bed. He noticed she carried his service blaster.

As she tossed the weapon on the bed, she said, "Oh good, you're awake again. Symptoms any better?"

He rubbed his forehead, remembering the pain and vertigo. "Yeah, I'm firing on all jets now."

"How's the shoulder?"

Mark flexed his arm, kneading his shoulder with the opposite hand. "A little sore. What happened? All I remember is breaking that globe thing under my foot and then a whole lot of hot wind—like being in a sandstorm."

"Exactly like it. Barent Kliin shot at you just as we were Traveling out of there, but the blast went wide—a near miss."

"Lucky for me. But why was I so sick? Near misses don't make you gut sick. Because let me tell you, I've had near misses and I've been shot before, and it's nothing like this experience."

She sat on the bed, close to him but out of arm's reach. Her face serious, the princess seemed to be studying him as she answered. "I don't think you're as good a candidate for the Traveling process as the Nelafinari led Lajollae to believe. Or else she didn't care. Traveling didn't affect me much beyond a bit of nausea, but you were in agony from the moment we arrived. Wherever we are."

"You're calm about it all, pretty sure of the facts." Mark straightened his tunic and reached for the blaster. He flipped the safety on and holstered the weapon. "You shot at something?"

Sandy shrugged. "Target practice. I'm at least a day and a night ahead of you on this planet. And I didn't take any ill effect from the trip."

"I'm sorry, but can we slow down and begin again? My ears are still ringing. Where is here? What is this place?"

"I don't know." She held up one hand. "You do remember Lajollae and the tent on Freemarket?"

Rubbing his forehead, he grimaced and made a motion for her to get on with her explanation.

"The tent began dissolving or transporting or something after you broke the globe. Barent Kliin and his men were right there as we were starting to Travel. Like I said, he shot at you, and then I couldn't see him or much of anything. The grit got into my eyes so I closed them and hung on to you, which is what you kept ordering me to do." She shook her finger at him, a smile on her face. "Quite vehemently. You give orders well."

"If me being in command got us away from Kliin, got us here in one piece with our gear, then I don't mind if you find it amusing." Struck by a new concern, he glanced around the barren chamber again. "*Is* my gear here?"

"Yes. And my bag, lucky for you. I left the luggage in the arrival chamber where we landed. I'm sporting some magnificent bruises, and you took the brunt of the fall, for which I owe you. I wonder if the original Travelers came and went the way we did?"

Temper rising at her insouciant air in this unknown-to-him situation, concerned she'd felt the need to fire his blaster, he took a deep breath. "Sandy—"

"What, you prefer factual reports?" She fidgeted with the necklace circling her graceful neck.

Scooting closer, he snagged the links with one hand. "Where did you get this?"

"It's the key to this place, I think. It hung on a hook right next to the circle of stone where we landed, as if someone left it there for us. The last Travelers through here maybe."

The gemstone did resemble a key, he had to admit. "So you found the key and I was laid out cold on the floor." He led the conversation to the facts interesting him the most. "Then what?"

She shuddered, wrapping her arms around herself. "I was frightened. It was pitch black and you were out of things, and I'd no idea where we were. I flailed around a bit, searching by touch for your bag, hoping maybe you had a handlamp, and I touched the necklace. The lights came on as soon as I did. You were convulsing, only semiconscious. So I tried to make you comfortable in here, and then I explored."

Rising, blaster in his hand, he paced to the open doorway, staying out of the line of sight. Glancing over his shoulder at her, he said, "You confirmed the place is deserted?"

"I don't think anyone has been here in a long time. The rooms have a musty, abandoned-building feeling." As she continued, she ticked off her points on her fingers. "I can't find any furnishings, no pots and pans—you know, none of the things you'd need to live here. All the furniture is massive, like this bed, or carved out of the rock, like the table in the dining room. The place is laid out like a cottage."

"Traveler vacation resort? At least the bed is comfortable." Another fleeting memory came to him. "I dreamt a medic gave me an inject. Was that you?"

She nodded. "ByutbitaneQ."

Troubled, he whistled. What was she doing carrying around such a powerful—and addictive—tranq? "Heavy-duty stuff."

Her calm response was matter-of-fact. "I had to stop the seizures, besides which you were frighteningly disoriented. I thought putting you under for about twenty-four hours might give your system time to recover on its own from residual effects of the travel."

He decided to let the subject lapse for now. But if she was addicted to such a vicious drug, he'd have real trouble on his hands when she started to detox. For sure the hidden cupboards of this odd dwelling didn't contain any illicit feelgoods, or an antidote.

Rumbling from his stomach reminded him how long it'd been since he last ate. "I need some nutrition. Where did you say my gear ended up? I have a couple of high-energy bars in there."

"I know. I hope you don't mind, but I ate most of one last night. But the fruit is so much better."

What was she talking about? He hadn't packed any real food. "Fruit?"

"Outside." She waved one hand in the general direction of the hall. "There's a garden outside. It's like an oasis. There's even a small lake, fed by cold springs directly from inside the mountain."

"We can't touch the local food until we know if it's safe for humans." As his blood pressure rose, he realized he'd fallen into lecturing her the way he would a raw recruit. Mark reminded himself she was an unschooled civilian and he should make allowances. He moderated his tone. "I've had the antidote injects for a lot of poisonous things, but you—"

"I promise I didn't eat anything unless I saw the birds and the ground rodents eat first, okay? And I had to drink from the lake. Neither of us has anything liquid in our bags. I don't believe Lajollae would send us to a place where we were going to die if we consumed the available provisions. That doesn't make sense."

"None of this makes sense," Mark retorted, a reluctant grin breaking out on his face. "All right, let me finish getting my boots on, and I'll be glad to tour your oasis, or whatever this place is."

"I think the lake has fish, so maybe we can figure out how to catch some dinner," she told him a moment later, strolling out of the bedroom into the next chamber. "This is where we arrived yesterday." She pointed at a raised, circular dais in the exact center of the room. His kitbag lay off to the side, her leather satchel lying next to it.

"Is that a second key?" he asked.

"I think so. I left it for you."

He pivoted, assessing the place they'd been sent to through the auspices of the mysterious Lajollae. He saw no decoration anywhere, no inscription, nothing to provide any hints about who'd built the dwelling or why.

He wasn't as comfortable in this place as Sandy seemed to be. Worry that they'd ended up in a trap of some kind, or even a shared hallucination, thrummed through him. But his bruises, aches, and pains felt real enough. Her assessment about the long-deserted aspects of the place summed conditions up perfectly. "Does anything look familiar outside? Do you have any idea what planet we might be on?"

"Nowhere I've ever been. I haven't traveled much in my life, as you can imagine."

"I've been all over the Sectors and into some of the Mawreg territory, but I don't think any one sentient could possibly know all the worlds where humans can survive. How many moons does this place have?"

"I saw two rising by the end of the day yesterday." She shrugged. "To tell you the truth, I was reluctant to stay outside and count celestial bodies. Once the sun set, I shut the door and spent the night sitting on the bed next to you, with your blaster in my hand."

"I'm sorry you had to endure the night by yourself." No wonder she had circles under her eyes. Mark guessed the long hours between sunset and dawn had been more unsettling for her than her calm recital would indicate. He'd forgotten how gutsy she could be. Pivoting in the hall to survey the small expanse of their new domicile, he said, "What's behind the other doors?"

Tapping one fingernail on the portal she lingered beside, she said, "Here's the door to the oasis. The next door over opens into some kind of huge, empty space." Sandy frowned. "When I walked across the threshold, I became a bit disoriented, like Traveling almost, but on a smaller scale."

Annoyed again, he didn't bother to moderate his tone. "I wish you hadn't done so much exploring while I was unconscious. What if something happened to you? I would have awakened today with no idea how to find you."

"And what exactly should I have done while you slept? Nothing happened to me. So, obviously, my decision was fine." She pointed her finger at him, and her tone grew a bit strident. "Don't treat me like a breakable, helpless imperial princess. Don't expect me to be anything but an equal partner on this weird adventure we've been flung into."

"I never treated you as if you were like the other women in the imperial family."

"Well, don't start now."

"Truce." He held up his hands as if warding off a blow. "What about the last door?"

"It doesn't open with the key. You can feel a vibration in the rock, and I think I heard humming, like machinery."

"I'll take your word for it." Rubbing his chin, wishing he could shave, Mark said, "Could be the mechanical room for devices keeping this place functioning."

"And the tourists aren't allowed in to mess with the settings?"

He nodded. "Exactly. Right now all I want is to see the outside, breathe some fresh air."

"Right this way, then." Eyebrows raised, a mischievous smile on her face, Sandy waved the key. "Ready?" With a flourish worthy of the best magician, she held the lavender key toward the center of the portal. The panel slid aside.

Warm, scented air and the inviting sounds of a breeze, birds calling, and water flowing drifted in through the opening.

He walked onto a wide ledge of variegated stone, his senses assaulted by the richness and beauty of the surroundings. Lush greenery dotted with exotic flowers of different colors, and trees laden with unidentifiable fruits stretched as far as he could see. A lapis lazuli sky arched above the peaceful scene. There were no clouds, not even wisps.

"A yellow sun," he observed as she joined him on the ledge. "Only one?"

Shading her eyes, she stared at the planet's star for a moment. "There's a small binary companion with a different orbital cycle. Come on, I want to show you the whole complex, and especially the lake!" She flashed the key at the doorway, shutting off access to the interior.

"Damn it, all our things are in there."

Spine rigid, face unsmiling, she keyed the door open again. "I've been in and out a dozen times. The key works, all right? You have to extend some trust here."

"Didn't you say you wanted to show me the gardens?" he parried, not willing to get drawn into another debate.

Sandy stepped off the ledge and walked across the thick green turf.

Sighing, he followed her for a tour of their private oasis. She led him to the small lake first, pointing out iridescent fish swimming in its shallow depths. Along the way she picked some fruit, handing Mark a tempting red sphere so juicy he found it hard to avoid making a mess of his tunic. Mood improving, he sat beside the water to eat.

"I didn't dare go deeper into the oasis on my own yesterday," she said, picking another piece of fruit for herself and joining him on the soft turf.

Tossing the core into the bushes, Mark leaned back to eye the mountain rising so far above them the peak was lost in the clouds. "I think our pocket paradise was built into a plateau. Took master builders to carve all this. Let's explore the boundaries, shall we?"

After another few moments of walking through a haphazard orchard of various types of fruit trees, they reached the outer wall. A ten-foot wall of stones stacked together with no mortar, yet linked perfectly, formed the barricade, running in both directions as far as he could see. He couldn't insert so much as a fingernail between the blocks. Troubled, he gave her a look. "The zoo-like aspects of this bother me."

"Zoo?"

"Perfect human habitat enclosed by a stone wall, male and female specimens trapped inside. The confined surroundings don't concern you?"

Eyebrows raised, she stared at the wall. "Now that you mention it, yes."

"I still have my antigrav pads. Let's see what's beyond the edge of our enclosure, shall we?" Suiting action to words, he activated the boots and rose to the top of the stone ringing the pocket oasis. A long, low whistle escaped his lips, and he descended, holding a hand out to her. "You have to see this. Let me lift you to the top."

"What is it?"

"I think we might have this planet to ourselves after all. There is nothing, but nothing, anywhere."

She made the short ascent in his arms. The two of them stood on the wall, staring across the rugged landscape. As far as Mark could see, stretching all the way to the horizon, was a semi-arid expanse, close to being a true desert. A solitary bird—hawk, eagle, some kind of predator—circled in the sky, drifting on the thermals, the only other living thing besides them anywhere. There were no roads, no signs of any other habitation, no lights. Mark lifted off and floated beyond the wall, both to assure himself nothing prevented him from doing so and to assess the possibilities of using the grav boots or attempting an old-fashioned manual descent.

"Sheer walls as far as I can see, disappearing into the clouds." He staggered a bit as he landed next to her again, the antigrav flickering off in one boot. "Well, we won't be using antigrav to escape. One pad by itself doesn't provide enough lift, and I wouldn't risk it failing on us." Reaching down, he yanked the useless antigrav insert from his boot and flung it out into the void. "I'm glad you like it here so much, because I'd say we're marooned." He eyed the bird, far above even their perch. "Unless we grow wings like he's got."

"Where would we go anyway?" she asked.

"I object on principle to being cooped up anywhere I can't get out of, no matter how beautiful. Makes me wary."

"Maybe the Travelers had some way of going to another place when they got tired of this one," Sandy suggested as she started walking back to their new domicile. "We can't fault them after the fact just because we don't. Now we know it's not a zoo. Don't try to scare me." She patted his arm as he walked beside her, taking some of the sting out of her warning. "You'll figure this out. We won't stay trapped in the oasis for the rest of our lives."

"Fair enough." He had no idea at the moment how to escape this beautiful cage, but was pleased by her faith in him.

Even if some of the features of the dwelling built into the cliff were for cooking, it was beyond either Mark or Sandy to find anything to use. Around twilight, he gathered fallen branches, built a stone fire ring, and coaxed a small blaze into existence on the broad patio outside. He roasted the fish he'd managed to spear with his combat knife while wading in the shallows of the lake. She sat, watching him in companionable silence. The primary sun had gone down in a raging blaze of scarlet and purple skies before he could prepare the main course. Fruit served as an appetizer.

"I'm sorry you got dragged into all this," Sandy said, taking the last few berries and rolling them in her palm.

Mark slid one of the fish off its skewer and onto a broad green leaf, placing the offering in front of her. "I got dragged into this, as you elegantly express the concept, one hell of a long time ago. The present adventure is nothing but another chapter in a long tale."

"Smells terrific." She broke the fish apart and started removing fine bones. "We can't avoid the subject forever. Do you know what my grandmother did to you?"

Her question broke a dam inside his heart, and the answer poured out. "Had me arrested, tortured, my brain scrubbed clean by her damn, clumsy techs, and then had me dumped in the Sectors as part of some half-baked sleeper-agent experiment. I was a seriously confused person for a lot of years, almost psychotic, with two sets of memories. A set on the surface making sense for the Sectors. One even more vivid set buried but trying to get out. I'd have flashes of recall at the weirdest times, couldn't control it."

"And you've been in the Sectors ever since?"

Rolling his shoulders, he said, "Her agents planted me in a destroyed colony, as if I was the only survivor of a Mawreg attack. I sure believed it for quite a few years. The Sectors authorities who process older survivors said I tested off the charts for military aptitude. Not surprising, since I'd been in training as a warrior in Outlier since I could walk. My body remembered even if my mind couldn't. And of course Outlier human stock age somewhat differently, so the Sectors authorities pegged me as younger than I am. The bureaucrats recorded me as having been a cadet in the militia on the destroyed colony and sent me to the Star Guard Academy."

Head tilted, she eyed him clinically for a moment. "But you obviously regained your true memories. How?"

"It happened the first time I underwent treatment in their rejuve resonator. I was in critical condition after a tricky mission, so the medics authorized the treatment. I argued with them about keeping the scar along my ribs. I knew the mark formed an essential part of my identity, a link to something, even without access to my memories. My commanding officer ordered the medics to comply with my demand just to get me to shut up. He wanted me to take the treatment before I bled out and died. I came out of the tissue-regeneration field with complete memories." Instinctive caution had made him keep his mouth shut in that bleak moment even as his mind had reeled under the assault of his true Outlier memories.

She discarded a tiny bone on the side of the leaf. "And then?"

"Got sent on another mission." He concentrated on filleting his fish for a moment to buy time. He never talked about himself. He kept those doors in his mind shut, and no good ever came of peeking behind them, in his experience. Yet how could he refuse to answer her questions? She was the cause of all his misfortunes. "I did my twenty in the Sectors Special Forces, got mustered out recently, in fact. The brass decided my skills and resistance to orders I didn't like made me too spooky for them, too unpredictable. I didn't know what to do next until your grandmother had me kidnapped. Ekatereen and I had a cozy little reunion – I'd have probably killed the old witch if she hadn't had half the palace guards in the room. I hope the snatch-and-grab job on me cost her a solar system's ransom." Bitterness burned in his throat. He wanted the empress to suffer, even if nothing would ever compensate for all she'd done to him. "She set me up as a mercenary, thanks to your madcap journey with Portuc."

Dropping her fish, Sandy recoiled. "She paid you to bring me to Throne?"

This discussion was veering perilously close to emotions he'd locked away in order to survive. Hurtful words came to his rescue. "Why else would I have bothered going to Freemarket? She offered more credits than I could spend in a lifetime." He chewed his fish and hoped his surliness would end the conversation for now.

Sandy pushed away her plate.

"So, most of those years in the Sectors, you knew who you were? But you made no attempt to return to Outlier? To me? Until someone—my grandmother, of all people—paid you?"

Listening to the shock and pain in her voice made him remorseful, so he offered a piece of the truth. "I didn't even know who the real Mark Denaltieri was until long after I graduated from the academy and commenced active duty, carrying out missions. If the Sectors authorities ever suspected me of being an Outlier soldier, I'd have been thrown in prison and never let out."

"But you weren't tempted to come for me before this?" Her voice was tight, and she eyed her dinner away as if the food had suddenly spoiled.

"I didn't know what your situation was. News doesn't filter from Outlier into the Sectors, especially not about minor members of the imperial family. You've no idea how impossible it is to travel from the Sectors into Outlier. Sectors citizens are expressly forbidden to cross the border. It takes huge piles of credits, connections, and sheer luck. Even if I'd somehow gotten to Throne, what could I have done? Empress Ekatereen would have had me executed the moment I crossed the Outlier border." Why couldn't she see he'd had no choices? He'd done what he had to do to survive. How could she blame him for all the things out of his control that blocked him from returning to her? "I made the best of my situation and persevered in the Sectors. At least I had a place there, a purpose."

"You could have come for me." Keeping her voice low, Sandy averted her face, contemplating the rising quarter moon, a glowing reddish dot, far over the horizon.

"You were the direct cause of my losing everything." Mark tried one last time to explain. "My final memory of you was the fight we had because I wouldn't join your household guard, remember? For all I know, *you* betrayed me to the empress. The secret police arrested me not two hours after I'd left our secret spot. The empress supervised my torture personally—did she tell you that? And one of the things she threw in my face while her men were doing their damnedest to break me was the information that you'd decided I wasn't worth risking yourself and your status for any longer."

"Do you really believe I'd betray the man I loved to her secret police?" A sob caught in her throat. "Why would I do such a thing?"

He couldn't maintain his self-imposed distance any longer. Rising, he touched her shoulder, turned her around to him. Back straight, she remained stiff against his body, her fists pushing against his chest. His lips close to her ear, he said, "Once I had my true memories firmly in place, I thought about you all the time. In some ways, remembering what we shared hurt worse than your grandmother's physical torture. If there'd been one single hope in seven hells of seeing you, of asking you to tell me the truth, I'd have found a way to get to Outlier, or died trying."

"Grandmother never told me who betrayed us. She just told me you were dead. She said she had you executed." Sandy unclenched her fists and wrapped her arms around his waist, resting her head against his chest. She wouldn't look at him. "Your punishment and death were all because of me, she said. On my head. My 'escapade,' as she called it, had cost her a good soldier. I never forgave myself for causing your death."

Mark didn't know what to say. Her words certainly had the ring of truth. He held her closer as more details poured out.

"I believed her at first. I wept and I raged. I demanded to see your body, but she said you'd been cremated. She assigned special guards to watch over me during my yearlong exile to her most distant estate. To consider my foolishness, she said. When my sentence ended, I stayed as far away from her as I could." Now Sandy's voice held a touch of proud defiance.

"You cut your hair." He felt like a fool the second after the words left his mouth, unable to block his memories of her long, silky blonde hair, falling around both of them as they lay together. Now he slid his fingers through the soft curls, massaging her neck.

"One of my minor rebellions over the years. Princesses of the Blood are never supposed to cut their hair, but it interfered with my work."

"Work?" The word was incongruous in a discussion of anyone from the imperial family.

"I'm a doctor," she said with visible, quiet pride.

It took him a moment to absorb the revelation. No member of the Zhivanov family had ever dabbled in real work, to his knowledge, much less undertaken something as demanding as medicine. Remembering his initial awakening on this new world of theirs, he laughed.

Apparently taking offense at his amusement, she held herself rigid and shoved away from him. Hands on her hips, voice like ice, she said, "What's so amusing about me being a doctor?"

"Nothing, I promise you. I thought you were an addict. I've been watching for the shakes, waiting for you to start detoxing on me."

"An addict?" She raised her eyebrows as comprehension dawned. "Are you talking about the inject I gave you to put you out? You believed I shared my private stash?"

"I apologize for misjudging you. I never dreamt you were a doctor."

"Oh yes, I can see how imagining me as a hopeless tranq abuser would be so much more in character for a Zhivanov." She walked away. Seating herself on the ledge, legs and arms crossed, her body language was closed off.

He walked after her, kneeling by her side. "I said I was sorry. My good luck to have you as my private doctor on this trip." The remark won him a small smile. Encouraged, he pursued the topic of her career. "The empress allowed you to deal with the sick and injured?"

"She didn't pay much attention to me for a long time after she took you away. She'd made her point, and as you know, she had many potential heirs at that time. My name was far down the list. I don't think she ever took my dedication to medicine seriously. Maybe she thought I was after drugs as well. She did say she found it politically useful to have the people see one of her heirs in a healing role." Again, Sandy's voice dripped acid. "In '07 an epidemic broke out, some new virus we'd never seen before. The Imperial House proved especially vulnerable to it—genetic predisposition, we think. There's research going on. I guess now I'll never know the results."

"Why did you go with Portuc?" The choice puzzled him. She'd never been able to stand Portuc when Mark had lived at court.

"What did Grandmother say when she had you kidnapped?" she wanted to know first.

"Some cock and bull story about Portuc helping you in an attempt to find me. But you thought I was dead, so tell me your real reason."

She shook her head. "I told you. After you were gone, I was inconsolable at first. I stopped eating, lost interest in all the activities I used to pursue, avoided those friends who were still willing to associate with me. I was on a dangerous downward path." A flush of embarrassment rose in her cheeks.

Justifiably or not, he'd been completely self-absorbed in the tragedy of his life, the destroyed hopes and dreams. He'd bitterly assumed she'd continued her privileged life after he disappeared. If she wasn't the one who'd betrayed him, maybe at best she might have cried a few tears. He'd had to believe Sandy indifferent to his fate or go insane. Confronting the reality now challenged his self-control. Needing a distraction and some distance, he went to tend the fire, feeding the flames a few sticks.

She had more details of her story to tell, raising her voice to carry over the crackle of the renewed fire. "Whenever my grandmother talked about your death it was as if she withheld a secret, even as she forced me to hear horrific details. She could never meet my eyes when we talked about you, and evasion's not Ekatereen's style. When I conducted my own medical research, I also hunted for any trace of your medical records, any clue about what happened to you."

"Surely she had those destroyed."

Sandy shook her head. "Ekatereen is ruthless, not subtle. The men who did the experiment on you were killed. The records in their lab were destroyed, but it never occurred to her that the scientists would be proud of their work and make copies in defiance of her orders. Who disobeys the Outlier empress, right? The backup records were hidden deep in the Throne medical database. The researchers were clever about it, but I took care to learn how to search the nooks and crannies of all the data warehouses as part of my medical training. Told my instructors I might go into research and needed mastery of the databases." She buried her face in her hands for a moment. "I wept when I read the details of what they did to you."

Silence fell between them for a few moments. Mark sat next to her.

She rested her hand on his thigh. "Was it so awful for you, there in the Sectors?"

He clasped her fingers. "Awful?" He considered. "No, once I got into the academy, I channeled my confusion into the training. I became one of the best damn Special Forces operators the Sectors ever had, doing nothing but wet work. Assassinations. I didn't care if I lived or died, even after I got my true memories back. I had a hole where my heart should have been, which made me unstoppable. I'd take any risk. And every time, I came through. The medtechs would patch the physical damage, and I'd volunteer for another assignment even more dangerous." He couldn't stop the flow of words.

"Was there—did you have someone in your life?"

He put his free hand under her chin, gently tilting her face up to his. "Have I been with other women? Yes, I'm no monk. Could any woman compete with my memory of you? No. I formed no permanent attachments in the Sectors."

She blinked, and he took his hand away from her chin, embarrassed at his own vehemence.

"I was getting blind drunk after Command mustered me out against my will, when four D'nvannae Brothers picked a fight with me in some dive bar. The next thing I know, it's a week later, I'm sick as a dog from cryo-sleep lag, lying in your grandmother's sitting room on Throne, listening to her ordering me to Freemarket to rescue you."

"But you did come for me."

Reluctant to say too much, he hung on to his self-control by a thread, unsure of himself. Unsure of her. This conversation had pushed a lot of buttons. He tried to lighten the tone. "My rates for rescue service are exorbitant. She paid. I'm a rich man if I ever get to Freemarket to claim the reward."

Head tilted, Sandy pointed her finger at him. "I'm on to you now. I see how you try to avoid the truth. I'm not going to let you push me away. You reappear in my life after twenty years, rescue me from Portuc and Barent—we need to talk, to figure this out. Figure us out."

Mark stood, stretching to unkink his back. Staring at the sky, dotted with stars but not in any formation he recognized, he said, "I couldn't leave you on Freemarket, not with Barent Kliin on the scene, hatching his lethal schemes. My heart held nothing for you but hatred for a long time. I couldn't keep my sanity any other way. Your grandmother made such a mess of my life because of what happened between us." He glanced at her. "Can you blame me?"

"No. I hated her too. But we're stuck here, wherever here is. I didn't get the impression Lajollae planned to drop in on us with another globe to take us somewhere recognizable. We've both changed, that's become obvious tonight. Can we take it one day at a time for now and see what happens?"

He stuck out his hand. "All right, I can agree to those conditions."

Her handshake was surprisingly firm and matter-of-fact, not like a pampered princess with airs and graces.

"What was the rest of your plan, back there on Freemarket?" she asked.

"You mean the half-assed plan?" He gave her a lopsided grin. "Well, either I sent you to Throne on your grandmother's preprogrammed ship, safely locked in cryo sleep, then made my own escape to the Sectors. Or—" His voice trailed off.

"Or?" she prompted.

There was silence. The faint breeze blew. Some night bird trilled a soft song.

Mark blew out a gusty sigh. "Oh hell, some small part of me always harbored a faint hope. Depending on how things developed, I thought maybe you'd want to try your luck with me in a two-person starspeeder I'd bought with her tainted gold. I had it parked in a hangar off the beaten path on Freemarket. See if maybe we could make it across the Sectors border together."

"Claim veteran's acres and homestead?" she asked after a surprised silence.

"Get to know each other again, see if we had any common ground anymore. Well, what was your plan in going to Freemarket with Portuc?"

"I couldn't think of any other place where I might be able to get a rogue freighter to take me into the Sectors, if I paid enough. I didn't plan much beyond reaching the Sectors, but I hoped I could—I don't know, find you, somehow. I identified the planet you'd been taken to originally, to be planted as a sleeper spy. Obviously the trail started there."

The idea of her entrusting herself to the kind of sentients who flew smuggling runs back and forth through the DMZ made him shudder. He was glad Portuc had kept Sandy under lock and key, preventing her from carrying out her scheme.

"And instead we're here, wherever this place is." He tried to divert the conversation away from the highly charged personal topics. "Maybe we've homesteaded an entire planet. Although our deed is restricted to this high-altitude oasis at the moment."

"The whole world can't be deserted, can it?"

"Until I find a way to get us off this mountainside, we might as well be alone. Ready to go inside?"

She shivered a little, hunching her shoulders and glancing at the trees. "How long will it be before we know if there are other people, other sentients here? Will we ever know?"

"Bored with my company already?" Taking his canteen, he smothered the fire, making sure the embers were well doused.

She gave him a look he recognized from the old days, one of exasperation mixed with amusement. "Not yet."

"All right then, do your magic with the key, lock us in for the night, and let's see what tomorrow brings." He swung her to her feet, holding her for just a heartbeat longer than necessary.

Settling in together on the large bed later had its awkward moments. He was acutely conscious of her lying so close, but she made no move that could be construed as an invitation to intimacy. Neither did he. He felt bruised from their frank conversation. Self-protective and uninviting, her body language spoke louder than words. He gave her the Kliin coat for a blanket and fell asleep on the opposite side of the mattress, taking care not to accidentally invade her space.

Sandy slept later than he did the next morning, no doubt making up for her all-night vigil the cycle before. Mark took the duplicate key from its hook, eager to pursue his hunch about the fourth door, the one opening into an empty room. Gritting his teeth after the black key opened the portal for him, he stepped into the darkness. A sharp, hot pain flickered through his nerves, gone as soon as the sensation registered.

The lights and ventilation responded to his presence. Striding into the huge space, he pondered the purpose of such a generous room. A garage maybe? Several hundred feet across the sandy floor from him stood a double door outlined in the stone wall. Holding the key in front of him, blaster drawn, he made his way to a spot that would be out of the direct line of fire. The portals slid open.

He gazed across the arid wasteland he'd seen from ground level the day before. Walking a few paces out from the entry, all senses alert, he assessed the situation. Their door opened onto a narrow mountain pass, with another steep slope rising across the way. Only a few hundred yards wide, the valley ran to the right as far as he could see from his cursory inspection. Checking the compass setting on his wrist chrono, he confirmed that was west. There were no tracks or any other signs of sentient beings.

I knew there had to be a way out.

The day was already hot outside the confines of the Traveler dwelling, and there were no breezes stirring. He took another quick glance in all directions and then closed the outer doors, going "upstairs" to waken Sandy and share this welcome news with her.

"What good does it do us?" Apparently, she was determined to be practical today. "You said yourself there's no sign of other life out there. We've no idea how far we'd have to travel to find anything worth leaving here for. For all we know, the entire planet is deserted."

"We can't live out our entire lives in this aerie."

"Why not? Can't you relax and enjoy this for a while? It's peaceful, we have food, water and total privacy. I don't comprehend your insistence on leaving. I thought we wanted to get to know each other again. What better setting could there be? What's your hurry to leave?" Tapping one toe, she glared at him. "Are you tired of me already?"

"Of course not. We don't have to leave today. I'm merely saying we can leave whenever we want. Come and see," he cajoled, holding out his hand.

Obviously humoring him, she grabbed a piece of fruit from the stash they'd stored in the "kitchen" area and followed him to the door under discussion. "Definitely Traveling," she said with a sharply in-drawn breath as they crossed the threshold. "You're right."

When they emerged in the hot and wind-blown pass, she did a slow 360-degree spin. "Did I really have to come down here with you to confirm how desolate the place is?"

Hand in hand, they walked out into the flatter portion of the valley. Shielding her eyes, Sandy said, "What do you suppose is causing that dust cloud? Are we going to have a storm?"

Unfastening one pocket flap on his utilities, Mark brought out distance viewers and scanned the area she indicated. "*Tzerde*. The question has been answered. We're not alone." Lowering the viewers, he grabbed her elbow and steered her toward the cliff wall where the opening to their temporary residence lay.

Sandy yanked her arm from his grasp. Standing with one hand on her hip, she gestured with the other. "I want to see for myself."

Exasperated, he handed her the viewers and drew his blaster. "Look fast."

"Two groups of people," she said a moment later, adjusting the focus. "One bunch chasing the other. What are those things they're riding in?"

"Low-tech civilization. Let me think." Dredging up the memory of a long-ago class at the academy, he said, "I believe they're called chariots."

"How do you know?"

"I had an entire course of study on primitive peoples. Technology tends to evolve in similar ways from world to world. Sometimes we'd have to run a mission on a planet early in the civilization cycle, stuff like this, so we had to know how to survive, blend in. You can't go around using your M27 indiscriminately if you want to stay undercover."

Still gazing fixedly at the horizon through the viewers, she said, "Seems I ignored a vital part of my education. I see this world has horses. I like that."

"The Sectors exploration teams have found humans, whales, horses, cats, roses—a number of common-denominator species co-exist on the thousands of planets where our kind of life-forms hang out. Lots of theories, of course. Never mattered much to me. The people and familiar animals exist, along with a million unfamiliar ones, fact of life, end of story." He grabbed at the viewers, wrenching them none too gently from her. "We need to get inside. We don't want to be here when these people go careening through the pass." Giving her no chance to protest, he picked her up and carried her to the base of the small incline that led to the opening in the mountain.

As he set her on her feet, Sandy said, "You're the one who wanted to find out if there were inhabitants here. Now you want to avoid them?"

"There are no circumstances in which I'm allowing you to be seen by chariots full of armed warriors."

"There was a woman in one of the vehicles." She climbed the slope, bare feet sinking into the loose sand.

"I saw her." Mark half turned, taking another look through the viewers.

"The horses pulling the first three chariots are getting tired. Not going to be able to outrun the others much longer, even if their vehicles are lighter in build. And I doubt if they were meant to carry three people. Too crowded, no room to fight. Seven hells, one just crashed!"

He swore again as one of the three chariots in the lead hit a buried obstruction and rose into the air, crashing down with bone-jarring force. The left wheel splintered. The chariot veered, throwing two of its occupants onto the hard plain. The driver's face was taut with concentration and fear as he reined the two horses in. The panicked team managed to drag the broken chariot at least another hundred yards before coming to a stop. The other two chariots circled around. There was a rapid conference among the fugitives, with much nervous glancing at the oncoming enemy.

The two good chariots rolled slowly away toward the base of Mark and Sandy's mountain. The driver of the damaged vehicle cut the traces and pulled and tugged his spooked animals in the direction his companions had gone. One of the people who'd been thrown from the chariot scrambled to his feet under his own power and limped after the rest, stopping to make a cursory check of the other crash victim.

"Dead. Broken neck." Mark's assessment was matter-of-fact.

"What's going on? Who has a broken neck?" She tugged at his arm. "If you plan to hog the viewers, at least tell me what you're seeing." Hand over her eyes, squinting as if to improve her vision, Sandy stared at the approaching dust cloud.

"We're getting to the safety of our door and closing it behind us now." He shoved the viewers in his pocket, holstered the blaster, and half carried Sandy the rest of the way to the entrance.

"Can't we stay, see what happens?" she said. "If we take cover behind these rocks, they won't know we're here. They certainly have no reason to be on the lookout for us. I understand you're worried about me, but we need to gather information, don't we?"

Blaster in his hand again, Mark surveyed their position. Sandy was right. The rocks in front of them would provide good cover. "All right, close the door, and then I want you to sit right here and don't make a move." He indicated a spot that was shielded but would afford her a view of the valley immediately below. "If I tell you to open the portal and go inside, promise you'll obey without question."

"I promise." She crouched where he'd indicated, holding the key in her hand.

Mark took up a position next to her, his blaster trained on the pass below as the party being pursued wheeled into view.

"Getting ready for a last stand." Mark's hand tightened on the grip of his M27 as he watched the smaller group. He admired the unknown officer's crisp, efficient manner as he directed his meager forces to deploy, using the mountain as a shield at their backs. "Must realize he can't escape the superior force with those tired horses. Not enough vehicles now anyway."

"We should do something." Sandy touched his arm, gave him a pleading glance.

"We don't know who the good guys are. We might not want to take either side. Although if I had to make a guess, I'm betting on this set, the smaller one."

"Why?"

"Can't explain it. Soldier's instincts maybe." Safe behind the rocks, he watched as the seven warriors formed a defensive ring behind the two remaining chariots, which had been drawn into a woefully inadequate barricade. The six horses were off to the side now, tethered to some scrubby bushes growing at the base of the mountain.

The officer took the woman by the hand and led her to the spot farthest away from where the enemy assault was going to hit. The couple stared at each other for a moment, exchanging words before the man leaned down for a long kiss, after which he directed her to the meager cover amongst the brush. Then, sword in hand, he strode to the barricade.

Apparently touched by the tender scene, Sandy grabbed his arm and said, "We have to help them!"

Flights of stubby black arrows came arching in from the pursuers. Three archers among the desperate escapees sent a return volley, but to what effect Mark couldn't tell, being at the wrong angle for a clear view. The exchange of arrows went on for a few moments, one of the defenders screaming and falling limp when a chance shot managed to penetrate their barricade of shields.

Three of the heavier, four-horse vehicles rushed in, sweeping to a halt in front of the makeshift barricade. Jumping from their conveyances, the soldiers engaged the hunted in fierce hand-to-hand combat with short swords. Drivers pulled their plunging teams out of the way. A fourth chariot drove up, the horses sweating with exertion in the heat. This driver seemed about to attempt a smashing assault on the defenders' makeshift wall but swerved at the last second. He waited impatiently as his complement of soldiers left the vehicle, avoiding engagement with the men already fighting. As soon as he was clear, the newcomer headed for the woman's hiding place, her colorful dress giving her position in the brown, dry underbrush away.

The officer in charge of the fugitives dispatched the man he fought with a fierce stroke, half decapitating his enemy. He ran to help the screaming woman as she was dragged toward the waiting chariot. Two more of the enemy troopers closed in from behind him, as if intending to capture him as well.

"I've seen enough. Get inside the mountain, seal the door, and wait for me. Now!"

Sandy scrambled to obey. Taking careful aim with his blaster, Mark drilled one attacker, then the other. Both fell to the sand. The officer spun around, seeking the source of this unexpected rescue. While he was distracted, another enemy soldier rushed in, striking him with a sword. The officer collapsed as Mark shot this new assailant.

Screaming, the woman struggled as her captors threw her into the waiting chariot. The driver whipped his team into a gallop, heading toward the open plain to the east. The departure acted as a signal for the other soldiers, who disengaged, running for their own chariots. Mark picked off as many as he could from his hiding place, then half ran, half slid down the incline, blaster in hand, sprinting into the open valley.

The dazed, battered defenders stared at him with mouths open.

As Mark ran to where the horses were tethered, he holstered his blaster.

Drawing his combat knife, he slashed through the traces, freeing the closest horse. Slamming the knife into its sheath, Mark took a firm grasp of the animal's coarse black mane. Gathering the reins in his other hand and stepping onto the framework of the chariot, he mounted. The horse took violent exception to carrying a person, bucking and kicking. A determined, skillful rider, Mark established control in the man-versus-beast battle of wills. Wheeling the animal in a tight circle, without checking to see if any of the soldiers would follow his lead, Mark gave the terrified horse its head and galloped at full speed after the four departing chariots, now spread out in a wedge, the one carrying their captive in the center. He drew his horse even with the chariot and fired one close-range shot at the driver, who lost the reins and slumped over, apparently dead. The woman lunged for the straps, but they slipped away, dragging in the sand under the horses' pounding hooves.

Blessed by ancestors from a fierce, horse-riding warrior clan, whose skills their descendants proudly maintained on his world even in the modern age, Mark didn't hesitate. Gripping his horse with his knees, Mark leaned over to grab the loose reins. He brought the team to a halt, yelling at the woman. "Come on, we haven't much time here, lady." He leaned over, prepared to pluck her out of the chariot. She cringed before taking a closer look at the horse he rode. Then she held out her hands to him, and he managed to hoist her behind him onto the horse, where she locked her arms around his waist.

He kicked the horse's flanks and headed to the base of the oasis mountain, where her own people waited. The enemy chariots were making wide turns and attempting to follow him. Mark fired off a few shots, aiming at the chariot drivers. He managed to wing one man, who lost control of his vehicle, which crashed into the one next to it. The remaining chariot came to a halt, its passengers apparently intimidated by his ability to deliver death long range.

Satisfied, he galloped back to the scene of the recent battle.

The apparent second-in-command met him. As the woman called out to him, this soldier gave Mark a searching look, continuing his study as he assisted the rescued lady to dismount.

The local asked a question. The language had an annoyingly familiar sound, Mark thought, as he dismounted, hanging on to the broken leather straps. He got about half the gist of what the man said. He'd been given hypno implants on many languages during various missions in the Sectors, and the babel sorted itself out in the unconscious part of his brain as the master implant analyzed the input. One language came to the fore out of the cacophony.

High Chetal.

Well, better than nothing.

"We've got to get inside before your enemies return," Mark told the soldier.

"Thank you and the lady for coming to our assistance, my lord." The man saluted, fist over the heart.

"The lady—" Mark spun around. Sandy had disobeyed his orders. She must have gone upstairs to the aerie to retrieve her medical kit, which now lay open beside her as she worked over the injured officer

Livid, he couldn't honestly say he was surprised. She was a doctor, so of course she'd come to help. Handing the horse off to an open-mouthed soldier standing nearby, Mark strode over to the princess. "How is he?"

Clearly in professional mode, Sandy answered matter-of-factly. "Head trauma. Probably a concussion. Nothing he can't recover from. Those two over there are dead. The others have superficial wounds."

The soldier holding Mark's horse shouted and pointed to the east, where a new dust cloud sprouted on the horizon. Mark caught the arm of the man who had greeted him. Switching easily from Outlier to High Chetal, he said, "We need to get the horses and ourselves to a safe place right away, before your enemies come back."

Eyeing him, but apparently willing to take sensible orders, the warrior hastened toward the horses, calling to his few remaining troopers.

Mark gave his attention to Sandy and the unconscious patient. "We have to move this man inside the garage."

She stood, drawing the other woman with her. "I understand. Try not to jar him too much."

"Get going!" Mark gave her a not-too-gentle push in the direction of the incline leading to the garage door.

Two of the soldiers came to carry their fallen officer across the narrow passage, up the hill, and into the opening in the side of the mountain. Mark and the others brought the horses and as much of the gear as the men could carry. The broken chariots and the fallen soldiers of both sides had to be left where they were, for now. He heard the sound of the approaching enemy chariots as Sandy keyed the portal door closed. Pivoing on his heel, he faced their motley assortment of new guests.

CHAPTER THREE

The four surviving soldiers had gone to one knee before Mark, heads bowed, right hands to their left shoulders in a salute. The woman remained standing, staring at him in a mixture of defiance and fear. Her hands were clenched at her sides, and her chest heaved as she breathed heavily.

"You can talk to them?" Sandy knelt beside her patient, taking his pulse. "Is this a planet you've been on after all?"

"No. The language is similar to one I had hypno implanted for a mission a long time ago. I'm not getting everything these people say, so they're probably having just as much trouble with me."

"Why are they kneeling to us?"

"I'll ask." Mark found translation duty tiresome. He hoped she was good with languages and learned fast.

The woman he'd rescued spoke first, before he could get a word out. Her tone was proud and regal, her voice low and musical. "I am Princess Tia, daughter of the last King of Nakhtiaar. My thanks to the Lady of the Star Wind and her consort for choosing to intervene in this humble matter of our lives."

Mark bowed to the woman. "My lady's name is Alessandra. I'm Mark."

"Your magic has been mighty, to bring us forth from death and into the safety of this place." Tia glanced around. "Surely there's more to your dwelling, Exalted Ones?"

"We'll take you to the living quarters," Mark said. "Your officer needs medical attention."

Tears trickled through the dust on Tia's cheeks "You don't intend to send us into the afterlife?" She pushed her black hair away from her wan face.

"Into the—no, quite the opposite. We want to help," Mark said. He gave the impatient Sandy a quick synopsis.

She grinned. "Lady of the Star Wind, hmm? Has a nice ring to it. What do they call you, then?"

Mark could feel his face reddening. Glad the lighting in the garage wasn't too bright, he said, "Your warrior. Concepts don't translate word for word."

"We need to get this man upstairs where I can treat these wounds." Sandy smoothed the strap of her medical bag where it dug into her shoulder. "The sooner, the better."

"This is Rothan." The woman gestured at the unconscious officer. "He's more dear to me than life itself. These men are his personal guard, what's left of them." She indicated the man who'd taken command after the officer was stricken. Although short, the man had well-developed arm and shoulder muscles. "Djed, chief archer of the Western Border."

The archer bowed. "I'm yours to command, Exalted One."

Mark wanted to get the locals to stop referring to him in such lofty terms but needed to have a better grasp of the situation before he corrected anyone's assumptions. He and Sandy could have made a huge mistake by intervening in local politics on the side of the refugees now standing in their garage.

"All right, Djed, I need your men to carry your captain farther into our dwelling, so the—the Lady of the Star Wind may continue her healing. Then we'll need to get the horses rubbed down. We can bring them some water and fodder later."

"Excellent." Rising to his feet, released from obeisance by the receipt of orders from one plainly used to giving them, the chief archer examined his surroundings, brow furrowed. "I see no exit, my lord, no water or grazing for the horses."

"This is a place of magic, exactly as you said." Mark gestured at Sandy. "She'll make it all plain to you." Then, in Outlier, he said to the princess, "Go ahead and open the portal to the dwelling, okay? We'll carry the wounded guy into the bedroom, and I've told Djed to get food and water for the horses from the oasis, once you let him out there."

"Just tell me what you need me to do. I have to get to my patient before he loses any more blood."

Mark touched her satchel. "How much in the way of medical supplies do you have?"

She frowned as she walked toward the portal. "Not as much as I'd like, but enough to take care of these people. I packed it practically to bursting when I left Outlier, because I wasn't ever going back. There must be local medicines I can learn to use or adapt, as my stock is exhausted." Flashing the lavender crystal key at the wall, she opened the way for them to proceed into the dwelling.

"The locals apparently believe you're some kind of a goddess or magical being. I think we need to be careful not to dispel such a useful impression right now," Mark said as he gestured for the awed refugees to follow Sandy through the portal.

After Sandy treated Rothan's wounds under Lady Tia's close scrutiny, Mark left Djed sitting with the unconscious man. Mark and Sandy escorted the noblewoman outside to the patio for something to eat. Tia accepted a leafy plate full of fish, fruit, and berries from one of the soldiers and then sank cross-legged onto the terrace across from Sandy.

Mark brought her a drink of water. "When you've eaten, we'd appreciate knowing what's going on. Why were you here in the desert? And why did these soldiers try to kidnap you?"

"We're on our way to the Lost City in search of the Crown and Scepter of Khunarum. If we can't locate the treasures and convey them to Nakhtiaar in time, our failure will mean disaster for my brother Hutenen and our people."

When he translated for Sandy, it was plain from her expression that the summary failed to enlighten her any more than it had made sense to him. "Do you understand the significance of anything she said?"

"I'm missing words here and there," he reminded her. "Let me try for a more complete explanation."

"There's a usurper on the throne. How is it you aren't aware of this fact?" Tia's surprise betrayed her puzzlement at being asked for a lesson in current events. "You've been absent from this land for at least three thousand years. Not a single mention of you in the scrolls of recent history. Yet here you are, in the Oasis of the Traveler. You chose to come to our rescue—unless this is all a dream or a vision. But you know nothing at all of what has been transpiring? You don't even speak the language as we do today!" She made a graceful hand gesture toward Sandy, who sat with a smile plastered on her face as the discussion occurred in a language she didn't comprehend. "Please don't mistake me. I'm grateful to meet you and find you kindly disposed to our cause. But I'm perplexed nonetheless."

Mark pondered how best to answer their guest's qualms. "Are you, then, one of those who fled this Lost City?"

"Of course not! The fall of the city occurred many generations ago." Tia laughed merrily at the idea. "Some three thousand years or more."

"Well, she isn't the Lady of the Star Wind who lived then either," Mark said, pointing at Sandy. "And I'm not the warrior from that legendary time. The events happened a long time ago even for my people. And we've been busy with other concerns in far-off places."

This explanation appeared to satisfy Tia. "Nakhtiaar needs your help to free the people from those who oppress and enslave them, so you've timed your return well."

Mark decided it might be best to let the discussion end there. Sure that he could obtain more intel the longer he spent with the Nakhtiaar, he didn't see a need to push the issue now.

He volunteered to sit with the injured man through the night. Sandy had discovered how to raise and lower the ambient lighting in the various chambers, so he had enough illumination to see the man's face. The patient lay under the folds of his own deep blue cloak in the bedroom. The women were asleep in the dining room, and the troopers were bivouacked outside in the oasis. A single man was stationed below with the horses.

Somewhere in the wee hours of the night, Rothan stirred. He opened his eyes, blinking a few times, moving his head restlessly on the makeshift pillow constructed from another cloak. He licked his cracked lips. "Water?"

Djed had filled a crude canteen at the tiny lake earlier in the evening. Mark offered it to the patient, holding the waterskin so the other could drink. "Just a few sips. You don't want to be sick."

Obediently, the man gulped a small amount of the water. "Thank you." Mark put his arm behind the man's shoulders to assist him in reclining.

"How are you feeling? Does your head hurt? How many fingers am I holding up?" Sandy had left Mark with a short litany of questions to ask if the patient awakened. She probably hadn't meant for him to ask them all at once, but being a nursemaid wasn't in his skill set.

"One finger. And no, my head doesn't hurt, which is a miracle, since the cursed dog of a Maiskhan must have struck me with his sword. I forgot what else you asked." The captain stared at Mark, his brow furrowed. Then his expression cleared, and his eyes opened wide. "I remember now. You came out of nowhere, out of the mountain, shooting magic arrows of death." He struggled to sit. "Tia! Where is she?"

Mark pressed him against the pillow. "She's safe, asleep in a room across the hall."

Closing his eyes as if the dim light bothered him, Rothan asked, "How many survived?"

"Tia, Djed, and three of your archers. Sorry, I don't know their names." Mark waved his key at the proper panel on the wall to dim the lights further.

"The horses?"

"We've taken good care of them, don't worry. I acquired a few extra mounts when we were cleaning up after the battle. Unhitched them from an abandoned chariot, one of the—the Maiskhan, you call them?"

Expression sour, as if the name itself brought a bad taste, the other man nodded. "Then all is not yet quite lost, if we're together and if we retain the means to reach the Lost City. There's so little time." He moved his head on the pillow.

"From the condition of your horses, you've been pushing them hard. How many days have you been traveling?"

"Seven days, with yet another three or four to go, if this is the mountain pass into the Empty Lands. And then we must get home to Nakhtiaar."

"Yeah, Tia said something about a deadline to us at dinner. She wasn't too forthcoming about the details."

"Your accent makes my head ache," said Rothan, distaste in his tone, opening his eyes to study Mark's face in the gloom. "Who are you?"

Grateful Lajollae had dropped them on a world where a readymade identity was available to adopt, Mark said, "I'm the warrior who guards the Lady of the Star Wind. She and I've come to this world for now."

"A good omen, to have the Star Wind at our backs in this time of crisis." The injured man sank against his pillow as if all mysteries were now explained to his satisfaction. "Is there any more water?" Fading fast, Rothan had a hard time keeping his eyes open, but seemed determined to pursue the issue of his quest to the lost city. "We must journey onward in the morning."

Mark shoved the cork into the waterskin. "I doubt if Sandy—the Lady—will let you leave the bed, much less agree to you riding in a chariot over rough ground."

"But I've told you, the time grows short. We can't forfeit a day, not an hour of a day. I'd drive at night under the moons as well, if the horses didn't require rest."

For the second time, Mark pushed him onto the makeshift pillows. "It won't do your cause any good if you die of a cerebral hemorrhage brought on by impatience."

"Die of a what?"

Not finding a word in High Chetal to fit the medical condition he wanted to describe, Mark hedged. "We'll see how you're doing in the morning, okay? I promise, word of an officer, we'll leave the moment my Lady gives you the medical clearance."

"In the morning," the other man insisted drowsily.

"We'll see." Mark was relieved to be done arguing for now as Rothan slipped into sleep.

A few hours later, the women walked into the chamber together, both anxious to see how Rothan fared. Mark stood, stretching, and moved aside for Sandy to examine the patient, who snored off and on.

"Did he regain consciousness at all?" She ran a rapid scan with one of her instruments.

"We had a regular gabfest in the middle of the night," Mark said. "And water was all I let him have." He anticipated her next question. "Rothan wants to travel today."

"It might be possible, I think. His head wound appears ugly enough on the surface, but there were no signs of skull fracture, no indication of more than a mild concussion. His vitals are good." She showed Mark the readout, though the figures meant nothing to him. "He could go on if he doesn't try to travel too fast."

"He'll be glad to hear the news. I'd have to knock him out to keep him in bed, if those were your orders. He's determined."

"We can go today?" Tia looked from one to the other, not comprehending a word of the rapid Outlier dialect.

"Yes, my lady, but we'll have to go with caution," Mark told her in High Chetal.

Eyes wide, Tia said, "You'll come with us?"

He was surprised at himself. He hadn't made a conscious decision to leave the oasis with these people, but plans revolved in his mind, all centering around a journey. Now he backtracked a bit. "I need to discuss the subject with the Lady of the Star Wind. Will you excuse us?"

As Rothan stirred groggily and Tia bent to tend to him, Mark took Sandy by the elbow, leading her out of the room. Mark strolled in silence across the central chamber and into the oasis, Sandy following his lead and not attempting to talk. Djed and one of his archers were preparing breakfast over a small fire.

The chief archer saluted as Mark walked onto the patio. "My captain is well this morning?"

Returning the salute, Mark nodded. "I think you may be able to continue on your journey today. Are the horses rested enough?"

"They must be," Djed said with a fatalistic shrug. "Will you share our breakfast?" He pointed at the frying fish and some kind of journeycake, spread out on one of the glossy green leaves.

"Later, thanks. The Lady and I need to have a conversation." Mark led Sandy away from the living quarters, stopping at the lake. Even though the locals didn't understand Outlier, he had a longtime aversion to being overheard.

She laughed at him as she seated herself on a big flat rock at the water's edge, dangling her toes in the clear water. "Afraid the Nakhtiaar got hypno training overnight?"

Mark frowned. "We need to make a decision."

"Did you find out more about why these people are fleeing?"

Skipping a rock across the calm surface of the pond, he said, "Pretty standard stuff. Rothan was conscious enough to talk a couple of times during the night, and I pieced the situation together from what he shared. In a nutshell, Tia's brother is the rightful king, but one of his late father's wives seized the throne. This brother strikes me as not the brightest strategist." Mark laughed. "Before he'd fully consolidated power after his father died, he departed on a previously planned two-year expedition to explore the region to the south, which gave this woman Farahna her chance. She acted as regent and then took over completely."

Sandy plucked a yellow and red variegated flower and began idly pulling the petals off, one by one, dropping them into the water to drift away. Frowning, she said, "So far this reminds me a lot of Outlier politics. I didn't expect to get ensnared in this kind of scheming and backstabbing here."

"Oh, it gets worse. Rothan and the real king recently came home in triumph from the trip, and on the night of the welcome-home banquet, the king falls mysteriously ill."

Tossing the final petals into the pond, she sighed. "Don't tell me—poisoned?"

"Rothan and Tia suspect foul play. The queen's personal doctors are treating him. No one can get in to see him, not even his sister. Who, by the way, scheming Queen Farahna intends to marry to her own son without further delay."

Sandy pulled her feet from the water as tiny fish came to investigate her wriggling toes. Drying them on the hem of her gown, she said, "Which explains the pursuit we saw and the attempt to kidnap Tia." She grimaced. "I can relate. Rothan must not like the queen's idea much either, since he stole her away. But why this mad dash to the lost city? I don't understand, unless he and Tia are eloping and planning to live there?"

Mark batted a large, slow-flying insect away from his face and stretched his arm to pick some fruit for his breakfast. "The tale takes an unusual twist. Rothan's after some artifacts, a crown and a scepter belonging to their ancestors. He says—no, he swears—the scepter has the power of life and death, can cure all ills, including poisoning, and whoever wears the crown is automatically the ruler. Apparently, the crown possesses its own magic, whereby it recognizes the true ruler, and the people will follow where the crown rests."

"Convenient." Tilting her head, Sandy said, "You sound like you believe the mad tale?"

Offering her the second red fruit he'd picked, he said, "I've seen stranger things on some of the worlds I've been to." He shrugged. "I mean, was what Lajollae did to send us here magic? Or ancient technology we don't comprehend?"

"Fair point." Biting into the juicy offering, she abandoned the flat rock and strolled along the edge of the water.

Mark followed her, slinging another stone into the lake and watching it skip five times before sinking from view. "I'm intrigued by the fact whoever lived in this oasis has a place in the legends of Rothan's people." He sat on the grassy bank to eat his own "apple" as she kilted her dress and waded into the water up to her knees. "There's another angle too," he said. "This Queen Farahna is from someplace else, the nation of Maiskhan. She's bringing in soldiers and priests from her home by the boatload, and Rothan suspects she's planning to convert his birthplace into a Maiskhan satellite."

"And we should care…why?"

Her confrontational tone rubbed him the wrong way. The Sandy he knew, or thought he'd known, wouldn't have been so dismissive of other people's problems. "The Maiskhan sound like a nightmare bunch. They believe in human sacrifice, and commit atrocities." Mark rose to steady her as she stepped from the lake so she wouldn't slip on the slick grass.

"According to Rothan." Sandy dropped his hand. "Not saying I don't believe him, but we both know the techniques of deploying negative propaganda to rally the populace. My grandmother's lackeys are accomplished liars."

"My assessment so far is he's a straightforward, no-bullshit guy. An honest man trying to save his best friend's life and throne. Wants to do right by his people." Her skepticism bothered him, but he had to admit neither of them had firsthand knowledge of the facts on this world. Rothan impressed him, had the kind of military background he could relate to, was comfortable with.

Unsmiling, Sandy faced him, her gaze direct. "So this decision you want me to make boils down to going with them or staying here, right?"

"Yes."

She stared across the lake, watching a flight of graceful white birds take wing into the sky, soaring easily beyond the barrier. "And you vote to go?"

"I do."

Pivoting on her heel to confront him, she said, "Why? Persuade me, *bogatyr Denaltieri,* remembering you're sworn to place my well-being uppermost."

Surprised and irritated by her reversion to haughty royalty, as well as her reference to his blood oath of allegiance, given decades before, Mark stayed silent for a moment, marshaling his thoughts. His readiness to sign on to the cause of people he'd just met was out of character for him, he realized under her prodding. "It's beautiful here, but we can't live the rest of our lives cooped up in this pocket-size oasis of greenery on the side of a mountain. Maybe it worked for the real Travelers, maybe they dropped in and spent their vacations here and then Traveled home to their real lives, or on to somewhere else. I don't know. But we—well, I think we're here on this planet forever. These seem like good, honest people and, furthermore, have horses, food, and water, maps for the terrain—who knows when another likely group might come along? I say we throw our lot in with them, see where it takes us."

"From what you've translated for me so far, it could take us deep into trouble. I guess I'm not as eager to leave this refuge as you are." Sandy dusted off her turquoise silk skirt, pausing to examine a couple of small rips and stains. "But what you say makes sense. If we're going to be on this planet for the rest of our lives, we can't hide from the people who live here. And I don't think we can be neutral either, do you?"

"Rothan said the Star Wind always showed favor to the side he's on. These people are so sure you're this legendary Lady returned to them. They view it as a positive omen, which is a point in our favor."

"I'd hate to disappoint them." Her laugh sounded forced, which Mark decided to ignore, pleased not to have to argue with her further about leaving the oasis.

There was a hail from the direction of the dwelling. Djed beckoned, while Rothan stood in the doorframe, leaning on Tia.

Mark waved a hand at the others. "Your patient's ambulatory whether you like it or not. Shall we go back?"

"Please remember this isn't another mission you're on," Sandy said. "This is the rest of our lives you're talking about." She walked past him without another word.

Over breakfast, the discussion dealt with strategy. Rothan expressed his gratitude for Mark's plans to accompany them to the Lost City.

"You've a house there as well," he informed Sandy. "The Lady of the Star Wind attended the court of King Khunarum from time to time, or so it says in the oldest scrolls."

Amused disbelief seemed to be Sandy's reaction as this was translated. "I'm inheriting things right and left, aren't I? Excellent news, I suppose, to have yet another place of our own on this planet. I may be reduced to one dress, but at least I have real estate."

Mark picked bones from the fish on his plate. "I hope the Traveler keys work there."

Eyebrows raised high in disbelief, she said, "Surely whatever kind of a dwelling or building they're talking about must have fallen down a long time ago. You said this city we're going to was abandoned over three thousand of their years ago."

Mark waved his hand at the oasis beyond the patio where they sat. "This place must be the same age or much older, and it's all functioning, once you found the keys. Why should the dwelling in the city be any different? I've seen Ancient Observer installations guesstimated at over a million standard years old, humming away, doing whatever AO technology does. In no way does this place resemble an AO installation, but similar idea. I'd like to get my hands on some high tech, even the alien kind. My blaster's only going to last so long. The civilian popgun I took off Kliin's merc will be exhausted even sooner. Your medical supplies are limited. Maybe at the house in the city, the Travelers left the pots and pans behind, unlike here."

"And the weapons and the medicines?"

"Right. A man can dream, can't he?"

After breakfast, Mark led the soldiers to the garage to check on the horses. While the men were busy with their tasks, he and Rothan strolled across the pass to examine the chariots.

Rothan tipped one to the upright position. "We can't all fit into two chariots, my friend."

Mark helped him with the second. "You probably noticed I rustled a few of the Maiskhan horses. The animals appear to be a sturdy breed. Sandy and I'll ride them."

Frowning, Rothan tried out the unfamiliar syllables. "Rustle? Ride?"

"Rustle as in steal. And ride as in on the horse, rather than standing in a bouncing chariot being pulled by a team of them. You'll see," Mark said, full of confidence in the bright morning and happy to be facing action. "These horses aren't used to riders, but we can manage."

Rothan knelt to examine the axle on the nearest chariot, running his hand over the wheel's spokes. "What Tia told me about you pursuing the Maiskhan on the bare back of a horse is nothing short of miraculous. Can you teach us? Or is it magic?"

"Riding's an acquired skill, nothing magical. But I think for now we should concentrate on getting to the Lost City the best way possible, which means using the chariots. No time to teach all of you to ride. Later. Cavalry is a definite advance in military strategy. It might come in handy if we find ourselves battling Farahna and her allies. Be a surprise she won't be expecting."

Moving to inspect the second chariot's harness, Rothan glanced at Mark over his shoulder. "You know of other such strategic advances?"

"Yes, but not all of them will be of any use to you in the middle of a desert. I promise to share whatever will work here, word of an officer."

Mark and the soldiers carried out a burial detail after breakfast. Before making the short return trip inside, he lingered alone for a few moments and buried his black key in an unobtrusive spot he knew he could find again, beside a variegated outcropping. If he and Sandy ever needed to seek sanctuary in the oasis, he wanted a key where he could find it, in case Sandy's key got lost during the expedition.

Departure took place after the noon hour, Sandy flashing the lavender crystal key at the garage portal. The door slammed closed faster than the human eye could follow. She stood staring at the barren flank of the mountain for a long moment, no sign left of the entry to the Traveler oasis.

Mark helped her mount on the least skittish of the horses, then got onto the animal he'd chosen for himself. Riding was a favorite pastime of the nobles on Throne, so she was at home on horseback, even without a saddle. Rothan watched all this with a critical eye, leaning on the rim of his chariot, Djed at the reins, holding the eager team in place. Tia stood braced against the opposite side of the basket. The second chariot, carrying the three remaining archers, waited slightly to the rear. Mark had the two other Maiskhan horses on long lead, burdened with makeshift packs constructed from cloaks taken from the dead enemy soldiers. The bags carried the items he'd salvaged from the wreckage of the third chariot, as well as from the Maiskhan. Full canteens of water from the oasis and as much fruit as the men had been able to pick from the low branches supplemented the original supplies.

"The fodder you provided has given them new life." Djed smiled at his eager team of horses. "The Oasis of the Travelers has magical powers, as the legends told."

"There'll be one full moon tonight, Amrell the beauteous. She's said to favor travelers. We can continue until Amrell begins to set, and thus make up some of the time we lost after skirmishing with the Maiskhan." Rothan provided his assessment as his chariot took the lead, moving to the west, deeper into the mountain pass.

"I don't like the appearance of the sky, my lord," the chief archer called out as the chariots and riders proceeded. "There could be trouble."

Mark glanced at the clear, flawless blue bowl of the sky. Maybe a few wispy clouds far, far out on the horizon. "What kind of trouble?"

"Sandstorm, my lord." Apparently detecting skepticism on Mark's face, the archer provided details. "Bad weather comes from the east with scant warning. To be caught in a storm is certain death. But perhaps the winds will batter themselves into oblivion against the mountains."

"Or we'll be far enough into the Empty Lands to escape the full fury," Rothan said. "The gods and omens have favored us so far, my friends. Let's not divine new catastrophe in a few clouds."

Mark could tell Djed remained unconvinced, as he and the other archers exchanged glances but said nothing further on the topic.

Another concern was bothering Mark more than issues of chancy weather. "What about the Maiskhan? Do you think they'll persist in following you?"

Rothan shook his head. "Doubtless, the enemy believes you were a demon from the underworld. You took Tia from them. I've been told by my men that you slaughtered many of the enemy with invisible arrows. Also, the Maiskhan believed me dead and saw our other casualties lying on the sands, so their leader will report a largely successful outcome to Farahna. Even she wouldn't expect soldiers to pursue a demon to the underworld in an attempt to secure Tia for her." He paused for a moment to kiss his lady on the cheek as she blushed. "No one travels in this desert without desperate cause. Paid mercenaries aren't loyal enough to proceed into the Empty Lands when they can convince themselves of our removal from the playing board."

"Would you look at that?" Cresting the final rise, Mark rode away from the foot of the towering mountains. He whistled and reined in his horse, stunned by the vista. Ahead on all sides stretched hundreds of square miles of scrub brush and golden sands, baking in the sunlight. Towering dunes marched to the horizon. There were no signs of life.

"This area is well named the Empty Lands," Tia said.

"We're following the ancient trade road." Rothan took a drink from one of the waterskins before passing it to Mark. "The route runs straight and true through the desert to the city we seek. There'll be an oasis about one day's travel from here."

"And there'll be water?"

Taking the waterskin back and raising it to his lips, Rothan answered seriously, "The gods must continue to favor us if we're to succeed. Not too late for you and the Lady to change your minds, go home to your oasis."

Mark heard the challenge hidden in the mild offer. "We've made our choice. We ride with you, wherever the decision takes us."

The day grew even more scorching. Under Sandy's eagle eye, constantly evaluating his recovery from the head wound, Rothan didn't push the horses too hard. Scrubby brush dotted the terrain, with small dunes here and there. The genuinely immense dunes lay ahead of them, shimmering golden in the sunlight. Distances were deceiving in the desert.

"This path we're on does resemble a road," Sandy said as her horse trotted beside the lead chariot.

Mark translated the remark.

"Yes, we're following the main caravan route dating to when the city of Khunarum was inhabited. For many hundreds of years, the traders brought goods inland from the coast over this road and other items back to the coast to sell. The Empty Lands were much more fertile and friendly to life eons ago," Rothan said.

"So no one lives out here at all? No nomads?"

Rothan shook his head. "The people of Khunarum either fled or died when the city was destroyed."

"But why didn't the survivors take this scepter and crown with them, if they're such important symbols?" Mark found this the most puzzling aspect of the legends he'd been told.

Rothan frowned. "The ancient tales aren't clear about how the city met its doom, nor about what happened on the final day."

"The civilization ended all in one day?" He supposed a cataclysmic event would expain the loss of even the most significant relics.

"So the old scrolls say. There were floods and the earth shook for moments on end. Buildings collapsed or were washed out to sea. Chaos reigned. The temple where the crown and scepter were housed sat in the hardest-hit area of the city."

"Maybe no priests survived to bring the items to safety," Tia said.

Mark frowned, guiding his horse past a large rock formation jutting from the hard-packed dirt. "But you think you can find these things three thousand years later and get to Nakhtiaar in time to save your prince?"

"We must." Rothan was as stubborn as he'd been the night before in the oasis. "Our land can't be ruled by a person not fit to sit on the throne. We won't submit to the Maiskhan overlords, nor honor their bloodthirsty gods, as Farahna wishes to do. Hutenen must retake the throne, proclaim his status as king, and put affairs into order and balance."

Mark was happy to see the pitiful little oasis ahead as the sun moved steadily toward the horizon. A handful of scrubby trees surrounded a small, brackish pond. The horses drank eagerly, but the humans were more reluctant. Djed got a fire going, and the group huddled around it, eating the rations brought from the Oasis of the Travelers.

Rothan neatly refolded the maps he'd been studying while he ate. "Tomorrow's journey includes a loop around a lake where we can refill our canteens again. There's nothing else before we reach the city on the coast."

"No sandstorm today," Mark reminded Djed.

The archer shook his head. "The clouds are mares' tails, and the moons have red rings. Tomorrow may be a day of demon weather, my lord."

"Too bad you don't control the weather, Lady of the Star Wind," Mark teased Sandy.

"I hardly feel in control of anything at the moment." She walked away from him to sit with Tia.

Mark let her go without comment, watching her chat with Tia in broken Nakhtiaar, trying out a few linguistic tidbits she'd picked up during the day, both women laughing. Sandy's attitude puzzled him, chafed at his nerves. She was polite to him, friendly, but nothing more. There was a reserve, some emotional barrier. Did she harbor resentment because he hadn't wanted to remain in the oasis? But if so, why hadn't she said something else? He reviewed their discussion, satisfied he'd made a compelling case for journeying with Rothan. She'd said yes, after all.

Rothan joined the women, apparently teasing Tia about something, and all three laughed. Rubbing his chin, Mark considered for the first time the fact Sandy didn't have to stay with him now that they'd joined other people. She was perfectly free to choose another man. And he was free to bed other women. They had no agreement to remain together, a state of affairs made painfully explicit after the discussion in the oasis.

The idea roiled his gut.

Sandy glanced in his direction, raised her shoulder, and pointedly gave all her attention to Tia.

Next day the small procession passed through the empty lake bed in the late morning, pausing to refill their canteens. The lake was mostly gone, the landscape marked with the signs of historical and ever-retreating water levels. Rothan had to proceed way out onto the dry lake bed to get at the water, leaving the road and traveling at a slow pace over the uncertain surface. The ground was crusted and white in spots with leached minerals. At one point the lead chariot broke through the thin top layer of hard dirt and became mired in muddy quicksand. It took an hour or so of hard work to get the vehicle loose before they could continue the trek toward the diminished lake.

After filling the canteens and watering the horses, Rothan circled the chariots on the long trek to the road. For several hours the path followed the shoreline of what had been a massive lake at one time in the distant past.

Rothan kept referring to the map, apparently not wanting to miss the point where the road diverged from the shore. Ancient, drawn on supple leather, the guide was rolled around a carved wooden spindle. When not perusing it with Djed, the captain kept the map in a pouch fastened to the side of his chariot.

"How did you get the charts?" Mark asked while Rothan stowed his charts away again. "I don't imagine you kept them handy all the time in case some day you decided to make this journey."

"No." His companions exchanged wry glances before the captain explained. "We broke into the royal library. We weren't even sure maps existed. I asked one of the priests an idle question at dinner one night, concerning his knowledge of old legends. He boasted he knew where such a map could be found."

"We were nearly caught the first time we entered the building. We had to sneak in again the next night, and then we found the archive." Djed slapped his knee, seeming amused as he discussed the adventure.

"We've a number of petty crimes to atone for. Hutenen will have to give us clemency as one of his first acts." Rothan smiled as well, like a boy who'd successfully robbed a cookie jar.

"No one at court believes the legends, I fear," the chief archer said. "Even the priest was scornful."

"But it's a powerful legend." Tia's voice held conviction and resolve. "If my brother holds the crown and scepter of our ancestor, no one will dispute his claim to rule."

Mark withheld his own skepticism. As he'd told Sandy earlier, for all either of them knew this token of ancient royalty had mystical powers for Tia's brother to wield against Farahna. Stranger things happened on many worlds.

Rothan stopped for late lunch in a tumbled ruin of a village. Scrawny trees growing in an abandoned garden on the edge of the settlement provided welcome shade. Tia declined all but a few morsels, despite much coaxing from her beloved. Sandy watched this byplay with a slight frown, whispering to Mark behind her hand, "I think Tia might be pregnant."

"Quite a complication. No telling how this society views children born out of wedlock. He told me they don't have permission to marry." Mark chewed his bite of fruit. "You have anything to help with the nausea?"

"I think so, but I can't offer it to her without some conversation and a diagnosis." The mere suggestion appeared to offend Sandy's medical ethos. "Maybe tonight when we camp, I can broach the subject with suitable finesse."

Mentally marking the topic dealt with, since he was sure she'd take care of Tia, Mark eyed a heated discussion occurring between Rothan and Djed, standing next to the vehicles. "I better go see what the two of them are arguing about."

"You do that." Sandy sipped her water as Mark walked away. Sighing, she capped the canteen and stowed it securely in her makeshift saddlebag. What would Mark have done if she'd decided to stay in the oasis by herself, rather than join this expedition? Anger fueled by hurt feelings had tempted her to make the choice. He'd known who he was for all those years he lived in exile in the Sectors? Yet he'd never tried to return for her? Hearing him admit these truths hurt like a knife in the heart. An even more devastating blow was his belief that she could have betrayed him to Ekatereen in a fit of pique. How could he think such things of her, if he'd truly loved her?

Unable to sit still with her bleak thoughts, Sandy rose and strolled farther along the road, staying in the shade. She found a tiny stone altar propped against the trunk of the sturdier trees, and paused to admire the carving. Although smoothed by wind and sand, the main piece of the altar bore discernible stars and moons surrounding a vaguely female figure. Remnants of colorful pigment lingered in the grooves, purple and red.

"Nuet."

Startled, Sandy realized Tia had joined her. "I'm sorry, what?"

The other woman touched the carving and repeated what Sandy now understood to be a name. "Nuet." She touched her belly and said, "Mother."

"A fertility goddess?" Although she had bits and pieces of the Nakhtiaar language now, Sandy spoke in Outlier, not having the words for her question. At least now she didn't have to hold back on the subject of Tia's pregnancy. She decided she'd better wait for Mark to translate that medical discussion, which would probably make him uncomfortable. Smiling to herself at the idea of Mark's discomfort, she peered more closely at the details of the altar.

"You and your warrior fight?" Tia asked, touching her elbow. "Not happy?"

She shook her head and made herself smile, all the while thinking she'd need to be more careful not to let her feelings show so openly. She was indeed unhappy with Mark Denaltieri at the moment, exercising a lot of restraint not to say bitter, hateful things to him, permanently ruining any chance of a reunion. Her heart might be bleeding from emotional wounds he'd inflicted, but she couldn't quite bring herself to close the door forever.

"No need to tell me." Tia pulled a piece of fruit from her pocket, placing it carefully in the center of the tiny altar, and drew a symbol in the air, bowing her head for a moment. Then she extended one hand to Sandy, as if inviting her to make a similar offering. With a smile, raising her hands as she stepped away, Sandy declined. Making sacrifices to an alien symbol of motherhood and fertility wasn't going to solve the problems burdening her heart.

"What are we waiting for?" Sandy was puzzled why they'd stayed so long at the ruined town, given Rothan's compulsion to reach the abandoned city as soon as possible. Pleasant as the respite was, time to sightsee and stroll was an oddity.

"Djed argues. He fears the storm." Tia shrugged, pivoting as Rothan called to them from the vicinity of the chariots.

"Must be time to go," Sandy said.

Since Rothan was in command and refused to listen to Djed's misgivings about the weather, they proceeded down the road somewhat after noon. On the outskirts of the abandoned town, the chariots passed a large structure in much better repair than anything Mark had seen previously, although an indisputable ruin. A double row of statues flanked a short passage to the wide steps. The figures were defaced and crumbled, rendering it impossible to tell what kind of creatures the sculptors had created. Half the building lay in a messy pile of jagged slabs and toppled columns, but the impressive main area remained intact, although in disrepair. Faint remnants of colorful murals marched across the pocked walls. Several large trees grew inside and through the wreckage.

"A temple to one of the oldest goddesses, I'm guessing," Tia told them as the chariots rumbled past. "Nuet, the Mother of All. We found a small altar to her earlier in the village. With none left to worship her, her power would be much depleted. But enough lingers to keep the most sacred portions of the building standing against wind and weather."

"This whole society is about superstition and mysticism," Mark observed to Sandy in Outlier. "A mythical explanation for all events. Typical for a culture at this stage."

Then the chariots and riders were on the open road again, and Mark gave no more consideration to the nameless village and its shrine until an hour later, when the wind began rising.

One moment, the weather was hot, bright, and dead calm. A few heartbeats later, distant thunder rumbled and the light became brassy. Rothan called the column to a halt. The horses were nervous, stamping their hooves and chewing at their bits, ears flicking back and forth as they sidled. The chariot drivers had to stand beside their teams, holding the rains while the officers conferred.

"The storm comes, my lord." Djed didn't allow any hint of triumph in his voice or demeanor, merely pointing toward the east. Mark swung around to follow his gaze, appalled and amazed to see gigantic, dirty yellow clouds boiling on the horizon, anvil-headed tops reaching for the outer stratosphere already. The weather front advanced with terrifying speed. Flashes of lightning sparked below the massed clouds.

"I've never seen anything so ominous." Sandy stared at the wide-open plain around them. "No shelter of any kind out here."

"Scarier than hell," he agreed.

The wind was now steady from the east, with gusts.

"I threw the gaming sticks and chose poorly for us in my haste," Rothan apologized, his face grim. "I hoped Djed read the signs wrong, and I should have known better. Interpreting weather omens is his gift."

"The question is, what are we going to do now? Wind's rising." Mark gathered his borrowed robes more closely around himself.

"Winds like shrieking hordes of devils will surround us soon," Djed said. "Do we not take shelter, our skin will be stripped from our bones and we'll die here unmourned."

"Shelter, huh?" Mark cast a sardonic eye around at the flat territory they were riding through. A towering dust devil swirled by him, spooking his horse, before dissipating a few feet away. "How far to the city?"

"Too far." Rothan shook his head. "Our only chance is to retreat, hope we can reach the village where we ate lunch today before the storm advances to meet us."

Mark and Sandy mounted their horses as the drivers took the chariots in a wide loop. The horses were reluctant to go toward the storm, but there was no choice. All too soon, Mark rode into the teeth of a rising gale. Visibility became limited. The wind-borne sand stung any exposed skin, and Mark realized Djed hadn't been speaking metaphorically about the power of the storm to strip a man to bones. The group stopped for a few precious moments to link themselves together. Anyone straying from the main party would never be found again. Sandy dismounted and huddled in one of the chariots. Mark took point, leading the horses, head down, concentrating on putting one foot in front of the other on the barely visible road. If he deviated from the road and missed their one chance at shelter, he and his companions would perish.

"We won't make the village before this becomes a full-on storm!" Mark shouted as he came abreast of the dilapidated statues lining the path to the temple. "We need to shelter here."

"We can't risk entering such a place." Djed's protest was nearly inaudible over the wind, even though the man shouted.

"We're going to die before we get to the damn village. This temple is better built than those huts anyway," Mark said, his lips close to Rothan's ear.

"Lead the way, then, Warrior."

Mark realized he'd never had such an intense five minutes in his entire life, not even in a running gun battle on foot against the Mawreg on Intriff VI. He clawed his way from one statue to the next, getting a death grip on the pedestal and pulling on the reins looped over his shoulder to indicate a direction to those following him. He stumbled and fell over the first step of the temple and scrambled up the sixteen risers on all fours, unable to stand against the wind. He rolled out of the way as the first chariot crested the threshold and barreled into the larger space of the temple, horses mad with terror, driver sawing at the reins to stop the team before crashing into something. The second chariot came right behind and the loose string of horses with it.

There was plenty of room in the center of the temple for their small party since the building had obviously once been a mighty place of worship. This portion of the stone block building was intact, roof holding in place, even against the shrieking winds. Mark lifted Sandy from the second chariot. She shook from exhaustion and tension. Holding her, Mark searched for Rothan and Djed in the gloom.

"How long do these storms usually blow?" He was sure Rothan couldn't hear him clearly over the gale but hoped he or Djed could get the gist of his question.

Djed shook his head and held up one finger, then two, which became three. Based on the intensity of the storm so far, Mark wondered if the archer indicated days, not hours. If so, a hell of an ordeal lay ahead.

"We must make a sacrifice," Tia said, her words snatched away by the winds. "We must give thanks for the shelter."

"This temple is long abandoned. We don't even know with certainty which goddess the people worshipped here." Rothan was impatient, busy with the horses. "There's no point in wasting provisions."

"Nuet. I tell you the place must belong to her." Shaking her head, Tia grabbed the bag of foodstuffs from one chariot and headed toward the altar at the far end of the chamber. "We must not offend, even by omission."

"I'll keep her company." Sandy followed Tia.

Preoccupied with helping the other men get the horses free of their harnesses and tethered to a hastily strung line, Mark glanced to where the two women were setting a small offering of fruit and water on the edge of the cracked altar.

Sandy rejoined him a few moments later, nibbling on a small piece of the fruit.

Mark attempted to make her comfortable in a sheltered corner beside a young tree growing from the ruptured basin of an ancient fountain. "Why'd you help her make a sacrifice?"

"The effort was obviously important to her. And somehow significant to me, as well." Sandy's tone conveyed her puzzlement, as did the frown on her face. "I don't know—I felt welcomed when we got here." Gazing at the tumbled ruins surrounding them, she shrugged. "It'll be a gift from some higher power if we manage to stay safe through the storm, won't it?"

Mark didn't detect any welcome directed at him, but he'd settle for being out of the driving wind and sand. He didn't begrudge the small amount of food and water spent on the sacrificial offering. Tia hadn't used enough to make a difference in their long-term survival on this trek.

Although he didn't agree, he didn't argue with Rothan's decision not to post a guard. The captain was in charge of this expedition, and more important, no one could make a move in the intense storm, not without an armored personnel carrier. He coughed, dust coating his throat. The air was full of it, coming in through cracks in the walls, or sifting from the roof above, shaken free by the force of the gale. The wind shrieked outside, tearing at the edges of the ancient building. The temple had stood for many centuries against such forces, so most likely the edifice would endure one more storm, and protect them. He could see faint murals on the wall near them, snakes winding through the stems of large flowers, stars and moons above.

Figuring a nap offered the best way to pass the time, he settled against the packs and eased Sandy onto his shoulder.

Wakening hours later, he told himself maybe the wind howled a bit less forcefully. Sandy stirred and sat up.

"Water?" Her lips were close to his ear.

He shook the canteen. "Empty. Wait a moment, and I'll bring some from the chariot." Stretching to unkink his legs, Mark crossed the sand-swept floor toward the vehicles.

Sandy's scream behind him penetrated even the roar of the storm. Pivoting, he drew his blaster as he ran back to where she sat. Skidding to a stop on the gritty floor, he did a doubletake at the menace threatening her.

A large, milky white snake faced the princess, its body a powerful coil, head swaying six feet above the floor, fangs bared, hood flared. The hood was more than two handspans in width, pulsing as the serpent contemplated Sandy. The moment was one of those times when the world seemed to stop then flip into hyperdrive. Mark shot from point-blank range, but the blast went unaccountably wide, as if the reptile had a force shield. As he watched, the serpent lunged forward and bit Sandy on the arm. He shot again, but this blast also missed its mark.

The snake launched itself at him, sinking huge fangs into his wrist. The bite hurt like hot electrodes stabbed into his flesh. Hand already paralyzed and swelling as the snake released its grip, Mark dropped the blaster. He fell to his knees, holding his numb right wrist with his left hand. The snake stared at him for a long moment at eye level, hood pulsing as it considered its next move. The intensity of the reptilian intelligence in those turquoise eyes was frightening. With unhurried contempt, the snake uncoiled and slid away, into the debris-filled basin. Slithering behind the tree, the reptile disappeared from sight.

Crawling one-handed on his knees, Mark's only thought was of reaching Sandy. She'd toppled backward, hitting her head on the edge of the pillar. Blood flowed freely from the graze on the back of her skull. She was unconscious, eyes rolled back into her head, but still breathing. Red and puffed, her bite wound bled sluggishly, ominous purple-black streaks progressing up her arm.

He groaned, resting his head on her stomach for a second in sheer frustration and pain. He checked his own wrist, but the damage appeared less severe than the wound Sandy'd received. The snake must have discharged most of its available venom into her before biting him.

His eyes weren't focusing well. People tugged at him, pulling him away from Sandy. He fought Rothan and Djed as the pair moved him, all the while both of them trying to get a glimpse of the wound on his wrist. Tia pushed past him to lift Sandy's arm, showing the bite to Rothan, shaking her head.

Stomach cramps and nausea assaulted Mark, and he fought to stay conscious. His guts were trying to turn themselves inside out. Convulsions swept over him, and the two men lowered him to the floor.

The wind continued to shriek outside, making conversation difficult. Tia ran to the chariots and fetched a small sack, from which she extracted a carved, salmon-pink stone vial and began to swirl paste of a matching color onto Sandy's arm. Next, she rubbed the remainder into his wrist. Foaming as it touched his skin, the ointment soothed the exterior inflammation, but the venom kept burning in his veins. He realized the pain must be much worse for Sandy.

As Tia bound Sandy's head wound with fabric ripped from her cloak, Mark staggered to the chariots and managed to retrieve her medical bag. Even as he undid the clasp, he admitted it was a useless gesture. She must have something for snakebite, but he'd no idea what. Blinking furiously, he stared at the injects and the other, sealed ampoules and packets, and cursed. In the Sectors, the military made the sergeants take field medicine, but officers like him didn't receive any instructions.

In the course of his years of service, he'd endured countless injects designed to protect him from lethal bites and poisons found on a wide variety of worlds. The cumulative immunity offered him limited protection now, he realized. But Sandy obviously had no such reserves.

Slamming the bag shut, he realized the rest of the party was staring at him, varying degrees of sadness and distress on their faces. Stricken by a sudden intensification of the nausea, he leaned over and threw up everything he'd eaten earlier. When he progressed to dry heaves, Rothan and Djed half carried him to where Sandy lay, lowering him to sit beside her, resting against the cold stone wall.

Djed urged him to drink a few sips of the warm, brackish water, which he then spat out as his stomach heaved again.

"I'm so sorry." Tia hugged him hard before seeking her place next to Rothan again.

Despite the numbness in his right arm, Mark gathered Sandy close. Head lolling, she was pale and in a cold sweat, but alive. Her eyelids fluttered, and her breathing was slow. He rocked her gently back and forth, ignoring the pain in his own arm, cursing his helplessness. Why had he coerced her into this mad journey into the Empty Lands? He'd rescued her from Kliin only to bring her to a painful death here on this alien planet.

Rothan checked on them some indeterminate time later. "Probably a desert viper, deadly. Although I've never heard of a white one. Nothing we can do, my friend. The poison must work its course. If she has a strong heart, she might survive. Try to keep her warm and yourself as well."

Mark found himself unable to speak past the lump in his throat. With Rothan's help, he wrapped them more securely in the cloaks.

He risked a glance at her arm, a vague idea of attempting a tourniquet on his mind. The whole arm was swollen twice its normal size, with purple streaks beneath her skin, spreading onto her chest now. Even he, with no medical training, realized it was far too late for a tourniquet to help. Mark grew lightheaded, the edges of his vision going black, and despite the self discipline his training provided, he couldn't hang on to consciousness any longer.

When he woke up with no idea how long he'd been out, the storm raged unabated outside and all his companions were asleep. He put two fingers to Sandy's neck, relieved to find a pulse, faint but steady.

Blinking, Mark tried to clear his head. Afraid he was suffering hallucinations, he stared at the opposite wall, which appeared to be moving. Four shapes emerged from the shadows, convincing him this was no vision, but reality. He tried to yell a warning as he struggled to rise, fumbling for his blaster. Reflexes severely impaired from the venom, he couldn't make the transition from kneeling woozily upright to a standing position.

To his relief, Rothan and Djed leaped from their bedrolls to face the intruders, knives at the ready, the three soldiers hastily closing ranks behind them. Rothan engaged in a dialogue with the newcomers, involving a lot of gestures on both sides. The wind snatched away the sound. From his steadily less militant stance as the conversation went on, Rothan didn't appear to find the mysterious arrivals a threat. After a particularly spirited burst of dialogue, the captain came to Mark, urging him to stand. The four newcomers, heavily swathed in robes and hooded cloaks, followed.

"I was wrong, you were right," Rothan yelled to Mark, right in his ear. "There *are* people living in these lands. These men are Mikkonites, ancestral allies of the Khunarum."

"Can they help Sandy?" The princess's life was all Mark cared about.

The wind died down a bit.

One Mikkonite stepped forward, throwing back his red-striped hood to reveal intricately braided blue hair. "The woman was bitten?"

"Yes, a big snake bit us both, got her first," Mark answered in High Chetal. "Must not have had much venom left when it got to me."

The man studied the bite marks on Mark's wrist before giving an order over his shoulder. He met Mark's eyes. "I don't recognize this fang pattern. Describe the serpent."

"White. Long, maybe six feet, with a flared hood, iridescent diamond pattern on its scales. Turquoise eyes—listen, do you have anything to relieve her symptoms? Counteract the poison?"

The man stared at him. Mark began to think he hadn't been understood. The dialect the strangers spoke sounded one step more removed from High Chetal. If not for the language lessons from Djed over the past few days, he wouldn't have been able to communicate at all.

The Mikkonite leader shook his head. "We must get to our village. I've nothing with me to help her."

"Forgotten about the storm?" Mark jabbed his thumb at the entrance to the temple, where sand swirled and winds howled with renewed ferocity. "How did you get here anyway?"

"The deserts of Khunarum are laced with secret tunnels, my lords. In the old days, the tunnels were used to keep trade going during the storm season. Why came you during this time?" he asked Rothan. "No one is safe to travel long distances above ground at this season."

"The records regarding the Empty Lands are spotty. We'd no idea about the storms." Rothan's voice was defensive, as if the newcomers were accusing him of carelessness or poor planning.

"Our need is great." Tia tucked the cloak tenderly around Sandy. "We had to risk it."

"This storm will blow itself out in another day or so. Till then you may shelter with us in my village." He bowed to Rothan and, with a shade less deference, to Mark. "I'm Jagrahim, headman of the Mikkonite."

"Tunnels?" Mark considered the possibilities. "How big?"

"The passages were constructed to allow horses and carts to travel in safety, but nowadays there are too many cave-ins. We'll have to leave your animals and send men to retrieve them later. Come, we must get the woman to the village where our healer can attempt to help her. We face a hike of several hours. I realize you must be weary and hungry, but there's nothing I can do to lessen the distance."

Mark wanted to carry Sandy himself, but the task was beyond him, as debilitated as the venom had made his body. Jagrahim directed his men to make a litter from some wooden panels and carry her on that. One by one, each person stepped behind the sliding wall of the temple, carefully descending a crumbling set of stairs. Djed supported Mark once they reached the tunnel floor. Ahead of them, the Mikkonite leader set a fast pace, going north in the dimly lit corridor.

Mark and Djed lagged behind, hampered by Mark's condition and lack of coordination. He realized his mind was far from clear, but he pondered how Jagrahim had known Rothan's party had taken shelter at the abandoned temple. His suspicion about coincidence made him wonder how trustworthy these new players were. Rothan might be happy to accept them as allies, but what did he know about the desert dwellers beyond legends? Rothan hadn't even believed anyone lived in this area until half an hour ago.

And what provided the light in these tunnels? Mark didn't see torches or lamps, yet there was enough ambient light for him to avoid obstacles and fallen stones with ease. He breathed fresh air too, which was puzzling since they were deep under the surface. Nothing added up satisfactorily for Mark, and his inability to concentrate on the situation frustrated him. He wasn't used to being incapacitated and out of control. He brushed his free hand against the butt of his blaster for reassurance—as long as he had his weapon, he could protect Sandy.

The lingering effects of the venom struck him again like knives in the gut, and he doubled over, in the grip of dry heaves. The archer let him slump to the stone floor of the tunnel and called to the men ahead for someone to assist him. Aware they were hoisting him to his feet, Mark realized he was stumbling forward, but then his vision went black, and he knew no more.

Chapter Four

The pain from the snakebite was intense, like she imagined being shot with a blaster might feel. Agony raced with the venom through her veins from the site of the puncture. Sandy heard herself screaming, understood Mark was trying to hold her, but gradually the world grayed, and she felt more and more distant. The sensation was as if she stood off to the side, watching someone else slump to the floor, hitting her head on the base of a column. No anxiety, no medical urgency occurred to Sandy as bright red blood pool around her unmoving form. *Someone needs to take care of the bleeding.*

A compulsion pulled at her, drawing her away from where her body lay. She half turned to see a bright green light over the altar where she and Tia had placed food and drink. Curious, Sandy abandoned Mark and the spot where her body lay bleeding, and walked through the ancient temple. As she got closer to the intricately carved altar, she realized a woman stood in the center of the light, beckoning to her. The woman reached to take her hand, easily lifting Sandy into the air and drawing her inexorably deeper into whatever corridor the light provided.

"No, wait, I have to stay with Mark," she said, frightened now, trying to retreat, tugging at the woman's hand, struggling to remain in the temple. "I can't leave him."

"He'll be fine. Come abide with us for now—we've missed you." The woman touched the center of Sandy's forehead, and she knew no more.

When she woke, she reclined in a comfortable, white, cushioned chair, feet propped on a footstool carved in the shape of an intricate flower, a brightly hued, tufted cushion as the bloom. A bewildering variety of beverages in cups and goblets rested on a wooden table at her side. As she pulled herself from a slumped position, she realized she no longer wore the turquoise gown. At some point, she had donned, or been dressed in, flowing robes of pure white dotted with tiny iridescent stars. Adrenaline soaring for a moment, she checked for the Traveler key, reassured when she found the chain still looped around her neck. Sandy ran a hand through her hair, pleased by how clean and silky the strands were, only vaguely alarmed she had no memory of a bath.

The brightly illuminated room was empty, although there were four other chairs close to hers, as if company was anticipated. Voices came from somewhere, and Sandy decided her best course of action was to seek out the other people. Before she could leave the chair's deeply cushioned embrace, however, four women entered the room as if dancing, so light and graceful were their movements. The newcomers were dressed in clothing similar to what she had on, embroidered with symbols other than stars. At the moment, all four were arguing in a language Sandy didn't comprehend, talking over each other.

"Excuse me," she said in Outlier, cutting through the chatter as she rose. "Where am I? Where's Mark?"

All four women swung to face her, and Sandy was struck by the likeness each had to the others, clearly sisters, although the eye and hair colors differed. The tallest stepped forward and answered her in the unknown tongue.

Sandy shook her head. "I'm sorry, I don't understand."

"Selata menorasta tintre—" Tone definitely one of irritation, eyes narrowed, the woman thumped Sandy's forehead with two fingertips. "We haven't time to waste before we're interrupted." She tilted her head, eyebrows raised. "Is that better? Do you understand me now?"

Raising her own hand to stroke her brow where a faint headache throbbed, Sandy nodded. "Yes, thank you."

"Be seated, refresh yourself." The woman made a graceful gesture at the waiting beverages. "We brought all your favorites."

Sandy sat. Inside, a tiny voice took umbrage at her own meek demeanor, when she'd clearly been kidnapped and separated from Mark, but she felt an overwhelming sense of peace, lassitude almost. Studying the drinks, she wondered if she'd been drugged. "I've never had any of these before, to my knowledge."

"See? I told you she wasn't who we believed her to be." The diminutive redhead spoke, voice triumphant. "We've made a mistake."

"She has the key," answered the blonde, sinking into one of the empty chairs.

The first woman made a shushing gesture. "Let's begin again, shall we?" Turning to Sandy, she said, "We're the Moon Sisters who watch over this world—Amrell, Terali, Lifnid, and Tresa." She'd pointed her index finger at each woman in turn. Now she raised her eyebrows. "And you are?"

"Alessandra of the Outlier Empire." She thought at least one of the names in the introduction sounded familiar. Hadn't Rothan made some reference to an Amrell a couple of days ago?

The sisters exchanged glances. "Outlier is a place unknown to us," said the spokeswoman.

"A name we've never heard before and a mortal we don't know." Tresa, the redhead, poured herself a drink. "We're going to regret this rash proceeding."

"I'm the senior in the sky at the moment, let me handle this." The leader, Amrell, seemed annoyed, frowning, tapping her toe on the mosaic floor. Gazing at Sandy, she said, "How came you to own the key?"

"I found it in the Oasis of the Travelers, inside the mountain dwelling when we arrived," Sandy said. "Mark and I were sent to this world by Lajollae, with one of her globes. Maybe you know of her?"

Her audience gasped. The three who'd remained standing hastily sought chairs.

"We believed you were the Lady of the Star Wind, returned at long last," said Amrell. "We've much missed your—her company, and when it became known you were waiting in the temple, we had no other thought but to bring you here as we did in olden times."

Sandy found herself getting used to the title by now. Maybe a star wind was what Lajollae had used to send her to this world. Somehow, the idea made sense in her current situation. Her reception by these women was cordial enough on the surface. Again, that nagging internal alarm sounded. Mark wasn't here, and she didn't know where he was or where she was, so things couldn't be fine. She dug the fingernails of her right hand into her palm, hoping the tiny prick of pain would help her throw off the lassitude.

"*What* have you done?" The new voice rang strident and accusatory. Sandy shifted in her chair to see a fifth woman had now entered the room. Older than the sisters appeared to be, she was also taller, standing at least two feet taller than Sandy. Set in intricate braids, her long black hair was decorated with emerald and sapphire clips. Most startling to Sandy were the gracefully arching golden horns growing from the woman's head, rising above her in a perfect curve, with a sparkling diadem suspended between them. The effect should have been odd or even grotesque, Sandy realized, but on this imposing being, the horns were somehow right and proper. Her deep-green dress had golden embroidery, and a belt set with opals in intricate patterns flashed rainbows in the bright light of the chamber.

The four sisters went to their knees, heads bowed. After a moment, Amrell raised her eyes to the newcomer and spoke. "As we were just telling our guest, we knew she waited in the temple so we sent Sherabti to welcome her as in days of old. Her reaction was not as expected, so I decided to personally conduct her and her consort." Biting her lip, Amrell frowned. "His reaction was also unexpectedly odd, as if his blood fought Sherabti's elixir. I couldn't bring him through the barriers into this place."

"Is Sherabti the snake? You had the snake bite me to get me here?" Sandy was outraged. The emotion gave her energy, broke the spell holding her so calm. These women were more dangerous than she'd realized.

"We meant no harm, Exalted One Haatrin," Tresa said, getting boldly to her feet and speaking to the horned woman. "We merely wanted to renew our acquaintance with our old friend." Now she cast Sandy an angry glance. "But this woman is an impostor. We should let her continue into death's embrace, since loss of life is how her body is reacting to Sherabti's kiss in the mortal world."

"Now you want to kill me?" Fight-or-flight response fully engaged, Sandy chose to go on the offensive, leaping to her feet. "I didn't ask to be bitten by a snake, and I certainly didn't ask you to bring me wherever this is. Send me back, make me whole, and we'll call it even."

"Yet she has the key," Amrell said, as if Sandy hadn't uttered a word.

Haatrin raised her hands, and the sisters subsided. "You were foolish and hasty," she said to them, her tone chiding. "Now you must bear the consequences." Pivoting on her heel, one eyebrow raised, she looked Sandy up and down. "Peace to you, daughter of queens. Matters will be sorted. While it's certainly true you're not the Lady of the Star Wind from eons ago, your arrival might be timely, might be part of a larger whole." Over her shoulder, she addressed Amrell and the others. "You know the balance is in jeopardy. Those who dwell in darkness gather and plot. This woman could be a key herself, a useful component of our strategy."

"I'm not a tool to be used by others," Sandy said, drawing upon her imperial heritage to sound haughty and disapproving. "And neither is Mark."

"Yet you plan to dwell on the world Lajollae sent you to." Haatrin made her assessment calmly. "Already you've chosen a side, made alliances. There's a cost to such decisions."

Sandy bit her lip, regretting all over again having agreed so easily to Mark's desire to leave the oasis and throw their lot in with Rothan and Tia. The stakes had been higher than she'd realized at the time.

Hands folded across her stomach, Haatrin maintained her calm, detached demeanor, in stark contrast to the excitability of the younger women. "All will be decided soon. Sherabti has gone to inform the Mother of these occurrences and She comes to this place to judge."

The Moon Sisters grew pale, exchanging furtive glances, and the light in the room dimmed. Goose bumps made Sandy shiver.

"We never meant to disturb Her," Amrell said, biting her lip.

"Yet you took action in a place dedicated to me from ancient times." The voice was like the crack of a whip. An elderly woman, clad in flowing garments of black, stood on the threshold, leaning heavily on an ebony cane, her withered hand clenched on the flared snake's head carved at the top. Emerald eyes winked in the carving, and Sandy had the unsettling impression that the eyes fixated on her. "You feckless children summon me to attend to matters I resigned long ago and left behind."

Thunder rumbled outside the room, and the sisters cringed away as the newcomer hobbled closer. Haatrin bowed her head but appeared less afraid, less gripped by awe than Amrell and her Moon Sisters. "Grandmother Nuet, this interruption is unfortunate but may also have potential. We may have a new Lady of the Star Wind." She gestured toward Sandy as if presenting a rare treat.

Now the crone's attention switched to Sandy. Her eyes were bottomless pools of black, sparks of gold flashing in the depths as Sandy stared. Instinctively, she bowed her head as she would have to her own grandmother, the empress. No question, but this newly arrived being commanded respect, whoever she might be. The name had a familiar sound as well. Remembering the altar in the abandoned village, Sandy speculated whether she drifted in a venom-induced dream, constructed from bits and pieces of her recent experiences. But this crone facing her could never be mistaken for a fertility goddess.

"Have you nothing to say?" Nuet's voice was impatient.

"I think this is all a mistake." The key hung heavy around Sandy's neck, and she wished Mark stood at her side.

"The balance of the universe demands correction of true mistakes." The elderly woman slammed the tip of her cane on the floor for emphasis and spoke as if making a pronouncement.

"I said we should let her die." Tresa spoke boldly. "All the problems would be solved."

The crone spun to glare at her, moving faster than Sandy would have dreamed possible, and thunder shook the room. "We don't yet know the outcome," Nuet said as the rumbles died away. "Haste only gets you in more trouble, youngest moon." She raised a cautionary hand as Tresa opened her mouth. "Silence would be well considered at this moment. In fact, you're dismissed, all of you. Having done your unthinking mischief, your presence is no longer desired." She waved one hand in a curt, shooing motion. "Be grateful I don't choose to reclaim my domain here. I might hurtle your namesakes away from this world as my first act." Her voice echoed in the room, as if they stood in a much larger space.

Like children released from school, the sisters fled in a pack without backward glances, leaving Haatrin, Sandy, and Nuet, the crone.

Sandy studied her. Was it her imagination or did the woman stand taller, her spine not as bent? And her hair had definitely been a wild tangle of dull gray curls, but was now more silver blond, wavy rather than curly. The eyes were the same, deep and unfathomable, but the wrinkles surrounding them were now fewer, the cheeks rosier. The hand holding the cane was smooth, the blue veins nearly unnoticeable, where before the vessels throbbed and drew the eyes.

Haatrin stepped to Sandy's side, taking her left wrist and gently rotating it to display the angry puncture wounds. "Here is Sherabti's mark, Mother of Us All."

The elder leaned closer, peering at the bite. "My servant is never mistaken, regardless of the foolishness of those girls. Sherabti saw potential."

"And the woman and her mortal companions were in your temple," Haatrin said as if citing a point in Sandy's favor. "She made proper sacrifice."

"We took shelter there from a sandstorm." Sandy felt compelled to clarify. The stakes in this room were high, with her life and maybe Mark's in danger. She didn't want any further misunderstandings between these beings and herself. Had her simple gesture of helping Tia place water and fruit on the broken altar gotten her into this jeopardy? "Please, whatever's going on here, don't hurt Mark. Neither of us meant any harm or disrespect. Take your anger out on me if you must, but not him." She might be angry with him for personal reasons, but she didn't want the foolishness of the younger women to cause his injury or death.

Haatrin shook her head. "There cannot be the one without the other. If you're the Lady, or to become her, he must be your warrior, your consort. Live or die in unison, the twined fate is inescapable if you claim these titles."

"Potential and problems, this girl carries both," said Nuet. She traced lines across Sandy's palm, her touch cool. Sandy's skin tingled where the woman's fingertip had been, and faint golden runes glowed for a heartbeat. "The scales are not yet balanced and may tip either way." Nuet stared at Sandy. "You'll need my mirror. And yet the gift may not be enough." Dropping Sandy's hand, she stood tall, the vestiges of age dropping away like veils. Now she appeared luminescent, beautiful, compelling in a way that made Sandy want to fall on the floor and worship as the Moon Sisters had earlier. Locking her knees, Sandy refused to bend, fighting the compulsion to grovel. The Zhivanov family *ruled*, they didn't make themselves subservient to others.

"You have the strength," Nuet said, as if aware of Sandy's inner resolve. "Can you apply it to the choices you and your consort make?" Not waiting for an answer, she addressed Haatrin in sharp tones. "This is not my concern, not my battle. Don't entreat me to be involved." The vehemence in her voice was powerful. "I've fought the chaos and the darkness here in my time, vanquished the evil I faced, and moved beyond to greater purpose."

Haatrin inclined her head. "Understood. I'd no intention of reaching out to you. The Moon Sisters are young and heedless, as everyone knows. My comrades among the Elder Gods and I are well seasoned, ready to carry the battle to the enemy ourselves."

"None may summon me from my refuge again," Nuet said, "especially not those ridiculous children. I won't be merciful if there's a reoccurrence of this unwarranted situation. The paths will be blocked, and I will take Sherabti with me away from this world, as I ought to have done long ago." A half smile flickered on Nuet's lips. "But she retained her fondness for the activities of mortals, which I'll no longer indulge." She shook her finger at Haatrin. "Any attempt to invoke me will rebound with deadly effect on those making the effort. I no longer have mortal worshippers to consider, no priests, no temples, no one speaks my name. All is as it should be. The cup has passed to you and your siblings. I've other duties to manage, responsibilities beyond your comprehension." The woman walked toward the door, no longer needing to guide her steps with the cane, which she cast aside. The wood struck the floor in a burst of purple and gold sparks, and Sandy gasped as the cane became Sherabti, the white snake, coiling sinuously for a moment.

Nuet was as youthful now as the Moon Sisters had been, in demeanor and appearance, and her robes transformed to shades of purple, from deepest amethyst to pale lavender, as if dye poured over the fabric. Masses of silver-blond hair tumbled over her shoulders.

Haatrin raised a hand. "And the mirror?"

Pausing on the threshold, the woman stood with her back to them for a moment. Sandy thought she wasn't going to answer Haatrin's hasty question. Half turning, Nuet stared across the room, her gaze locked on Sandy's face. "I've said she may have the mirror. Whether she can wield its powers in part or in full, or at all, remains to be seen, depends on her choices. And those of her warrior."

"I'll try not to disappoint you," Sandy said, feeling as if she'd been given some treasure to safeguard, although as yet there'd been no sign of this mirror the others spoke of in such respectful terms.

"You have the rare chance to affect the balance," the woman said, shaking a finger at her. "Such opportunities are not often granted to mortals. Don't waste it." Without another word, she crossed the threshold and disappeared as thunder rolled outside the chamber.

Sherabti raised her hooded head and hissed before following her mistress from the room. As the snake's tail disappeared into the corridor, or whatever lay outside the boundaries of the space, a wall appeared, joined smoothly to the other three as if it had always been there, leaving no visible door.

"I'll send you safely into your body," Haatrin said. "But first, there are some things I ought to tell you." She drew Sandy to the nearest pair of chairs and sat. Selecting two of the waiting goblets filled with shimmering swirls of blue and green liquid, she offered one to Sandy. "Drink, this will help ease your spirit's reunion with your body and ameliorate the effects of Sherabti's kiss."

Unable to refuse the offer, Sandy reluctantly took a sip, then another as the delicious liquid hit her palate. She voiced the issue concerning her most at the moment. "All this talk of balance and opportunities, involving me and my warrior. I have to tell you the relationship between Mark and me is unsettled. Old matters lie between us."

"You must have a warrior, a consort, if you are to be the Lady," Haatrin said, her tone firm. "But this Mark you speak of doesn't have to be the one. You can choose another, a warrior of Nakhtiaar perhaps. What matters is your choice." Leaning forward, she touched a fingertip to Sandy's chest above her heart. "Your choice here." Retreating, she drank from her own glass.

"How much time do I have to decide? To see if things can be worked out with us?"

"You're already too late for some possibilities," Haatrin said. "But time remains for other paths." She shook her head. "You aren't going to remember all of what I share with you, as you're mortal and not the being the Moon Sisters hoped they welcomed. As they learned, to their sorrow."

"Then why tell me anything?" Sandy's throbbing headache grew, and she had wavy sparkles in the center of her field of vision. "Let me reenter my body now."

"Even if you lose the detail of what I reveal, you'll retain the essence. And the mirror holds immense power. Nuet's agreement to allow you to attempt the use of it is an amazing boon." Haatrin was unmoved by Sandy's request to leave. She pushed another glass closer to Sandy's elbow. "Try this one. Sit back, listen, don't allow your anxiety to rule your heart. Soon enough, you'll awaken."

On the surface above, the sandstorm raged for the third or fourth day—he'd lost count. In this room where Sandy lay so close to death, a quiet and cool atmosphere prevailed, suitable for an invalid. The flames of the massed candles hardly flickered. She lay motionless beneath the red, blue, and yellow striped wraps, her hair curling against her head. The dose of some mysterious liquid administered by the local healer had made her breathing less labored. Mark had received the same potion to drink and found relief from nausea and dizziness within moments. His arm burned, but the swelling subsided. Mark rolled his sleeve up again, checking to make sure, as much as he could tell in the dim torch light.

He lounged on the low chair next to the bed, oblivious to the continued comings and goings of the Mikkonite women. He ignored the tray of food and drink placed at his elbow. When it was removed, hours later the serving woman clucked her tongue in dismay to find the offerings untouched. To please his hosts, he sipped the fruit juice and took a few bites of a meat-stuffed roll. Only then would the servant take the rest of the food and leave him alone.

He held Sandy's hand, so cold yet with a reassuringly steady pulse at the wrist. He stared at her serene face, noting the fine lines above her eyebrows and around her eyes. She was a remarkably beautiful woman now, not the girl he'd loved. So many long years had passed while he'd been in exile in the Sectors and she'd been enmeshed in her grandmother's dynastic schemes. Becoming a doctor, of all things. He admitted he hadn't given her enough credit for the accomplishment, wondered what drove her to make the choice.

He couldn't believe he might lose her now, on a world alien to both of them, among strangers. His heart stuttered as he considered how much was unsaid between them. His fault too, all his fault. She'd been ready to welcome him right back into her heart where they'd left off over twenty years ago, but he'd held himself aloof, stubborn, blaming her for things she was innocent of. Afraid to tear down the walls he'd constructed for himself. He'd said some deliberately hurtful things to keep her at a distance until it suited him to seek rapprochement, if it ever did.

Lajollae had sent them into their own private Eden, and he'd been impatient to break free, frightened of the confinement. Action over emotion. His stupid, self-defeating motto.

Sandy had kept her own thoughts and wishes to herself, accompanied him on this wild goose chase with people she didn't know, committed to a cause she didn't believe in, rather than lose him again.

"Please, you have to survive this. Come back to me. We can sort out the barriers between us." Smoothing the damp curls off her face, he brushed a kiss on her forehead. "I promise on my life—" He broke off, hearing a faint stirring in the hall behind him.

"She remains unconscious?"

Mark realized Jagrahim stood on the threshold, one hand holding aside the leather curtain trimmed with cascades of amber beads. "No change."

"Come, I wish to show you something," the chief told him.

Incredulous anyone would expect him to abandon Sandy while she was helpless, he knew his tone skirted rudeness. "I can't leave her. It'll have to wait."

"My wife will sit with her. You remember her? She is our healer."

Robes fluttering, the shy village woman stepped from behind her tall husband and moved to the bedside. She laid one graceful hand on Sandy's brow. Frowning, the princess muttered something and shifted on the mattress to avoid even such a light touch.

The healer showed no sign of dismay. "I'm pleased by the progress the wound on her arm shows." She peeled back Sandy's sleeve much as Mark had done a few moments ago. "The marks are fading and receding. The swelling subsides by the hour. The poison leaves her system."

"Please," the chief said to Mark, "this will only take a few moments. Surely you trust my wife to watch over her patient?"

"What is it I need to see?"

"Just come and perhaps you will understand."

Mark squeezed Sandy's hand and laid it by her side on the colorful blanket. Rising, he stretched muscles cramped after the long hours of motionless vigil. He allowed the chief's wife to slip past him and sit in the chair he'd vacated.

He followed Jagrahim into the corridor, deserted at this hour. His companion walked without talking through a succession of hallways. The chief led Mark into a large chamber filled floor to ceiling with shelves holding thousands of scrolls. A long, shiny table occupied the middle of the room, its legs graceful depictions of some birdlike creature. A scroll had been partially unspooled and spread out, waiting for them, the edges anchored with glimmering green and blue stones carved into fanciful shapes of birds and fish.

"What is all this?" Mark paused on the threshold, breathing in the musty but not unpleasant smell, stunned by the sight of thousands of scrolls.

"The Library of Khunarum himself." Jagrahim's voice held pride. "When the great city perished from the lives of men, and the people fled away to the south, my tribe received the duty and honor of preserving the knowledge. We even have some of the oldest books known to man." He gestured to a far corner of the room, dark and shadowed. "Stone tablets. No one can decipher them any longer, yet we preserve them."

"Can you read these?" Mark had been in the great Archives of the Sectors once, and its keepers had been no less proud of the accumulated knowledge.

"Three are appointed in each succeeding generation to learn the written language. We used to maintain a cadre of five readers, but my people are dwindling in number. Life here in the Empty Lands is hard. We can't spare so many these days who don't contribute to the direct work of keeping the village alive. But yes, I can read the scrolls."

"This is fascinating," Mark said with a diplomacy he didn't feel. "Rothan and Tia will want to see this. But why did you bring me here tonight?"

"After hearing your description of the serpent in the temple, I remembered a reference to such a creature. I've spent the night searching the pertinent scrolls." He gestured at the scroll spread open on the table.

"Is there mention of an antidote for the venom?"

Jagrahim didn't answer but drew him to the table. "Is this the creature?"

Moving a candle closer, Mark leaned over the page and swallowed hard. There on the parchment, depicted by the brushstrokes of some long-dead master artist, lay the snake, drawn half life-size. "Oh yes, I'd know it anywhere." He was fascinated by the sparkling turquoise eyes, almost alive on the paper, staring at him. Tightly coiled, the milky white body was limned with some iridescent substance, to suggest the eerie transparency of the actual reptile's scales. "What does the text say?"

The desert chieftain regarded him with an odd expression. He didn't answer, but carefully unrolled the scroll a few more turns. Mark could see the edges were crumbling. It must be beyond ancient. Long lines of elegant symbols surrounded the depiction of the snake.

The desert chief repositioned the anchor stones. "Read for yourself."

Mark shook his head. Even if this was High Chetal in the written format, which he doubted, his hypno training covered spoken languages only. He could no more read this than the well-meaning man opposite him could speak Outlier. "I can't. Translate for me, please."

"This is Sherabti, companion to the Goddess Mother Nuet, She Who Came Before. She who gave birth to the parents of the gods who now guard the world and the underworld, the life and the afterlife. The Goddess Mother was powerful, all knowing. You took shelter in her temple, you know. Sherabti served as her messenger, her watcher—"

"Wait just a moment." Mark held up his hands against the flood of words. "You're talking about this snake as if it's a myth."

Jagrahim seemed to be in unmistakable agreement. "Myth, legend, divine being, who can say?"

Mark shook his head in quick, hot denial. "No, I stood this close to it. Then it bit Sandy. Hell, it bit me—look!" Mark shoved his sleeve aside to reveal the twin fang marks above his wrist on the inside of his left arm. The marks were red and purple, surrounded by a spectacular black bruise. "Lucky it ran out of venom, or

I'd be in a coma too. The snake was real, all right. Mythical creatures don't leave damage like this."

"Did the others see it?"

"Well, no. I think Rothan caught a glimpse maybe. I'm telling you, a real serpent attacked us."

"There's no such creature known to my people, my lord, and we live in this desert. There are snakes, yes, and many are deadly. But this"—he tapped the crumbling, painted surface—"doesn't exist, save in the oldest scrolls of a long-dead religion. The Goddess Mother isn't served by any now. I remembered this picture because, as a child learning to read, I enjoyed the old stories. You were sheltering in what was her main temple, eons ago, when the Empty Lands were green and fertile and heavily populated." He started to roll the document onto its ornately carved wooden spool.

Mark reached out to stop him. "Hang on a moment. What does it say about this Sherabti?"

"Sherabti's role was the messenger of the Lady, as I told you already. The serpent could bring good or bad tidings—or warnings—as the Lady willed. It could kill, and it could bring life."

"Confusing. And not one whole hell of a lot of help right now." Mark permitted Jagrahim to complete his delicate task.

"I'm sorry. I assumed you'd want to have the details of what you were dealing with. Was I wrong?"

Mark accepted the chief had meant well. "I'm out of my depth here. I'm a soldier, you know? I can take a collection of hard facts and make them add up like a stack of bricks. You want to attack some kind of fortress, I'm your man. You want someone assassinated or kidnapped, I can do it. But what am I supposed to do with this kind of magical construct? And how do I use it to help Sandy? Do I go back there and tell her to wake up, quit faking it, because, hey, you were bitten by a mythological snake, not a real one?" He bit his lip against the flood of words. Panic over the possibility of losing Sandy was uncomfortably close to the surface of his emotions.

Jagrahim inserted the scroll into a jar with others and fastened a thin leather cover over the opening, knotting a string around the jar's neck. "I regret having confused you more than I helped. You and your Lady of the Star Wind are sadly unprepared for what you've found upon your return to our world."

Mark was unwilling to go into the whole discussion again of their actual identities. It wasn't going to make any sense to Jagrahim, any more than stories of goddesses and their snake messengers made sense to him. Sometimes old truths were well buried in the mythology of a planet, but he didn't have the training or the aptitude to try to ferret out from the deteriorating lore what might be of use in the current crisis. Frustrating to know there might be answers hidden from him in this room, but he had to accept defeat. "May I return to Sandy now?"

"Of course. Tomorrow I'll have the readers search through more of the older scrolls, see if any further details can be gleaned about Sherabti."

"I'd appreciate the effort." Mark was being more diplomatic than truthful again. He didn't think any myths or legends about snakes were going to help Sandy recover. His frustration was going to grow if people kept arguing with him about whether the snake existed. Damn it, he could prove the fucking thing had been real—didn't he bear the fang marks? He rubbed at the ache where the snake had struck him.

Jagrahim led him through the winding corridors in silence.

"She hasn't moved." The chief's wife slid from the chair to make room for Mark to resume his vigil. "She's neither worse nor better. We can hope for no more at this stage." She patted him on the arm in a maternal fashion. "You need rest as well."

He gave her a tired grin, which was the best he could muster, and muttered his thanks.

"We'll retire to our own chambers now," Jagrahim said, arm around his diminutive wife. "Should you need anything in the night, a servant waits outside your door."

"Thanks." Mark sank into the vacated chair and took Sandy's hand in his, not turning his head to watch his hosts leave. He harbored lingering doubts about the Mikkonite, questions he wanted answered, but he had to admit the tribe was taking good care of Sandy.

The seemingly endless night hours continued to drag by. The candles guttered. He didn't mind sitting in the semidark. At some point, he fell asleep, unable to resist the demands of his tired body any longer.

"Mark?"

Her soft voice brought him awake hours later. He sat up, still holding her hand, and now she squeezed his. Examining her face intently, he asked, "How do you feel?"

She furrowed her brow. "I don't know—sort of dizzy. Strange. I've been dreaming for the longest time."

He laughed, not sure yet whether to be relieved. "You've been out for two and a half days."

With one hand, she explored the back of her head gingerly. "Well, I guess I didn't dream this. I smacked my head on the base of a column, didn't I?"

"You sure did, as if the snakebite wasn't injury enough. Is there anything I should do, check your reflexes or get you something from your medical kit?"

"No, if I made it to this point, I'm probably okay. No double vision, no weakness. Slight headache." Eyes narrowed, she attempted to see through the gloom. "Where are we? Not at the oasis?"

"No, we're in the village of the Mikkonite. Old allies of Rothan's ancestors. The tribe rescued us from the sandstorm. It's a long story. Do you want more light?"

"No." She clutched at his hand as he made to rise from the chair to rekindle the lamps. "Don't leave me again."

"Never. Not in this lifetime. I've been a total fool. I'm sorry. I've had nothing to do but think while I've been sitting here. I prayed to the Lords of Space to pull you through, even though they probably don't listen for appeals from this place."

He swallowed hard. "You were all I ever wanted, and then when I find you again, I waste the opportunity. I was being stubborn, holding your grandmother's crimes against you. Not being willing to let my shields down and tell you—"

She reached with her free hand to touch his lips, stopping him in midsentence. "The past is finished, done. We agreed to start over and meet each other as we are now, remember? Besides, she told me we had to accept the situation here, since we'd made the choice already."

He paused in the middle of plumping the pillows to make her a better backrest. "She?"

"I was dreaming. Maybe it wasn't a dream. I went somewhere…else. Not this planet at all, but not like the Traveling. A beautiful room full of light."

"Don't tell me if remembering the dream distresses you." The hairs on the back of his neck rose at the eerie way she was talking.

"I can't remember the details now." Sandy closed her eyes for a moment, long lashes brushing her cheeks before she blinked and stared at him. "The experience or vision is fading, piece by piece. But there was a woman, or maybe several women, from this world we're on. She said she'd known me before, in another time, and she'd know me again in the future. She told me so many things, and now I can't remember. I can't even picture her face. She was so beautiful—it almost hurt to be in her presence. And there were others there too, but silent onlookers most of the time, watching me. And then the truly terrifying Mother arrived." She broke off, laughing. "I must sound deranged to you."

"Since we've been here, there've been so many strange things going on. I don't discount anything anymore." The way she talked of her experiences disturbed him. "The people here say the snake doesn't exist. Not as I described it anyway."

"Sherabti? But she does. She served the Mother. The young ones had no other way to bring me to them. But you weren't there. You didn't come." She stared at him, wide-eyed.

"Sandy, I didn't have any dreams at all. The venom sure affected us differently. I've had a lot of inoculations against native toxins in a wide range over the years, which probably shielded me from the worst of the poison."

"Some of the people there argued against letting me return to this life. I think at least one wanted me to die." Sandy's eyes filled with tears, and she reached for him.

Mark moved onto the bed, enfolding her in a comforting hug. She clung to him and cried. At a total loss now, he wondered how she knew the name of the mythical snake. Had he said it to Jagrahim once he reentered the bedchamber? He didn't think so. Mark stayed silent, content to hold her and stroke her hair.

Wiping her eyes on the sleeve of the tunic the Mikkonite had dressed her in, she leaned against the pillow. "The choice was left to me at the end," Sandy said with a small hiccup.

"What choice?"

"Whether to die or come back here." Her words indicated she was somewhat disoriented.

"Thank you for choosing life, for choosing me," he said, gratitude warming his heart even as he worried about the stability of her recovery.

"We can't ever go home, you know." She rested her head on his shoulder.

"I didn't think we could. Lajollae made it pretty clear she sold one-way tickets."

"I'd kind of hoped we might find a way, in the oasis. I know better now. We've got work to do here. We're not the right people, not truly Star Wind and her consort, but we have to be, if we're going to be on this world. We've got decisions ahead of us." She worried at the fringe of the blanket, knotting and unknotting the strands.

Mark laid his hand over hers. "Sweetheart, don't concern yourself about it now. I'm not pressing you for any decisions. You're remembering remnants of dreams, as you said."

"I'm afraid to sleep again." She sounded drowsy. "But I can't stay awake any longer either. My eyes won't stay open. So tired—"

"I'll be right here, I promise. I'll wake you if the dreams seem to be distressing you."

She moved over on the bed and patted the mattress beside her. "Please, hold me. I'll feel safe then. I could always sleep in your arms."

"Whatever you want." He took off his boots, then adjusted the pillows against the headboard. He sat, cradling her. She was already asleep again, but in a normal fashion, be believed, not comatose.

Jagrahim's wife found them curled together on the bed in the morning. She clapped her hands once with pleasure, pleased to find Sandy conscious. The healer directed the serving girls with crisp efficiency as they set breakfast on the low table at the far wall.

"Eat, regain your strength, both of you," she admonished. "For your warrior would not leave your side, nor would he eat more than a bite or two while you wandered in your dreams, my lady. I'll share the good news with your companions while you breakfast."

"Thank you." Mark surveyed the platters of fruit and other delicacies. "What can I bring you? She's giving excellent advice—you do need to get your strength back. As soon as the sandstorm ends, Rothan's going to be impatient to get to the lost city. I'm sure he'd have left us already, if the storm hadn't been blowing."

"Yes, we need to get there, the sooner the better," Sandy said. "Time's growing short. We're already too late for some things."

She didn't expand on her remark, accepting the plate of fruit he'd selected for her, some bread, and scrambled eggs, and a mug each of juice and of water. He fixed a more generous helping for himself, realizing with a sudden pang in his gut how hungry he'd become after two days of standing watch over Sandy.

"We rejoice in your recovery, Lady."

Rothan and Tia stood in the doorway, Jagrahim behind them. Mark gestured for them to come in.

"Other than a huge appetite, I'm fine today, no aftereffects." Sandy waved the roll in her hand.

Mark made the introductions. "This is Jagrahim, chief of the Mikkonite. He and his men rescued us from the sandstorm, brought us to their village. His wife, Merbek, has been taking care of you."

"My thanks to you and your wife." Sandy always exuded regal grace. "I'm grateful."

"The storm abates. By tonight we should be able to ride to the lost city." Rothan's eagerness reverberated in his voice. "The chief tells me it's a few hours from here, to the west. We're close to our destination at last."

Jagrahim bowed at the waist. "It's my honor to guide you the rest of the way and get you past the city's safeguards."

"Safeguards?" Mark paused, the bread in his hand forgotten. "What danger can there be now, after thousands of years?"

The chief shook his head. "Those who came before left powerful curses and spells to prevent looting, to deter men who have no right to set foot in Amaraten from doing so. There are great secrets locked in those ruins. Treasures beyond imagining."

"I want two things from the ruins," Rothan said. "And I've the right to claim them for my king, Hutenen."

Jagrahim regarded him gravely. "I agree. You've the right to search for the Crown and Scepter of Khunarum and make your attempt to take them for his descendants. Otherwise, I'd be sending you on your way to die in the desert or to be struck by the curses, should you be lucky enough to find Amaraten's gates."

"And we have a house there, or so Rothan told us." Mark meant his contribution to the conversation in jest, but Jagrahim's response was measured and somber.

"Legend speaks of the Lady of the Star Wind, grieving over the death of Khunarum and the destruction of his city. She abandoned her house, and departed to the sky, promising to return if ever his heirs had need of her."

"I'll need the mirror." Sandy broke into the history discussion. She sipped her juice while staring at Mark over the lip of the mug.

The non sequitur surprised him, since he'd never known Sandy to be vain about her appearance. He brought her the small mirror lying on the side table.

"Not that one." Tossing aside the tiny silver mirror without glancing at it, she frowned as if he'd committed a serious error. Chills spiraled along his spine, because she had an uncanny resemblance to her grandmother, the empress, for a moment. It was as if another woman looked out of Sandy's blue eyes. Even her voice had an altered timbre—deeper, more husky, with an accent he had never heard before. "The Mirror of the Mother—I have to find it."

Tia questioned her declaration. "But Nuet's mirror is a legend, a fable for telling children."

"No, I need it." Blinking, Sandy fell against the pillows. A half-eaten piece of fruit rolled from her hand, bounced off the side of the bed, and flew across the floor, coming to rest at Mark's toe.

Frowning, he retrieved the fruit, throwing it onto the tray. "Are you all right?"

She stared at him, brow furrowed in a bewildered frown. She put one hand to her temple. "I'm sorry, what was I saying?"

"Something about a mirror. Maybe you're not as recovered as we believed. You should rest." Mark prepared to escort the guests from the room.

"I thought you didn't speak our language?" Rothan watched Sandy with mild suspicion.

Mark realized she hadn't been speaking in the High Chetal he used to get by, but was expressing herself perfectly in the actual language of this planet. Dismayed by yet another mystery, he stared at her.

Speaking in Outlier, to him alone, she said, "I don't know. Maybe I've been subconsciously absorbing it since we met Rothan and Tia? Or maybe it came to me in the dreams."

"Maybe you have an amazing facility with languages. Don't distress yourself." Mark was shaken enough for both of them. He didn't like unexplained phenomena, especially when it came to things affecting her.

"We'll leave at full moon. Amrell rules the sky tonight, and she's the most brilliant of the moons," Jagrahim said.

"Brunette." Sandy said idly, toying with the small mirror she'd rejected a moment earlier. "She's brunette."

Realizing their new friends were staring at her, Mark tried to cover the awkward moment. "She's still a bit woozy from the venom and the blow to the head. Nothing to worry about. We can travel."

Later the same evening Jagrahim escorted them through a series of tunnels to the surface outside the village. There, Mark found their chariots waiting, horses already harnessed, as well as a cluster of Mikkonite warriors and their mounts.

A tall warrior in blue robes strode to meet them, saluting Jagrahim. "All is in readiness."

Mark was surprised to find the soldier was a woman, since he'd observed only male fighters in the tunnels and the village. Women fought for the Sectors in all kinds of combat units, so he was used to running dangerous missions with mixed teams, but he hadn't expected that on this world.

Jagrahim rested one hand on the warrior's shoulder. "I'm pleased to present my daughter, Sallea."

She pushed the hood of her cloak onto her shoulders and saluted. Sallea had a strong face with high cheekbones and well-defined brows. Her eyes were the same vivid blue as her robes, and she'd outlined them in kohl, or something similar, the touch of femininity not detracting at all from her general air of military discipline. Her midnight blue hair had been coiled into a tight braid. She wore soft, black leather riding boots, and a heavily padded black glove covered her hand and forearm. "I'm honored to lead your escort on the trip to the lost city," she said.

"My daughter is a Hunter." Palpable pride sounded in Jagrahim's voice, and the extra emphasis he put on the last word made it sound as if it were a title. "Can you summon Lakht for them to meet?"

"Of course, it'll be my pleasure." She stepped a little away, holding out her arm. A moment later, there was a swooshing sound of wings and a loud call of *keeeeooooo* from the sky. An imposing bird of prey came in low across the ground, rising to land on Sallea's outstretched arm. Once it had settled itself, the bird leaned over to give her a quick caress along the cheek with its closed beak. She stuck her free hand into a pouch at her belt and retrieved a fragment of meat that she fed the bird from her open palm.

Mark marveled she could bear the weight of the bird, which was about three feet from the tip of its beak to end of its tail. It clung to her padded arm with talons like thick knives. The dense plumage started off gray on the head, darkening to ebony black at the tail and trailing wing edges. A crisp white vee of feathers accented the neck, and the huge eyes were outlined in vivid yellow, along with the upper beak. The legs were feathered in soft, downy gray, but there was nothing chicklike about the creature, or the scythelike talons now gripping the glove over Sallea's arm. Mark bet she needed to replace those padded gloves fairly often.

The wingspan as it swooped to answer whatever summons Sallea had made was easily eight feet. This bird could do a lot of damage to a man if it decided, or was ordered, to attack. He realized Lakht was eyeing him in the same manner he was assessing the bird. "Impressive," he said. "What do you hunt?"

Sallea laughed, stroking one finger across the bird's back. "Anything we wish to find. Lakht is my eyes on the desert. When we're linked, I see what he sees and I tell him what to search for."

"A true Hunter can speak to his or her bird," Jagrahim said. "Mind to mind."

"To some extent." Sallea laughed as the bird shifted and lifted its wings. "Lakht's mind is full of the urge to drink the hot blood of desert rodents most of the day. But we can communicate well enough."

"He's magnificent. What's his range?" Mark asked.

"About ten miles, depending on the thermals." Sallea lifted her arm as if throwing the bird, who launched himself into the air with grace and soared into the night sky, briefly outlined against the moon as he flew off to the east. "We should go, Father."

The full, silvery moon called Amrell cast so much light Mark could almost believe he was riding at midday, except for the night chill. The sandstorm had blown over and taken all the clouds with it. Jagrahim, Sallea, and nine more warriors kept their horses reined in to match the speed of the chariots. The Mikkonite leader guided the party by some set of landmarks that he didn't share. He did tell them Amaraten was located to the north, on the coastline, having originally been a major commercial hub, as well as Khunarum's capital. Lakht flew above the column in endless circles, sometimes going ahead, but primarily staying with the party. Mark could detect no evidence of the old trade road, nor did he see signposts. The area they rode through was nothing but featureless desert to his eyes, although the farther they rode, the more vegetation he saw dotting the hills. Clearly, Amaraten was situated in a more temperate zone than the rest of the Empty Lands.

Drawing his horse even with the lead chariot, planning to exchange a few words with Rothan, he was struck by Tia's distress. She clutched the railing, her eyes shut. "Are you all right?" He raised his voice to be heard over the sound of the wooden wheels rattling across the hard ground.

She opened her eyes. With dismay Mark observed how pale she'd become, even allowing for the effect of the moonlight. "I'm fine, thank you for your concern. I had a small attack of nausea, some dizziness. Perhaps the dinner we ate right before leaving the Mikkonite village was unwise, at least in my case."

"Don't be hesitant about telling us if you need to stop," Mark urged her. "I know Rothan's in a hurry, but he wouldn't want you to be ill."

"Indeed," the captain said from his position on the other side of the chariot, handling the reins. "And the same applies to your lady, if she needs a rest."

Mark gazed at Sandy, riding in company with Jagrahim. At ease in the Mikkonite saddle, she chatted with the chieftain in her freshly acquired local dialect. Her command of the language bothered him, but he couldn't deny her sudden aptitude made things easier and did no harm.

One of the Mikkonite outriders stood tall in his stirrups and called out to the chief. "The walls of the city lie ahead."

"How much farther?"

"Perhaps an hour."

"I'd have said we were closer." Mark was surprised to hear how much travel time remained.

The rider glanced at him. "Distances are deceiving on the desert, my lord."

"Good, I'm pleased with the time we've made." Jagrahim waved one hand at Sallea. "Daughter, ride ahead and prepare the gate for us."

The girl was gone in a flurry of sand, her horse lengthening its stride into a gallop. One rider followed her.

"Prepare the gate?" Mark restrained his horse, which wanted to go for a run in pursuit of Sallea.

Jagrahim said, "As I told you this morning, the city has its safeguards. We can't ride straight in."

"I thought the site was abandoned due to some catastrophe many centuries ago?"

Nodding, Jagrahim had the benign expression of a teacher listening to a clever pupil recite lessons. "That is true."

"But the refugees took time to set safeguards while running for their lives?"

"The city yet contains countless treasures. It's a graveyard as well, for many who died in the fall of the city. The entire site deserves respect, not grave-robbing." Jagrahim guffawed, startling Mark, given the grim nature of what he'd been discussing. Spreading his arms wide, the chief shared the amusing idea making him laugh. "Although who would venture this far into the Empty Lands to despoil the city is a mystery. Not many are brave enough. We don't rescue those who go astray either. I made an exception for your party."

Mark whistled. "Lucky for us."

"Your banners and the chariots told us you were of Nakhtiaar. We had to investigate your reason for entering our territory before allowing you to proceed or leaving you to die."

The walls of the city loomed before Mark for a long time before they arrived at the gates. Distances were indeed deceiving on this wasteland. The fortifications appeared to be in excellent condition and stretched in both directions as far as the eye could see. Sentry towers rose high above the battlements at regular intervals. Mark felt as if he was being watched. The repeated assurances about how long the city had been deserted didn't diminish his unease.

Sallea and her companion stood waiting for them in front of a massive set of dull black metal gates three stories tall. Mark saw no inscription or decoration of any type.

"I've spoken all but the last spell, Father," Sallea said to Jagrahim as the entire party reined to a halt.

The chieftain nodded. "Proceed then and let us enter this place."

"As you command." Facing the gates, she held her hands up. When she spoke, she used a normal tone, pitched for conversation. "Open now, mighty guardians, part for those who have come to see your secrets, in the name of Khunarum and of the ancient gods. Let no harm be visited on us during our time within thy walls. We will leave all things as we find them, save for the items which are the basis of our quest."

She made a slight gesture, as if pushing the air in front of the gates.

For a long moment, nothing happened. Mark contemplated how the party might be able to scale the walls if required to do so. Sallea frowned and made the pushing gesture again, with more force. Lakht came winging in from behind, landing on her arm, beating his wings, and fanning air toward the portal.

The gates opened inward, inch by inch. The process was eerie, soundless, and intimidating. Lakht took to the air with a harsh cry. The horses reared and balked, forcing the riders to delay for a few moments until the animals could be calmed.

The gates stopped at about half open, but there was room for the chariots to squeeze through.

The air inside the walls had an odd quality as Mark's horse sidestepped through the open portal. Unnatural, chilled. He thought he detected a slight tang of the salt air from the as-yet-unseen ocean. The surroundings were too quiet. He had a hard time catching his breath as soon as he crossed the boundary, as if the air was heavier than normal, making his lungs labor. There were no birds, other than Lakht, at the moment riding on a special saddle perch. No one spoke.

Jagrahim led the column away from the gates. The road was clear of debris here, as if it had been partially cleared of obstructions. Mark shifted in the saddle to check the entrance one more time and found the massive gates closed, which bothered him. He hoped Sallea had a chant for reopening them, even as he made sure his blaster was close at hand.

As they proceeded through the streets of the lost city, there was a little bit of conversation from Rothan and Tia, who were marveling at how well preserved some sections were. The city planners had evidently relied on the outer wall to keep them safe and allowed the dwellings and public buildings themselves to sprawl over the land between the ensorcelled boundary and the ocean. Other areas were nothing but empty land, wiped clean by the ocean's fury millennia ago. Then there were patches of jumbled rubble, dense and impenetrable, no way to tell what kind of buildings had been there. Yet the road they traveled remained quite clear, the stones in good repair and the path unobstructed. Being exposed, an easy target if there was surveillance of any kind going on, made Mark nervous, running contrary to all his training and experience.

After a few moments, Jagrahim reined in his horse at a cross street, stopping the slow-moving procession with his upraised hand.

"Your house lies at the end of the thoroughfare, my lady." Bowing in the saddle to Sandy, he pointed with his coiled whip.

"How do you know?" Mark could tell from the way Sandy bit her lip she was trying not to laugh. If she'd told him once, she'd said it ten times—she found the idea of owning a specific ruin in the lost city unlikely and amusing.

"I had the readers go over the maps of the city from before the catastrophe and locate the place." Jagrahim's answer was mundane and practical. "I'm sure you wish to examine your property."

Glancing in Mark's direction, Sandy raised her eyebrows in a silent question.

"I think we probably should." Curiosity was getting the better of him. Would they find more Traveler relics? He hoped for clues about the real Lady of the Star Wind and her consort.

"We'll be at the harbor," Jagrahim said, pointing in the direction he'd been leading them. "Join us when you're finished here. Follow the road, and you'll find us at the water's edge."

"We won't be too long, I'm sure," Mark said. "Good hunting!"

The rest of the party continued along the broad thoroughfare, to the east. Tia gave a wave, and then the group drove around a wide curve in the road, moving from sight behind a complex of fallen pillars and broken statues.

Mark and Sandy turned their horses and rode at a cautious pace down the indicated street, which ended about a quarter mile later in a half circle in front of an imposing structure. Even in ruins, the building was majestic, surrounded by what might have been gardens or orchards. One side of the ornately carved wooden door had fallen off the hinges and lay in jagged, rotting pieces on the steps. The other half of the door sat half open. Part of the roof had fallen in to their far left. An impressively large tree grew through a gap it had forced in the walls and roof, towering far above the ruined dwelling.

Dismounting and waiting for Sandy to do the same, Mark knotted his horse's reins around the half-broken pillar at the east end of the terrace, registering the remnant of a carving appeared to be some kind of winged beast. Checking his blaster, he took the lead on the flight of shallow steps to the half-open door. When he rested his hand on the gilded panel, it swung open on silent hinges. "After three thousand years, the hinges don't need oiling?"

"Didn't need the key then." Sandy allowed the lavender pendant on its thin chain to fall between her breasts. "This is nothing like the oasis."

"Nothing outworld about it, for sure. Matches the architecture in the rest of the city, or what's left of the place. Maybe the Travelers went native when they dropped in?"

"I hope we'll find something to tell us more about them. About who we're supposed to be." She sounded eager.

"You mean who we're masquerading as?"

"The situation has been fine so far," Sandy answered. "Why does it bother you so much?"

"Posing as someone else might come back to bite us. Come on, let's see what we own here. Watch out for snakes."

Disappointment met Mark when he walked into the foyer of "their" house. The walls were painted with stylized, faded frescoes, much as he'd seen on other vertical surfaces elsewhere in the ruins, lacking any depiction of people. A partially collapsed staircase would have led to the now destroyed second floor.

He shone his light around the room and then at the floor. A few sparkling points caught the glare and reflected it.

"A mosaic maybe?" Sandy added the light from her lamp.

"Maybe." Mark scuffed his boot across the portion in front of him. She knelt and wiped the rest of the dust away with the hem of her flowing Mikkonite robe. She sat back with a gasp. "Wow."

"Yeah, you said it."

The large area where she'd removed the top layer of dirt now glowed in the light with multicolored, flat, cut gemstones set into a glossy black enameled surface.

"If I didn't know how fantastic it would sound, I'd say it was meant to be the Tiandromedi galaxy cluster, on the far side of Outlier," Sandy said. "The pattern and color of the major stars are quite distinctive. Can this whole floor be a star map?"

"Could be."

"Do you see any clue on the mosaic to indicate where the Travelers came from? Any special markings?"

Mark shook his head. "You can't see Tiandromedi from the local night sky of this planet, no question there. We'd have noticed that detail for sure. Maybe thousands of years ago you could. We've no idea where Lajollae dropped us. It could be a coincidence we think this is a map of a galaxy known to us."

Dusting her hands, Sandy gazed around the rest of the large foyer. "Shall we clean the rest? Find out?"

"I don't think we have the time. And what would we do with the information anyway?" He held out his hand to her and helped her to her feet again. "We didn't come to do housework."

"I suppose you're right." She brushed the dirt off her robes. "It's tantalizing."

"Like so many things on this planet." Mark swung his lamp to illuminate the walls again. "So far it's all been a mystery wrapped in myth."

Three gaping doorways opened off the entry. Choosing the one straight ahead of them, he shone his handlamp into the room. The light reflected off more painted walls.

"Nothing in there," he reported over his shoulder to Sandy. "Someone cleaned out all the furnishings here too, just like at the mountain."

"Why would they take the trouble? And when? Jagrahim said the records had no mention of anyone returning to the city after it was abandoned."

"Well, someone went to a lot of trouble to make sure the streets stayed clear. I suspect there's more to the reality about how life in this city ended than what the legends tell." Mark shrugged. "What's your preference—left or right doorway next?"

Sandy considered. "Left." She suited action to words and took three steps to the portal.

Mark hastened to get in front of her, blaster ready. Moonlight pouring through a skylight illuminated this chamber. Like a visible stream of light, the beams slashed across the mosaic floor tiles to focus on a table against the far wall. One object sat on the table, reflecting the light so strongly it glowed.

Sandy ran across the room to scoop up the relic before he could stop her or utter any cautions. "It's the Mirror of the Mother!" She held it out to him. "I've been hoping to find this today."

Her fixation on mirrors concerned him. Holstering the blaster for a moment, he held out his hand. "May I see?"

She passed it to him readily enough. Mark turned it over in his hands as if it were a booby trap ready to explode. About six inches in diameter, the round mirror had been set in a solid-gold frame. Carved vines and flowers unfamiliar to him twined around the edges. Two female figures and one man comprised the handle. Exquisite attention had been paid to the details of their faces and clothes. Together, the three balanced the mirror disk in their upraised hands. He rotated the treasure in his hand and exclaimed in surprise. Instead of reflecting his face, the surface of the mirror was dark and streaked.

"Maybe it's just dusty?" He handed the mirror to Sandy. So far he didn't see what the fuss was all about, but he had the sense not to say so. He could appreciate the mirror as a work of art, beautiful, but only a woman's accessory, not his idea of a weapon.

She tried cleaning the reflecting surface with a fold of her robe but had no luck shining it up.

He stubbed his toe on something in the dust on the floor, which slid across the mosaic. When he chased the item, he found a small box lying on its side, leaning against the table leg. He picked it up, rotating the box in his hands. The container was an intricately layered assembly of different-colored types of wood polished to a high gloss, gleaming in the moonlight. On each flat surface, in variegated stone inlays, there was a rendition of the soaring bird of prey he'd seen over their oasis, surely a cousin to Sallea's hunting bird. "Looks like a ring box."

"Open it," Sandy urged, not taking her gaze from the mirror. She was examining each detail of the three figures on the handle as best she could in the available light.

Mark set his handlamp on the table, then fumbled with the latch on the box. He didn't want to force it, or damage the thing. At last the cover sprang open with an audible click. Now he was the one mesmerized by treasure gleaming in the moonlight. The box held a man's ring, solid, heavy gold, set with a massive dark blue lapis. The top of the stone had been carved into a star, with the stylized shape of the bird of prey in the center. Mark stripped his riding gloves off and plucked the ring from the prongs holding it. He slid the ring onto his left-hand ring finger where the band fit as if made to measure for him.

He'd never been one for jewelry or adornment. Yes, he'd worn the heavy ring symbolizing his place in his Outlier Clan with pride. The empress had ripped it from his hand personally at the beginning of her attempt to break him with torture and mind games. He supposed she'd had it destroyed. He'd never worn another until this moment, scorning the Star Guard Academy class ring. Pawned that bit of jewelry the day after graduation, bought drinks for his cronies and never thought about it again. But this ring of unknown provenance felt right and proper. He curled his hand into a fist. This ring was his.

Eyebrows raised, Sandy gazed at him. "Found something?"

"A ring." He held out his hand to show her. "It fits like the goldsmith made it for me."

She leaned closer, touching the bezel. "Interesting star and hawk motif. Am I the star and you're the hunter?"

"It could mean nothing," he said. "I just like it. And this is our house, or so we've been told over and over. Let's go see what's in the last room across the foyer."

"Anything is likely to be a letdown after the mirror and the ring." Sandy tucked the mirror into her side pocket. "But we might as well see it all."

"Odds are we'll never be back this way so we shouldn't waste the opportunity," he agreed.

He paused on the threshold of the last chamber. This room was a mess, as if most of the household inventory, other than the table with the mirror and the ring, had been thrust, thrown, and stacked in the available space by people in a great rush. There were pieces of furniture, dishes, and goblets, scrolls such as the ones Jagrahim had pored over at the Mikkonite settlement, and dozens more items. There was no order or sense to the collection.

"Nothing here like what we found at the mountain," Sandy said after they'd spent a few moments sifting through the stacks and pulling out items at random. "No high tech."

"This is all local stuff for sure. Jagrahim might want the scrolls." Mark wished he could read the local language. The answers he sought might be on the papyrus in front of him and he'd never know.

"We can ask him. He wasn't too keen on taking anything more away from this city." She wandered off to examine something else that caught her eye.

"Though why not—" Mark broke off in midsentence. "Come look at this."

"What?" She came across the room to him, following his pointing hand. "*Tzerde!*"

Three of Lajollae's bubbles lay scattered on the threadbare remnants of a once-lush carpet.

Sandy retreated as if to avoid even inadvertent contact. She tugged at Mark's elbow.

"I wonder where the globes would take us?" Mark said.

"I wonder why they're here. Did Lajollae stop in Amaraten at some point? Or did the Travelers carry a supply of their own?"

"Well, we're never going to know." He sought her concurrence. "Are we?"

"No. We've done all of her kind of Traveling I ever want to do. And you don't tolerate it well. Don't touch them." She grabbed at his arm again. "We can't take any chances."

Sandy's wide eyes and shaky voice conveyed her deep concern, compelling him to remind her that Traveling hadn't been simple to initiate. "I had to smash the one on Freemarket to make it work."

"I don't care. The globes make me nervous."

"At least we've established the people who lived here had some connection to Lajollae and the Travelers." He shone his lamp fully on the globes, noting how each appeared to contain clouds.

"I want to show you what I found, over here." She led him across the room and pointed at the wall. "What do you see?"

At first he couldn't make out a thing, but the longer he stared, Mark began to see two silhouettes in the moonlight—man and a woman. The woman was seated, the man's hand on her shoulder. He moved closer. "Like a sketch, as if the artist was beginning a commission when the disaster struck."

She reached out and brushed the wall with her fingertips. "If only he'd drawn the faces. I want to know, to see—"

"I don't think we're meant to."

Ignoring him, Sandy moved farther along the wall, shining her lamp at the next figure that stood behind the man. "This one doesn't seem human. A local god maybe?"

Mark studied the faded outline. "Definitely reptilian. Unfinished like the others. No one said all the Travelers were human. Lajollae sure wasn't."

"Oh, surely you don't think alien beings walked the streets here?"

A loud shout from outside interrupted their discussion.

"Time to go, I guess." Mark took her by the elbow and guided her out of the room. "Hope Rothan and Tia found what they traveled here for."

"The two of them and their allies have gone to a lot of trouble," Sandy said.

"Hard to believe this crown is going to make a difference in the political situation." Mark was curious to see what Sandy's opinion might be.

"I don't know." She shook her head. "Sometimes symbols have a lot of power to influence the people. Depends on many factors."

"Depends on this person we've never met, this prince of theirs, Tia's brother. He's the unknown quantity."

"We don't know enough about any of it to say for sure." Before mounting her horse, Sandy took a lingering look at the ruins of the dwelling. "So frustrating. I think we might find some real answers in there if we had time to sift through the one room full of stuff."

"Which Jagrahim won't let us do." Mark heard another yell from the general direction of the main street. "We'd better rejoin the others."

When he and Sandy walked their horses toward the sound of the shouts, Djed came running along the street alone. Short of breath, agitated, and upset, the archer saluted Mark. "You must come at once, my lord."

"What's up? Did Rothan find the crown and whatever it is?"

"Scepter." Djed corrected him. "No, my lord. The Mikkonite led us to a complex of buildings, part of a palace, half fallen into the sea. Jagrahim told Rothan what he seeks is in a room drowned under water at high tide. Once the tide withdrew from the ruins, my captain went to retrieve the treasures but hasn't given us any sign as to how he fares. Jagrahim says he can't help or hinder. He and his people are allowed by ancient treaty to act as guides only, on penalty of death. I'm afraid for Rothan—what if he's gotten trapped in the ruins? The waters will come in, and he'll drown."

"Does he swim? Do you?"

"Swim? You mean like a fish of the deep?" The mere idea apparently astounded Djed. "No, nor do any of my archers. You haven't seen the creatures swimming the waters. Legend says one of Khunarum's own daughters was tipped from her pleasure boat and killed by the fanged hunters in the river. When even a boat isn't safe, no sane man risks himself naked in the waters."

Sandy pulled her horse away from grazing on nearby brush. "Sounds like we'd better stop wasting time."

"Right." Mark held out a hand to Djed.

The archer backed away, shaking his head. "I'll run beside your horse."

"Suit yourself. Let's go."

A few moments later, the road ended at the edge of the harbor. The Mikkonite were clustered beside the chariots and the other horses. The men were playing a game of chance, while Jagrahim and his daughter chatted off to the side. Tia and the rest of the archers were close to the edge of the muddy tidal flats, gazing at the ruins revealed by the low tide.

Mark brought his horse to a halt, stood in the stirrups, and reconnoitered. The pavement ended at the cliff edge. There were parts of enormous buildings and immense statues, broken rotting ships, and unidentifiable rubble protruding from the wet sand below as far as he could see, all the way to the horizon. Slimy, dripping, green and brown seaweed festooned the ruins like glistening carpet. Another long fragment of the road stood about thirty feet from the base of the cliff, leading to a cluster of ruins perched crookedly on a small rise, as if the seas had tried to remove them and tired of the task. The blue and green ocean gleamed in the soft predawn light, waves breaking in the distance. The sets broke closer each time.

Mark dismounted. "Where's Rothan?"

"He's gone to what remains of the inner palace of Khunarum." Jagrahim pointed with his chin at the cantilevered ruins way out in the harbor. "The crown and the scepter were left there, in the vaults below the throne room."

"Below?" Mark leaned cautiously over the cliff's edge, gauging the high-tide mark on the rocks below, and then straightened to assess the advancing ocean. "How long till high tide?"

"The tides run on six-hour cycles, my lord. We began this venture at low tide."

"So we have some time but not much. All right, I'll go out there and see what's keeping him."

"I'm coming too," Djed said. "You may need help if he's trapped." He addressed Tia. "With your permission, my lady."

She waved one hand in consent. "Rothan insisted this task was his alone, but now I'm afraid for him. Surely it can't offend the gods of this place for you to go to his aid."

"Be careful." Sandy dismounted and came to Mark's side, staring at the ruins. "I don't like this at all."

"We'll be fine, I promise. I swim like a fish, learned at the academy." Mark kissed her cheek, breathing in her sweet scent. "Come on, Djed, let's get going."

The two men rappelled down the cliff, using ropes Rothan had affixed earlier for his own descent. As soon as he reached the ground, Mark yelled for the Mikkonite to toss him another coil of rope.

He checked the charge in his blaster, shouldered the new rope, and marched off, the archer on his heels.

The muck and wet sand made for torturously slow going, but as soon as he got onto the road, broken and disrupted as the pavement was, Mark quickened the pace. The slippery surface was strewn with seaweed, but it provided better footing than the muck. Exhilarated by the smell of fresh salt air, he filled his lungs without irritating them the way the dead air in the city itself had done. Mark drew in a second deep breath.

"We have any idea where we are going once we reach that pile?" he asked Djed.

The archer shook his head. "My captain had instructions from the ancient scrolls. I believe he knew what he had to do, but I'm not sure. It was his task alone, he said."

"Fortunately, we can follow his tracks." Mark pointed to where the seaweed had been trampled or disturbed.

When he reached the pile of ruins, Mark waved to the watching party on shore, and then he and Djed scrambled into the tumbled blocks of what had once been a massive building. He proceeded with caution, reminding his companion to do the same. "Must have been some hellacious earthquake to raise parts of the harbor and sink others—the land here moved a good thirty feet in spots." He pointed at the broken escarpments and heard Djed gasp at his estimate of the earth's raw power. "Here are Rothan's footprints, going down these stairs."

The two men descended what had been a broad stairway in the distant past, now choked with huge pieces of masonry and broken statues. Barely enough clearance existed for a man to pass between some of the chunks of debris. At the bottom, Mark faced the dark entrance to a corridor extending under the building. When he shone his handlamp into the cavernous opening, he realized the tunnel descended at a gradual slope.

"I'm not crazy about this." Mark cupped his hand beside his mouth, leaned into the corridor, and yelled, "Rothan!"

He received no reply, only the odd and distant echo of his voice. Mark's instincts pushed him to find Rothan in the shortest possible amount of time. The tunnel remained in passable condition, although the walls were covered with seaweed, barnacles, and slime. The ceiling dripped, and there were numerous puddles. "Must flood to the top at high tide." He aimed his light at the tiled ceiling. "We have to be out of here well before then."

"Indeed," Djed said with a nervous glance at his surroundings.

After a few moments of walking, Mark came to a spot where the walls had fallen in somewhat. He poked his light through the narrow opening. "Gets better ahead but not much. I'll go first, and then you can hand me the torch and follow."

The tunnel was quiet, only the constant *plink plink* of dripping water and the sound of their own footsteps. The two men passed more piles of rubble. The passageway kept going downward, the angle of descent becoming steeper.

"We'll be in the Underworld at this rate." Djed clutched at his amulet of brown and green beads.

"Whoever the builders were, they understood how to construct for the ages. This place endured pretty well over the centuries. Hello, what's this?"

He stood at the top of a flight of stairs leading into the depths of the ruins.

"Rothan rigged a rope for a handrail." Mark grabbed at the strand and tugged. "One good sign."

Djed swallowed hard and began his descent on Mark's heels.

About halfway down, Mark paused, raising a hand to signal Djed to stop. "Did you hear something? There it is again!"

A faint yell repeated from the inky dark below. The two men exchanged glances. Mark drew his blaster and moved out, taking extra care on the slimy steps. The stairs ended with no warning, leaving him balanced on the narrow edge of a glowing azure pool. There was no way to gauge how deep the water might be. Mark raised his torch and peered across the obstacle while both men called out for their missing comrade.

"Over here," came the reply, a weak voice from the right.

Mark swung the lamp in the proper direction. Rothan sat on a ledge about a yard above the water level, sword balanced across his knees, left leg bleeding sluggishly. An odd slash cut across his left cheek.

"What the hell happened?" Mark said.

"There's some creature in the depths," Rothan answered in a low voice. "Extinguish the torches, quick. The hell spawn is drawn to light."

Too late.

A large aquatic creature came from the bottom of the pool in a sudden surge of cold water. Mark and Djed went reeling as a wave broke around them. The beast flailed with heavy black tentacles, knocking the already off-balance archer into the water. Cursing, Mark blasted the two sinewy, suckered arms coming at him. A third tentacle wrapped around his ankle, tugged him off the ledge and into the water. He lost the lamp, which flew from his grasp as his elbow struck the step with bone-bruising force, but he kept a death grip on the blaster as he was submerged. The creature dragged him deep before releasing its grip momentarily, only to clutch Mark again, suckers sliding off the impenetrable fabric of his offworld fatigue pants. While the beast was stymied by his clothing, Mark managed to fight to the surface for one huge, desperate breath. As the animal hauled him under for the second time, he fired a tight pattern of blasts into the water where he hoped the main body was located. The tentacles tightened unbearably for a second before the creature convulsed. Tentacles drifted aimlessly now, the beast sinking into the murk. Mark kicked completely loose of one lingering ropy fragment curled around his ankle and shot to the surface, floating there for a second, gasping for air.

He stowed his weapon, took a deep breath, and dove, trying to locate Djed, who hadn't surfaced. Cloth brushed past his fingertips, and he surfaced with a mighty effort, dragging the dead weight of the archer with him. Mark managed to get himself and Djed onto the lowest stair. Rolling the unconscious man onto his back, Mark worked to resuscitate him. The hand torch had come to rest against the stair and provided light for the effort.

Sputtering, Djed convulsed, retching copious quantities of water. After the spasms stopped, he wiped his mouth and clutched at his legs, nearly toppling into the water. "I can't feel my left leg!"

Mark played the torch over Djed's extremities, finding an even pattern of oozing gashes running the entire length of his leg from ankle to hip. "Creature must have claws mixed in with the suckers."

"The numbness goes away," Rothan said. "I was ensnared in the same fashion as I swam across the pool. I stabbed it in the eye with my dagger, and it released me. I got to this ledge but couldn't go forward or retreat to find an alternate route. The creature lurked in the water. It couldn't find me with the torch extinguished."

"Is there only one?" While he talked, Mark made quick work of bandaging the archer's leg with rags torn from his borrowed Mikkonite robes. He tried to shield the light with his body, preventing stray beams from falling on the tide pool beside him.

"I only saw one. I heard you coming and tried to warn you."

"Don't worry, I believe you. The echoes are funny in here." Mark tied off the bandages with a quick knot and clapped Djed on the shoulder. "Can you stand?"

"I think so."

"Then I'm sending you to report." Mark held up a hand to forestall the archer's immediate protest. "You can't swim, remember? I can tow you across this pool, but like as not, we aren't going to get out of this pile of rubble here before the tide turns. I can't take a chance with a total nonswimmer. Also, I want Tia and the others to have some status. They need to know we're in one piece. You can tell them Rothan and I are moving onward. I don't want anyone else coming in here, risking their necks. I'll get him off the ledge, and we'll get to the other side of this damn sinkhole."

Djed argued for a moment against being ordered to retreat from the action. He finally admitted there was no way for him to continue, between his injury and the undeniable need for swimming skills. Mark watched his hobbling progress on the first few stairs, then pivoted to scan the depths of the tide pool for any signs of life. Finding none, he raised the torch. "Room for two of us over there?"

Before Rothan could answer, the creature surfaced, remaining arms thrashing the air. Waves of water washed over the step.

Mark fell back, retreating three risers, swearing, yanking his blaster out with one hand, playing the torch over the animal, trying to find a vulnerable spot. He realized another, even larger animal had the first one in its grasp, and the two were fighting to the death. "This is our chance! We can get across while the beasts distract each other," he yelled to Rothan. "Can you move?"

"With help. My leg remains somewhat numb."

Stowing blaster and handlamp on his belt, Mark made a shallow dive into the menacing pool, keeping to the edges, trying to avoid the two thrashing beasts. A few quick strokes brought him to the ledge. He hung on while Rothan slid gingerly into the water, Mark bracing him so he wouldn't go under, and then Mark struck out for the far edge of the pool. The two men crawled onto the broken stairs while the combat to the death continued behind them, playing out in eerie silence, as the marine creatures appeared to be mute.

"We need to get away from this water and those animals." Mark slicked his hair away from his face and shook the water off. "There might be more of them. I'll check your wounds when we get to the top of the stairs."

Rothan shook his head, already staggering to the next stair. "My wounds can wait, nothing life-threatening. We have to find the vault, get the crown and scepter, and escape before high tide."

Knowing time was running out, Mark didn't argue. Shining his handlamp on the staircase in front of Rothan, he said, "Lead on, let's get this done."

At the top of the stairs, he found himself in another corridor, facing a door cut from a single slab of black rock, resembling the metal city gates. "Now what?"

"Legend states there were three ways to open the door. There was a key"—Rothan gestured at an ornate golden lock—"which I don't have."

Mark eyed the door. The lock had a shape similar to Sandy's key from the oasis. Not having brought his key, there was nothing he could offer. "And the second method of getting this open?"

"A spell."

"Let me guess, you don't know it?"

Rothan rubbed his forehead. "The scrolls Djed and I found in the palace library were ancient beyond time, crumbling as I tried to read them, eaten away by insects in other places. Parts were missing. No, the words of the spell were obliterated."

"So no key, no voice lock, what was the third way in?"

"Khunarum and his direct descendants could prove their right to open the door. I'll have to try. My mother is the daughter of the last king. And the blood of the kings of Nakhtiaar traces to Khunarum in an unbroken line." Rothan laughed. "Or so the legends state. We'll have to hope none of the ancient queens played their husbands false."

"I can try blasting it open." Mark drew his service weapon.

"Acting as tomb robbers will be my last resort." Rothan's voice held distaste.

"Is this the guy's tomb?"

"No, I don't think so. But it's the same principle. He didn't mean the crown and scepter to be removed for any but a dire need, which ancient prophecies said might arise long after his time. Well, the two items were purposefully left here after the destruction of the entire city after all."

"Good point. How does this third method work, then?"

Rothan ran his hand over the door's surface, searching for something. "Legend states Khunarum left a sign for his descendants—ah, here! See, it is the imprint of his open hand."

Mark leaned over, directing his handlamp where Rothan pointed at a spot beside the keyhole. The shallow indentation was the silhouette of a man's open hand, surrounded by symbols. A similar concavity next to it was a more feminine shape. Mark admired the way the ancients had provided for either a man or a woman to make their claim for the artifacts. Showed a lot of forethought.

Rothan took a deep breath and set his right hand into the center of the larger carved handprint. For a second, nothing happened. Then he grunted and yanked his hand free, staring at his thumb, where a large teardrop of blood quivered. No blood could be seen anywhere on the door, as if the stone had absorbed the droplet.

"Shh, hear that?" Blaster at the ready, Mark backed up a step.

A quiet hum came from the door itself.

A voice boomed in the corridor, uttering six short syllables. None of Mark's hypno-implanted languages offered even a partial or suggested translation. Although he was obviously listening intently, Rothan seemed just as perplexed, the words apparently meaningless to him as well. The door rose. A rush of perfumed, intoxicating air came rushing out with a noticeable hiss. Dizzy, Mark held his breath after one surprised inhalation while he and Rothan retreated.

"DNA testing?" Mark theorized out loud. "Primitive DNA testing to open the door when all else failed? This Khunarum had a lot of help from someone more advanced than his own civilization."

"Your words are gibberish." Rothan sneezed.

The door stopped its leisurely ascent, then jerked into life again for another few inches. Progress stopped with a harsh grinding noise that was painful against Mark's eardrums. When nothing else happened, he said, "Guess it's done all it's going to do. We'd better crawl under if we want to get in." He dropped to his knees on the slimy floor, peering under the slab into the room beyond

Rothan went first. Mark crawled under the huge door slab hot on his heels. He refused to think about how much the stone must weigh as he passed over the lintel and rolled clear.

"Lords of Space!" Mark came to his feet and half drew his blaster, fearing a living being faced him in the gloom. After one horrified moment, he realized it was a statue painted with incredible realism, detailed even to the lashes on the open eyes. Mark decided to forgive himself for being fooled in the gloom. "Khunarum?" he asked as Rothan got to his feet.

"I would imagine so." Eyes wide, the other man stared at the statue. He made a gesture with his right hand, as if in respect or worship.

Mark played his light over the contents of the apparently water-tight chamber. Khunarum sat in the middle. Baskets, bins, and crates were stacked to the ceiling. Some were sealed, others held tightly rolled scrolls, fabric, jewelry. A set of shelves on the far wall was crammed with statues, vases, and small boxes. Many of these had toppled over, fallen to the floor, and broken, probably during earthquakes over the centuries. Mark ran the torchlight over the floor. He stood on a woven carpet, its rich colors undimmed by time. To his left on the floor lay a small wreath of flowers and a scarf or veil, gossamer thin, half covering a child's clay pull toy in the shape of a lion. The walls of the vault were covered with stylized paintings—garden scenes, hunting scenes, a river expedition—Mark couldn't take it all in, and the decorations had no special meaning for him. Ancient weapons had been hung with great care on one wall—swords, shields, a massive bow and quiver of arrows.

The disarray and quantity of goods reminded Mark of the way "their" house had been, elsewhere in the city. An unfathomable mass of items. "All his worldly goods?" he asked.

Rothan shook his head. "Khunarum and his city were rich beyond the understanding of man, according to legend. These items stored here under the watchful eye of his statue would have been his most prized possessions but by no means all he owned. What I would give to speak to him across time and ask his advice about defeating Farahna and her schemes."

Mark directed his torch at the statue again. The king was depicted sitting on a carved version of a simple woven chair, flanked by a lion on the left and some kind of aquatic animal on the other. The sculpted beasts appeared to be life-size and gazed with a daunting stare at whomever walked through the door. The king's portrayal was larger-than-life. Studying the man's clean-shaven features, Mark detected a familial resemblance between this person and Rothan. The hair was long and caught in a single braid. His lips were parted, as if to speak and grant Rothan's fervent wish for ancient wisdom. On his carved brow sat the crown they'd come to find, a golden circlet set with a dozen unfaceted green gems that glistened as Mark's light played over them. A golden sun disk was the crown's centerpiece, encircled by a snake that reared above the disk with bared fangs and a flared hood. Khunarum's left hand rested on his lap, holding a rolled papyrus. Mark tried to imagine what kind of significant information had been preserved on the scroll. The statue's raised right arm extended toward them, as if in invitation. The hand bore the carving of an elaborate signet ring. The statue's fingers were curled, presumably to hold the scepter. Khunarum was missing the tip of one finger, lost in combat perhaps. The bare chest of the figure bore some serious scars, testifying to the fact that the legendary king had lived in perilous times.

The scepter itself was nowhere in sight.

Mark searched the floor, passing behind the statue and re-emerging. "No scepter. If you want the crown, you'd better take it. The tide's coming in outside, and we have to make our escape."

Rothan put his hand to his temple as if rousing himself from a dream. "Standing here at last, I find myself reluctant to take what we sought. The crown should stay here, where it belongs." He gave Mark a sideways glance. "Do you understand? Even though we fought so hard to get here?"

"I get it. We can leave the crown, you know." Mark had no desire to touch anything in the room. Nerves tingling, he felt an urgent impulse to leave, and a headache pounded behind his eyes. Bad air maybe. "No sign of the scepter. If it's in one of those boxes in the stacks to the side, we probably don't have time to search for it."

"No." Rothan's voice sounded regretful as he answered the comment about leaving the diadem. "I must take the crown. I must have it to save my people from

Farahna and the Maiskhan. When Hutenen is shown to be the rightful ruler, when he appears wearing this crown, all doubt and indecision will be erased. The people, the priests, and the army will rally to him and realize the utter folly of aligning with her and her foreign allies."

"I get the power of symbols to move men to action," Mark said. "Whatever you've decided, we need to do it and get out of here, is all I'm saying."

"Pragmatic. A pity about the scepter, but I'll rely on your Lady of the Star Wind to heal my prince with her magic when we arrive in Nakhtiaar." Rothan advanced to stand in front of the statue. "There were words on the parchment for the taking of the crown. Some were missing."

"Voice-activated." Mark found it less unnerving to think of what was happening in terms of his own world.

"I don't know what will happen when I take the crown without completion of the proper chant." Rothan glanced at Mark and laughed. "I have to guess at the pronunciation anyway. The words were written in symbols I recognized, but the meaning…" He crossed his arms over his chest and bowed low to the statue, which continued to gaze serenely over their heads. "We crave pardon for disturbing thy rest, Exalted One, but our need is dire. The plea I make is to take the crown forth, to use its power for the benefit of the descendants of thy people."

After completing the heartfelt prayer in his own tongue, Rothan chanted a short set of words. Mark's hypno training didn't translate. He thought he caught a fragment here and there, but Rothan stumbled over the syllables. Finishing the required sounds, he took a deep breath and removed the crown from Khunarum's brow. As if waiting for some catastrophe to befall him, Rothan froze for a moment.

Nothing broke the silence but the sound of water rushing into the tunnels far away as the high tide neared.

Mark stirred from his contemplation of Khunarum's likeness. "We'll need a box or something to carry the crown. Let me see what I can find." He rummaged through the contents of the room nearby and found a heavy wooden chest of about the right size that had potential as a water-tight container. The seams were sealed with strips of some dark metal. When he dumped out the contents, golden coins or medallions clinked and clattered across the floor. Mark held the box toward Rothan, so he could set the crown inside.

Studying the pile of coins, Mark had another idea. "Did you bring any money on this excursion from Nakhtiaar?"

Adjusting the crown in the box, Rothan frowned and looked up. "We left in the middle of the night after stealing the chariots. We pretty much had the clothes on our backs and stole food and water on the way."

Mark gestured to the pile of coins on the rug. "Mind if I take a few of these, then?"

"Why?" Rothan's tone was surprised and a bit suspicious.

"We might need funds to get home to your city. We can't expect free lodging and services from everyone just because Jagrahim has been so generous."

"Sounds reasonable. Good idea."

Mark was slipping a fistful of the coins into one of the pockets of his utilities when a loud cracking sound emanated from the walls on all sides. Mark's hand light dimmed to a pinpoint. The ground beneath his feet rumbled and shook, sending him reeling. A harsh grating noise rasped behind them.

"Set the crown in the box." Mark spun, aiming the yellowing light of his torch at the door. The great slab was sliding downward in fits and starts, grinding and grating. He shoved Rothan in the direction of the exit. "Move, or we'll be trapped."

Rothan stumbled toward the door, dropping the crown in the box and snapping the lid shut. Mark scrambled to follow him. As he passed the statue, he swore, reaching to grab the papyrus. Something, some deep instinct, told him he had to have whatever was written on that scroll. Tucking it in his waistband, he crawled at the best pace he could manage, desperate to get past the huge slab before it slammed shut. He heard a sound behind him. As he shoved the box under the door, he gazed at Khunarum's face. The statue's right hand had retracted to form a close-fisted salute over the heart.

What happened next shocked Mark so much he forgot all thoughts of self-preservation and escape.

The statue stood and took one pace forward. Khunarum's eyes were alive, glowing. He stared straight at Mark and nodded once, majestically. The animals flanking him tossed their heads and growled. A voice rang in his head.

As commanded by the gods, my most precious artifacts have been sent into exile with my people, one to each of the Twenty Families for use either singly or in unison in dire times. I repay my debts of loyalty and now am done.

Rothan reached in from the corridor and dragged the box out of danger before yanking on Mark's sleeve, yelling, "Come on, you'll be crushed."

Mark closed his eyes, rolled frantically out of the way, and the door slammed inches from his face. "Lords of Space." He tried to forget his last glimpse of the occupants of the vault. "Close call."

Rothan coughed. "Are you all right? Why did you hesitate? Were you stuck?"

Mark lay on the floor, breathing hard, the world spinning around him. He had *not* heard the voice of a man dead thirty centuries. Hallucination, nothing more mysterious, brought on by bad air in the small room. He staggered to his feet with Rothan's help and fought the nausea in his gut, taking deep breaths. This place was too spooky for him. "I'm fine. Let's get out of here. The tide won't wait."

With Rothan carrying the precious box, the two men retraced their steps as the small quakes continued. Once or twice, Mark had to stop and clutch at the walls to stay on his feet as a stronger tremor hit.

"These damn tunnels can't take much more of this pounding," Mark said after one jolting shake, as a portion of the wall ahead crumbled and fell apart. He took a few more steps, moving past a bend before halting in dismay. The waters were already coming up the corridor toward them. The water advanced and receded and advanced again. He retreated. "We can't go back the way we came in."

"The tunnel continued on to the right, beyond the vault." Rothan reversed direction, sprinting the other way. "No time to lose!"

Mark ran down the corridor right behind him, dodging fallen stones and stumbling on the slick surface. Behind him, the water crept onward.

"Stairs!" Mark grabbed Rothan's arm and ascended the damp, slimy, seaweed-strewn staircase. He hoped against hope it would lead them out of the maze of tunnels. Behind them, the water continued to rise, coming faster and faster. The swarm of quakes threatened to knock him off the precarious staircase. There were loud crashes as more portions of the tunnels collapsed. Then, so abruptly he almost plunged off the edge, the staircase ended in midair, hanging over the water. He steadied Rothan to keep him from falling into the harbor.

Mark gazed over the green water, ruins and wrecks now hidden under its deceptively serene surface. "Can you dive?"

"I never have." Rothan pushed his hair out of his eyes with a subtly trembling hand. "When we were on a trading expedition in the jungles to the far south, one of the tribes we spent time with insisted Hutenen and I learn to swim so we could participate in a game played for honor. But to dive as you did at the tide pool—no."

"We can't stay here till the tide turns again. This building is going to come apart around us. All these centuries, and the damn thing shakes apart today!"

"It must be because I took the crown. I couldn't complete the sacred incantation, remember?"

Mark didn't care what was causing the old structure to self-destruct. He wanted to survive. "Yeah, well, here's what we're going to do. You better go in feet first and strike for the surface as soon as you hit. I'll toss the box as close to you as I can, and then I'll dive in. We'll swim to shore together. Tide's going in, so the current ought to carry us, making the trip less arduous."

Rothan took a deep breath, then another.

"Don't think about it too much," Mark advised. While his companion focused on preparations for jumping into the water, he took the papyrus from his belt and stuffed it under the crown in the box for safekeeping.

Swearing or calling upon his gods for help, the captain took a giant step off the ledge, plunging into the murky green waters below. Mark had an anxious moment, waiting for his companion to reappear from the depths. Rothan was struggling a little, but he raised one arm and waved, so Mark heaved the wooden box out and followed it in a smooth dive, cutting through the water without raising much of a splash. He resurfaced. A few strokes brought him close to Rothan, floating with the aid of the box.

"Let's get to dry land!" Mark got a mouthful of the salty water and spat it out.

"No arguments from me." Rothan released his grip on the box, pushing it through the water to Mark before swimming, his strokes awkward and inefficient, but he made progress. Even with the handicap of the box, Mark had no problem matching the other man's pace. He'd gotten a few yards away from the ruin when Rothan shouted and disappeared under the water, bobbing up again and trying to yell but getting water in his mouth. The current grabbed Mark a second later, sweeping them both sideways in the grip of a powerful riptide.

Rothan wasn't panicking, but he fought to continue straight to the shore. Mark worked with the flow, overtook him, and yelled in his ear, "Go with it, don't try to fight the current. We have to swim parallel to the shoreline till we can get clear."

Mark managed to stay afloat himself, all the while encouraging his companion and keeping him from drowning. He also kept track of the precious wooden box. As he'd expected, the riptide lost its power a few hundred yards farther along the coast, and Mark was able to direct them both toward the shoreline. Now the tide worked in their favor, and after a few long moments, Mark washed up on the beach. Exhausted from the struggle, he forced himself to rise and check on Rothan, facedown in the foam.

As Mark rolled him over, the captain coughed, retching. Overhead Mark heard Lakht's harsh cry. Shielding his eyes with one hand, he stared into the sky until he spotted the bird, and then he waved vigorously, hoping Sallea would see him through Lakht's eyes.

Rothan leaned with his head on his knees. "I never want to swim again. Is the box safe?"

"Got it right here." Mark tapped the lid.

"Open it, check the crown." Leaning over, Rothan vomited copious quantities of seawater. He wiped his mouth. "We must not let the salt water corrode it."

Mark worked the complicated latch and swung the lid open. The interior was tight and dry, the crown gleaming in the early morning sun, the parchment scroll nestled underneath.

Frowning, eyes narrowed, Rothan touched the note with one fingertip. "You took this too?"

"Yeah, I can't explain why, but it seemed like a good idea at the time. Somebody made an effort to leave it there for anyone who came after the crown." Maybe his unusual fixation on the scroll was why he'd had the hallucination about the long-dead king talking to him.

"Good point. I hope we can find someone to read it for us."

"Here come the others." Mark retrieved the scroll, put it back inside, and resealed the box.

Jagrahim led the charge over the beach at a gallop. The chief reined in his stallion with a swirl of sand and hit the beach to run the last few steps. "Are you all right?!"

"The ocean did its best, but we managed to survive." Mark stepped aside to greet Sandy, who hugged him as if she intended to never let go.

"I wouldn't have survived without you." Rothan stood with help from two of the archers and Tia. "I owe you much. Nakhtiaar owes you much."

"Glad to be of service." Mark had never been comfortable accepting thanks. "What next? How do we get to your city to give the crown to your prince?"

Rothan gazed at the ocean for a moment as if hoping to find an answer, before pivoting to regard the ruined city. "I don't know. We were ignorant about the season of storms in the Empty Lands. Yet we must journey home with all haste to ensure Hutenen survives whatever Farahna is scheming, or all this effort might be for naught. Any suggestions?" he asked Jagrahim.

The chieftain nodded. "Leave this to me, my lords. We'll procure a fast ship for you and get you home faster than you came, if the sea gods favor you."

"A ship?" Mark waved his hand at the harbor in front of them. "How can a ship put in here with all those ruins waiting under the surface to tear a hole in the hull?"

"Didn't you say the city was forbidden territory?" Sandy asked.

"Indeed, and so it is. My people carry on an extensive trade from a secret harbor located on the coast two days' ride from here. Our trading partners arrive on a regular schedule, or I can set a summons beacon if no ships are due this week."

"What do you trade?" Mark's assessment was that the Mikkonite chief possessed many secrets and relished surprising them one revelation at a time.

"The rest of the world craves our crimson and purple dyes to make themselves beautiful." Jagrahim gestured at his robes, covered in multicolored whorls.

"You can't get the spices we grow anywhere else," Sallea said. "You tasted them in the cooking at our village. But, Father, the merchant captains want gold to transport passengers and drive hard bargains."

"Problem solved." Mark unfastened a side pocket on his fatigues and pulled out one of the gleaming coins from Khunarum's vault. "There are a few more where this came from."

Stroking his beard for a moment, Jagrahim pondered before giving his consent. "It is well. The bounty of Khunarum can pay to transport his crown and scepter."

"Rothan and I reached the same decision, although we didn't get the scepter." Mark restored the coin to his pocket.

"But we must have that to cure my brother." Tia's eyes were wide as she looked from Rothan to Mark. "Why didn't you take it as well as the crown?"

Rothan folded her hand in his. "The scepter wasn't there, beloved. The gods favored us only so far." He pointed at Sandy. "The Lady of the Star Wind can cure your brother's ailment when we arrive home."

The center of attention, Sandy said, "I probably can if the illness hasn't progressed too far. I've got a few things in my bag equivalent to generics for organic poisons, but—"

Mark put his arm around her shoulder and leaned closer, whispering in her ear, "I wouldn't say any more right now. Let's evaluate the medical situation when we arrive."

Rothan's party left Amareten by the main gate after traversing the abandoned city again. Jagrahim insisted they stay in a tight formation and didn't suggest any side trips. Sallea reopened the gate for them, and she and one man stayed behind to seal the portal with the secret rituals, rejoining the column later. After a day of riding along the coast, Jagrahim called for spending the night in a sheltered cove. Dinner consisted of plain but filling journey fare, after which Mark made a tour of the sentries on duty, checking their level of situational awareness before he allowed himself to drift to sleep with the sound of the waves in his ears.

He woke in the middle of the night, realizing Sandy wasn't in her bedroll next to him. Anxious, he grabbed his blaster and prowled through the camp. She stood on the beach, gazing out to the horizon.

Relieved but concerned that she'd wandered off, he joined her. "Don't take strolls on your own—it's not safe. What are you doing out here in the middle of the night anyway?"

"I couldn't sleep, so I got up to watch the waves and think." She turned her head toward him. "You know how much I loved the water when we lived on Throne."

"Thinking what? You're freezing!" Mark took her in his arms, appalled at how chilled she'd gotten in the night air. He took off his borrowed cloak and wrapped her in it.

"Thinking about what it must have been like in the city, on the day when the earthquakes and the tidal waves hit. Did the residents have any forewarning? What else was going on? Jagrahim said the city had been at war. And something must have happened to Khunarum himself. No one has talked about him leaving the city."

He didn't want to think about the legendary king. "The city died a long time ago and probably not the way these people have heard the story told. Funny how events become distorted and altered over the centuries. Does it matter anymore?

Let's get back to the fire before you catch some local disease. I'm a lousy doctor, no training, remember?"

She accompanied him willingly, holding his hand. "Don't you wonder about why the Travelers left the mirror and your ring in our house, not even locked away? Or what happened to all of the people?"

"Rothan told us, the populace fled through the Empty Lands, and the survivors ended up founding new cities in Nakhtiaar." Ancient history on alien planets didn't much interest him, new home or not. He was jaded after spending years being dropped on strange worlds for brief missions and then moving on to the next place, the next urgent job. "Maybe the Travelers didn't set as much store by the mirror as you do. I mean, the crown is a beautiful piece of artwork, but it's just an object, not a weapon."

"I feel as if we have a connection to whoever lived here before, as if the items were left for us to find." She paused, wrapping his cloak around herself more securely. "You didn't see anything unusual when you were in the vault with Rothan?"

Mark repressed the disturbing memory of those moments, glad she couldn't read his mind. "No."

"I wish I could have gone in there with you." She lifted the mirror from her belt, stared at the blackened surface in the moonlight, and let it fall. "If it could only tell us. I think all the answers are there." She stared at the two moons in the sky. "Amrell and Terali tonight." She sighed as she sat. "I can't remember my dreams anymore from the venom-induced coma. I knew things when I first awakened, and now I can't recall them, which is frustrating."

"What kind of things?" Mark searched for a blanket, wrapping her securely in the one he located, then sat beside her, poking at the fire to make it provide more heat against the chill of the night.

Sandy glared at him before rubbing her forehead as she did when she had a headache. "Don't laugh. I received so much knowledge, heard so many important things, and now it's mostly lost."

"I'm not laughing." He moved behind her and massaged her shoulders as best he could through the blanket.

"You're skeptical, though."

"Don't build too much on whatever the neurotoxins in the snake venom made you dream," Mark said. "But if you need to know something, it'll come back."

"You think so?" Sandy seemed to find the idea comforting.

Mark hadn't thought the remark through before he said it. He wanted to end the conversation, which was making him uncomfortable because he didn't like any discussion of the strange things she'd hallucinated in her coma. He wanted to avoid reminders of the whole episode. Now he took a second, adding twigs to the fire while he searched his mind for something innocuous to add. "It's like me and my hypno training on languages—I don't remember them all, all the time. It takes a trigger, a...a need, and then the right one comes up, like the High Chetal did on the day we met Rothan and Tia."

Sandy appeared to find the concept reasonable, saying, "Makes sense. And the harder I try to remember it, the less I'll be able to recall."

"I think so, yes. Come to bed now and rest, even if you can't sleep, okay?"

A moment or two after he'd tucked her into her bedroll, he realized she was snoring. Reclining, he soon drifted into sleep again himself.

In the morning, in the bright sunlight, all the talk of the ancient past seemed as if it belonged to another world. Jagrahim's warriors prepared a quick breakfast of journeybread and salty dried fish.

"May we see the crown just once, before you bear it away to Nakhtiaar?" Jagrahim made his request humbly as his men broke camp. "My people have been responsible for the city and its contents for so long, I should like to gaze upon Khunarum's greatest possession."

"Of course. I should have thought to show you yesterday," Rothan said in an apologetic tone. "My mind and my body were worn out from our endeavors in the sunken palace."

He pulled the box out of the pack it was stored in and opened the lid. The crown gleamed in the sun.

Leaning over, Jagrahim peered at the small scroll. "What's this?"

"It was in Khunarum's hand. Or, rather, the statue's hand, and it seemed to me at the time we'd better take it along. Is there a problem?" Confused by his own spur-of-the-moment decision, Mark was defensive. Not being able to offer crisp reasoning for his action annoyed him.

"No, of course not. You were there, not I. If the scroll wasn't meant to go with the crown, you wouldn't have it. May I see?" Jagrahim didn't wait for permission but fished it out of the box and unrolled it.

"Can you read it?" Sandy crowded close. "What does it say?"

"Is it a message of some sort?" Rothan asked.

Jagrahim held up a hand for silence. "This ancient script is hard to read. I need quiet to concentrate. Sallea, come translate this with me. You're more proficient on this alphabet than any other reader."

His daughter strolled over, taking a quick glance. "It's a list of some kind."

"Yes, that's my conclusion as well," her father agreed.

"A list?" Disappointed because he'd been hoping for some message from beyond the grave, something dramatic, Mark silently chided himself for letting himself get lost in the myths.

"Yes." Sallea nodded. "Khunarum's Artifacts, it says at the top, and then see here, it says Crown, Scepter, Sword, Goblet, Dagger, and so forth. About twenty items. The words opposite are family names, I believe."

"Some overzealous scribe worked overtime. Imagine sticking around to make a list like this when the whole city was shaking apart, falling on your head." Mark vented his disappointment in the prosaic nature of the scroll by being sarcastic.

Rothan plucked the scroll from Jagrahim's hands, rolled it up, and handed it to Mark. "This is yours."

"Mine?" Mark had to juggle not to drop it in the sand.

"You were moved to take it, and Khunarum allowed you to have it. Therefore, it's yours." The captain was matter-of-fact. He sealed the box and stowed it safely in the chariot.

The Mikkonite drifted away, returning to their chores breaking camp.

"I guess you have another souvenir." Sandy laughed at him.

"What do I do with it?"

"Oh here, give the scroll to me. I'll tuck it in my medical bag for safekeeping. Maybe we can frame it someday, proof we really were here once upon a time. It's too unique to throw away."

"You want it, it's yours. Gift from me to you." Mark bowed. "I think we'd better mount up now. Looks like our friends are ready to get out of here."

"We should reach our trading post in midafternoon," Jagrahim told them as they rode out of the sheltered cove. "And if we're in luck, there'll be a ship in port. I'm hoping for Captain Demari. He's a Minolan, and I trust him above the others. He'll get you to Nakhtiaar without asking too many questions."

"Demari is a scoundrel." Sallea didn't sound like an admirer of the seafarer.

"He keeps his bargains, which is what matters here. And he's an excellent seaman."

"How much trading do you do?" Mark guided his suddenly skittish horse past a clump of seaweed.

"Not much. I prefer to keep a low profile. And the traders are never allowed beyond our small coastal enclave, so none gain the knowledge of where my villages lie. But there are certain things we can't grow or make for ourselves. It's also wise to have at least limited contact with the rest of the world, to hear the news."

"The legend says the first trading ship was driven ashore in our cove when the city of Khunarum was destroyed," Sallea said. "Our people helped rebuild the ship after signing a treaty between the Mikkonite and the captain to maintain the relationship. And so it has gone, through the ages to now."

"Yes, and the first trader captain married a daughter of our people." Jagrahim winked.

"Well, I wouldn't marry a seaman. I've no desire to go onto the ocean on a tiny ship. The treaty will have to survive without such a sacrifice on my part." Hand on her hip, Sallea fumed, indignant. "I'll take a husband from our own people when I'm good and ready."

"Any danger of the trading relationships breaking down?" As he asked the follow-up question, Mark realized he'd automatically shifted into data-gathering mode. Collecting hard intel was good, familiar, far removed from mystical artifacts and strange messages from long-dead kings.

Jagrahim frowned. "Sometimes the ships don't come on schedule. Certain captains no longer make landfall, and no one has heard of them. More are missing than the storms and reefs of the ocean usually account for in a given time."

"Any idea what's going on?"

The chief shook his head. "Rumors, no more. The men of Maiskhan are known to seek extension of their influence to those who sail freely on the oceans."

Rothan spat. "They're greedy, and their god is evil. I've no trouble believing Maiskhan seeks dominion over those who have freedom of the seas. I can't believe Farahna invites them into the heart of our land. How can she be so foolhardy? So stupid?"

"Hutenen will set it all right." Tia's sunny smile showed how unconcerned she felt. "As soon as we bring him the crown and Lady Sandy cures him of the poison."

Mark and Sandy exchanged glances but said nothing. The longer this expedition went on, the more Mark wondered if Hutenen remained alive to take possession of the crown. How long would a despotic usurper queen wait to kill her rival? But Tia and Rothan seemed confident, so they must have known something he didn't about the situation. Perhaps Farahna had other plans for Hutenen than a convoluted assassination.

Jagrahim spoke up. "And the completion of my task is to get you there. See, there's a ship waiting." He pointed down the coast, where Mark saw a mast extending above the headland. "No more talk, we need to ride hard, lest the captain set sail before we arrive."

When Mark rounded the headland a short time later, he found a large ship at anchor in the cove. Five Mikkonite and three or four sailors were taking a meal break beside a fire, rising as the newcomers arrived in a flurry of sand.

Jagrahim got his wish about which free trader would be in port. Mark liked Demari once introductions had been made and the bargaining commenced. The seaman had an easygoing manner and didn't ask too many questions.

"I don't carry passengers as a rule." Stroking his short beard, Demari wore the air of a man considering his options. "Cargo has less risk and fewer complications in this unsettled time."

"We can pay well for the passage," Rothan told him impatiently. "We must get to the city as soon as possible."

Demari took a moment to eye Rothan as if assessing his potential as an adversary. He yelled some instruction to his first mate about the loading of the cargo, and then reopened the subject of their passage with him. "It'll be rough for the women, but they can share my second cabin. Cramped quarters."

"We'll be fine." Sandy apparently had no doubts. Tia nodded but without conviction. She glanced at the *Lady Dawn*, rolling from side to side in the waves even in the sheltered cove. Apprehension was plain in the tense set of the Nakhtiaar noblewoman's shoulders.

"How long is the journey?" Mark asked.

"If the sea god favors us and the winds blow well, a week, maybe two. First, we sail out to the open sea to avoid the reefs, set a course westward along the coast, and navigate into the mouth of the river."

"So long?" Hands on his hips, mouth a thin line, Rothan looked to the sky as if hoping the gods would deliver a better alternative.

"Better than trying to go overland again, what with the sandstorms," Mark answered. "This stacks up as our best bet."

Some spirited negotiation followed over the price. A quantity of the gold coins changed hands, and the matter was settled.

"You can go out to the ship in the next boat, then, my lords, ladies." Demari shook hands with Rothan and then with Mark. Excusing himself, he strode down the beach to direct his crew.

"We'll stay to see you off," Jagrahim told them.

"We couldn't have completed our quest without your help, sir," Rothan said. "I'm grateful, and my prince will be as well."

"You had the right to request our assistance, my lord." Jagrahim hesitated for a moment. "My people owe you allegiance because you hold the crown."

Rothan made a gesture as if waving the remark away. "I took the crown for my prince, for Hutenen, not for myself."

"Nonetheless, I'm honor bound to place my tribe and myself at your service. Should you ever have need of our assistance in any way, you have but to send a summons. Mikkon will answer, this I swear by our gods."

"Thank you. And the reverse is true," Rothan said. "Can we ever be of assistance to you—"

"We'll send word." Jagrahim bowed. "There's another matter." He glanced at Sallea. "I wish to send my daughter with you, as my ambassador. The recent events you've shared with us tell me we lack sufficient involvement in the affairs of the wider world. Your people are so ignorant of mine, of what conditions are here in this area. And for my part, I want to know what transpires with your prince, with the Maiskhan. Sallea can send Lakht to me periodically with word. It would be good for her to spend time at a royal court, see how others live in different fashion. Then she can return to me in a few months' time, when matters are settled in Nakhtiaar."

"It would be my honor," Sallea said as she became the center of attention.

"I'll personally guarantee your safe passage as an ambassador," Rothan said.

"The matter is settled then." Jagrahim bowed again. He and Sallea stepped aside for some private conversation.

Mark only overheard the beginning of the chat as father and daughter moved out of earshot. "And if reinforcements are needed…"

He wasn't surprised the desert chieftain had the same kind of qualms he did about whether the would-be Queen Farahna and her Maiskhan allies could be removed from power so simply.

About an hour later, with all cargo stowed and passengers aboard, the *Lady Dawn* raised her stone anchor and hoisted sail. Mark stood at the rail and watched the land grow smaller and smaller in their wake.

Sandy joined him. "You may have suffered from Lajollae's Travel, but I have to say, Tia isn't a good candidate for this kind of journey. She's been vomiting already, and we've hardly left the harbor, much less hit the deep-water swells."

"I never sailed on water before. Only in space." Mark stared at the billowing sails and then across the blue-green waves. "I like it."

The princess leaned on the rail. "Grandmother has a fleet of pleasure boats on Throne, on Lake Baikum, so I've sailed. I've never been on an ocean before. The waves are imposing. Makes me wish the boat had power, not just sails and oars."

"Sailing agrees with you." Mark studied her rosy-cheeked face with pleasure. "Do you have something you can give Tia?"

"Well, she's pregnant, which makes things worse in the nausea department. Limits what I can prescribe too, but I have an inject or two. Captain Demari said his cook can make special soup for her as well."

Mark watched a pod of sleek gray marine dwellers pacing the ship, cutting in and out of the jade-green waves as if at play with the *Lady Dawn*. "Jagrahim's worried about the situation with Farahna, the same way I am. I overheard him talking to Sallea before we left. I wish Rothan wasn't putting so much stock in this crown to work magic. And in his prince, who's an unknown quantity to us. I have confidence in Rothan, but I've yet to meet the other guy."

"Want to know what I think?" Sandy said.

"What?"

"I think Rothan and Tia were so desperate there was nothing else left to try, especially when the queen hatched her plan for Tia to be married off against her will." Sandy gave him a sideways glance. "When you're out of options—sensible options—you give up or you go for the farfetched hope."

"Like taking Lajollae's offer to send us somewhere else?" Mark grinned.

"Exactly." Sandy stared out to sea, where a vee of birds flew against the cloudless sky. "So far, by throwing our lot in with Rothan and Tia, we've apparently fallen into a similar situation to the one we were escaping. Only Lajollae isn't coming to our rescue this time."

Disturbed by the dryness of her tone, he eyed her. "You're not going to reopen the argument about staying at the oasis, are you?"

Leaning on the rail, she said, "It's too late to regret the decision or reconsider. There are inevitable consequences to choosing sides, however."

CHAPTER FIVE

"I'm just saying I don't think it's a good idea to march into the city tomorrow morning after weeks away without knowing the current state," Mark argued. "Captain Demari said he's seeing much more Maiskhan presence in the harbor than even a month ago."

"True." Rothan frowned, his voice tense. "I'm impatient to get the crown to Hutenen. The stewardship of such a powerful relic weighs heavily on me. Nothing must happen to it before I can deliver the box to the prince."

Mark gazed toward the quiet shoreline, where torches and oil lamps flickered in the capital city. He didn't have a good feeling about the situation. "But you and Tia are fugitives from Farahna, remember? You can't go openly to find your prince in her palace. There'll be people who'd recognize you."

"True again. What do you suggest?"

"Let Djed and me go into the city tonight, see what we can find out, do a quick recon."

"Mark—" Sandy's voice rose in immediate protest.

"Recon missions behind enemy lines to scope out the lay of the land are what I do. Or did. The Sectors spent a lot of credits training me to be outstanding at secret operations. With Djed as my local guide, it'll be simple." Mark took her hand. "We have to know. We can't go in there blind."

"I can send Lakht to view the city and the palace from the air," Sallea said. "Report on troop movements."

"Good idea." Mark rubbed his hands together. "But we need boots on the ground to gather detailed intel."

"You don't look like a citizen of Nakhtiaar, my lord," Djed said, his first comment in the hasty strategy session being held on the *Lady Dawn's* stern.

"True enough, but I can pass for a foreign sailor, especially if I wear a head covering." "I'll lend you the small rowboat," Captain Demari said. "I advise you to be back aboard by dawn."

"You think this is a good idea?" Rothan asked him.

The *Lady Dawn's* captain leaned against the railing of his ship. "Always better to know what you're sailing into, my lords."

"It's settled then," Mark declared. Rothan made no further protest.

Mark and Djed climbed down the netting into the dinghy shortly thereafter. They rowed to shore, beaching their craft alongside other small boats to the side of the main docks. The two men sauntered to the waterfront district, where the taverns were brightly lit and loud voices could be heard.

"Best if you don't talk much," Djed said apologetically as the two hiked an uneven street toward the closest tavern. "Your accent is still strange."

"Fine. We don't want to attract attention. Our job is to find out as much as we can about the situation in the city and the palace."

Mark walked into the Blue Cobra behind Djed, blinking as the smoky air in the crowded inn hit his eyes and lungs. Djed led Mark to the bar and demanded two mugs of ale, throwing down some Minolan coins. The archer worked his way through the crowd of sailors and soldiers and took a table toward the rear of the low-ceilinged room. Satisfied with the arrangement, Mark sat with his back to the wall, sipping his beer, which had a surprising kick to it.

Two girls were dancing halfheartedly, barely in sync with the music. Some sailors at two tables were making ribald comments. A ragtag group of Nakhtiaar soldiers sat at another set of benches nearby. Mark homed in on the conversation, while appearing to be enthralled by the charms of the dancers.

"Aye, I'm assigned to the funerary procession, curse the gods." The soldier appeared drunk. He slammed his mug on the table, sloshing the foamy liquid on himself. "I want nothing to do with it."

His companions tried to shush him. Someone handed him a fresh mug of beer.

The man was in the grip of strong emotion, fueled by his alcohol. "It's a travesty, I tell you. This princeling has only been dead a short time. The palace staff and the priests can't possibly have done all the proper rituals for embalming and said the prayers in such a short time. And why me, I asked the officer? Why do I have to accompany the coffin? Let me do crowd control."

"Ah, it's not such bad duty, Osork. You'll get to see the queen up close. She might take a fancy to you." The man nudged him and winked. He made some joke, which Mark only got part of as High Chetal failed to translate the local slang. Hand gestures made clear the crude nature of the remark.

"Yes, which is the path this foolish princeling traveled, and look what happened to him." The soldier took a drink from the mug, ale dripping through his beard. "It's bad luck, I tell you. This whole thing reeks." He leaned in to his mates, but since Mark sat so close he could hear too. "Gossip in the palace says she murdered him."

At this, his friends abandoned their drinks, took him by the arms, and bundled him out of the inn, plainly frightened his words might have been overheard and cause them all trouble.

Mark could tell Djed was shocked by what he'd learned. The archer took a deep swallow of his ale and closed his eyes for a moment. Mark put a restraining hand on the other man's wrist and shook his head slightly. Djed swallowed hard, trying to relax as he settled his back against the wall behind him, stretching his legs and giving every sign of contentment with his surroundings. Both men leisurely finished their drinks and then strolled into the street about half an hour later. Only when they were well away from the lights and heading to the docks did either say anything.

"My poor Prince Hutenen. We feared Farahna was trying to kill him and now apparently she's succeeded." Jaw clenched, voice tight, the archer was in the throes of strong emotion as he untied their rowboat for the trip out to the *Lady Dawn*.

"We have to keep Rothan and Tia from walking into a trap." Mark climbed in and unshipped the oars. "We can't do anything for this other guy now, but we have to protect them."

"How?"

"We'll have to keep a low profile tomorrow while the ship's cargo gets unloaded. Maybe Demari can take us down the coast to another harbor and we can work our way inland to your home. Didn't you tell me Rothan comes from a province to the south of here?"

"True, Rothan's mother married a southern noble and raised her son away from the court intrigues."

"Would we find sanctuary there?"

"Indeed. General Intef, his grandfather, holds the area with a strong army. Farahna wouldn't be able to move against him easily, and he'd never surrender my captain or Tia. You've concocted a sound plan, my lord." The archer calmed a bit, contemplating the idea of safety in his homeland. As Mark rowed, Djed had a question of his own. "What of you and your lady?"

"We'd go too, for now." Returning to the aerie was always hovering at the back of Mark's mind as a last resort, but he preferred to remain embedded with his local allies.

"Good." Djed had a smile on his face. "We can always use another stout warrior."

As he rounded the stern of another cargo ship, Mark stopped rowing and cursed under his breath, stabbing his oars into the water to stop their forward progress. "*Tzerde*! Too damn late."

While he'd been gone, a large black Maiskhan ship had locked itself to the side of their merchant vessel with grappling hooks. The two ships rose and fell together on the dark waves. Lit by torches, the deck of the *Lady Dawn* was crowded with people.

"By the gods," Djed said as he eyed the situation. "Who boards a merchant ship at night, when there's peace in the harbor? My lord and lady should have been safe."

Mark rested on his oars, considering the next steps. There weren't a lot of options. Briefly, he contemplated raking the archers on the enemy ship with blaster fire, or precision sniping at the enemy officers on board the *Lady Dawn,* but either strategy had too many flaws when it came to ensuring Sandy's safety. Without equally well-armed reinforcements, he couldn't singlehandedly overwhelm the enemy, even with his high-tech weapon. Too many opponents. The guards ringing Sandy and his friends had swords, spears and knives, clearly menacing the prisoners. She could be dead in an instant. Rowing back to shore and trying to set up some kind of ambush in an unknown city, hoping to achieve a rescue with only Djed, wasn't a viable strategy. Abandoning the half-formed ideas as futile, he said, "You have to stay clear. Stay in the rowboat and keep watch."

Djed's jaw dropped. "What will you do?"

"I'm going on board the *Lady Dawn.*" Mark unbuckled the blaster's belt and kicked off his sandals.

Djed tried to talk him out of the idea. "You won't be able to rescue them, not even with your magic weapons. The Maiskhan guard our people too closely, and there are too many aboard."

"I know, but I can't sit here and do nothing." Mark stripped off his tunic, wrapped the blaster securely in its holster, and offered the weapon to the other man. "I want you to keep this safe for me. If I take it with me, the Maiskhan will confiscate it."

With a firm hand, Djed pushed the bundle back at him. "Please reconsider, my lord. You can't rescue them by yourself. And even if both of us reboard the ship, we can't prevail against so many enemies."

"Which of us knows his way in this city? Who is more likely to have a prayer of finding someone to help us? Not me. Come on, Djed, admit it. You're the one who needs to stay free to operate and plan rescues, and I'm the obvious choice to surrender himself to stay with my lady, Rothan and Tia. I'm more likely to find an opportunity to make a break for it if I'm inside with them."

Silently, the archer took the blaster.

"Do what you can for us," Mark said.

"I'm not sure what can be done, my lord. There weren't many I trusted in the city. My men on the boat may now be dead or taken prisoner as well. To go to my captain's grandfather in the south, raise an army, and march to free you by force would take weeks. By then Farahna will have executed all of you or sold you as slaves."

"I have to be with my lady to try to protect her." Mark wasn't compromising. "Safeguard the blaster. I'm going to need it later, I promise you."

"Gods be with you, then. I'll watch from afar tonight and undertake what can be done to help tomorrow."

Mark stood cautiously, concerned the crude boat would tip over. He scanned the black water for a moment, trying not to think of the giant snakes he'd seen sunning on the riverbanks during the day as the *Lady Dawn* had cruised down the main river. One had dragged a large, horned bovine to its death with minimal effort while he and Sandy watched in astonishment. Hoping the creatures didn't hunt at night, Mark dove into the water and swam toward the conjoined ships. Reaching the anchor chain, he climbed hand over hand, pausing at the top to peer over the edge of the deck railing.

Rothan was on his knees by the wheel, hands bound behind his back, a ring of spears pointed at his throat by Maiskhan soldiers. Heavily guarded, Tia and Sandy stood off to the side. The women were barefoot, in their linen night shifts, clinging together.

Captain Demari, Sallea, and his crew were clustered at the far end of the deck, standing silent and uneasy behind a line of enemy warriors. Relieved to see the other woman and the three archers were safely mixed in with the crew, Mark assumed Demari hadn't betrayed them. Djed might have a few more resources to tap in any eventual rescue attempts.

Glancing at the deck of the Maiskhan ship, he saw a squad of archers with bows at the ready, should anyone on the *Lady Dawn* attempt resistance. As he'd figured, his blaster wouldn't have been effective in these close quarters against so many of the enemy. Too much risk that Sandy, or their friends, would have been caught in the field of fire.

Fingering Sandy's blond hair, a burly officer made some rapid comments while his comrades guffawed. She slapped his hand away and cursed at him in Outlier. Before she could strike his face, the man caught her wrist and twisted it behind her back.

Mark judged the time had arrived to make his entrance.

Getting a firm grip on the slippery rail, he vaulted onto the deck. The soldiers shouted to their commander as he landed.

He already had his Special Forces knife out, hilt forward in a gesture of surrender. "I'm the Lady of the Star Wind's warrior." He spoke in fairly smooth Nakhtiaar to the officer in command of the operation.

"Ah, the missing man we were told about," answered the Maiskhan calmly, also in the local language.

Mark ignored Sandy's instinctive cry of protest at his surrender, keeping his focus on the officer. "I claim the right to accompany the Lady wherever you take her. She's not to be harmed in any way."

"Bold words for a prisoner." The officer in charge accepted the knife. Brows drawn together in a frown, lips pursed in a sneer, he said, "I'd never surrender myself so. If this is some trick, I warn you there's no chance of success. Your woman will be the first to die."

"I took an oath to protect her which I must honor even unto my own death."

"You'll suffer her fate at her side, then. We go to see your queen, who'll decide the outcome." Tucking the knife into his waistband, the officer gestured to his troops. "Tie the fool up. Get the others onto the small boats. We've wasted more than enough time." He walked away, going to the portside railing.

"Can I be about my business now?" Captain Demari called out. "I'm an honest merchant, and I've perishable goods to land at dawn."

The Maiskhan glared at him. "Consider yourself lucky to be sailing under the flag and seal of Minolos. We've no quarrel at present with him, or I'd seize your cargo and sell you, your woman, and your men into slavery besides. Give me a reason, and I still might. You aided traitors."

"Unknowingly, my lord." Hands spread in supplication, Demari protested as if he was an innocent bystander. "These people were presented to me as common passengers and paid their fare in anonymous gold."

One of the other Maiskhan officers made an urgent request in his commander's ear. Giving his subordinate a surprised look, the man raised his voice again. "I require the possessions of these prisoners. Queen Farahna will want to examine anything retrieved from the Empty Lands. Rothan may have found something she should claim."

Demari gave orders for the requested items to be brought above deck. He stood with one arm casually encircling Sallea's waist while his sailors hastened to do his bidding. Mark eyed the Mikkonite, wondering how Demari had persuaded her not to wade into battle when the ship was boarded. Outwardly docile, with downcast eyes, Sallea was going along with Demari's ruse to keep her safe for now.

The Maiskhan soldiers bound Mark's arms tightly behind him, while his companions were being lowered in nets to a smaller boat waiting alongside. When Mark's turn for the uncomfortable descent came, he employed his excellent peripheral vision to see if Djed lurked in the vicinity of the *Lady Dawn*. To his relief, the archer was nowhere in sight. He didn't have much genuine hope for Djed to find a way to get them out of the current situation, but it was a shred of comfort having a clandestine ally He didn't know how much help, if any, he could anticipate from Demari or his crew.

The prisoners were rowed to the long docks and then pushed into separate chariots for the torchlit ride to the palace. As the vehicle holding Mark left the docks, he saw their possessions, including Sandy's medical bag and the chest holding the Crown of Khunarum, loaded onto yet another chariot.

The caravan galloped through the empty streets of the city. When they reached the palace, uninterested Nakhtiaar guards watched the group climb the many stairs. Mark noted with professional interest this was the only spot where the Nakhtiaar were guarding their own. Everywhere else in the palace there were Maiskhan soldiers, made distinctive by their dark red uniforms and elaborate helmets, exhibiting the discipline of tough, experienced warriors.

When Mark entered the formal audience room deep inside the labyrinthian palace, the chamber was empty. Foaming water from a small fountain ran into a tiled fish pond at the far end, covered with lily pads and fragrant purple and white flowers. An impressive gilded throne topped a four-step dais. Large, ornately decorated columns supported the roof. Covering the walls, bright murals depicted a variety of pastoral scenes involving what he assumed were local deities.

Two tall Nakhtiaar guards appeared, flanking a short, chubby, bald man. The latter had the appearance of one just awakened and hastily dressed, fussing with his robes and straightening an intricate gold and enamel pendant dangling from heavy gold links around his neck even as he came into the room. "I received your messenger. The queen consented to deal with this matter tonight," he informed the Maiskhan officer in charge of their party. "She'll be here soon."

"And Gaddaf, my own commander? He's been notified?"

Frowning, the official appeared to take offense at being questioned. Straightening his spine, he brushed nonexistent dust from his collar. "All has been arranged as you requested in your message from the docks," he replied, his tone arch.

The man in charge of the prisoner detail smiled, revealing a few missing teeth, and patted the newcomer on the shoulder. "Excellent and efficient as always, Seroj. Our mutual masters will be pleased."

The Maiskhan soldiers forced Rothan and Mark to their knees, side by side on the hard tile directly in front of the throne. Tia and Sandy were allowed to stand, ringed by the enemy soldiers off to the left side.

"What happened?" Mark whispered to Rothan, keeping his eyes focused straight ahead.

"Soon after you left, the enemy boarded us. Routine inspection, the officer said."

"In the middle of the night?"

Rothan kept his voice low. "We've been betrayed somehow, perhaps by one of Demari's sailors. We tried to pass ourselves off as ordinary passengers, but the Maiskhan seemed to be expecting us. They knew who Tia and I were. Demari wouldn't fight, although he did tell lies to protect Sallea. He couldn't raise sail to flee either. We'd nowhere to hide. "

Mark eyed the bruises on Rothan's face. "You fought, though."

"To no avail, and once the women were surrounded, I could only surrender."

"I'd have done the same. Overwhelming odds."

"But you were free, off the ship." Rothan shifted on the hard floor. "Why give yourself up?"

Mark clenched his jaw. "I can't do anything to help my lady if I'm not with her."

"You can't do anything to help her at present anyway," Rothan pointed out.

"Silence!" The Maiskhan officer emphasized his command with swift kicks. Mark went sprawling on the floor, Rothan falling across his legs as he too was buffeted by their captor.

More people trickled into the room, two or three at a time—several ladies-in-waiting, two tall fan bearers, nobles, several scribes. Each yawning newcomer was rubbing sleep from their eyes, adjusting their garments, much as Seroj had done when he first arrived. A trio of musicians sauntered in bearing flutes and a stringed instrument and, after a false start or two, played quietly. The Maiskhan high commander marched into the chamber as if on parade, accompanied by a bevy of bearded priests in long fringed and striped robes. Hands behind his back, the enemy leader inspected the silent prisoners, pausing first in front of Mark and then Rothan.

"Excellent work, Captain Farun," he said over their heads to the man who'd captured them. Gaddaf was evidently well satisfied. "Her Majesty is most pleased by what you've done, locating and capturing these fugitives."

Chest puffed with pride at the accolade, Farun strutted to where Mark could see him. "Thank you, sir. When I received word of the ship's arrival in port and that it was carrying passengers, I deemed it worth investigating immediately."

"Prudent. The fugitives might have gotten away entirely in the morning, as busy as the port gets. Yes, indeed, a generous reward shall be yours, and a more important assignment to follow. We'll discuss the details later, over wine." Leaning closer to Farun, Gaddaf lowered his voice. "Let's get through this audience with her. Her moods can be uncertain."

Farun nodded. "I understand, sir."

"Be ready for anything." The commander assessed the prisoners. "Not an impressive lot, for all we've heard about this Rothan. She may want them executed on the spot."

A horn fanfare sounded in the hallway to the left. A squad of Nakhtiaar guards marched smartly into the room, drawn swords held flat over their hearts. Four small, fat dogs gamboled and tumbled across the floor, threatening to trip the solemn soldiers. The Maiskhan commander kicked at one who came too close to his ankle. Unruffled, the dog waddled over to sniff at Rothan and Mark, before losing interest and sinking bonelessly on its side for a nap.

Queen Farahna made her entrance.

She was shorter than Mark had expected, and definitely on the plump side, gowned in gracefully flowing robes. Her apparently hastily made-up face featured three colors of eyeshadow, rosy cheeks, and ruby red lips. The artificial coloring only made her pale features appear harsh, not beautiful to Mark's eyes. Her black hair was drawn into a sloppy chignon, accented with a curved white enamel crown. Rubies and pearls were set ino the crown at intervals, forming an intricate pattern, and a large sun-shaped medallion adorned the center. Tangled gold, turquoise, coral, and jet strands covered the queen's ample chest. Brushing her shoulders, golden snake earrings hung from her extended earlobes. All the waiting Nakhtiaar in the room—except the guards, prisoners and priests—saluted smartly.

Staring at Farahna, Mark was reminded of Empress Ekatereen so long ago on Throne Planet. The two women didn't look anything like each other physically, but both had the arrogance of absolute power in their stance and expression, laced with cruelty.

Rothan struggled to his feet, while the crowd stared at him, apparently aghast at the breach of court etiquette. "You're not my queen. I swore no oaths to you, owe you no allegiance. Where is Hutenen? I demand he be summoned and I'll explain my actions to him. It's my right as an officer to report to my superior."

Pausing in midstep for one breath, Farahna didn't turn. With a shrug, she swept up the steps of her dais and seated herself on the throne, resting her elbows on the wide arms of the ceremonial chair. She arranged her skirts in graceful folds and stuck out one sandaled foot, admiring the jeweled straps for a moment. Then she raised her extravagantly outlined eyes to inspect Rothan head to toe, as if he was a horse for her stable. "Poor fool. All your efforts in the Empty Lands have been for naught—your ineffectual prince is dead."

Mark, of course, already knew of Hutenen's death, but he was sure the news rocked Rothan and Tia to the core. He heard the girl's gasp from across the room and Sandy's murmured condolence.

As if he'd been struck by a spear, Rothan retreated a step, shaking his head in denial. Chin raised, eyes narrowed, he said, "You lie."

Farahna cackled in amusement, the sound grating and unsympathetic. "He died shortly after you left the capital without permission. Perhaps if you'd been here, you might have changed his fate, Captain."

"You murdered him." Face red and contorted in anger, Rothan struggled against the hands of the Maiskhan guards grabbing at him as he advanced toward the dais. "How could anyone, even I, have prevented such treachery?"

Farun, the Maiskhan captain, backhanded Rothan across the face, knocking him to the floor before placing a savage kick in the defenseless man's ribs for good measure. "Speak with respect to your ruler, dog."

"Surely you knew Hutenen was unwell." Farahna sighed, the sound echoing in the chamber. She toyed with the golden tassel attached to a loop at the end of her elaborately enameled scepter. "His bloodline ran weak and thin."

She's reveling in this moment. Mark studied the queen's face, seeing scant possibility of mercy or any opportunity to bargain.

Farahna continued her recitation of her supposedly well-intentioned efforts. "I summoned my personal physicians for your prince, time after time, but he only grew worse. And then he died. But it matters not—Hutenen was a grain of sand blown away by the desert winds. Of no consequence." Leaning forward, she pointed her beringed finger at Rothan. "I'm the ruler of this land, chosen by the gods to occupy this throne. You've shown much disrespect to me—a month ago and now tonight—and therefore disrespect also to the Exalted Ones. The gods demand your death, Captain Rothan. There'll be no easy passage to the next world for one who committed treason against me and insulted the gods."

She rose, slinking down the stairs, skirt fanning out behind her. "Give me your whip," she said to the nearest guard, snapping her fingers. The man unhooked a coiled flail from his belt, and she grabbed it. Running the leather strands through her fingers, Farahna circled Rothan as the Maiskhan soldiers yanked him to his feet, restraining him firmly. The queen stopped a pace or so in front of the defiant prisoner. "You're no officer of mine, traitor." She struck him across the face with the flail. Studded leather thongs hidden among the ribbons opened bleeding weals on his left cheek.

Rothan sagged in the hold of his captors but didn't utter a sound. He shook his head, trying to throw off the effect of the blow, and spat blood that stained the edge of the queen's skirt.

Lips curled in distaste, she twitched the stained fabric aside. "No plea for mercy?"

"Burn in hell."

She touched Rothan's chin with the flail. "I condemn you to death. You'll be taken to the courtyard for punishment at the conclusion of this audience and whipped to death for your crimes."

Screaming, Tia slipped through the loose circle of guards and ran to her lover, clutching his arm but glaring at Farahna. "You've no right to sentence him."

Unflustered, the queen stepped away, swinging the whip in a lazy circle. "Ah yes, Hutenen's bereaved sister. You've been foolish and disobedient, girl. And after all my efforts to make a home for you at my court. I took you into my own household, made you a lady-in-waiting. Gracious, I was. But I'll forgive you in my great compassion for your loss of a dear brother, for I can be kind and merciful."

There was a ripple of murmuring amongst the ladies-in-waiting and the nobles, who echoed, "Great and merciful is our queen."

Farahna acknowledged the fawning with a tilt of her head and a perfunctory wave but kept her focus on Tia. "You'll be wed to my son as we originally planned. Such an honor, such happiness will console you for the loss of both the brother and the unworthy lover. Let there be no further delay in accomplishing this felicitous union! I want to see you wreathed in flowers and smiling as a bride, for I love you as a daughter, despite your wayward behavior. Seroj, where are you?"

The chubby little man edged a step or two away from the nobles, fidgeting with his collar. Cringing as if he feared she'd attack him with the whip, he made an awkward bow. "Here, Your Majesty. What is thy will?"

"Send couriers to the royal hunting preserves where my son is entertaining his friends. Tell him and his companions he must make his way home immediately. I wish him to marry this girl before the sun sets tomorrow."

Rothan and Tia exchanged despairing glances. She wrapped her arms around his neck more tightly.

Grinning as if enjoying their task, the Maiskhan soldiers pulled the couple apart.

"I'll never marry your son. I'm wed to Rothan in the sight of the gods." Tia wept copiously, striking the Maiskhan soldiers with ineffectual blows of her small fists. Her tear-choked voice stayed firm and loud. "The Exalted Ones approve of our union."

Making her way to the throne again, Farahna paused for a moment. Her frown left no doubt about her displeasure, but her voice remained calm. "Unfortunate. You'll be a widow by the dawn of this new day, and I'm sure my gods will smile even more joyously on your next marriage."

"I'm pregnant with Rothan's child." Tia made the announcement through tears, her voice proud.

"Now you have made me unhappy," Farahna hissed. She made a beeline for Tia, who stood straighter, putting her hands over her abdomen as the queen approached. Pausing a few feet away, the ruler tilted her head, assessing the younger woman. "Yes, I see the signs now that I know to look more closely. You fool, you could have claimed your place at my son's side, helped him rule your country when I'm gone, but he won't be eager to bed you now. Nor am I inclined to continue offering clemency." Farahna rubbed her forehead. "Let me think." Turning on her heel, she walked in silence to the dais, pausing to gaze at Mark as if seeing him for the first time.

"Who or what are you? How came you to be in company with this wretched traitor? Speak up!"

"A warrior for hire." Mark wasn't giving away any intel to this woman. The less she knew about Sandy and him, the better.

"And this woman?" Farahna eyed Sandy.

"She's the Lady of the Star Wind, come to fulfill the ancient prophecies," Tia said, going to link her arm with Sandy's. "She stands with us."

"Silence!" Farahna made a chopping motion with her hand, pointing the whip handle at Tia. "The Lady of the Star Wind is a story for children, a fable. Don't try my patience."

"We've seen pale women with hair such as hers before on our travels in the far north. The seas run colder than hell, the sun rarely shines, and men must dress themselves in the fur of animals to survive," the Maiskhan commander told Farahna. "She's obviously lied to these gullible traitors, as Your Majesty surmises."

Farahna sighed gustily, like a woman pushed to the edge of her endurance. "I'm not amused by fanciful recitations at this late hour." Allowing a sly grin to show, she said, "Well, it matters not. You've both chosen the wrong side of the gaming table, soldier for hire and alleged Lady, whoever you are and whatever your true motives might be." Dropping the whip, she pointed the scepter in her other hand at Mark. "You stand allied with a traitor. Therefore, I must count you as the same. Condemned by your own words." She waved the symbol of her rank at Seroj. "Execute this man tonight along with Rothan, his companion in treachery."

"And the fair-haired woman?" asked the Maiskhan commander.

Farahna considered Sandy, who met her gaze ice for ice. Looking over her shoulder, the queen frowned at her military ally. "You've some use for this person, Gaddaf?"

"Myself? No, Your Majesty. I'd give her as a reward to the men who captured her."

His answer was prompt and smooth and well calculated to please Farahna.

"And the pregnant princess?" asked one of the Maiskhan priests, speaking for the first time. Black robes rustling, he walked over to Tia, who shrank away from him. Sandy positioned herself in an effort to protect the princess from whatever the priest might have in mind. The man reached past Sandy, extending a hand to rub Tia's slightly rounded stomach. "This child would be the perfect sacrifice for the dedication of the new temple to our gods after the construction is complete. What more glorious gift for the gods than the blood of a royal Nakhtiaar babe? Will it be a boy?" he demanded eagerly. "The gods prefer firstborn boys."

"Get away from us!" Sandy stared at him in horror and revulsion, cradling a shaking Tia in her arms.

All the Nakhtiaar in the room were watching the priest in varying degrees of visible distaste, even Farahna, Mark observed. The Maiskhan commander apparently realized the point at about the same moment. He rushed to head off potential disaster.

"Peace, Nebuc." He came to take the priest by the arm and walk him away from Tia and Sandy. "We needn't worry about the sacrifices for the temple now. Completion of construction is many months away. I don't think it pleases Her Majesty to make such a gift to our gods."

"Indeed, it does not," she said, ascending the stairs to sink onto her throne. Running the straps of the flail through her stubby fingers, she pondered for a moment. Then she waved the whip in Tia's general direction. "On further contemplation, I've decided since she's *not* fit to wed my son, she and her unborn child will accompany Hutenen into the afterlife."

"You can't kill Tia!" Given strength by his desperation, Rothan took one step forward, nearly breaking free of the guards. "She's of royal blood and must be treated with the respect due to one of her rank. I don't care what you do to me, but let my wife and child live. Send them into exile if you must, but grant them mercy, I beg you."

Farahna was scathing and scornful. "Hutenen is being interred tomorrow in a royal tomb. It will be Tia's honor and duty to accompany her beloved brother into the afterlife." She contemplated the assembled Maiskhan and her own courtiers, frowning as her gaze drifted over Gaddaf, still standing close to Sandy. The Maiskhan commander caught her glare and moved away. Mark wondered if the man had the dubious privilege of sharing the queen's bed. Farahna certainly acted like a jealous woman where he was concerned.

Narrowing her eyes, smiling as if struck by an amusing thought, the queen said, "I'll send this so-called Lady of the Star Wind on the tomb journey with Tia and her brother to watch over and care for them in the next life. Does such a high honor please you, oh Lady?" Her voice dripped scorn. "I think nothing of disappointing my allies' lustful impulses, if it will honor one of such storied rank."

Mark's gut twisted. He'd never imagined a set of circumstances where he'd be glad to hear Sandy sentenced to death by being entombed alive. But at least she'd be safe from the Maiskhan soldiers in the room, who made what kind of fate they preferred for their beautiful captive all too clear with their lascivious glances and muttered remarks.

"What of the items brought from the Empty Lands, Your Majesty?" The speaker was Seroj, who apparently loathed loose ends. "What are we to do with those?"

Eyebrows raised to her hairline, Farahna looked at Rothan in a sort of amazed respect. "You actually retrieved the crown and scepter? Bring the sacred objects to me at once. I must see them!"

The Maiskhan soldiers carried the whole pile of belongings forward and placed them in some rough order at the foot of the throne. Seroj came to fumble through the pile for a few moments before extracting the wooden box. He ascended the first step of the throne to offer it to Farahna, who'd settled onto her throne while waiting.

"You open it—there may be a spell or a curse." She poked the scepter at him, as if to herd him farther away.

Seroj had the hang-dog air of a man going to his death, but he did as ordered, struggling with the golden hawk clasp and finally getting the box to open. Mark couldn't see the contents from his angle so he settled for watching Farahna's face as the lid rose. At first she was taken aback, and then she laughed. Unable to stop laughing, she took a sip of wine from a cup offered by a lady-in-waiting and finally caught her breath. "Oh, you pitiful fools. You ruined your lives for this piece of trash? Display the thing!"

Turning in place, Seroj tilted the box. Mark leaned forward, appalled to see the rich fabric lining of the box gone, shredded by time, discolored, rotted. The crown itself lay pitted, speckled with green verdigris, gaping holes where the fabulous jewels had been.

"This cannot be!" Rothan said, voice horrified. He stared at the wreckage in the box. "When we found the crown in the city, it was perfect!"

"Well, it's nothing but old junk now. Perhaps you were ensorcelled there." Farahna shrieked with renewed mirth. "I'll bury this relic with your beloved Hutenen. It's too late to crown him with these tomb robbers' loot, but he can carry it to the afterlife to console himself for his failures here. Perfect, the spice on the dessert." She collected her robes. "Enough amusement. We must rise with the dawn sun to prepare for the funerary procession through the city." She waved one hand at Gaddaf. "Take these traitors to the courtyard now. Carry out the sentence I decreed earlier. No further delays." Her gaze fell on Sandy and Tia, standing together at the foot of the throne. She pointed her scepter at Seroj. "Their women will bear witness to the queen's justice. How appropriate. They'll testify to the gods of my wisdom and even-handed judgment."

Seroj bowed, fist over his heart. "It shall be done at once, all as you order. I'll see to the details personally."

"You can't do this, you must not do this." Tia lunged forward and grabbed Farahna's sleeve as the queen walked by. "Rothan also carries the blood of kings in his veins. The gods will be offended if he's whipped to death like some common criminal! The Exalted Ones avert their faces from you, Farahna, and bring doom to Nakhtiaar."

"Enough talk, enough empty threats. He's a traitor and deserves whatever death I choose for him." Farahna ripped her sleeve away from Tia's clawed fingers so violently the fabric tore. "I tire of all of this drama. I'll watch this sentence carried out to ensure no more time is wasted."

The Maiskhan guards dragged Mark through an antechamber and outside into the crisp night air. Their destination was an enclosed courtyard. Rusty bloodstains from previous executions marred the walls and floor. Farahna and the courtiers followed, silent for the most part. A few of the Maiskhan guards made taunting comments to the prisoners. Sandy clung to Mark until the jeering soldiers dragged her and Tia away, positioning them against the far wall inside a ring of spears.

Soldiers slashed the ropes at Mark's wrists, carelessly cutting him in the process. Two Maiskhan guards fastened stout leather restraints at his wrists and ankles until he was stretched between two thick pillars. Blood trickled down his arms. His shoulders ached from the exaggerated stance they'd forced him into. Agony rippled down his arm in waves from the spot where the healing snakebite was now constricted by the tight bindings, making it difficult to stand still and appear stoic. He wasn't giving his captors the satisfaction of seeing how much pain he was in. Rothan was strung up between the next two columns. The executioners demonstrated a few practice cracks of their iron-tipped whips, striking fat sparks off the courtyard stones, while waiting for Farahna's signal to begin the execution.

Swallowing hard, Mark prayed to the Lords of Space for a swift, merciful death once the executioners were ordered to inflict the punishment.

Sandy witnessing his death was beyond his worst nightmare.

"I was proud to serve with you, my brother," Rothan said quietly.

"An honor for me as well." Mark took a deep breath, intending to die with as much dignity as he could muster.

An odd quiver vibrated through the stone columns, jerking his restraints, threatening to dislocate his shoulders.

A low rumbling burst from the ground below the bloodstained stones. A crack of thunder boomed, and lightning flashed through the night sky above. Next moment, the courtyard rocked in the grip of a moderate earthquake. Held upright by the implacable bonds at his wrists, Mark felt blood flowing freely as the restraints cut into him. From what little he could see, people were staggering in the small courtyard, most falling where they stood. Terrified courtiers and soldiers crawled in a vain search for safe shelter. Screams could be heard above the thunderous sound of the earthquake.

A large portion of the Palace façade crumbled and toppled onto the courtyard with a crash like an explosion, followed by more masonry. The two executioners and a number of the Maiskhan soldiers were caught in the avalanche of stones, screaming as they fell under tons of rubble. Gaddaf pulled Farahna to the dubious safety of the palace entrance. Sandy and Tia scrabbled on hands and knees away from the crumbling wall at their backs, taking shelter under the other doorway's arch.

The shaking lasted for a good thirty seconds, stopped for a heartbeat, and then an aftershock rumbled through the ground with a single sharp jolt. Crashing sounds could be heard as more walls collapsed and columns fell in other areas of the palace.

"As I foretold, the gods don't wish these men to die!" Tia screamed to anyone who might be listening as she rose to her feet.

Another small aftershock rattled the palace.

"Release them, or the gods will bring this place down on your head, Farahna." Tia made this dire prophecy at the top of her lungs as she struggled to keep her footing.

Mark heard a yelled command from the queen. "Do it, release them!"

Staggering like a drunk, Seroj regained his feet. He took two steps toward Mark and Rothan, drawing his belt knife to cut the ropes, and was crushed by a toppling statue as another, more powerful, aftershock rolled through the bedrock under the palace.

Abandoning their attempt to reform a line around the prisoners, the surviving Maiskhan soldiers broke ranks and ran from the area.

"Sandy, quick, grab a knife and get me down," Mark said, straining against the restraints to see her. "We've got a short window of opportunity for escape here."

As the trembling underfoot faded and the earth steadied, Sandy and Tia each gathered a belt knife from a dead or dying guard. The women sawed at the restraints holding Mark and Rothan to the columns. The second he was free, Mark took Sandy in his arms and held her tight, burying his face in her soft hair. She was shaking so hard she dropped the knife.

"I'd have gone insane watching them execute you. These people are barbarians!"

"We're not out of the woods yet." He drew Sandy behind him, shielded by the pillar as Gaddaf, the Maiskhan commander, reentered the courtyard. He drove a squad of his men with him, cursing and beating them with the flat of his sword.

Mark checked for potential exits, but there was no hope of escape from the enclosed space. The Maiskhan were coming at them from both doorways.

"You possess the luck of the gods, at any event, traitors." The Maiskhan commander stared at them from his position behind the ranks of his soldiers. "The queen has altered her decree. You're to be interred alive with the women after all, entombed with Hutenen's body tomorrow." Lowering his voice, he leaned closer. "No doubt it would momentarily displease the queen, but I've no compunctions about killing all of you right here." Eyes gleaming in the torchlight, Gaddaf ran his finger along the edge of his sword. He made a beckoning gesture with his other hand. "Give me an excuse."

Surrounded by edgy guards, the four prisoners marched under Gaddaf's supervision through halls full of frightened courtiers, fallen walls, and damaged statuary to a cell in the lower depths of the palace.

"Dawn arrives soon, bringing the hour of your funeral procession. Make peace with your gods." Gaddaf left one torch in a wall sconce and slammed the cell door as he departed.

A heavy bolt locked on the other side, the sound echoing in the small space. Mark assessed the situation, which took a depressingly short time. The room was a large rectangle divided into four open cells by partitions. There was a stack of lumpy, straw-filled mats by the door, a couple of benches, and nothing else. He did a quick reconnaissance of the entire room, noting chains and bloodstains in several alcoves. Pacing to the entry, he said, "We're not getting out of here. Not even a window."

"No, we're well and truly caught," Rothan agreed. "What of Djed? He didn't return with you to the *Lady Dawn*."

Pondering the potential for ambushing a guard the next time anyone entered the cell, Mark said, "I ordered him to stay on the loose. I hoped he could manage something, some kind of rescue."

"At least he won't suffer our fate."

"My head spins. I'm dizzy." Tia moaned, sagging against Rothan suddenly. "I need to lie down."

While Rothan carried his swooning wife, Mark dragged two of the mattresses into the far corner, piling one on top of another so Rothan had somewhere to place her. Kneeling on the grimy floor beside the rearranged bedding, Sandy took her pulse.

"Rapid. I think she's a bit in shock after all we've been through. She needs to rest and be kept warm. I wish I had my medical bag."

Rothan sat on the lumpy mat next to Tia, folding her tenderly in his arms. "I'll provide such warmth as I can, and comfort, till the guards come for us."

Mark took Sandy by the hand, raising her easily to her feet. "Let's give them some privacy, as much as we can in this dungeon."

She held his wrist and peered at the cuts in the torchlight. "I'd better bandage these. Nothing to wash them with, no antiseptic."

"I don't think I'm going to have time to worry about infection." Returning to the entry, he got a grip on the best of the remaining mattresses and dragged them to the farthest corner, inside the least disgusting cubicle. Sandy followed. "Might as well be comfortable ourselves. Have a bit of privacy." He sat on the hard surface and reached for her. She folded herself into his embrace. They sat in silence for a few moments.

"You're freezing. Such a flimsy nightgown." He rubbed his hands up and down her arms to warm her.

"You're half naked and soaked from swimming!"

"We're a fine pair, all right. Still alive, though." He bent his head and kissed her softly on the bare shoulder.

Sandy stared at him. "When you came on board the *Lady Dawn* tonight, I was so frightened for you, afraid the Maiskhan would kill you right there. Why didn't you stay with Djed? Try to rescue us later?"

Smoothing her hair away from her face, he said, "I'm never going to be parted from you again. There were too many Maiskhan on the ship for me to be able to rescue you. Using my blaster against all those archers on the enemy ship would have left too much chance you'd be injured or killed. Blasters are no good in close-quarters combat. I figured the next best thing was to be captured along with you. More chance of being able to make something happen, since I'm lacking situational intel on this world and have little hope for reinforcements." He realized he'd clenched his fists. "Not that I'm having much success extracting us from danger so far."

"I'm glad you're here." She tore strips from her gown and did the best she could to wrap his wrists, tsking over the renewed damage at the site of the snakebite. He flexed his arms when she'd finished. "Thanks."

"On the house." She lay back against his chest.

He hugged her. "Listen, I don't know how much time we have before they come to take us, but I need to tell you two things."

"Yes?" She faced him when he didn't immediately continue.

Mark brushed her lips with a kiss. "One, I'm sorrier than you'll ever know for dragging you into exile on this planet, bringing you into danger after danger, risking your life for total strangers—"

"I've heard enough." She placed her fingers on his lips. "We made the decision together to take the chance Lajollae offered. You were facing certain death on Freemarket, and as you said at the time, my fate wasn't going to be much better." She gave an exaggerated shiver. "Barent Kliin is a monster. At least here we've been side by side. I wouldn't give up sharing the dangers with you if Lajollae appeared in this cell right now and offered to send me to Throne."

Mark kissed her fingertips and then her lips. She returned the embrace but wasn't finished speaking her mind. "All those years when I believed you were dead, I was merely existing, walking through life, losing myself in my work, and caring for others so I wouldn't think so much about what I'd lost. Since you came for me, and brought me here, well, I've lived. I'm happy." She spared a quick glance at the dingy, smelly cell. "No matter what we're going through."

Mark studied her face in the flickering torchlight. "Which brings me to my second item. You're the only woman I've ever loved. Even when I tried to make myself hate you, in the Sectors, my heart was yours." He linked his fingers with hers. "That's why I never found anyone else. I belong to you."

"I understand." She raised her face to his, and they kissed for a moment.

Attempting to get more comfortable, Mark leaned against the wall, Sandy curled on his lap, her head pillowed on his chest. Although his shoulders and back ached from being strung up in the courtyard, and buffeted by the earthquake, he endured the discomfort to be close to her. He drew in a deep breath of her perfume and her warm, womanly essence, the scents easing his mind and body down from the edge of adrenaline stress.

After a moment or two of this, she lifted her shoulder to break free of his embrace. Instantly, Mark moved his hands away from her, and she turned, repositioning herself on his lap, her legs wrapped around him, arms circling his neck. The curves of her soft bottom pressing on his cock aroused him even in this situation. Mark lowered his head and leaned into a caress, his tongue probing gently at the invitation she offered with her parted lips. They kissed passionately, tongues exploring, twined in a sinuous, hot dance. After a moment, he withdrew, trailing soft caresses along the curve of her warm and sensuous neck, always one of his favorite places on her body. Tilting her head for him, Sandy allowed him to nuzzle the sexy, soft hollow where her neck curved into her shoulder. She slid one hand between their bodies, cupping him.

Unable to stop himself, he thrust against the pressure as she massaged his shaft through the fabric of his damp kilt. He took her mouth for another deep, long kiss. "I want you," he whispered.

"Can we? Here?" Sandy glanced at the dank prison walls as she caught her lower lip in her teeth. "What about Rothan and Tia?"

"They're probably doing the same thing about now."

"Aren't you in a lot of pain?" She searched his face. "The Maiskhan weren't any too gentle. I don't want to aggravate your injuries."

"Let me worry about my injuries. Don't be the doctor for a few moments." Seeing consent in the way her eyes softened as she smiled at him, he rolled them over onto the lumpy mattress, so she lay pinned beneath him, his penis nestled in the vee of her legs, separated by the layers of their clothing. "We don't know what will happen tomorrow, but at least we have the rest of the night." Keeping the weight of his upper torso on his elbows, he smoothed her hair across the mattress. "I don't want to die without loving you again."

She put her hand on his lips. "I'm with you all the way, my *bogatyr*. This moment is what we have, so let's savor it."

Capturing his lips with hers, she tenderly explored his mouth while working his clothing off. She ran her hands over his thighs, massaging and caressing, until she was squeezing his butt. Her fingers brushed his balls through the coarse fabric of his undergarment. Responding to her ministrations, his shaft pulled the fabric taut. She pushed him over onto his back, Mark yielding to her without reservation. Sandy stroked his nipples, making him shiver, and ran her hands across the taut muscles of his abdomen, Silky hair caressing his skin as she lowered her head, she pulled the drawstring of his loincloth loose with her teeth. Moving away a few inches, she tugged at the garment with her hands, arousal making her hasty, a bit rough as she rendered him naked.

Freed, his shaft immediately jutted out, ready for action.

"Come here," she ordered, wrapping her hands around the base of his penis to stroke him, base to tip, holding him prisoner, not that he had any intention of complaining. She swirled her tongue across the engorged head, lapping up the first pearly drops of arousal. He fisted his hands in her hair to pull her closer as his hips bucked. She took him into her mouth, sucking, releasing, teasing.

After a moment, he realized he was going to finish if he didn't slow her down. Gently, he disengaged. The possibility of being interrupted by the guards stayed in the back of his mind, curbing his ardor somewhat as he repositioned them so she lay under him. Rather than risk having her naked in the cell, he hiked her skirt to her waist and lowered himself to fit in the vee of her legs.

His shaft nudged against her body, the caress of her soft folds increasing his desire. His whole body craved what she was offering him, but despite his brave words, the aches and pains forced him to move slowly, gently. She held him as tightly as she could, kissing his neck, his chest. Her hips rose and fell under him. He slid his ironhard erection the first few inches into her body, finding her so hot and tight he could hardly bear it. He brought one hand to where their bodies were joined, pushing through her soft blond curls to stroke sensitive places to heighten her arousal.

He moved his hips slowly, advancing inside her as she clenched her inner muscles to hold him, then withdrawing only to drive forward again as she matched his rhythm perfectly. Sandy locked her legs behind his back, keeping him imprisoned deep within her. Whispering his name, she hugged him tight. He stopped exerting iron control and pumped harder, faster, driving into her body as deeply as he could.

A storm of emotion and sensation blocked all thought, leaving nothing but the intensity of the shared pleasure that overtook him as they both climaxed. Exhausted and sweaty, Sandy went limp against him, breathing hard. Savoring the pleasure of their bodies locked together, he stayed where he was for a few moments. Then he rolled them onto their sides, his cock slipping out of her body. Sandy murmured a little sigh of regret, resting one hand palm down on his stomach. He settled her into his shoulder and reached one hand to pull her nightgown down, covering her as best he could. She snuggled closer, draping one leg over his body.

"Loving you was even better than I remembered," she whispered, kissing his cheek. "Of course, the surroundings and the bed leave a lot to be desired."

His arms tightened. "We should have done this at the oasis on our first night here. So much wasted time—I was an idiot."

They lay entangled for a few moments, breathing deeply. Sandy curled as close to him as she could get, whispering little endearments in Outlier. After a few moments, he knew she slept. Cautiously he pulled free long enough to put his clothing on, before taking her into his arms again.

Mark stayed awake the rest of the night, keeping watch over his princess and attempting to formulate some desperate option that might get her out of danger tomorrow.

The door creaking open a few hours later sent him into high alert, although his body was stiff and aching from the mistreatment the day before. Mark hastily untangled his legs from hers, got to his feet, fists clenched, ready to shield Sandy as best he could. Over the partition, he saw Rothan rising on the far side of the cell to do the same for his woman.

"You will assemble here to meet us now," said the Maiskhan officer in charge of the guard detail, pointing at the floor in front of him. "Or my men will enjoy subduing you and your women."

As slowly as he dared, Mark walked hand in hand with Sandy to obey.

"I truly regret we've come to this moment." The Nakhtiaar official accompanying the jailers bowed as Rothan and Tia approached the door.

"Not as sorry as we are, Sapair," Rothan said, shaking his head. "How much time do we have?"

"The burial procession is to commence in an hour. You must be bathed and dressed. We've brought basins of warm water for you and appropriate clothing." Sapair gestured at the small piles of garments now being carried into the cell by servants. The squad of tense Maiskhan soldiers spread out to line the walls, on the alert for any offensive move on the part of the prisoners. The official glanced at the soldiers and then away with a small shudder. Leaning closer to Rothan, he said, "It was the most I could get away with. But don't tarry in your preparations. We're pressed for time."

"You expect the women to get undressed in front of these leering jackasses?" Mark said glared at the Maiskhan. "Better think again."

"We appreciate your efforts," Tia told Sapair softly. "Leave the basins and the clothing, and we'll be ready at the appointed hour. I give you my word. I wouldn't dishonor my brother by going to his burial dressed like this." She gestured at her crumpled and bloodstained night shift.

The courtier bowed to her. "As you wish, of course, my lady." He clapped his hands. "Leave us," he said with a shooing motion. The servants and the soldiers, including their scowling captain, withdrew.

Mark gave Rothan a sideways glance as the group was exiting, wondering if Sapair would be a valuable enough hostage to buy their freedom if he were to grab him.

The Nakhtiaar captain shook his head decisively in answer to the unspoken question.

Apparently unaware of his jeopardy, Sapair watched his companions file into the corridor before fumbling in his robes to retrieve four hard rolls and a small brick of cheese, which he handed to Rothan. "Eat quickly. I'm sorry I couldn't bring anything else."

"Sapair?" came a peremptory call from outside the cell.

"Coming," he said, voice tense as he glanced toward the door. "Giving them instructions for the procession!" Lowering his voice again, he said, "Farahna wanted you to go to your deaths starving. But I remember when my own sister was pregnant. She'd get ravenous and faint from hunger at times. I wanted to spare you public embarrassment, Lady Tia. My sincere condolences on the loss of your brother." He bowed his head and strode rapidly out of the cell before anyone could thank him.

The door slammed emphatically shut behind him, and Mark heard the lock click. "I could have grabbed him."

"And the Maiskhan would have cheerfully killed him to get to you. Our freedom can't be won by holding a mere official hostage. Farahna would just appoint someone else to the duties." Rothan walked to the pile of clothing and lifted out a finely woven blue tunic and a pair of black leather pants. Setting those aside, he took out an intricately worked leather belt studded with golden falcons at intervals. "Sapair does us great honor. I am sure it was his idea to bring us clothing befitting our ranks. The queen would have us die dressed as slaves, prisoners, in dishonor. Thanks to Sapair, we'll go to Hutenen's tomb properly attired."

"A small rebellion but brave on his part," Tia answered. "He was always a good person, one I trusted." Brushing a tear from her cheek, she reconsidered. "As far as I could trust anyone in this palace."

"Excuse me if I don't find the information consoling. I'd prefer actual help. I don't imagine he hid any weapons in the wardrobe?" Mark grabbed a belt and showed Sandy the empty slot where a knife would customarily ride. Disgusted, he dropped the accessory onto the pile of clothes. "Any chance there might be some help for us from the crowd? Or the local soldiery? Enough men who might not want to see you die? We should have some plan in case there's a break in our favor."

Rothan shook his head. "When we were brought in the other night, I was looking for friendly faces, hoping perhaps some of my own soldiers might have infiltrated the palace guard, but there was no one."

"Yeah, I saw how the Maiskhan soldiers occupied all the strategically important entries and exits, as well as guarding the queen. And us."

"What about Djed?" Sandy asked in a low voice. "He's still on the loose, isn't he?"

"One man with only a few hours to plan and no one to trust?" Rothan shrugged. "I think the world of my chief archer, but unless the gods themselves intervene, we're going to the tomb this morning."

"And we need to be dressed," Tia said, kneeling beside the heap of clothing and sorting through the garments. "I don't want to die today, but I prefer to walk with dignity."

Mark took a deep breath to control the anger and frustration running roughshod over his nerves. "Just all of you promise me to stay alert, and if by some miracle we get the chance, we make a break for freedom." He glanced at his three companions as they each nodded. "Pass me whatever I'm supposed to wear, and let's get on with this. And hand over a roll and some cheese for Sandy, please."

"Considerate of him to bring food." Sandy accepted the bread from Rothan, broke it in half, and gave part to Mark.

"Yes, it was. But we'll dine in the afterlife with my brother." Tia took her chosen dress and accessories, and headed to the farthest corner to change. Rothan grabbed two basins of water and followed her.

Mark and Sandy exchanged glances but said nothing, retreating to their portion of the cell to wash off the worst of the dirt and grime. Nibbling at the rolls and cheese, they dressed in silence.

As if going to some grand court function, Sandy and Tia were soon resplendent in gold-tinted linen sheaths, soft leather sandals, with lightweight, fringed shawls to carry. Mark and Rothan were arrayed in the more military garb, bareheaded, with the sturdy sandals and blue cloaks of warriors.

Sapair and the efficient armed escort showed up promptly as the captives were finishing the last touches on their clothing.

"Good." The official surveyed them head to toe with a critical eye while the Maiskhan exuded boredom.

Tia rested her hand on Sapair's arm for a moment. "We appreciate the kindness, but have you considered how angry Farahna will be with you?"

Sapair shrugged, although he wore a frown. "There's already enough about this situation I find distasteful, my lady. This issue of the clothing is the one thing where I had a chance to intervene." He leaned closer to her ear. "Farahna needs me since Seroj died in the quake. I'm the only one who knows the details of a number of ongoing projects she cares a great deal about. Farahna isn't the most patient woman. Punishing me would delay her efforts—I can afford to tweak her a bit." Straightening and raising his voice, he continued. "You're to march in the procession directly behind the bier carrying Hutenen's coffin. Maiskhan soldiers will escort you, and their orders are to kill all of you, starting with Princess Tia, should any attempt be made to escape. I wouldn't recommend taking any inappropriate action."

"Like going for Farahna's throat?" Mark made the offer in a low tone.

"You can march in chains." Sword drawn, Farun, the Maiskhan captain, pushed past Sapair to go face to face with Mark. "Your choice. Your woman will be the first to die, while you watch. I won't warn you again."

Mark shook his head. "No need for threats, we'll see this through."

"Sensible." Farun shoved his sword into the sheath.

"You better hope I don't come back as a ghost, though," Mark said, pointing at his tormenter. "You'll be one of the first people I come for."

The Maiskhan soldiers muttered, shuffling a few steps farther away. Several fingered amulets or made hand signs in Mark's direction.

Despite the dire situation, Rothan laughed. "The enemy will quake in their boots for weeks now that you've cursed them. Warrior of the Star Wind, you never cease to fight, do you?"

"Never," Mark told him as they were escorted out of the cell and led down the corridor toward daylight. "It's the motto of my clan."

"And I love him for it," Sandy said, kissing him on the cheek.

He clasped her hand and walked steadily forward with dignified resolve to meet whatever fate Farahna had planned. Unless, of course, fate gave him an opportunity to thwart her.

CHAPTER SIX

For a few moments, the prisoners were kept waiting under heavy guard in the spacious open patio in front of the palace's main entrance.

There was a stir behind them as eight hulking, muscle-bound servants carried the funeral bier of Prince Hutenen from the palace and into the square. Even under the dire circumstances, Mark couldn't help but stare in awe. The wood top of the oversized coffin gleamed with gold leaf in the ruddy sun of morning. A mosaic of finely crushed stones had been set in a golden frame on the top of the sarcophagus, depicting the visage of a handsome young man, calm and serene, eyes closed. Enameled details glinted on all sides of the coffin. The bottom half was burnished, fine-grain wood inscribed with line after line of the local language in gold-painted calligraphy. More of the precious metal was on display in the huge hinges on one side of the coffin and the lock on the other side, topped with an elaborate insignia.

"An abomination," Rothan said with disgust. He spat. "Her seal shouldn't be imposed on Hutenen's coffin. She insults him in the smallest details. Wasn't murdering him enough for her?"

The coffin was loaded onto a waiting cart drawn by four nervous horses, elaborate red and black plumes on their harnesses. The queen got into a wooden chair painted with flowers and birds in brilliant colors and was lifted into the air by four men. Surveying the crowd from her vantage point, Farahna proclaimed in a stentorian voice, "Today we mourn the loss of one for whom I was regent, one with whom I'd have gladly shared the throne. Yet it was not to be—the gods called him to dwell with them. Our loss and our grief are their happiness, and we mustn't ask why. As a sign of my benevolence and enduring obeisance to the ancient ways and the traditional gods of this land, I've agreed to the heartfelt pleas of Princess Tia and Captain Rothan to accompany their beloved Hutenen to his new life, rather than linger here broken-hearted with us."

A murmur ran through the crowd. Rothan cursed under his breath, and the guards closed in on the prisoners.

"It's a custom dating back to the founding of Nakhtiaar, though not much practiced any longer." Farahna was continuing her remarks as the assembled citizens gawked at the scene before them. "Yet when the request was made of me with such affecting sincerity and grief by the closest mourners, I'd no choice but to allow the sacrifice. And now we go to praise Hutenen and bury him. I ask you to say a prayer for the late prince today as our procession passes, and then turn to the duties of the living, for such is what he'd request of us. The palace will serve the ritual bread, meat, and beer at sundown, also as tradition dictates."

There was a ragged cheer at the news of the free meal. Farahna waved her left hand languidly, and the procession moved out of the temple gates and into the city streets to the slow beat of drums. The captives were marching behind the funeral bier. The crowds were silent for the most part. Occasionally, a woman would throw flowers at the coffin. Mark was sure the populace feared Farahna and her Maiskhan guards, so the lack of public emotion didn't surprise him.

"Usually, the family hires private mourners." Tia glanced at the quiet throng lining the street. "The spirit of the deceased needs to follow the weeping and wailing of mourners to be sure it will be drawn to the proper tomb. But even I can't cry for my brother today. I'm too full of rage at the woman who killed him and stole his throne."

"Clever speech she made," Mark said. "I doubt if many people believe all that bullshit she said about the sacrifice we're allegedly making, but I've got to give her credit for telling the story the way she wants our deaths perceived. She might create reasonable doubt in some of the more credulous and gain herself supporters."

Once the parade was outside the city gates, Mark and the others were loaded into a cart drawn by oxen for the last part of the journey. The procession traveled into the countryside at a slow pace for about an hour, crossing a dusty plain before entering the mouth of an arid valley. An imposing building loomed out of the hazy heat as they progressed through the valley.

"As I surmised, our destination is Farahna's personal temple." Rothan pointed at the structure ahead. "The final irony."

"What's the significance of having her own temple?" Sandy asked.

"She shows Hutenen contempt yet again. He's to be buried in an antechamber to her own planned tomb, which lies in the mountain behind her temple. She intends to keep him under her control in the afterlife and deprive him of his due, even there." Rothan shook his head. "My prince underestimated her, to his eternal regret."

"You tried to warn him," Tia reminded her lover as the guards chivvied them out of the cart and to the foot of the first flight of stairs. "He wouldn't listen."

Rothan was silent.

Mark trudged up five sets of stairs to the platform at the top, level with the entrance to Queen Farahna's temple. Eight priests carried the coffin into the building as the prisoners arrived. Armed temple guards pushed and shoved Mark and the others into the cool dark of the building, guiding them through a set of polished pink marble columns. Looming at the far end of the first chamber was an altar dominated by an elaborate, three times life-size carving of Farahna. She was depicted on her throne with two female deities on either side. The goddesses were portrayed gazing at her adoringly, while the queen stared straight ahead at any who approached. Giant scented candles provided the illumination. A phalanx of priestesses stood in a cluster beside the altar, chanting some kind of hymn.

Farahna performed a short ceremonial ritual with her priests and priestesses, who did most of the work. She picked at her fingernails as if bored but mouthed words when required. She left the dancing and gesturing to the others. The four prisoners waited in a cluster, surrounded by guards alert for any sign of last-minute resistance. Mark thought Tia was praying. Rothan stood as if ready for action, jaw clenched, but no opportunity arose. The Maiskhan were too numerous, highly vigilant, spears aimed at the women in particular.

Rituals over, Mark and his companions followed as priests took the coffin farther into the depths of the temple, past the altar, and down a long corridor stretching deep into the mountain from which the building had been carved. There were doors along either side of this wide hall. Most were blank, with rough, unfinished surfaces. One or two had been smoothed and painted with pictures and inscriptions that were hard to see in the gloom.

Rothan indicated the painted door he was marching past. "Her favorite body-guard, who died saving her life in an assassination attempt."

"And you say her own tomb is here too?" Sandy asked with a sort of fascinated horror.

"Oh yes," Tia said. "At the end of the corridor, in the heart of the mountain, with many tricks and traps for any man foolish enough to disturb her in the afterlife. She executes her architects and tomb builders on a regular basis. No one other than herself will know the entire set of plans."

"Why would anyone work for her, then?" Mark was puzzled. "Sounds like certain death."

"She provides for their families. She gives rich funerals to her victims. The workers will be well-off in the afterlife." Tia's explanation was matter-of-fact. "And, of course, each man and woman hopes to outlive her."

"What's going to happen to us?" Mark asked Rothan.

"We're going into the afterlife with the prince," the captain answered. "To serve him, as she said this morning in the square. It's an old custom, long abandoned. Farahna's conveniently reviving the practice to execute us without public outcry or repercussions."

"Most people are interred with pictures of their loved ones and tiny statues of servants to keep them company," Tia added, wrapping herself tightly in her shawl.

A young priest diverted the procession into a branching corridor, where Mark found himself walking on a downward slope. The surface underfoot in this area was much rougher, unfinished stone. Huge blocks of raw, gray-and-black veined marble were suspended above their heads. He glanced at Rothan. "Booby traps?"

"To be triggered after the tomb is sealed and the queen and the priests have reached safety outside the tunnels. We're to be trapped for eternity, my friend."

Mark hugged Sandy as the mourners halted again, this time at a doorway deep in the mountain. Frustration and anger at having led her into this death trap raged in his heart. "I'm so sorry."

She shook her head and squeezed his hand. "We took the chance and the risks together."

He wished he could forgive himself as easily as she'd apparently forgiven him yet again.

Farahna came to stand close to her prisoners, remaining well out of arm's reach, protected by the Maiskhan guards. As the queen contemplated her prisoners, Mark realized she reminded him more and more of the Outlier empress.

"You do my prince the final dishonor, I see." Rothan's whole demeanor was contemptuous as he stared at the inscription above the door where the flickering light from the torches picked out the freshly cut characters.

"He Who Strove and Failed," Farahna read, a mocking tone in her sultry voice. "Where's the dishonor in my statement? It's the truth—Hutenen couldn't prevail against me in the end. He's the one being buried here today, not me."

"You killed him through vile treachery," Rothan said. "Leaving aside the issue of who belongs on the throne, he'd have won in any kind of fair trial or contest."

"There are no rules when one is taking, then keeping, a throne. Only strength and guile, both of which he lacked." She laughed, walking ahead into the tomb's antechamber.

The guards shoved the prisoners into the room behind her.

The first chamber was small and jam-packed with household goods. Objects of all description, from cooking pots to a gilded bed frame, had been piled against the cold stone walls. Jewels and spices spilled together on the floor from jars stacked too haphazardly, leading to minor disaster. Broken shards littered the priceless woven rugs thrown in the dust. More goods were added now, brought along in the funeral procession. The queen's attention rested on the items being given to Hutenen as final tribute. Frowning, she ordered several things returned to the palace.

Mark considered making an attempt to grab Farahna, hold her hostage, the ransom being freedom for all of them.

As if reading his mind, Gaddaf stepped between him and the queen, pressing the tip of his knife to Mark's throat. "I know you're the most dangerous man here," the Maiskhan commander said in a low voice, staring into Mark's eyes. "I've been watching you make and discard plans all morning. But even the wiliest and most skillful of warriors has his weakness, and yours is the woman from the north. She's good in bed no doubt, but no warrior to match your skills. My spearman has orders to slay her if you make a move, no matter what chaos might be happening. Try anything, and your woman will die." He didn't wait for Mark to acknowledge the threat but slowly retreated, sliding his knife into its sheath and rejoining Farahna.

A few moments later, the captives were hurried past the mess into a second, bigger room, also crammed with goods. There were spears, shields embossed with the royal crest, a bow and quiver of arrows, chairs, unlit lamps, chests of drawers—too much to see. A realistic door had been painted onto one side wall in vivid blue, although it was clearly nothing but an illusion. The coffin had been lowered into a massive stone receptacle in the middle of the chamber. Four priests were cursing under their breath and struggling to push the flat top onto the tomb, sealing away the unfortunate young would-be king.

As his eyes adjusted to the level of light in the chamber, Mark noticed a lavishly dressed woman slumped in a chair across the room, her hand resting on the flank of a brindled hunting dog curled by her side as if asleep. Her eyes were closed, and her head lolled against the cushions. He had no doubt she and her canine were dead.

The queen followed his line of sight. Her painted lips curved, and she sighed theatrically. "Kiramyen, his favorite concubine. She asked to go with him, and how could I in good conscience refuse the piteous request?"

"And the dog? Did it ask to die?" Mark said. "Or did you make the decision for it?"

"Prepare them and let us be done." The queen ignored Mark's last question. "We must be in the city before the sun sets to preside over the feasting. I'm satisfied here." She walked out of the chamber without another word, her sandals clicking on the hard stone. The Maiskhan guards followed.

Mark moved in front of Sandy and stood facing the half circle of priests and temple guards. Hands fisted, he settled into a combat stance, done being manhandled. "Leave us alone to meet our fate in here as we see fit."

Rothan stepped to his side, face grim. "As my brother says, walk away."

"Even unarmed, we can make mincemeat of you," Mark threatened the priests, who backed away, some making signs in the air against the evil eye.

"You do no honor to your prince to behave this way in the presence of his mortal remains." Gesturing at the granite enclosure where Hutenen now rested, the oldest priest was scornful.

"This is about us now, not him," Mark said. "And we don't need any additional 'preparation' from you. No poison, no drugs, no chaining us to the wall, or whatever your bitch queen has in mind. Go on, get out of here!"

"Before she seals you in the tomb with us," Rothan suggested.

The priests and the Nakhtiaar guards exchanged nervous glances. Holding his sword in front of him as if to ward off any attack from Mark, the leader of the troops retreated toward the door. "It matters not to me. You'll die no matter what is done or undone." Stumbling on the threshold, the man fled.

His act set off a mass exodus, soldiers and priests crowding through the narrow entry, frantic to leave the room. A moment later, the heavy stone door, easily a yard thick, rolled into place. Shortly thereafter, Mark heard the muffled boom of the outer chamber closing.

"Find your peace," Rothan said, taking Tia by the arm. "We'll have scant time before the air is gone and our lives in this world with it."

"Put out all but one torch, conserve the oxygen as long as we can." Mark extinguished the one closest to him, smothering it in the dust underfoot.

"I don't want to die in the dark," Sandy said. "I've always been afraid of the dark." She swallowed hard. "I know that sounds ridiculous, considering the situation."

He hugged her close. "We'll have some light, don't worry."

Rothan moved away to deal with the other torches. He'd taken two steps across the chamber when a series of low, rumbling shock waves could be heard and felt. Dust rained on Mark from overhead.

"She released the sealing stones," Rothan said with a shrug. "The guards and priests surely lacked sufficient time to make their way to safety."

"She killed them?" Coughing, Sandy brushed dust from her hair.

"Probably. Priests—even those who know the sacred writings—are simple to replace. Temple guards have no value at all to Farahna. You noticed she took her Maiskhan soldiers with her? And the priests had seen the riches with which Hutenen was buried and had the secret of locating the chambers within the mountain. She wouldn't want such knowledge to exist. A few more Nakhtiaar lives one way or the other don't matter to her." Rothan finished his task, leaving only the smallest torch lit. He crossed the chamber to Tia. In the dim light, he took her into his arms and kissed her. "Let me prepare a comfortable resting place for you, my love."

Holding Sandy close to him, Mark could feel her straining to take in air.

"I-I'm already having trouble breathing," she told him. "I think it's nerves. The air can't be running low already, can it?"

Mark spotted a stack of rugs and cushions against the far wall next to the dead concubine. Taking a moment, he grabbed an assortment. As he sorted through the pile, he noticed some of the household goods that had been brought were in less than pristine condition, a few threadbare rugs, some dented cooking utensils, figurines chipped or broken, furniture missing paint. Farahna had apparently padded the funeral goods with discards. Shaking his head at the depth of her duplicity, he took the pillows he'd selected and turned.

"I won't sit there," Sandy said.

"No," he agreed, guiding her to the farthest spot in the chamber away from the sepulcher, in line with the now sealed door.

Mark made a nest of the pillows and rugs before inviting Sandy to recline against him, her head on his chest. Silently cursing Farahna and the Outlier empress, he was alarmed by the effort his beloved exerted to draw every breath. They lay in the dank room, not talking, drawing what comfort they could from each other's touch.

The torch guttered and came back to feeble life. Mark blinked, peering across the room to see how Rothan and Tia were doing, but it was growing dark. Or else his eyes were failing as the oxygen was depleted. He couldn't feel Sandy breathing against his chest any longer, but raising a hand to check her pulse required too much effort. The roaring in his ears was deafening, and the room spun around him.

Some indeterminate time later, Mark awoke with a start. He sat up, easing Sandy onto the pillows beside him, relieved to find her still breathing. The chamber was filled with a dim, steel-blue light from an unknown source. Dust motes floated in the air, sparkling like small sapphires. The heavy lid of the sepulcher sat ajar, half off. Chills running down his spine, Mark glanced across the room at the door.

A man stood there in the now open portal, facing away, looking into the next chamber. As if sensing Mark's scrutiny, the man slowly turned his head. They stared at each other for a moment. He didn't speak, gazing at Mark with an expression on his handsome face conveying mild regret. The same general age as Rothan, the newcomer had long black hair curled at the back of his neck. Strong, slashing eyebrows provided the setting for a pair of coal black eyes. His thin lips parted to say something, then closed again, the words unsaid.

Holding Mark's gaze with the intensity of his own stare, the apparition beckoned. Rising, compelled to obey the silent summons by some power he didn't understand, Mark walked across the cold floor, skirting the half-open sepulcher in the center. He glanced at the details of the mosaic representation of the prince's face and then evaluated the man in the door.

Hutenen. Or his ghost.

The prince had moved on by the time Mark reached the open door. He crossed the threshold to find the portal opened into a long corridor filled with the same uncanny metallic-blue light. Tendrils of fog or smoke curled along the floor. Walking a few yards ahead, Hutenen nearly brushed the narrow walls of the corridor with his broad shoulders as he paced toward whatever awaited them.

Mark opened his mouth to say something, ask the prince to wait, ask what the seven hells was going on, but closed his lips without making a sound. It didn't seem appropriate to break this silence. Maybe even dangerous to do so. Not even glancing back to check on his unconscious companions, Mark proceeded down the corridor in Hutenen's wake. At the next corner, the prince disappeared.

Hurrying now, Mark came to the end of the straight hallway and jogged to the left where the prince had gone, stopping five paces later on the threshold of yet another chamber and taking in the scene.

Prince Hutenen bowed in front of a being half again as tall as he was. This man was pale, his hair a mix of white, black, and midnight blue. His high-cheekboned face was calm, the thin lips set in a neutral line, neither approving nor disapproving. Under thick white eyebrows, his blue eyes practically glowed, the same color as the light illuminating the corridor. Attired in sweeping robes of midnight blue with touches of silver, the sleeves lined with wine-red satin that looked like blood, the man reminded Mark of a judge. He carried a scepter of highly polished silver set with large cabochon gems of varying shades of blue. The top bore a many-faceted iridescent crystal, inside which colors whirled and spun like caged lightning. As the prince bowed, a breathtakingly beautiful woman stepped from the shadows.

Clad in fine white robes more elegant than anything Farahna had worn, the woman's swanlike neck was adorned with many intricate necklaces forming a multicolored collar. A scarlet ribbon headband threaded through her glossy black hair. Two golden horns spiraled from her head, an elaborately inscribed diadem suspended from golden chains looped around the horns. A second man sat behind her, cross-legged on a padded bench. He held a sharp quill pen poised in one well-formed hand, white feather curving gracefully, and a small oblong tablet thick with what appeared to be sheets of cream-colored paper cupped in the other. Instead of hair, he had fine green iridescent feathers all over his skull and following the bony line of his spine.

No one paid any attention to Mark

He saw thousands, if not millions, of brilliantly colored, small glass jars lining shelves beyond the three uncanny beings. As he watched, the woman said something to Hutenen, who answered in a low but firm voice. The scribe, or clerk, scribbled a note before setting his instruments on the table and striding to the shelves. Tracing the small bottles with his finger as he strolled along the endless cases, searching high and low, the scribe finally chose one, clutching it in his fist as he made his way to the waiting woman. Bowing low, he handed her his choice. Mark saw a golden crest attached to the neck of the container by thin, twisted wires. She held the bottle out to the prince, who glanced at it before nodding.

The woman dipped a golden spoon into the glittering purple crystalline powder heaped like a small sand dune on an alabaster plate to her left. She shook the powder into a golden bowl on the table in front of her, followed by a few ounces of luminescent blue liquid from a nearby carafe. Pausing, head tilted as if considering choices, she eyed Hutenen and made her final selection from a rack of oddly shaped containers behind her. Extracting a small vial glowing vibrant green, she shook a few grains of the powder into the mix. The final ingredient in this odd mix appeared to be plain water splashed from a crystal clear goblet. Then she reached for the iridescent glass bottle the scribe had selected earlier, breaking the red wax seal and discarding it. As her companions watched with close attention, she tipped the bottle over the bowl. A faint smell of flowers and woods came to Mark, extremely pleasant to the senses, almost mesmerizing. A ribbon of pearl-gray smoke rippled from the container, descending into the mixture in lazy whorls, until the bottle was empty. Setting it aside, the woman picked up a spoon with a handle carved in the shape of a flower, blue and ivory and green enamel inlaid in the petals, and stirred the mixture three times, uttering Hutenen's name.

She bent over the mixing bowl, gesturing to the prince to do the same. Biting his lip—the first sign of emotion he'd shown—Hutenen stepped closer until he bumped into the table. Eyes fixed on whatever lay in the bowl, he gripped the beveled edge of the table so hard his knuckles went white. Plainly, the outcome of this odd ritual had deep significance to him.

Thin mist full of sparkling points of white light rose to wreathe Hutenen's face, cascading down his entire body. He took a deep breath, face relaxing into a smile, as if all his hopes had been realized.

The scribe made intricate notes on his pad, as if recording the recipe the woman had used, the pen scratching across the surface of the paper. Then he set the utensil on the table, aligning it precisely with a stack of similar pens, and rose to his full height, close to nine feet tall, like the woman and the other being. He carried the paper he'd been writing with such attention to the table where the judge sat, and the woman joined them. All three examined the results for a moment before the judge sat back in his chair as if satisfied. He nodded, touching the note with the crystal at the end of his scepter, and as if that had been a signal, the paper burst into brilliant white flame and disappeared. The scribe pointed at Hutenen.

"You have accomplished that which you were tasked to do in this life, for better or for worse, whether the meaning was clear to you or not. Your heart and your soul remained strong and dedicated to honor. You may pass from this place with no further penalty or judgment and into the contented afterlife you've earned." The pronouncement had the sound of an oath or ritual.

The scribe's next words were prosaic, like a host saying farewell to a guest. "I'll escort you to the portal."

Prince Hutenen paused as he and the scribe began to leave the chamber, going to whatever came next in this series of events. He and the three beings stared at

Mark, who straightened, dropping his arms to his sides, feeling as if he should be at attention, perhaps even salute.

The prince said nothing but raised one hand in final farewell. Mark detected a flash of what he assumed was sorrow and longing on the man's face. The prince wanted to speak, his lips forming hushed words never to be given full voice. The scribe tugged at his elbow. Then the prince and his guide were gone, vanishing in the mist with only the fading sound of footfalls to mark their going.

Hands extended to Mark, the woman came forward, and with no hesitation, he laid his own hands, palms down, in her light clasp. She studied him from her greater height. Her eyes were the pure, intense purple of the river flowers, and she wore their perfume as well. Relaxing, Mark felt an inexplicable sense of peace and calm flowing from her into his soul. Then the woman drew him forward to face the remaining man and the golden bowl.

There was no mercy in the judge's face, nor in the unblinking blue eyes, as the deity stared at him. "You were not called and are here beforetimes."

Releasing Mark, the woman held her hand out flat. A small, opalescent glass jar materialized. The jar's stopper was a carved hawk's head painted in intricate detail. The symbol of Mark's Outlier warrior clan glowed red on the side of the jar.

As he gaped at the jar, he felt a tugging sensation in his chest, followed by a wave of dizziness. The woman smiled as if satisfied, unstoppering the vial and setting the lid aside with great care. She poured the contents into her golden bowl and added one of her own spices or chemicals.

A sense of dread crept over him. His gut told him he was in peril, but he'd no idea what defense he could mount.

There was a sudden displacement in the air next to him as Sandy joined him in this nightmare. He squeezed her fingers, fear for her overwhelmed by sheer gratitude not to be alone facing these beings and their judging of unknown things. Smiling, the woman raised her head, extending one flawless, beringed hand toward Sandy. Seconds later, a second jar had materialized in her palm. The jar top was also carved with the hawk's visage, but the golden plaque on the side bore the

Zhivanov coat of arms, incongruous in this place. Tracing the design with one fingertip, the woman laughed and allowed a plume of golden smoke to drift from the second bottle into the bowl. The two jars vanished into thin air.

"Your hearts are true," proclaimed the scribe, who'd returned unnoticed from wherever he'd escorted Hutenen. He stared at them from blinking black avian eyes, then focused on his pad, scratching a few notes.

In all his long years of exile and military service across the Sectors, Mark had never encountered beings like these. The gods of Nakhtiaar were more unfathomable in their power than anything or anyone he'd ever faced.

"No wrongdoing is recorded in your hearts, you've told no lies, encouraged no evil to spawn," the woman said in sonorous tones, as if proclaiming some small portion of a ritual. "Yet it isn't your time to journey to the destination." She exchanged glances with the judge, who gave an imperceptible tilt of his head while remaining silent. His agreement appeared to be reluctantly given, unable to be denied in the face of whatever lay in the golden bowl, which no one offered to let Mark and Sandy view for themselves.

The woman addressed them once more. "Another destiny lies ahead, much work to be done on the road you've chosen before you ever face the Ruler of Eternity. Go forth from us and do what you must."

She drew a small blue and green striped feather from her belt and touched first Mark, then Sandy on the forehead and on the left wrist. She raised the feather to her lips and kissed it, vanishing into the mist as she did so, her rich laugh lingering in the chamber with them. Another wave of dizziness and nausea assaulted Mark, as if her going had sucked all the air from the room. His knees gave way under him, and he fell, bringing Sandy with him as he lost consciousness.

Someone was shaking him so hard his teeth chattered.

"Wake up, my lord, we haven't much time!"

Mark opened his eyes with great reluctance. Djed pummeled him. A faint breeze of blessed fresh air flowed into the room from somewhere. He drew in three great breaths, expanding his chest as far as it would go, and the life-giving oxygen cleared his head. "How did you get here?" He struggled to stand. "There's a way out?"

"Of a sort, but we must hurry." Djed stepped back, talking to Rothan over his shoulder. "They live, my lord."

"Thanks be to the Exalted Ones!" Rothan said. "A miracle has been wrought here, in the midst of treachery and evil."

Mark squatted to help Sandy, stirring dazedly from her semicomatose state among the cushions. Now wasn't the time to speak of what he'd seen. He glanced over his shoulder at the great sarcophagus in the center of the chamber. The lid was in place, the queen's unbroken seal gleaming in the flickering light of Djed's torch. Goose bumps spread over Mark's body even as he told himself he'd known all along he'd been lost in an oxygen-deprivation hallucination.

"Where's Tia?" Mark hauled the half-conscious Sandy to her feet. She swayed against him drunkenly.

"We sent her on ahead with Djed's cousin." Rothan came to help with Sandy. "You were both hard to waken. I feared we were too late."

"Sent them ahead where?" Mental processes a bit foggy from lack of air, Mark thought for a moment of the corridor he and Hutenen's spirit traversed in the dream.

"I expected the queen would want to entomb you with our prince," Djed explained rapidly. "I have a cousin who makes his living as a grave digger by day, grave robber by night. His nocturnal occupation is the shameful secret of my family, but today it became a blessing from the gods. I sought him out and obtained the secret way into this place. It's narrow, difficult, but serves as your path to the world of the living, my lords."

Several chairs and tables had been stacked against the far wall as a sort of makeshift ladder. The breeze came from an opening about one yard square in the roof of the chamber.

"You go first," Mark told Rothan and Djed. "I'll help Sandy climb up to you, and then you get her to safety. I'll be right behind."

"My bag, I need my medical bag." She struggled. "I can't go without my instruments and medicines—they're irreplaceable."

"We'll get it," Mark promised her. "I took note where the priests dumped it when we were brought in here." He stepped away and found the bag in a pile of miscellaneous household goods by the door. He brought it to her.

Djed clambered into the escape tunnel with nimble athleticism. Now he reached for Sandy, but she handed him the bag instead. The archer grunted and disappeared from view, passing the leather satchel to someone farther up in the tunnel.

Sandy shook one finger at Mark. "Promise you won't be long?"

"I swear on my honor as a *bogatyr*."

"There's a rope ladder, my lady, to pull yourself along the steep incline," Djed said from his perch half in and half out of the tunnel. "You must climb to freedom, but we'll help."

Squeaking in dismay from time to time, she picked her way to the top of the stack of furniture. She reached for the first shifting rung of the rope ladder as the archer dropped it in front of her questing hand. Rothan climbed halfway up the precarious tower of tables and chairs and gave her a boost into the tunnel. The captain offered Mark a hand, but he'd moved away.

"My brother, what are you about?" Rothan jumped from the pile of furniture.

"We can't leave the Crown of Khunarum in here." Mark held the torch and rummaged among the boxes and bales and other household goods. "Hutenen may have no further need of it—trust me—but we do."

"We journeyed to the Lost City and brought the crown back for him." Rothan crossed the floor. "We must leave it here. There's no other to wear it."

"I don't accept your conclusion." Mark continued his search.

"You dishonor the prince by stealing from his tomb." Rothan grabbed Mark by the elbow. "Much as I owe you, I can't permit thievery."

Mark moved the torch in his free hand to allow an unobscured view of Rothan's face. The two men stared at each other for a long moment in the hot light, Rothan scrutinizing Mark's face. No words were uttered. Drawing a long breath and exhaling, the Nakhtiaar soldier released his grip on Mark's arm. "What have you seen? What happened to you, my friend?"

Mark found himself reluctant to give voice to the events he'd witnessed in his dream, a vision that had the clarity of reality. Even awake, he could see the room, the beings and the bowl in his mind's eye. "I can't even begin to tell you. Words fail me." The firmly sealed, giant sarcophagus drew his attention, and then his gaze traveled to the far wall, where the intricately detailed false door had been painted. Even in the flat painting, the door was closed.

Rothan followed the direction of his gaze. He swallowed hard, struggling for words. "Just tell me, is my shield brother Hutenen…safe? Did he…did his soul—"

"The scribe or court clerk said his heart was pure. He'd done no evil. I don't know what it all meant, or how real it was. Your prince is gone, and he doesn't need the Crown of Khunarum or anything else in this place anymore, but I think—I know—we do. Nakhtiaar does."

"My lords, what delays you? Time grows short, and once you reach the outer world, we still have to make our escape from this cursed valley." Djed's voice was hoarse and stressed, hard to make out.

Mark pressed his fist to his chest, seeking to ease the constriction low oxygen was causing. "Air's going bad in here, even with an open shaft. You go ahead. I'll be along as soon as I find the damn chest."

"I'll help."

Mark wasn't going to spend precious time in protest. The two men searched with increasing desperation among the jumble of things Farahna had ordered thrown into the tomb. "The crown has to be here." Mark ran his hand through his hair. "She said she didn't want it."

"We've missed nothing, my brother." Rothan kicked aside a stack of baskets. "Perhaps she changed her mind, or the priests left the crown in the outer chamber."

"Or maybe she stashed it in there with the prince." Mark indicated the stone sarcophagus. He took two steps. "I can't lift this damn lid off without your help."

Lips compressed, not uttering a word, Rothan came to assist. He plucked a gold and ivory knife from the mess on the floor and slashed through the queen's seal, red flakes of wax flying. Dropping the dagger, he said with satisfaction, "Even if I've become the lowliest of coffin thieves, there's a certain pleasure in breaking her name, which never should have been imposed on my prince."

"Look, I'm sorry to ask you to go against your beliefs, and I wouldn't suggest it if the needs of the living didn't outweigh the customary reverence for grave goods. I'm sure Hutenen wouldn't be upset by this act." Mark got a grip on the end of the heavy lid, while Rothan stood at the left side, and the two men struggled to move it. Rothan muttered prayers under his breath, and they made a second attempt. Mark felt the slab shift somewhat and redoubled his efforts.

"My lords, what are you doing?" Djed dropped into the chamber, landing like a cat.

Mark waited for Rothan to take charge. The latter gave crisp orders.

"Come and help us. We must take the Crown of Khunarum from this place or our beloved land of Nakhtiaar is lost to Farahna and her Maiskhan dogs forever."

Eyes wide, Djed recoiled, the expression on his face one of terror. "But to open the sarcophagus of our prince—"

"There's no choice." Rothan's answer was given in a harsh monotone. He didn't look at Mark.

Each step dragging, Djed walked to the other side of the bier like a man going to his own painful death. "We'll be cursed for this, my lords."

"I don't think so," Mark said. "I believe we're doing what Hutenen would want."

The lid gave way under the renewed effort of the three men, moving with surprising ease once it began to shift, and they pushed it to the sandy floor. The granite slab shattered into three pieces along some invisible fault lines as it hit the ground. The torchlight glinted off the great, gold leaf-covered coffin inside the sepulcher, and Mark gazed again upon the mosaic of the departed prince, marveling at the uncanny resemblance to the man's ghost. Eyes wide, tremors running through their bodies, Rothan and Djed retreated, transfixed by what they'd done, apparently against all their beliefs. Mark didn't blame them for being frightened. Uttering a crude Outlier oath to prod himself into motion, he leaned over the open coffin, running his hand along the side of the container. Nothing. Moving to the right side, he repeated the gesture. Three-quarters of the way, his hand rammed into something with bruising force. He grabbed the impediment with both hands, bringing the familiar wooden box from the depths of the sepulcher.

"Got it! Now we can go."

The three men delayed no longer. First Djed and then Rothan made the climb into the narrow mouth of the escape tunnel. Bringing up the rear, Mark was acutely conscious of the walls of the mountain pressing in on him as he climbed the rope ladder, pushing the crown's case in front of him. Claustrophobia had never bothered him before, but this whole night's events shredded his nerves in unusual ways.

Men reached into the tunnel to lift him the last yard, the box taken away from him and set aside by Rothan. Mark rolled onto his back on the stony slope, heedless of pebbles and roots digging into him, and took huge breaths of the clean night air, trying to clear the scent of unguents, smoke, and perfumes out of his lungs. He was vaguely aware of two or three men working hard to cover the entrance to the tunnel with flat slabs of rock and brush, concealing their access to the riches of the tomb below.

Grateful to be alive and free, Mark watched two of the moons and a skyful of unfamiliar stars high above him. After a few moments, Sandy sat beside him, her sandals scattering little rivulets of pebbles down the steep slope. "Are you all right?"

Leaning on his elbows, he nodded. "You?"

"Fine. I had a dream." Massaging her temples, she swallowed hard.

"Yes. I imagine we had the same dream. I'm not so sure it was *only* a dream. Who knows on this world?"

"The woman was Haatrin," she said. "I don't know who the others were, but now I remember her from the coma dream."

"We can talk about it later. Is that Sallea I see over by Djed?"

"Apparently, she talked Demari into putting her ashore in the morning, and Djed approached her, so she joined the rescue party." Sandy lifted her hair and twisted it into a ponytail. "I haven't had a chance to talk to her yet."

"Must have been some argument she had with Demari." Raising his voice, Mark addressed Djed. "What's next in this escape plan of yours?"

"We must get away from here before daylight. The queen has patrols of the entire area at regular intervals during the day."

"But not at night?" The gap in coverage surprised him.

"No." Djed's teeth gleamed in the moonlight. "The spirits of the dead are abroad at night, you know."

Quiet laughter greeted his joke, easing the tension.

"The Maiskhan are extremely superstitious about the night," said a nearby soldier. "They won't do anything after sunset, other than fuck. Indoors." More laughter greeted his sally.

"I don't think I know you?" Mark said to the man, who was standing next to Rothan.

"Lieutenant Khefer, from my grandfather's territory, assigned to my command," Rothan said, clapping his subordinate on the shoulder with open affection. "I'm anxious to hear what news he can give us about the events we missed."

"I can tell you some of what happened after you left the city, my lord, but may I suggest not here?" The other soldier appeared to share Djed's anxiety to be away from the tomb.

"Yes, let's go to my village, to my home," said the grave-digger cousin. "You can make plans there. My wives are cooking a large feast in your honor. We'll eat, and you can discuss whatever you want, but we must be away from here now."

An hour or so later, having walked out of the valley of the temple and tombs in the moonlight and then into the small village where Djed's cousin lived, the now-freed prisoners and their motley rescuers sat in the cozy safety of the grave robber's large hut. The cousin's wives served wine, olives, bread and cheese, and roast fowl. The simple fare tasted better to Mark than any meal he'd ever had, in Outlier or in the Sectors.

"What do we do next?" Tia inquired, politely refusing a second helping of the main dish. "Where can we go?"

"How many days' walking does it take to get to your grandfather's holdings in the south?" Mark took the platter from her and ladled a third helping onto his plate. Surviving to fight another day had had a positive effect on his appetite.

"Why?" Rothan wiped his lips with the back of his hand and studied Mark. "How is the length of the journey relevant? We can't go there."

"Word will get to Farahna if we travel home," Tia protested before Mark could answer Rothan's question. "We have to leave Nakhtiaar altogether and live out our lives in some foreign land."

"You'd be welcome to find refuge with my people," Sallea said.

"A kind offer, which I may well accept, although I loathe the inglorious end to our plans." Rothan leaned against the wall of the dwelling, sipping at his beer.

"There was nothing wrong with your original plan," Mark said. "The rightful King of Nakhtiaar needs to sit on the throne, not Farahna. Having seen her for myself, I pity the country that has to live under her rule."

"There *is* no rightful king, as you put it, left." Rothan sounded as if he were explaining something to a small child. He reached in front of Tia to snag a tidbit of cheese. "Hutenen was the last of his line. There's no other."

Mark sighed. The answer was obvious to him. "There's you."

The Nakhtiaar in the hut were silent. He got the impression his proposal stunned the audience, except for Sallea, who nodded as if the idea made sense to her.

Sandy also agreed with Mark's point, turning in her seat to stare at Rothan. "You told us your mother was in the direct line, a sister of the last true king."

"And besides those facts," Mark continued with what he felt to be irrefutable logic, "your wife is Hutenen's only sibling, right?"

"Yes," said Rothan and Tia in unison.

"So who better to sit the throne than the two of you?" Mark challenged them.

"My father wasn't of the royal blood," Rothan said in protest. "I'm only half royal, and inheritance of the throne doesn't pass through the female line."

"Time to change a few rules." Sandy dipped the crust of her bread into the broth on her plate.

"Alter the rules, restart the game." Mark sat on the edge of his chair, pointing a finger at Sallea. "Your father swore allegiance to Rothan, right? Not Hutenen."

Finishing her wine, the Mikkonite nodded. "By ancient treaty we owe loyalty to whoever rightfully holds the crown. The unseen forces guarding the lost city allowed Rothan to take the crown. Therefore, my father judged him to be king." She grinned. "Of course, he has to seize his kingdom."

Mark smiled at her excellent point. "I'm getting to that. Nakhtiaar has good allies in the Empty Lands." He stabbed his spoon in the air, aimed at Rothan. "You and Hutenen had the same upbringing, you told me, the same training in warfare and statecraft, the same experiences on your two-year expedition. Who pursued the Crown of Khunarum? And who found it, against all odds? Hutenen may have been a great person, but he didn't think on the grand scale of what would be best for the country. You did. If he was alive, I wouldn't argue against your sworn allegiance to the man. But he's dead. And we're still here, left to deal with the realities of the situation. Who has more right to sit on the throne, to rule? You or Farahna? Who has the best interests of these people at heart? You? Or that murderous bitch who can't wait to hand the country over to her Maiskhan allies?"

"The Warrior of the Star Wind speaks truth," Djed agreed vehemently. "You must listen to him, sir."

"Indeed," Lieutenant Khefer chimed in. "These are words of deep wisdom. It shouldn't require outsiders to make us see the situation so clearly."

Sandy spoke again. "The responsibility for an entire nation can be a crushing burden. But I think Mark's point is valid. Who else can be king? If you can name one other legitimate candidate, then we'll take the Crown of Khunarum to him or her, and leave you to find what peace you can achieve in exile with Tia."

Rothan stared from one to the next, the comments coming too thick and fast for him to get a word in edgewise until Sandy stopped speaking. He slammed his fist on the table. "Never did I seek to gain the throne. I swear to you, my loyalty, my concern was all for Hutenen."

"We know the truth well, my lord," Djed said. "But the situation is altered."

"Is there anyone else to lead the fight against Farahna? Any other potential leader of a rebellion?" Mark asked the company at large. "Anywhere in Nakhtiaar?"

There was silence. Khefer and Djed shook their heads. The cousin and his chief wife stayed quiet. Mark gazed at Rothan. "There you have it. Either you step up to the challenge, or your country falls into the hands of Farahna's Maiskhan allies while you learn to ride horses in the Empty Lands and your child is born in permanent exile. What's it to be?"

"The crown itself will tell us." Tia, usually so quiet, surprised them all with her fervent declaration. "Give me the case, if you please."

Mark, who'd kept the box close-by during their escape from the valley, placed it into her outstretched hands.

Sandy moved aside the plates and serving dishes on the rough table where their dinner had been set. Tia put the chest down. Taking a deep breath, she slid the hawk-shaped catch open, raising the lid, wincing at the creak of protest from the ancient hinges.

The golden crown was lustrous, whole and restored to its former glory, its large gemstones blinking in the light from the oil lamps.

Somehow, Mark didn't feel any surprise. Not much was going to amaze him after his encounter with Hutenen's ghost and the otherworldly beings in the tomb. Lajollae had sent Sandy and him to a world where strange powers held sway and unimaginable things were possible. He could go with the program.

Tia fell back a step. Even though unboxing the crown had been her idea, she appeared frightened to find the diadem intact. Sandy had no hesitation. She took the Crown of Khunarum from the box. Balancing it on her palms, she pivoted to face Rothan. "Do you take this crown and all the responsibilities it brings? Will you swear to protect and defend the people of this land?"

Rothan's face was set and grim, lines of strain around his eyes. He swallowed. "I will." He moved a step toward her, took the crown in both hands, and placed it on his own head, where the diadem sat as if made for him alone.

"Honor to the king!" Djed went to his knees on the dirt floor of the hut. "Long life and blessings to the new king."

All the Nakhtiaar in the room except Tia knelt and echoed the archer's salutations. Sallea saluted, fist over her heart. "Well done," she said. "This is the time to abandon old traditions of succession and pursue the better alternative."

Rothan laughed, breaking the tension. "Has any king ever had such an odd coronation?" His expression softened. "But with such good and loyal courtiers?" He took off the crown. "Rise, my friends. You do me honor, but it's early days yet for courtly ceremony. We have to get away from here, or else the reign of Rothan the First will be short and inglorious."

"How long to get to your grandfather's holdings?" Mark asked again.

"Two to three weeks' march on foot, as we are." Rothan glanced at Tia. "You shouldn't walk so far in your condition."

"If Your Majesty permits," said Lieutenant Khefer. "I took the liberty of stealing a team of four oxen and a cart. The conveyance and team are out in the stable. I wished for a chariot, of course—"

"Of course." The exchange sounded like an old joke between the two men.

"But I couldn't attract too much attention." Khefer's brown eyes gleamed with amusement, and the dimples in his cheeks deepened. "So oxen it was. At least Lady Tia won't have to walk."

"Excellent. We can take on the guise of spice merchants going to the mountain lands to trade." Rothan rubbed his hands together in anticipation.

"It's the time of year for merchants to travel, peddling their wares," Djed agreed. "No one will suspect, although we're a large group for traders."

"What about the three archers hiding on the *Lady Dawn*?" Leaving anyone behind went against Mark's code as a soldier.

"Demari planned to let them go in a hidden harbor he knows on the coast, since he didn't betray them to the Maiskhan the other night," Sallea said. "I would have taken them with me, but we feared I'd draw too much attention. One nomad warrior traveling alone isn't unknown, Demari told me when I'd argued him to a standstill, especially garbed in concealing robes as I was. Escorted by Nakhtiaar archers? Unwise. Better for us all to go separately."

Rothan said, "Our men will make for the sanctuary of my grandfather's lands. What of the soldiers who followed us from home originally? Hutenen's personal guard?"

Khefer laughed, a bitter edge to his mirth. "Chaos reigned in the palace on the day the concubine came screaming into the throne room. She was hysterical. We all ran to Hutenen's rooms to find him frothing at the mouth, in convulsions on the floor. Farahna and Gaddaf, the Maiskhan commander, were exchanging satisfied—no, gleeful—glances and whispers as the physicians strove in vain to save him. I didn't need to be tapped on the shoulder by the gods to see which way the winds blew. I called our men together in the barracks and spent an hour writing them official leave papers. I sent them off in ones and twos. By now they'll be home. I believed your grandfather could use any and all reinforcements, and our prince had no further need for loyal guards. We'd not been allowed near him for weeks."

Rothan said, "True, which was one reason Tia and I decided we had to go search for the crown. There was nothing else to be done."

"The prince died two days after you left." Lieutenant Khefer's face, usually so cheerful, reflected his grief. "He'd been so ill—"

"But you, what did you do?" Tia asked Khefer. "After you sent our soldiers on their way?"

"There's honor and brotherhood remaining in the Nakhtiaar army, my lady. There were those officers willing to help me, one in particular who took great risk—" Khefer broke off in midsentence. "We can speak of those events later.

Tonight isn't for the naming of names. I hid in the ranks, one anonymous soldier among the many, watching for your return. I hoped I could get to you, Captain—I mean, Your Majesty."

Rothan waved off concerns over his proper title. "Captain will do for now."

"I hoped I could somehow warn you before you confronted Farahna. I've those in the city who were my eyes and ears, who were to let me know if you were sighted."

"Spies? You have a network of spies?" The possibilities immediately appealed to Mark. He appreciated the way this warrior strategized.

"Yes." Khefer stood straighter, chest out with pride. "Never did it occur to me to watch for you by sea. I hadn't anticipated such an eventuality, my lord. I planned to wait till the festival began, for if you'd not come by then, I knew you wouldn't be returning. The gods would have denied your quest. Then I too was going home."

"A good plan and one which we'll carry out, beginning before first light today," Rothan said. "You've done well, Captain Khefer." He laid extra stress on the elevated rank. "There'll be recognition, medals for your service at my earliest opportunity."

"It was my honor, Your Majesty. And I'm grateful for the favor you show this night, promoting this unworthy one to captain." Khefer bowed low before continuing his story. "When I ran into Djed, met Sallea, in the crowd at the palace this morning, I realized things had gone awry."

"So the three of us left the city and came here in search of my cousin," the archer finished. "And you know the rest, my lord."

"We'll need disguises for the trip south," Mark said. "Sandy and I are too noticeable, being so fair-skinned. Everyone outside this room believes we're dead and buried in that tomb. And Sallea with her blue hair stands out as well. The mistaken belief about our deaths is our biggest advantage."

"If not for you, old friend, we'd be dead by now," Rothan said, clapping Djed on the shoulder.

"And the help of my cousin." The archer refused to take all the credit. "And Sallea and Lieutenant—I mean, Captain Khefer."

Rothan spoke to the cousin with gratitude. "I can't reward you adequately now, but I give you my word, you'll be generously rewarded for your assistance at my earliest opportunity in the future."

"To have the king in one's debt is unheard of for a man like me, and beyond price. My honor to be of service." The older man bowed as his wives curtsied. "But you must be well away from here as soon as possible, if I'm to survive and collect my debts."

"My cousin speaks the truth. If we're to be traders, we can't be seen leaving this village, for no trader would ever deign to set foot here," Djed said.

Now that the plan was established, everyone set to work. The grave robber's chief wife brought out a quantity of clothing for them to select from, telling Tia the entire village had donated their wardrobes to outfit the fugitives if necessary. The party wrapped themselves in robes and hooded cloaks, and Sandy took a veil to shield her pale face from close scrutiny if the need arose. Khefer and Djed went to the stable to yoke the quartet of oxen. After some spirited discussion, Sallea accompanied them, pointing out her expertise with animals of all species. The trio brought the cart to the hut's entry.

Rothan guffawed as he caught site of the top-heavy vehicle laden with sacks and jars. "Khefer, my faithful one, you've also stolen a spice merchant's entire inventory for us. Our disguise will be complete. We may even make a profit."

"Yeah, but is someone going to miss all this?" Mark wasn't as happy about the quantity of cargo as he circled the wooden conveyance, staying well out of range of the oxen's horns and hooves. The animals seemed placid enough, but he wasn't familiar with their habits. "Report it stolen? We don't need the authorities searching for a trader's cart and some overattentive guard observing us on the road. There might be awkward questions."

Khefer was all innocence. Showing a guileless face appeared to be a particular talent of the young officer's. "It seems, my lords and ladies, a grievous fire broke out in the trade warehouses by the harbor today. Much was lost in the way of trade goods, and the terrified horses and oxen scattered to the four winds as the stables burned."

"We don't carry a cargo entirely given over to spices." Djed lifted a few sacks out of the way and revealed a cache of knives and swords, and one bow, which he slung over his own shoulder. He plucked a small bundle from the hiding place and partially unwrapped it, holding his prize out to Mark. "I've something for you, my lord."

"You don't know how grateful I am to retrieve this." Marc reached for the blaster and checked the charge level. "The Maiskhan are never going to see me surrender again, word of a Denaltieri *bogatyr*," he said to Sandy as he holstered the weapon and buckled the belt. Grinning at Rothan, he added, "Farahna and her lap dog Gaddaf better stay out of my way."

Rothan took his pick of the swords and belted it on. "Much better to be armed and able to fight, I agree. Let's proceed with this journey."

Mark took two knives to replace his lost Special Forces blade, refusing the swords as being too unfamiliar. "I learned to fence as a boy, but with much more slender blades than your soldiers use," he told Rothan. "I can do more damage with weapons I understand, and in hand-to-hand combat." He patted his blaster, riding at his hip. "This is weapon enough for me."

"When we reach my grandfather's province, I'll arrange sword lessons for you, and in turn, you can teach me these other techniques you speak of," Rothan said.

As dawn broke, they were well on their way along the road leading away from the capital city, headed south at the best pace the team of oxen could or would manage. Mark estimated the animals could cover a couple of miles in a standard hour, maybe ten miles a day. Nowhere near as fast as horses would be, but on the other hand, the sturdy beasts demonstrated endless endurance.

After leaving the valley of tombs along a twisting back road, remaining undetected, the route they had to follow took them past the colossal temple the Maiskhan were constructing to their own gods, using Nakhtiaar slave labor. Mark felt an icy trickle between his shoulder blades the entire time it took their slow team to plod past the turnoff to the place. Even this early in the morning, he saw gangs of men working on the stone terraces set upon a giant, reinforced earthen mound. He pitied the prisoners, hoping as many as possible would remain alive by the time Rothan brought an army from the mountains to liberate the country and its people.

Sandy and Tia were drowsing on the cart, cushioned by the sacks of spices. Khefer guided the team, Sallea perched beside him on the wagon's rude seat. Lakht soared high above. Mark and Djed walked a few paces behind the cart before Mark realized Rothan had fallen even farther behind them. Their companion halted at the crossroads they'd passed a few moments ago and stared to the east.

"Hey, wait." Mark touched Djed's shoulder. "We've lost Rothan."

The archer followed Mark's gaze. "His Majesty," he said with extra emphasis, "does as he wishes, my lord."

"Royal protocol be damned, I'm going to keep him company. I know he's a fine warrior, but there's too much riding on his shoulders for us to leave him alone and unguarded." Mark jogged down the road to where Rothan stood.

When he reached his friend's side, Mark didn't say anything, but waited to see if Rothan intended to redirect their journey. He stood guard, scanning in all directions, blaster in hand.

At length, the new king sighed. "Do you know what lies over the horizon at the end of the road?" he asked Mark without lifting his gaze away from the other, empty thoroughfare.

"No idea."

"The Temple of Dendke, where the ceremony of the Golden Dawn will be held in a week's time. Where false Queen Farahna will again accept tribute, dispense her brand of twisted justice, worship the gods, the Maiskhan gods as well no doubt—" Now, eyebrows raised, Rothan studied Mark. "I know you were skeptical about the power of the crown."

Grinning, Mark said, "Hey, I was allowed to be skeptical before the magic trick right under my eyes. Pretty impressive, going from perfection to tarnished trash for Farahna's benefit. And then transmuting into treasure for you. I'm a believer now."

"Perhaps the crown would have done what I hoped, perhaps Hutenen could have used it to reclaim the throne. But now we'll never know."

Mark kept quiet, sensing Rothan had more to say.

A moment later, his companion continued sharing his thoughts. "If only Hutenen had seized the moment a year ago when we first marched home triumphant from the expedition. I think we might have been able to unseat Farahna. There were many in the army then still loyal to the proper order of things, many in the priesthood and the government unsure of her new claims to divinity. She'd not yet brought in more than a few of her Maiskhan dogs. The balance swung undecided for a majority of our people."

"But?"

"Hutenen wouldn't act. He hesitated. He wanted to negotiate with her, to ascend the throne in an orderly fashion. He wanted her to admit her wrongdoing. Being so stubborn was his undoing. It gave her time to consolidate power, all the while saying honey-sweet things to him, things he wanted to hear, to believe. She—she fascinated him, ever since we were boys. She was his father's last, youngest wife, you know. Decades younger than the king. Vastly more clever than any of his other wives. She took influential men as her lovers even when her husband lived. Led each to believe he was her chosen one to sit on the throne with her. She played them against each other for her favors—priests, generals, lords of the kingdom. Nothing is too twisted for her if it helps her keep control. Murder has long been rumored to be a favorite tool, and now we know the truth of the accusation since she poisoned my prince to get him out of her way." Rothan's hand clenched on the hilt of his sword. "When we marched home to find the illegal situation Farahna had created, he should have struck her down at her first blasphemous words about the gods giving her the right to rule."

Mark had no doubt Rothan would have taken direct action against Farahna if he'd been in charge.

They strolled toward the oxcart, which Khefer had stopped, waiting to see what the orders would be.

"I went to get Hutenen the Crown and the Scepter to instill in his heart the courage and decisiveness of Khunarum," Rothan said as he and Mark walked. "Tia thinks we were after the artifacts to cure the physical poison, but I wanted them to cure him in spirit and resolve."

"The crown may have magical properties, as you and I saw clearly during the audience with Farahna," Mark answered. "But it can't awaken the attributes of a king in the heart of a man who didn't possess the raw material. Hutenen wasn't you. He didn't have your strength."

"Will it be enough?" Rothan stopped again, rolling his shoulders. "When I wore the crown in the grave robber's hut, I felt no different than I do this moment, wearing nothing on my head but the hood of this humble merchant's garb." He glanced at Mark, eyes narrowed. "I admit this to you alone, because you helped me take the crown from Khunarum, but it brings me no extra power, no secret knowledge."

"You're the right man at the right time, and you know what you have to do. You're human, like the rest of us, crown or no crown. You're going to win this war, if it can be won, and we're all going to work hard to make it happen. We'll do the best we can, fight as hard and as smart as we know how, and then fate is out of our hands," Mark said, answering from his heart. "Unlike Hutenen, you have the guts to take on the challenge, to try to save your people and your country. Farahna and her Maiskhan don't fool or intimidate you."

"Nor you!" His expression lightening, Rothan clapped Mark on the shoulder. "You're an ally and a friend beyond price. More valuable in your own way than the Crown of Khunarum."

Ducking his head and giving a self-deprecating chuckle, never one to seek or accept praise easily, Mark said, "Now you're getting carried away."

"We'll see." Rothan lengthened his stride, motioning for Khefer to get the oxen moving again.

"What were you two talking about?" Sandy asked, hopping off the cart to walk hand in hand with Mark. "Is he having second thoughts? Are you?"

He squeezed her hand and hugged her close. "No to both questions. We're well and truly embroiled in a plot to overthrow the queen. I've no idea what's going to happen, but I have confidence in Rothan."

"My faith is based on your abilities," she said, poking a finger at his chest.

"The two of us together," he answered, pulling her close.

"And the mirror." Sandy brought the gleaming artifact from her pocket, examining the handle in the sunlight. "This is important, maybe as crucial to success as the crown." She glanced at him. "I know you're not a believer, but Haatrin told me the mirror could be a powerful weapon in the right hands."

Mark kissed her. "If anyone can convert an old mirror into a magical weapon, it'd be you. You used to love to read all those musty old books about magic and miracles, fairies and elves."

"I'm serious." Frowning, she slid the mirror into her pocket.

"So am I," he said with a laugh. "Come on, slow as the oxen are, the cart is getting ahead of us."

CHAPTER SEVEN

The first night they had to camp at a crowded oasis thronged with caravans and smaller groups of travelers. Khefer directed their cart to a spot at the fringe of the gathering under a scrubby palm tree and stood, rubbing the forehead of the lead ox while the group conferred in a loose circle around him.

"While it doesn't make me happy to be around so many people," Mark said, "there's some safety in the sheer numbers. What's the protocol here?"

"Set up a cooking fire, put out our sleeping mats. We can keep to ourselves, and no one will remark on the behavior." Rothan was calm. "Spice traders are known to be standoffish due to the value of their wares. Lucky for us, there don't appear to be any other members of the guild here. They might recognize our cart, or wish to socialize, and our disguise won't stand up to close scrutiny by experts." He looked apologetic as he made his next remark. "The women will have to go fetch the water for the beasts and us from the central well."

"Not by themselves." Mark's protest was immediate.

"You and Djed can go along as guards, but don't touch the water jars or buckets yourself. That would draw attention, as spice guildsmen never haul water if their wives are present. Khefer will procure fodder for the oxen, and Sallea and I'll stay with the cart, unload the necessities." The king assigned a role to everyone.

Mark found it telling that Rothan included Sallea among the warriors, not the water-fetching women. True, the Mikkonite was dressed like a man, wore a sword, and had her telltale blue hair hidden under complicated cloth headgear. Sandy murmured a similar observation to him as they walked behind Djed and Tia toward the center of the activity, where the Nakhtiaar had told them the well would be.

"I find it amusing," she said as they joined the tail end of a long line queued for the water, "that the queen and the Outlier princess are the ones with the clay jars and wooden buckets, hauling water. A nice reminder not to think too much of myself. I suppose we'll have to make several trips—the oxen must be thirsty after pulling the cart all day."

He was glad she was taking their mundane assignment in stride. Scanning his surroundings, he realized he and Djed were the only men in the vicinity. They were getting a lot of attention and some catcalls from the other women, which was unfortunate, but he wasn't letting Sandy walk around this oasis full of people without him. Djed seemed to be taking it all in stride, exchanging bold glances and winks with more than one woman, even as he kept his hand on his sword.

It took three trips to the well before the water detail was accomplished. They ate a sparse dinner around their small campfire and stretched out on mats laid between the cart and the tree. Sandy fell asleep at once, her head pillowed on his shoulder. Mark lay awake, listening to the clamor of the busy oasis—music, people singing and arguing, animals bellowing—reflecting on how different this world was from anywhere in the Sectors where he'd spent much time. The raw energy and the possibilities for change here appealed to him.

They'd divided the night into watches, and his was the last before dawn. Rothan wanted to be on the road again as early as possible, hoping not to be trapped behind a long caravan. Breakfast was rushed, and then they were on their way. The day was uneventful but nerve-racking, as Maiskhan patrols passed them more than once.

"Looking for us?" Mark asked as the most recent set of chariots thundered past in a cloud of dust.

"I doubt it," Rothan answered.

"You trust the grave robbers' village to keep our secret?" Mark glanced at Djed, speaking quietly enough so the archer wouldn't hear.

"I do. Betraying our secret reveals their own and destroys their livelihood. They'd never trust Farahna—she's killed too many of the tomb workers, who are also their extended family members. I think the Maiskhan are tightening their grip on the entire country, patrolling the caravan routes, probably getting ready to assess tolls and taxes once they're more fully in control of Nakhtiaar." Eyes narrowed as he considered, Rothan rubbed his chin. "I might go trade some spices for better foodstuffs, try talking to some of the caravan workers in the process at the next oasis tonight, get a sense of how they feel about the Maiskhan, what they're seeing as they traverse Nakhtiaar."

"Good idea, intel is always valuable. Just be careful not to arouse their suspicions by asking too many probing questions while you improve our diet," Mark said with a grin.

The oxcart slowed and stopped, Khefer pulling the team to the side of the road, leaving room for caravans or other travelers to safely pass.

Hand on his blaster, Mark jogged to the front of the cart. "Why are we stopping?"

Khefer handed the reins to Sallea and climbed from his driver's seat. "I think the left leader has something wrong with his hoof. His pace is off."

"Because the pace is so blistering," Mark muttered.

The officer heard the remark. Pausing, he said, "These animals are doing their best for us and deserve our care in return, my lord."

"Even if they're not pulling a chariot." Rothan's remark was made in a jovial tone. Breaking into a smile, Khefer nodded and proceeded on his way.

"What is it with all these references to Khefer and chariots?" Mark asked as he and the other two men took up positions between the cart and the passersby on the road. "Seems like an old joke that I'm not getting."

"Khefer is mad for horses and speed, has been since he was a boy," Rothan said, accepting a cup of water from Tia.

"He stole a chariot when he was about six," the queen added, waiting while her husband slaked his thirst. "Managed to drive it quite a way before his father caught up in another chariot and ordered him to halt. No amount of punishment could induce him to say he was sorry."

Wiping his mouth on his sleeve, Rothan nodded. "Even as a boy, he was the best judge of horses in my grandfather's province and won many a race against those who thought themselves his betters because they were older. He refuses to walk anywhere if there's a chariot and a road." He waved one hand at the dusty thoroughfare in front of them. "Yet here we are on a road, and he's driving stolid oxen, of all creatures."

"Riding the horse is better," Sallea said from her perch on the wagon's bench.

Mark nodded. "I'm in agreement with her—cavalry is the way of the future."

"We'd have a heated debate on the point, my lord, if this was the right time and place," Khefer said, patting the brown and white ox on the flank as the animal turned its horned head to carefully nuzzle his shoulder. "All set, just a pebble. Shall we continue?"

"By all means." Rothan stepped into the road to create an opening for the cart to move into the flow of travelers journeying south. "I want to get to my grandfather's stronghold in the mountains before the first snow falls."

Khefer frowned. "As we're only in midsummer, sir, I think we can meet that schedule easily."

"He's just casting more aspersions on your oxen," Sallea said, digging Khefer in the ribs as he climbed to sit beside her and took the reins. "My advice is to prove him wrong."

Mark would have preferred to avoid the crowded oases and camp somewhere more private each night. He felt the chances of discovery were unnecessarily high, but when he raised the issue to Rothan, the king made it clear they had no choice. "The only water along the caravan routes is at these stops. We can't carry enough for ourselves and the oxen to camp anywhere else. Eventually, we'll be leaving the track and setting off to the west, toward the mountains and home. Few journey there, as my grandfather's province is quite self-sufficient, not much trade to be done."

Mark eyed his friend. "But?"

"There are rumored to be bandits among those who traverse the main roads here. They might find a party like ours enticing prey, with our women and our spices. We'll have to be doubly vigilant the first few days we travel the more isolated track."

Mark kept the conversation firmly in mind as they continued on their way south. He didn't notice anyone tailing them or paying undue attention, not even in the caravans they passed or the ones that overtook them during the trek. Their group inevitably made some acquaintances among the people traveling in their direction, women they'd stand in line with at every well and a few caravan workers. Sandy provided medical care here and there, under protest from Mark, who worried about revealing their secret. She went heavily veiled, with him standing guard, limiting herself to remedies that were effective but wouldn't seem too miraculous. She kept the mirror concealed in its pouch at her belt at all times.

He was glad to see the landscape becoming greener and more welcoming as the days passed on the trek farther south. Finally, the day came that Rothan, Khefer, and Djed conferred before directing the oxcart off the main road and onto a smaller track that led west toward the foothills and the imposing, snow-capped mountain range beyond.

After an hour or so of walking, Sandy pushed her hood back, revealing her blond hair and pale skin. Running her hand through her hair, she sighed with a happy smile. "No more need for concealment. I'm so tired of this set of clothing. Maybe we can even take a bath somewhere."

"There will be small lakes and streams," Tia promised from where she lay on the cart. The queen was having a rough time with her pregnancy and rarely left the cart to walk. "Cold water from the mountains but fit for bathing." She stretched. "Once we reach our home, there will be hot baths and clean clothes again."

"And beds, in bedrooms," Sandy said, giving Mark a wink.

He felt his cheeks growing a bit flushed, but could he help it if he chafed at the lack of opportunities to deepen the physical relationship with his beloved? The time to stroll and talk without interruption was a rare gift after so many years apart, but fueled the fire of his passion for Sandy.

Rothan nodded. "All the comforts of my grandfather's palace will be welcome."

"How much longer till we arrive?" Mark said.

"Several weeks," was Khefer's discouraging answer.

They camped beside a small stream, and for once there was no need to haul water anywhere, nor to collect fodder for the oxen, who contentedly grazed in the lush grassland around the campsite. Djed took his bow and arrow to hunt, returning with some kind of small antelope, which he dressed and roasted over the fire, seasoned with their finest purloined spices. The evening felt like a celebration. Even Lakht seemed content, perched on a large tree branch, dining on entrails Djed had set aside for him.

Rothan raised his mug of wine. "A toast to exceptional comrades!"

Mark drank and even proposed a toast of his own, but he couldn't relax. Unease pricked at him, as if they were being watched. With a murmured apology to Sandy, he slipped away from the fire, speaking to Khefer, who stood guard, and then prowling through the nearby grassland and rock outcroppings, but he found no evidence of pursuit. When he eventually returned to the circle, she gave him a quizzical glance, eyebrows raised, but he shook his head. Leaning on his shoulder, she gazed at the night sky.

"Tresa is on the ascendant now," she said, pointing at the reddish moon beginning to peek above the horizon. "She was the most unpleasant of the sisters."

He wrapped her cloak more securely around her shoulders as a breeze sprang up. "Are you concerned?"

"I don't like her ruling the sky over me," Sandy admitted. "Any of the other moons and I'm fine, but I feel like Tresa brings bad luck." She shivered. "This is the safest part of the journey, right? So what harm can her influence do?"

Mark smiled, but in the back of his mind he remembered Rothan's warning that if brigands were going to attack, it would be in the first day or two after leaving the safety of the caravan route.

"The Moon Sisters aren't as powerful as the mirror," Tia said from her position on the other side. "And Tresa is the weakest of them."

"Which would be more comforting if I could make the damn mirror work," Sandy whispered in Mark's ear.

"We've got our blasters."

But the night passed uneventfully, as did the second day of travel. Mark continued to feel uneasy, doubling back more than once to check the trail behind them, without finding anything untoward. He still went to sleep with his blaster close at hand.

Close to dawn, he woke to Sallea's hand over his mouth. "Lakht has seen men circling, coming to attack," she whispered, releasing him.

"How many?" He turned to rouse Sandy as carefully as Sallea had wakened him.

"Twenty. Rothan thinks several gangs may have banded together, as we're such a rich target."

Sword in hand, she moved away.

Mark and Sandy crept after her, joining their fellow travelers behind the wagon, which Khefer had parked in a small grove of trees the night before.

"Plan?" Mark asked Rothan.

"Too many for us to attack them. I'm thinking we take the high ground, place the women there." Rothan pointed at the trees above them.

Bow slung over his back, Djed was already climbing nimbly to find a perch from which he could shoot.

Mark nodded. "Good plan. I'm going to try to outflank them, take out a few before the battle begins. Keep Sandy safe."

He kissed her, then slunk through the trees into the tall grass beyond, moving slowly. Pausing at the small creek, he smeared his face with mud so he would be less visible, and then set out to track the enemy. He drew one knife as he went. The blaster would be too noisy, alerting the bandits to the fact that their attack was no longer a surprise. Mark grinned. Aerial surveillance—Lakht, in this case—was always a soldier's secret advantage. He found the last man on the loose circle of enemies around their campsite, crept up from behind, and silently slashed the thug's throat. Moving on, he managed to kill two more before their leader gave some unseen signal, and the remaining bandits moved from their hiding spots, brandishing weapons, yelling curses, and charged the wagon.

Drawing his blaster, Mark saw several of Djed's arrows hit their targets while he himself was picking picked off five more men in quick succession. Then the battle became too close, hand to hand, as the ten surviving attackers launched themselves at Rothan, Khefer, and Sallea. Lakht came screaming from the sky to tangle with a man trying to assault Sallea from the side. Mark sprinted into the thick of the fray, stabbing and slashing as he went, reducing the odds against the defenders. With relief, he realized Sandy and Tia had climbed or been boosted into the safety of a tree, where Sandy now used her civilian blaster to kill a man attempting to reach them.

Djed fired a few more arrows before dropping to the ground, tackling one of several opponents concentrating on Rothan.

Mark stabbed another in the back, his blow glancing off a sturdy leather vest and slicing the man's sword arm. The assailant spun, sword flashing in the pearly predawn light, as he sought to kill Mark. Catching the blade with the reinforced, curved guard of his knife and diverting the thrust, Mark fired his blaster with the other hand. The man crumpled to the dirt. Mark was grabbed unexpectedly from behind, and his reflexes kicked in. He stabbed upward into the attacker's chest, threw him to the ground, kicking him savagely as he attempted to rise, and finished him with a short burst from the blaster.

Taking in huge breaths, he retrieved his knife and wheeled, ready to take on any remaining bandits, but his companions had finished off the rest. Lakht went screaming triumphantly into the sky in a show of acrobatic aerodynamics. Mark surveyed the other men and Sallea. "Everyone okay? Anyone hurt?"

Sandy dropped from the tree, landing lightly on her feet. "Let me get my bag, and I can treat any injuries."

Concerned, he moved to her side. "Are you sure you're okay? I saw you shoot that guy. Well done, by the way."

She leaned on him for a moment. "I was defending Tia. And myself. I can live with what I did."

He wasn't entirely convinced, but realizing how many adventures and dire situations she'd been through on this journey, he understood she'd become more hardened, to a degree, than she'd been on Freemarket. As she rummaged through their belongings on the cart, he looked at Rothan. "What do you want us to do with the bodies?"

Holding a rag to his bleeding arm, the king spat, "We leave them where they fell, for the scavengers and the demons. Scum like these men deserve nothing better."

Sandy's eyes were wide, but she withheld comment as she went to work cleaning and bandaging the deep slash on Rothan's sword arm.

Mark was fine with the decision, but concerned over something else. "I'm going to backtrack, make sure there aren't any more following our trail."

"I'll send Lakht to fly cover for you," Sallea said as she and Djed helped the queen to descend from the tree.

"Thanks, I appreciate the reinforcements. That's some ally you've got." Mark shielded his eyes with one hand, gazing into the sky where Lakht wheeled effortlessly.

"We'll be moving out as soon as Khefer gets the oxen harnessed," Rothan said. "We can eat journeycake and dried meat strips as we hike today."

"No problem. I'll catch up." With one more glance at Sandy to reassure himself she was holding up, he jogged to the east, swerving under cover in the grasslands as he reconnoitered.

Finding no one else following their trail, Mark rejoined the group a few hours later. The road was beginning to climb into the foothills, so the going was harder.

The oxen showed no distress, but Sallea mentioned having a headache, and Tia was short of breath.

"We're at a higher altitude," Sandy said. "Fortunately, we're going so slowly our bodies will have time to adjust."

"My grandfather's capital sits on a plateau high in the mountains," Rothan told her.

"Those of you who grew up there have an advantage, but the rest of us should be fine after a day or so." She squeezed Mark's hand. "The human body is very adaptable."

"Do you think Tresa is done with us?" he asked, smiling to show he was teasing.

Sandy frowned, not answering his grin. "She has a few turns left in the night sky. And we have days of journeying ahead." Lifting the pouch containing the mirror, she said, "If I ever figure out how to tap into the power of this, even Tresa will give us a wide berth and be tame."

Two days later, as they toiled up a steep grade, the bad luck of Tresa reached out for them again. Part of the roadway crumbled under the wagon. With a sharp crack that echoed through the mountain pass, the right wheel broke, and the wagon lurched toward the precipice. Luckily, Sandy and Tia had been hiking, not riding, as a few of the bags of spices went hurtling into the void. Khefer maintained an iron grip on Sallea at his side to prevent her from falling while he urged the oxen to drag the cart a few more feet to a wider spot in the road.

"Hold the cart, quickly," he yelled.

Mark, Rothan, and Djed hastened to grab at the wagon's side, pulling it upright again, although it tilted a bit on the broken wheel. Face white, lip bleeding a little where she'd bitten it, Sallea climbed across Khefer and jumped to the ground, steadied by Mark. She spun on her heel to watch Khefer dismount from the driver's seat.

Breathing hard, the group stood staring at the wagon. Tia sank onto a convenient rock. "What do we do now?"

Sandy shook her head. "I don't want you walking any more than you already have, if we can help it." She shot a glance at Rothan. "She's in enough physical distress as it is with the pregnancy and the altitude."

"Can we repair the wheel?" Mark asked.

Giving the reins to Sallea, Khefer gestured at Djed, and the two men edged carefully along the right side of the wagon to examine the spoked wooden hoop. "I think we can probably do a temporary fix, using wood from the cart itself to reinforce the cracked spokes, get where we're going," Khefer said.

As he finished speaking, the right rear ox gave a gusty sigh and collapsed onto the road in a heap. Sallea and Khefer both ran to the animal, the latter running his hand over the ox's heaving flank while Sallea rubbed its forehead and spoke in a soothing tone. Lowing softly, the ox flicked its ears.

Khefer looked at Sandy. "Can you help, my lady?"

"I'm not an animal doctor," Sandy said, moving to kneel in the dust beside the stricken creature. "But I'll see what I can do."

Lakht landed on the wagon with a whoosh and surveyed the downed ox, head tilted, eyes gleaming. Sallea sat back on her heels. Glancing at Khefer, she said hesitantly, "Lakht believes the animal is done."

Sandy lifted the small scanner she'd been using away from the ox's side. "I think its heart is giving out." She ran one hand along the rough coat. "Poor thing."

"So we fix the wheel and perhaps we lighten the load. We can manage with three oxen," Rothan said. "I'd abandon the cart altogether, but we have a few days' march ahead of us, and we need the supplies. Not to mention the issue of my wife not being able to walk so far."

"I don't want my problems to cost these animals their lives." Tia wiped away tears.

Rising, Sandy made quick work of scanning the other three beasts of burden standing patiently nearby. "I don't detect any distress. They should be fine. I think the one we're losing might have been older."

"Yes," Khefer said, beginning to unbuckle the harness on the downed ox. "I had very little time to pick and choose that night, or I'd have left this one in the city and taken another."

Mark moved to help Djed with freeing the wooden yoke from the fallen animal and unhooking the rest of the team from the cart. The archer led them up the trail a short way and fastened the reins to a scrubby tree.

Rothan placed a hand on Khefer's shoulder. "The ox has given good and loyal service, my friend, but we need to make our repairs and move on."

Mark turned to Sandy. "Can you end its suffering? Something in your bag?"

"I've been thinking what I might use," she said, pushing her hair off her face. "I don't believe it's in pain, which is a blessing."

Sallea held up one hand. "I can do this." She looked at Khefer. "I will do this, for you. I can see your heart bleeds for the creature, and I want to end the sorrow for you both." Changing her posture to sit cross-legged, Sallea rested one hand, palm down, on the ox's forehead and closed her eyes. She chanted almost under her breath in Mikkonite, extending her free hand to Khefer. He wrapped both of his around her fingers and bowed his head. The ox heaved a great sigh and closed its luminous brown eyes, a moment later going still.

Khefer helped Sallea to her feet, arm around her waist, escorting her to a place next to a small tree. Sighing, she leaned against the trunk and slid to sit. "I gave the animal our thanks and told it to lay down its burdens," she said, voice thready.

Mark brought her the waterskin. "Well done."

Khefer knelt to assist her with drinking since her hands were shaking. "I owe you, my lady warrior."

Mark left the two alone and rejoined Rothan and Djed. "Shall we get on with the repairs? We'll have to modify the harness for three animals now as well."

Rothan glanced at Khefer and Sallea. "I'll be glad when this journey is done."

"Amrell takes the sky tonight," Sandy said from her spot next to Tia. "As long as we arrive at your grandfather's home under her watchful scrutiny, we'll be fine."

As he started unloading sacks of spice from the listing cart, Mark hoped she was right.

Three days later, Mark faced closed gates, but with a sense of relief tempered by impatience. The large wooden portal in front of him was set into towering stone walls, anchored with metal hinges. Cautionary phrases warning off intruders, he surmised, were painted in red on the surface. Guards stared down from above, bows drawn, arrows nocked, at the ready.

"Is this the only way into your grandfather's territory?" Mark walked a few paces to the left in the area where the guards had told them to wait, admiring the workmanship of the wall builders. The giant cut stones comprising the walls fit together without mortar. There were no discernible cracks or obvious weaknesses.

"Yes, without going overland for hundreds of miles and trekking through dense jungle," Rothan answered. "What's taking them so long?"

"We've sent for the officer of the guard," one archer yelled as Rothan stood, hands on hips, regarding those on the ramparts with a frown. "General Intef closed the borders of our land to all from the north."

"You'll be on your way down the mountain within the hour." Another soldier laughed derisively.

"We've no need of spices," yelled a third. "You can leave the women, though."

Reaching for his sword, Khefer cursed. Rothan held his arm. "Patience. Once we're inside, out of the world's view, I'll make myself known."

"The louts insult you and your queen," Khefer said.

"These men have no way to know who we are. I'm not pleased by the lack of discipline, however. I'll have to deal with the issue at the proper time."

"How are you going to persuade the officer in charge to let us enter? If you don't want to reveal yourself yet?" Tiring of his scrutiny of the walls, Mark walked to the oxcart and perched on the tail next to Sandy.

"I'm hoping the commandant will be someone known to me. If not, I'll announce my identity as a last resort."

A small door set into the great gate creaked open. An officer in a crisp blue tunic and black leather pants, wearing a golden helmet with a blue horsehair crest, marched out, four archers at his back.

"Ah, good. Nemiah." Rothan recognized the officer. "We trained together." He moved forward, Mark and Khefer at his shoulders. Djed and Sallea stayed with the oxen and the cart.

"I regret to inform you our borders are closed, merchant," the officer said, much as his men on the wall had stated, but with more courtesy. "You'll have to turn those beasts around and retrace your route."

Rothan pushed the hood of his robe away from his face. "Don't you know me? We drank enough cheap wine together in better times."

The officer did a double take, face going white under his tan. He retreated a few steps. "Are you real? Or a ghost?"

"A man of flesh and blood, gods be praised. I don't want the entire border to know I'm here. Permit me to enter the gate while you send for my grandfather and my mother?"

Nemiah saluted. "Of course, Captain, at once. But we heard you'd died."

"Greatly exaggerated. I doubt you can believe any news coming from the north these days." Rothan grinned.

A few rapid orders from Rothan's old comrade, and the gates swung wide. Khefer prodded the stolid oxen into motion. The party walked into the border fort, gates closing behind them. At the solid sound, Mark took a deep breath, relieved, knowing he and Sandy had arrived at last in a place where neither Farahna nor her Maiskhan allies could touch them. He glanced over at Sandy, who smiled. His princess had courage to spare, but even she'd been pushed to her limit by their slow oxcart-enabled escape.

Nemiah took them to his quarters.

"If you and your party can wait here, my lord," he said, tone deferential but firm, "I'll notify General Intef and Princess Sharesi."

"Have you parchment or a tablet? And a writing instrument? I must send my grandfather a note with your courier." Rothan gazed at the small desk against one wall. "He'll be skeptical of this news."

The requested items were brought. Rothan scrawled bold, intricate characters across the scroll he was given, periodically dipping the quill into the ink. Watching his friend concentrate on the note gave Mark uncomfortable flashbacks to the scene he'd been a reluctant part of weeks ago, in what he felt sure was the Nakhtiaar version of the underworld. After sanding the ink to dry it, Rothan rolled the parchment onto a cylinder, sealing the communication with wax spilled from the candle on the table and the imprint of his signet ring.

Nemiah took the scroll, stowing it in a pouch at his belt. "I'll carry this myself. The errand will be my privilege, sir. Can I order the servants to bring you anything while you wait?"

"We ate on the road at the noon hour, thank you. But we're parched from waiting in the sun outside the gates. Wine would be excellent."

"Juice or water for Tia." Ever the watchful doctor, Sandy interrupted the conversation.

"At once." The border officer saluted and left the room.

Tired, Mark sat cross-legged on the floor, leaving the bunk for Tia and Sandy. He'd seen more of this planet, up close and marching across it, than he'd ever seen of any other world in his entire career. The novelty of hiking through the terrain, versus flying over it, wore off early in the trip. As he'd told Sandy more than once during their journey south, what he now missed most from their previous life was air transport. He envied Lakht.

"How long till your grandfather gets here?" he asked Rothan.

"An hour, maybe a bit longer. The main city where he resides lies south of the border. I'm glad he's not on his annual tour of the territory. My appearance will be complicated enough without him being absent." Rothan laughed at his own understatement. "We've one final, brief trek, through the pass and onto the plateau. Have some wine, relax. I think you've been on guard day and night without ceasing while we were on the road. Try to tell me there was a single night you slept with both eyes shut."

"Merely being cautious in case Farahna somehow learned of our escape." Taking the proffered wineskin, Mark knocked back a long swallow of the wine. "We weren't in a good position to evade capture or fight off a Maiskhan attack. Not on the open road. Chariots could have overtaken us any time."

"My oxen did their best." Khefer's weary retort came immediately.

Mark grinned to take the sting from his criticism. "I'm grateful to the beasts. Doesn't mean I ever want to see them again. Give me a good saddle horse."

"True words," Sallea said, holding out her hand for the wineskin.

She and the men continued the desultory conversation on the merits of chariots versus cavalry, more to pass the time than anything else. Sandy kept watch over Tia, drowsing on the cot with her head pillowed in the Outlier woman's lap. Sallea sat on the floor beside Khefer, leaning on his shoulder. Finally, Mark heard trumpets blaring from the fort's courtyard.

Moments later, the door flew open, hitting the wall with enough force to dent the panel. Mark was on his feet, blaster half drawn before he realized the guards streaming in were the advance force of Rothan's family.

Princess Sharesi entered the room behind the soldiers, a tall, austere woman in fine linen robes and tiers of golden necklaces, her long white hair elaborately dressed with jeweled pins. The resemblance between her and Rothan was unmistakable. As Rothan and Tia embraced the princess, General Intef strode into the chamber. The women were both weeping. Rothan broke free of his mother's clinging arms and stepped away, saluting his grandfather. "I've come home, sir."

General Intef answered the salute. "Long overdue. But welcome." He clapped Rothan on the shoulder. "And you brought Lieutenant Khefer and Chief Archer Djed as well, I see."

"But how?" said Sharesi, not releasing her grip on Tia's hand. "This is a true miracle, beyond comprehension, beyond even praying for, but I must know all the details!"

Rothan laughed, giving her a hug. "We'll explain, I promise. First, let me introduce several people to whom we owe much." He gestured to Mark, Sandy, and Sallea, who'd withdrawn from the family reunion. "This is the Lady of the Star Wind, Alessandra, and her warrior, Mark. I owe them my life, Tia's life—much more than I can ever repay. And Lady Sallea is the ambassador from the Mikkonite. Her father rules in the Empty Lands."

General Intef assessed them coolly, nodding as Mark saluted. "You're welcome to my province."

Princess Sharesi chimed in with less reserve in her voice. "But of course we're delighted to have you here. This is amazing. The men Lieutenant Khefer sent home told us rumors of a wild journey to find the city of Khunarum. I gather from the presence of Lady Sallea, the ambassador from the Empty Lands, you had a measure of success?"

"Indeed. Lord Mark saved my life in the lost city. The circumstances are a tale worth telling. But there's something else of higher priority, Grandfather, Mother." Rothan glanced at Tia for corroboration of his claim, and she gave him a tiny smile of encouragement.

"We're aware of Hutenen's death." Sharesi wiped away a tear, smearing her eye makeup. Mark remembered Rothan had said she'd raised the late prince along with her own son. "Sad tidings."

"The official report stated you were entombed with him because you wished to go to the underworld in his company," General Intef said, a question in his tone.

Rothan shook his head, meeting his grandfather's searching look without flinching. "We were entombed at Farahna's command, not by choice."

"Beats dying under the lash," Mark said. "Which was her first choice of death sentence."

"How did you escape, then? No, never mind, we'll discuss the details later." Sharesi waved her hands as if shooing insects away. "You must be exhausted from travel and the dangers you faced. I imagine the journey was hardest for Tia. I see there's to be a child."

"We're man and wife now." Rothan's declaration was simple, heartfelt. "The child will be my heir."

"This calls for a feast of celebration and proper thanks rendered to the Exalted Ones for so many reasons it makes me dizzy to think of it all." The princess gave Tia a hug.

"Followed by serious discussions of strategy in the morning." The general wasn't smiling. "If Farahna learns you're alive, I'm not sure what her reaction will be, but the range of possibilities is grim. We must be prepared."

Rothan laid his hand on the general's arm. "Wait, Grandfather, we've not told you the most important thing."

Brow furrowed in a frown, the general stopped.

"More important than the fact of your survival? More than Tia's pregnancy?" Princess Sharesi asked. "What else can there be to add to this momentous day?"

Rothan gestured to his wife. "My love, may I have the box, please?"

She brought the container, setting it on the table in front of her husband. He took a deep breath and slid the golden lock aside, flipping open the lid, extracting the Crown of Khunarum, and setting it on his bare head. Pivoting on his heel, he faced the staring occupants of the room.

"I am become king."

There was a moment of total silence.

Khefer and Djed knelt.

The general and Rothan locked eyes for a long moment. Mark would have given a great deal to be privy to the rapid thoughts and plans obviously whirling through the older man's mind. General Intef went to one knee a heartbeat later, hand over his heart. "Hail to the king, may the gods be praised!"

Then and only then, Mark observed, did the other men in the room go to their knees and take up the cry. He filed the fact away for the future.

General Intef regained his feet a moment later. "With Your Majesty's permission, we must keep this news quiet while we plan our next steps. The matter is even more urgent now. Farahna will take extreme measures against you once she receives this news. The Maiskhan won't welcome the idea of another legitimate claimant to the throne, either."

He addressed the officers and men who'd accompanied him. "This is not to be spoken of until the king decrees it to be public knowledge. I will have a blood oath on this from each of you. Do you all understand?"

"If it—if it pleases Your Majesty, let us leave this place and go on to the house." Princess Sharesi's voice was faint. Mark wondered if Sandy would have her as a new patient before the end of this family reunion. "A great feast will be prepared in your honor."

"My companions and I have journeyed far, and we're tired," Rothan said. "For tonight, an intimate family dinner is all we can handle, Mother. We'll be pleased to recite the tale of our adventures for you."

"It will be my honor to hear of them." She bowed her head and moved aside for Rothan and Tia to pass ahead of her. She and General Intef followed a pace or so behind.

Mark snagged Djed by the arm as the archer collected the wooden box holding the crown. "Is there going to be this much formality all the time now?"

"No. His Majesty can indicate he's present as a military officer. Then we can all be less constrained by royal protocol." Djed sounded wistful. "He may be more his old self when we're private with him. But he is king now, apart from all men, anointed by the gods, and there's no going back to the older, simpler times. None of us can ever forget his new status." He hefted the box and walked out.

"Thank goodness there's some hope, though, for less pomp all the time. Even your grandmother doesn't insist on all this bowing and scraping," Mark told Sandy as he held the door open for her to follow the archer from the room.

"She would if she knew someone else demanded it." Sandy packed her medical bag. "We'd better hurry, or they'll leave without us. Rothan shook them pretty badly with his announcement."

"Did you see how the locals didn't pay homage till the general made it clear which way he'd go?"

"Rothan taking the crown as his must be a lot for them to absorb," Sandy said, frowning thoughtfully. "But one thing my grandmother always used to say—if you have the key military officers behind you, you sit a secure throne."

Captain Khefer stuck his head through the open doorway. "The king asks for you. We can't leave till you are with us."

"We're coming," Mark said, ushering Sandy through the door ahead of him.

Chariots conveyed them up the long, easy incline of the mountain pass and onto the immense, miles-long plateau forming the core of the territory. The general's personal estate, including his sprawling house, official buildings, several temples, secondary residences, and various assorted outbuildings, all enhanced by well-manicured gardens and luxurious old growth trees, lay a few miles into the plateau. The compound sat at the edge of the capital city. Quiet, efficient servants escorted the newcomers into the house and to the banquet that had been prepared while the household waited for them to arrive.

There was much talk and laughter at the dinner, which lasted for hours and through so many richly varied courses that Mark lost count. Rothan recited the long tale of his adventures in the Empty Lands, of meeting Mark and Sandy, of the rescue by the Mikkonites, of the desperate search in the half-drowned city for the crown, the sea voyage aboard the *Lady Dawn*, and then confrontation with Farahna and the eventual escape from the tomb. The journey to the south took a brief time. Captain Khefer was allowed to share his adventure of burning the trading warehouses and stables when he stole the oxen.

"An epic tale," General Intef said at the end of the entire recitation. "We shall have to have the scribes record it for posterity. And now, King Rothan the First, by the grace of Khunarum and the gods, we must make some serious plans."

"Not tonight!" Princess Sharesi protested. "Tonight is for rejoicing and celebrating. No battle plans."

"You're right, Mother, but so is my grandfather," Rothan said. "Tomorrow, we'll need to count those we can rally to the cause, which provinces have treaties with us, or can be trusted to fight Farahna beside us. We'll have to sift through

Captain Khefer's information about the Maiskhan forces in the capital city and in the land at large. There's much to do before we can launch any kind of successful rebellion. We must be successful; we will retake our homeland."

"To the downfall of Farahna and all tyrants!" Mark stood and raised his mug in a toast. Rothan came to his feet, followed by their companions around the table, all lifting mugs and goblets and repeating Mark's cry with gusto.

The dinner party broke up quickly. Rothan and Tia withdrew first, as royal etiquette required. Princess Sharesi came to Mark and Sandy. "I've ordered a suite of rooms prepared for you in the same wing of the palace as His Majesty's. You need to be close should he have need of you. I hope the rooms I've chosen will be to your liking." She extended a hand to Sallea. "Your chambers are in the same wing."

"I'm sure the accommodations will be fine," Sandy replied graciously. "You're very kind, Your Highness."

"I'll walk with you." The elder princess and Sandy fell into step together as they left the large banquet hall and traversed a long hall. Mark stayed a step behind, Sallea matching him stride for stride, and a small crowd of servants trailed him, as if he was leading a parade.

Clearing her throat, Rothan's mother asked, "I notice what must be the Mirror of the Mother at your belt?"

Sandy stopped in the middle of the hall. "You know of it?" She half lifted the mirror from where it dangled on her hip.

"I'm a high priestess of the goddess Haatrin, daughter's daughter of She who created the mirror. I'm learned in the mysteries of my particular temple. This is a deep and old secret of a related temple."

"Do you know how to use it? To see with it?"

Sharesi missed a step in her surprise. Mark grabbed her elbow to steady her. "You carry it, and yet you don't know how to use it? How did this come about?"

He didn't like the trend of the conversation, much as he was drawn to Sharesi, who reminded him in an indefinable way of his own mother. He was wary of anything causing doubts about their assumed identities. Frowning at Sandy, he shook his head, but eager as always for knowledge about the artifact, she ignored his unspoken signal.

"We found the mirror in our house at the Lost City of Khunarum. I'd been searching for it ever since we were in the Temple of Nuet. I was bitten by Sherabti—"

Face set in lines of distress, Sharesi clamped her hand on Sandy's arm so hard her knuckles were white. "Forgive me, but to speak Names of Ancient Power is unwise. Even the names of those much removed in time can draw the focus of disastrous energies. You've established no safeguards, Lady."

"I'm—I'm sorry." Sandy glanced at Mark for help, rolling her eyes. "I'm frustrated because I don't know how to use the mirror, to make it reflect."

"A great pity. This is a secret lost to time, then, I fear," Sharesi said. "It's not recorded in any scroll I've ever read. The mirror always fascinated me, ever since I read of it as a child, but not much is known."

Mark tried to do damage control in case any was needed. "We did explain to Rothan, to the king, I mean, we're not the Lady of the Star Wind and her warrior who lived in the time of King Khunarum."

"How odd your predecessors left it there for you with no instructions. Legend speaks of it as a fearsome weapon as well as an instrument of farseeing." Sharesi strolled farther, drawing them with her. The servants marched solemnly behind. "I know of an elder wisewoman from the western provinces who used to serve me as a maid. She might have additional knowledge, coming as she does from an area where a large number of the most ancient scrolls and tablets survived. I know she trained under a legendary wisewoman who, it was said, searched all her life for the mirror because she'd found a document setting forth the conditions for its use. This senior mentor hoped to find it, of course, but never did, so she passed on what she knew to Babsuket in the last days of her own life. Many are the legends about where the artifacts from Khunarum's city ended up. I'll arrange for you to meet with her."

"Marvelous! Tomorrow?"

Appearing amused by Sandy's eagerness, Sharesi bit her lip in an obvious attempt not to smile. "My serving woman is old, half blind, and retired to live with her great-grandchildren in a village at the far edge of this territory. I'll have her summoned as rapidly as may be done with one of such age and infirmity."

"We could go to her," Mark said, conscious of Sandy's hunger to learn more.

Sharesi shook her head. "It wouldn't be proper. You are of the king's inner court, and others must come to you, my lord. It will be her honor to be summoned. His Majesty will reward her well for the service." Head tilted, quizzical smile on her rouged lips, the princess said, "I think you have many things to get used to here in Nakhtiaar of today. And now, here are your chambers."

Two servants swept the doors open as the princess gestured. Other people flowed around them, carrying lamps and torches, flooding the room with light. Their few meager belongings from the oxcart had already been laid with precision on top of a chest on the far wall. Exhaustion overtaking his willpower now that Sandy was safe in the general's stronghold and he could relax his vigilance somewhat, Mark focused on the great bed.

"I'll leave you now. Should you require anything in the night, guards and a servant stand on duty outside the door." Having assured herself all housekeeping details in the room were in order, Sharesi took her leave. "If you'll come with me, Ambassador Sallea, we've selected a room for you with a patio, so your hawk may come and go as he pleases."

Mark heard Sallea graciously thanking their hostess as the two moved away in the corridor outside.

Bowing, the servants left, the last man closing the door.

Sandy strolled along the wall, small oil lamp in hand, admiring the paintings of water lilies, birds, and fish. She stopped at a small piece of furniture. "What a beautiful chest of drawers. The drawer handles are birds! And how elegant these tiny bottles are." Sandy selected a small blue and gold blown-glass bottle from a collection of five sitting on top of the bureau and examined it in the torchlight. "Exquisite."

"Not what we grew up with, is it?" Mark vividly remembered the ornate, red and gold décor permeating Throne. The Zhivanov Dynasty had lavish, gaudy tastes.

"No, but I like it." She set the bottle with its fellows and strolled farther, exploring the room. "Kind of peaceful, reminds me of the time at sea on the *Lady Dawn*. I think we're safe here, don't you?" she asked over her shoulder.

"Yes, General Intef runs a tight, disciplined operation. I can see where Rothan got his military instincts. I've been watching—the soldiers are well trained, professional, sharp. Farahna and her Maiskhan allies would have a hard time taking this province."

Next moment, he realized Sandy was laughing at him. "Yes, but aside from all those excellent considerations, this place feels like a home. Princess Sharesi's treating us like her personal guests." She set the oil lamp on a small ebony table with cat-paw shaped feet and fell onto the bed with a gusty sigh. "No more sleeping on the hard ground or napping on a jolting oxcart!"

"For a while." Mark sat beside her on the bed and took her hand. "Rothan's going to have to start a war to take the throne for himself."

"I know. I helped talk him into it, remember? But may I please enjoy the peace and quiet—and a civilized bed—for one night?"

"Peace and quiet? I was contemplating something else."

Sandy laughed and scooted to the center of the large bed, extending one hand to him as invitation. "I'm tired, though, I have to tell you."

"Relax." He pulled off his tunic and threw it on the floor. "Tonight is for me to pleasure you." Unwrapping the kilt and loincloth took a moment longer. Kicking off the sandals, he stood naked before her.

"And what comprises this ambitious plan?" She watched him disrobe with a mischievous gleam in her eyes.

"Lie back on those pillows and find out."

"Sounds promising." Taking her time, moving with a languorous seductiveness he found hard to resist, she did as he'd requested.

He took her dress off in one quick move and guided her hands above her head, twining her fingers between the leaves carved into the headboard. Sandy gave him a little frown before smiling and adjusting herself to lie comfortably on the massed pillows. Mark trailed featherlight kisses all over her slender, silky body, pausing to suckle at her breasts for a few moments while she writhed under him, obeying his unspoken order not to move her hands while he played. He teased at her left nipple, kneading her breast gently while he pulled at the rosy bud, twirling his tongue as if tasting the rarest delicacy. He kept his hand where it was but moved his mouth to the other side, to give the second tightly furled nipple equal treatment.

Then he shifted position on the mattress to lie between her spread legs. Teasing her, he caressed her soft, sensitive folds with his probing tongue for a few moments, then penetrated more. She moaned and tightened her grip on the bed as he worked his tongue deeper, hot, wet, insistent.

Sandy fisted her fingers in his long black hair where it lay against her thighs, tugging gently but insistently. "I can't wait any longer. I want you inside me now."

He stopped what he was doing and raised his head. "Not too tired?"

"Wretch!" She tugged at him again, urging him to comply with her request.

He allowed her to pull him on top of her. She lifted her face for a kiss, lips parted, eyes closed in anticipation. Guiding his aching cock into the soft depths he'd prepared so thoroughly with his attention, he traced her lips with his tongue. She gave him entry into her warm mouth as she wrapped her body around his, holding him tight. Unable to delay any longer, he positioned his hips and drove deep.

Sandy climaxed, keeping him locked inside her. Mark waited through her orgasm, still hard and ready himself, till she relaxed the slightest amount. Then he began moving inside her with a tantalizingly slow rhythm, building momentum for her to finish again, in unison with him this time. Mark fell onto the rumpled linen sheets, holding her to him, exhausted in the best possible sense of the word.

He kissed her as he drew a thin blanket over them both, and then closed his eyes for the first untroubled night's sleep he'd had in a long time.

Ten days later, after Rothan was presented to the people of the province as the new king by General Intef, trusted couriers were sent with secret messages to various territories Intef regarded as allies, or with whom he had influence. Dispatched to the lowlands after a briefing from Mark on what kind of intel he wanted, Captain Khefer worked to reestablish contact with his network of spies in the capital. Mark was sure the clever young officer had his own ideas for strategies to foster success for the rebellion to come.

Mark spent a day inspecting the estate's stables, identifying a few spirited horses to break to the saddle. He and Sandy, along with Sallea, spent long hours with the general's harness maker, trying to explain the concept of saddles, bridles, and other tack. Then Mark and Sallea reviewed volunteers from the ranks who showed an interest in learning to ride as opposed to driving chariots. Not too many stepped forward in the first wave, but Mark knew even a small troop of cavalry could be useful and prove the concept, so he persevered. He also had to admit to himself that he liked the idea of something unique he could make his own in the midst of the Nakhtiaar military structure. Sallea served as his enthusiastic lieutenant.

After the initial flurry of planning and activity, those in command had no choice but to wait for their efforts to come to fruition. Rothan insisted Mark must learn how to use the local weapons. As an officer candidate, he'd been taught the elegant art of fencing decades ago, but this was slash, attack, and defend with shorter, heavier blades. Some of what he had learned so long ago was applicable, much was not. The use of the shield involved new techniques as well.

He was hard at work in the courtyard of the armorer, sweating and struggling through a one-on-one swordfight drill with an old but cunning warrior, while Rothan called out instructions and admonitions from the side.

About halfway through the scheduled time for practice, Djed came striding across the yard, and his voice intruded on the hot, dusty afternoon air.

"Forgive me, my lords, but you're needed in the main house!"

Mark saluted his sparring partner, not unhappy for an excuse to give his aching muscles a rest. Handing the sword and shield to a waiting servant, he joined Rothan and the archer. "What's going on?"

"Queen Tia says you must come to the house at once and see to the Lady of the Star Wind," the archer said. "I don't know what's amiss."

The three men headed for the women's wing of the general's mansion. "Wasn't this her morning to work with the elderly serving woman, Babsuket, on the mysteries of the mirror?" Rothan commented, lengthening his stride to keep pace with Mark.

"Yeah, I thought so too." Mark shook his head. "Sandy was looking forward to it, in fact. She's been absorbed by the riddle of the mirror and what it might be able to do for us. She couldn't sleep last night, she was so excited about meeting Babsuket today and picking her brain—getting instructions, I mean—on how to use this mirror."

But when Mark walked into the large audience room dedicated to today's initial session between Sandy and the old wisewoman, he realized at once things weren't progressing satisfactorily.

"Your Majesty must forgive me, but I'm compelled to tell the truth." Brow furrowed in a frown, Babsuket pointed a trembling hand at Sandy. "This woman will never be able to wield the power of the mirror," the old woman said, even as she bowed to Rothan as required by court etiquette.

"Rise, honored old one." Rothan took his seat at the edge of the room. "There's no need for apology if some barrier exists of which we were unaware."

"Wait, I'm missing something." Mark glanced from Sandy to Tia, and then to the old crone. Shoulders hunched, she'd hobbled to stand next to Princess Sharesi as if for protection. "The mirror came to my Lady. It was meant for her, so why the fuss?"

"Look at the mirror." Babsuket spoke in a harsh monotone.

He did as ordered and stared at the golden object now resting on a low table. The fan-shaped mirror's opaque surface gleamed as usual, not reflecting anything.

"See you not the handle?" Babsuket's tone was insulting, as if she addressed a backward child. "Pick it up, warrior, and examine those who stand there."

He took the mirror in his left hand. Lingering uneasiness about the way Sandy had come to have it in her possession made him reluctant to touch the artifact. The whole issue of the identities they'd inherited was unsettling and spooky in his mind.

Swallowing hard, he glanced at the handle as it lay in his hand. The core was a tight braid of three thick golden columns, a figure standing at the top of each, their upraised arms supporting the disk above them. Facing upward, the beautiful, serene face and form of a young goddess swathed in a swirling dress was revealed in intricate detail.

Babsuket spoke again, her voice guttural. "Your Lady was the untouched innocent when first you met."

Angry embarrassment flashed across his nerves, like a match striking flint, to be discussing these intimate matters in a room full of people. As the old crone stated, he knew Sandy's personal history, none better. Involuntarily, he glanced at the princess, who was staring at the floor.

Babsuket continued her recitation. "She'll also be the elder wisewoman in time. She has an unusual portion of knowledge now for one so young. I've been told how she does healing with her own magics, even saving the life of our king when you first met."

Mark spun the handle of the mirror clockwise, examining the depiction of the goddess in her guise as old woman, beautiful in her way but ancient, her face wrinkled. He clicked the handle clockwise one more time and stared at the warrior carved on the third side. The man's face was strong, determined under the elaborate crested helmet.

Babsuket sighed as she watched him turn the handle to the warrior. "Now that I behold you standing next to the one who would wield the mirror, I perceive it can never be. The foundation is flawed, the braid between the two of you not tightly woven."

Adrift, Mark found this conversation perplexing. Sandy shook her head, refusing to speak, and walked a step or two away from him, making a show of pouring herself some wine.

"Wait, are you saying Sandy won't be able to make this thing work because there's something wrong with *me*?" Anger spread through him like acid. "With our relationship?" "The scrolls from ancient days spoke of the need for the Lady to have a consort to bind the energies together, as the handle of the mirror itself shows. There were rituals, ceremonies, oaths between the two. She wields the mirror, the warrior consort wields other powers of his own, given to him by his gods. Ultimately, he protects her, and she draws upon him for the most exacting tasks." Closing her eyes for a moment, Babsuket reached out a hand as if parting curtains and said, "I see a jagged crack in the bond between the two of you, a crevasse, as if many years were spent apart. Perhaps if she'd already owned the mirror, she could overcome this, but with both of you untested, the fatal flaw must always prevent the power of the mirror from expression." Opening her eyes, the elderly woman gave Mark an unpleasant smirk. "Or if she chooses another consort and starts fresh, perhaps she might achieve the bonding required. But not in time to fulfill the prophecy and assist our new king in gaining the throne." Babsuket raised her hands, palms up. "Useless for me to pour two parts of the knowledge into a broken vessel. Why this great gift of the ancient goddess came to her I don't understand! Perhaps it was a mistake, perhaps it wasn't meant for her to have, despite what all of you believe. It cannot be the time of the ancient prophecies, for she can't use the mirror. What this means for the success or failure of your campaign, Your Majesty, I can't predict."

Babsuket peered at the assembled nobles and servants, most of whom were gawking at her. Smiling, as if satisfied to be the center of attention, she drew herself upright as far as her bowed spine would permit. "I refuse to be involved in this—this error. The woman's possession of the mirror offends." Her voice turned sickly sweet, her expression sly as she looked to Rothan. "Allow me to seek refuge in my garden at the home of my great-grandchildren. I pray thee, Your Majesty, don't summon me again to work with these flawed candidates. I fear the anger of the gods will smite me over this. Or give me the mirror." She spoke the last words lightly, as if they were a casual afterthought.

"We're grateful for your service to us in this matter, and you shall be rewarded." Rothan's voice was polite and formal. "It's not in my power to interfere with the mirror, nor would I second-guess the gods as to who is the rightful owner. My queen will give orders for your care and comfort in all ways this night. You can set out on the journey home in the morning. A suitable escort will be provided."

Tia took her cue from her husband and motioned to the waiting maids, who supported the old wisewoman on either side as she hobbled from the room. Babsuket paused beside Sandy, shaking her head. She reached out, as if to pat Sandy on the cheek, but the princess jerked back several steps to avoid the crone's touch. Wringing her hands, murmuring more misgivings to the flustered maids, Babsuket and her escorts disappeared through the curtains. Taking one last look at Sandy, Tia then followed, drawing Rothan from his chair to accompany her.

Mark felt at a loss. "Well, I don't get it. I guess it's too bad we can't use the mirror against Farahna, but if we can't, we can't. I was always kinda skeptical—" He set the item on the table, realizing he was talking to himself. Sandy had fled the room, going out to the garden.

"Follow her." Princess Sharesi came to stand beside him. She gave him a surprisingly forceful shove. "I'll safeguard the mirror until your Lady wants it again. Now go to her."

Mark walked outside to find Sandy, but she was nowhere to be seen. Frowning, he walked farther into the elaborate gardens, letting his eyes get used to the blazing sun until he found her by the lily pool, staring over the plateau.

"Are you okay?" he asked, coming up behind her.

She refused to turn, even when he placed gentle hands on her shoulders and tried to draw her closer.

He realized she was crying. "What's wrong? I know it's disappointing about the mirror thing, but maybe we won't even need it as a weapon. Let me help, talk to me." The depth of her emotion over this odd event worried him. "I know the old witch was pretty rude, but sometimes elderly people can be abrupt. And she believed in you from what I could tell—it was me she managed to insult. Although, clearly she coveted the mirror."

Sandy swallowed hard. She heard the concern for her in his voice but wasn't ready to discuss the subject, couldn't talk about it past the lump in her throat and the pain in her heart. She forced herself to stroll along the edge of the pond and to keep her voice from trembling. "That loathsome woman didn't hurt my feelings. I could care less about her or her opinions. And I won't be seeking out another consort just so I can use the mirror, if that part of what she said concerns you. Look, I just want to think in peace and quiet right now. I'll be in our rooms in plenty of time for dinner, all right?"

"Are you sure you're okay?" He sounded dubious, moving closer.

"Why wouldn't I be?" She bent to sniff a flowering bush, wishing he'd take the hint and leave.

He gave her an awkward hug, which she allowed, and then walked toward the house. She watched him out of the corner of her eye, and when she felt sure he wasn't coming back, she gave in to her vertigo and nausea and collapsed in slow motion to her knees on the soft grassy bank of the pond, hot tears pouring down her cheeks.

Next moment, Mark picked her up effortlessly. "Sandy, what the seven *hells* is the matter?" He carried her to the closest bench, on the far side of the pond under a striped awning.

Unable to speak past her grief, she wept as he carefully sat, adjusting his hold on her. She laid her head on his chest and allowed herself to give in to emotion. Blessedly, Mark didn't ask questions or try to talk. For the longest time, he held her close and rocked her slightly in his arms, stroking her hair, rubbing her back.

Eventually, she exhausted her tears, drained and tired. Hiccupping, she dried her eyes on her sleeve.

"Talk to me." His quiet voice was inviting, not demanding. "You know you can trust me," he said. "You could always trust me, right from the first time we met. I love you."

Where to begin? She took a deep breath, despite the tightness of emotion like bands of steel constricting her chest. After this disastrous afternoon, she was going to need some meds from her dwindling supply. The thought gave her the logical place to launch into the facts he was entitled to hear. "Why do you think I became a doctor?"

"I've no idea," he said. "When we were together on Throne, you never talked of such ambitions."

"I wanted to do something worthwhile with my life, to help people, not just spend my days in endless, meaningless court intrigues and social activities. To be brutally honest, I wanted a way to distract myself from my own tragedy and loss. When we came here, all the signs indicated the mirror was meant to be mine, not only as another way that I could help, but also as a task no one else alive could accomplish. After the experience with the visions, I felt it was meant to be, although Nuet did warn I might not be able to use it. We've both heard the prophecies, how the mirror is necessary to support Rothan's bid for regaining the throne. Then to have that harridan Babsuket tell me I'm doomed to failure because of how we began, because of all the years we were ripped apart, because maybe we don't really love each other enough—" She drew in a deep breath. "She picked at old wounds, I'll admit. It made me so angry because none of what she said is true. It can't be." Staring at him, she threaded her fingers through his hair, caressing his cheek. "I love you."

"Then what's all this about?" He seemed at a loss. "You're a doctor, the most highly trained physician on the entire planet. No one else can do what you do."

She shook her head. "It's not *enough*. I settled for being a doctor years ago, because that was my only choice, and I am good at it. Here, after Sherabti's bite and the visions, I had my heart set on being the Lady of the Star Wind. I wanted to fill the role, to use the mirror, to have my own power the way I never wanted anything before, not even to be Outlier empress. Anyone can learn to be a doctor, but only I can use the mirror. Or so I believed." She felt an aching pit inside her gut, a longing that was indescribable. She *needed* to be able to partner with the mirror, to use it. The longer she had possession of the artifact, the more the desire grew. The more sure she became that it was hers to command, if she could only find the secret. The mirror called to her, that's what Mark didn't understand. The magic wanted her, and she wanted it. But she was reluctant to explain that to him. He already looked askance at her attachment to the idea. But if the choice was between the mirror and Mark, there was no choice to be made, because she loved him with all her heart.

As if sensing her train of thought, Mark said, "I never had any regrets about us, you know, and I won't start now."

"Never?" Doubt crept in at the edges of her thoughts, sending traitorous tentacles into the surety of her love for him. "Not even when you regained your memories and realized what Ekatereen had done to you?"

"I tried to hate you. I told you that. I failed. Those months with you on Throne, loving you, were the best part of my entire life." His low voice vibrated with endless depths of emotion. "I could never make my way to you. Even if I could have infiltrated Throne's security measures, no possibility existed of getting past the empress's personal safeguards on her family. Nothing I could say or do would ever change Ekatereen's mind about my unworthiness to be your husband. I assumed you'd gotten married to someone else in due course." His voice trailed off. Clearing his throat, Mark finished his thought. "Deep down, where I wouldn't admit it to myself, I—I hoped you were happy."

She kissed him. "Not without you."

Leaning on each other, the couple sat for a few moments, watching the shadows lengthen as the day came to an end.

"So, you became a doctor—"

She sighed. "One of the female physicians showed great sympathy to me, braver than the rest. She spent a lot of time talking me through my grief and depression.

In time I wanted to be like her, to help others. Emulating her gave me a purpose and a focus. I hoped and believed if I kept myself busy with medical school and then practicing medicine, I could hold my emotions at bay."

"How can Babsuket know or guess this about you, about us?" Mark wondered out loud. "She said she saw it when I walked into the room—do you believe that? Are we somehow…broken?"

Sandy pushed her hair from her face. "This place is full of mysteries. I wonder why Haatrin wanted me to have the mirror if I can't use it. How could someone powerful enough to be regarded as a goddess not know?"

"I don't give a fuck about the damn mirror," he said. "I care about you."

"I'll be all right." She wiped her cheeks with the edge of her skirt. "I'm going to go to our room and lie down. I have a terrible headache."

"I think I'll sit here a bit. Unless you want company—"

"Not right now." She gave him a quick kiss to take the edge off her blunt refusal. "Will you make excuses for me at dinner?"

"Of course. I'll check on you after the meal."

Feeling curiously lighter now that she'd vented her wrenching disappointment over her inability to command the mirror's gifts, Sandy was sure he didn't understand the depth of loss she was feeling. He also probably didn't grasp the weight of the decision not to renounce him as her partner and go in search of a consort the mirror would accept. Hastening toward the house, Sandy pressed one hand to her forehead, where a migraine throbbed. Thank goodness she had plenty of the medicine for headaches left in her bag. A good night's sleep, and she'd be fine. She hoped.

Mark stared at the pond without seeing it after she walked away. Summoned by a servant, he endured dinner a while later. The conversation was desultory at best, punctuated by long pauses at the end of which he'd realize the guests were either looking at him or studiously away from him. He escaped to the garden again as soon as he could without offending his hosts. He wanted to be alone in the cool dark night to try to think things through.

Wandering to the bench by the pond, farthest away from the house full of well-meaning people, Mark sat, rubbing his forehead. He had a nagging ache behind the eyes. Sandy had refused dinner after all and had fallen asleep, according to the servant Tia sent to inquire. He'd checked on her himself before going outside to sit. She'd taken something from her stock of sedatives to help and had been snoring lightly.

He wished he'd asked her for headclear. A whole bottle of it.

As he sat under the stars, his mind a jumble of emotion, he realized someone was coming across the path to bear him company.

"Your heart is troubled, warrior."

Princess Sharesi stood alone in the twilight, with no attendants. He started to rise to bow to her as protocol demanded, but she made a slight motion for him to remain seated. "No need for ceremony." She sat at the end of the bench. "Old Babsuket shouldn't have been so blunt today. I think she wishes the mirror had come to her hand. Jealousy colors her speech," the princess said by way of an apology for her former servant.

"Her remarks were pretty insulting to me," Mark said. "And Sandy is really upset about not being able to use the mirror."

The elderly princess shook her head, elaborate golden flower earrings chiming. "Let me say this to you—there are tremendous powers here. Coming as you do from the stars, you've little to no comprehension of what we deal with in Nakhtiaar. Of who and what protects and defends us. You've faced those who guard the paths to the underworld and the afterlife of Nakhtiaar." Sharesi made the comment a statement, not a question.

Mark recalled his eerie dream in Hutenen's tomb. He found he didn't want to make denials about what had happened. "Yes, I've seen them. And Sandy believes she spent time with Haatrin and others after the snake bit her."

"Did you not feel their power? Did you believe in them at the moment you were judged?"

"The experience was as real as anything else in this world gets." He stared at her. "So?"

"The oldest tablets say the Exalted Ones guard more than one door to more than one reality. Persuade them of the worth of your quest and a path might be opened for you and your Lady of the Star Wind, allowing you to try to repair the schism of which Babsuket spoke, or at least to establish a proper foundation for the powers to flow to your Lady." She studied him for a long moment in the moonlight, her expression kindly. "Ask the gods to solve the problem of you being the barrier to what she's supposed to do. To what she craves, because I assure you, desire to be the keeper of the Mirror of the Mother must be running strong in her blood. The mirror is a thing of much power, and it seeks a vessel."

"Riddles." Mark dropped his head and scuffed at a pebble with his sandaled foot. His head ached more than ever. "Begging your pardon, but there are times when riddles are the primary language on this planet."

"She wouldn't have been chosen. She never would have seen Sherabti." Princess Sharesi made a gesture to ward off evil as she uttered the name. "The mirror wouldn't have come to her if there were some impossible barrier to her use of the weapon. She has to use it to fight on behalf of my son in his quest to take the throne. The prophecies are all clear about the need for the mirror to ensure my son's ultimate victory and successful rule, if he's to wear the Crown of Khunarum." Sharesi studied his face in the moonlight. "She could choose another Warrior, one with whom she lacks the painful history the two of you share. She is the fated one, not you."

Mark was speechless for a moment. "We've loved each other nearly all our lives. She'd never leave me for another man just to use the mirror. I don't care how much magic the fucking thing possesses." He realized his fists were clenched, and he made a conscious effort to seek calm. "I have to tell you it's bothered me from the beginning how obsessed she's been with this damn mirror. It's as if she feels she's going to be useless to everyone now if she can't make the mirror do its tricks.

Sandy has such a good heart, knows so many things—I hate to see her tearing herself up over what is to us merely an alien artifact."

"And you wish to fix this wrong for her, I know." She patted his knee as if sorry for him. "Even I, who studied in the service of my goddess for many long years, am woefully ignorant in this area. Even Babsuket, for all her wisdom and strange gifts, doesn't know the total of things. I think she knows less about the actual use of the mirror than she let on."

"The empress, Sandy's grandmother, took so much from us both—all those years of my life, of Sandy's life. I had simple dreams as a young man—do valorous deeds in the empress's service, accrue rank and honors, have a large family of sturdy sons and daughters." Hearing himself outlining the plan, he laughed. "Basically, repeat my grandfather's life, my father's life. Then with a wave of her hand, the empress took all I held dear away from me. But Sandy and I are together now. We'll have time to build a shared life, even if it is going to be in a place stranger than anything either of us could have imagined. We have each other again and we can make up for a portion of the lost years at least. But to somehow satisfy this requirement to overcome the basic fact of our separation—" He shrugged. "I've no idea what to do about that. If our love for each other right now isn't enough to satisfy these magical rules I never heard of before, then I'm at a loss."

Sharesi rose. To be polite, he stood as well.

"I agree with your assessment that she currently has no desire to choose the mirror over you, no thought of replacing you as her warrior, I'll ask the goddess to send me a sign as to what else may be done."

"Thank you, Your Highness." Mark watched her walk away. He resolved not to say one word to Sandy about this conversation. No need to upset her further. He was angry enough for both of them. And he hated the seed of doubt lodged in his heart like a dart that Sharesi had left him with. What if the magic worked its will on Sandy, influenced her to renounce her love for him? Brought her other candidates to be the Warrior, share the magic? How long could she resist? How long could he stand in her way? Uncanny events had already happened to her on this planet, anything might be possible.

"We didn't come all this way and suffer unbearable pain to give up on each other now," he said, as if challenging the unseen dieties in charge of the mirror. "You need to find a way to make *our* magic work for your fucking mirror."

There was no response. He didn't know whether to be relieved or regretful.

Close to midnight, he trudged inside the mansion, made his way to their suite of rooms, and climbed into the bed beside Sandy, trying not to wake her. She murmured in her sleep and rolled over, curling into him for comfort. He drifted off to the sound of her soft breathing.

Coughing as dank, cold air filled his lungs, he realized he stood in what he thought as the chamber of Judging, with no idea or memory of how he got there. He put his arm around Sandy, standing close beside him. The goddess Haatrin was waiting for them, although there was no sign of the judge or the scribe. "Why have you come here again, still before your appointed time?"

"To solve the riddle of how I may use the mirror I was given," Sandy answered before Mark could make a sound. He wondered if she'd arranged this dream through some means he didn't understand. A drug from her kit perhaps? But Sandy was still talking. "We wish to pass through your door—"

"To use our door." Haatrin was stern and unfriendly. Quite different than when Mark saw her before. "You don't belong to this place and this time, Traveler. You've no right to ask these things."

Sandy refused to yield an inch. "We do belong. We've been given rights through the grace of Nuet." She paused as the name echoed through the chamber, amplifying as the word reverberated against the stone walls. Haatrin winced. Sandy appealed to the goddess. "I may not remember everything you told me when we met before, but I remember Nuet. You asked her, and she said I had choices, had a chance to wield her mirror, so I beg you to help me—us—now."

Idly, Haatrin flicked the curling feather she held. "I detect the faintest hint of Sherabti's venom in the wounds you each bear, tying you to this world. The magic remains potent." Head tilted, voice low as if talking to herself rather than Mark and Sandy, she said, "True, I did raise the issue of the mirror with Nuet because I hoped this was the time of the prophecy. And I witnessed her agreement that you could have the mirror and attempt to use it. Consent grudgingly given but valid nonetheless. For all her age and disengagement from this world, she knows much we've yet to learn." Raising her head, she looked at Mark. "And you issued an ill-conceived challenge, did you not?"

Startled, he thought back to his defiant words in the garden after dinner, about the need to fit what was special about the two of them into the requirements of the Mirror. Rolling his shoulders, ignoring Sandy's surprised expression, he said, "I did, not that I agree with your term."

Haatrin chewed her lip for a moment before nodding and giving Sandy a direct stare. "Very well, you may pass. The success or failure of your quest is not mine to decide, understand? I open the door to possibility alone. Walking through the door is up to you. Achieving your goal is on your shoulders." The goddess flicked her attention between them. "Both of you."

"A door is all we wanted," Sandy affirmed. "Thank you."

"The door you seek is one we don't use," Haatrin said. "I don't know if anyone has ever crossed the threshold from here. This entire quest is unprecedented in our experience, but then, you're not of this world by birth or heritage."

"We've chosen to make our home here, though," Mark said. "We've committed to Rothan and his cause."

Haatrin placed the blue and brown feather in her hair rather absent-mindedly. "So you say. I accept you believe this." Straightening her spine, she said, "We must go quickly, while the omens and alignments which brought you to me tonight remain favorable to you. Such things change quickly."

She spun on her heel and walked rapidly into the corridor to the right. Mark and Sandy rushed to follow her.

The walls of the passage were blank, smooth gray stone. The farther he walked, the dizzier Mark became. Other halls branched away, but Haatrin didn't even glance at those. A few moments later, the corridor opened out into a huge room dimly lit by multicolored torches set into elaborate golden fixtures at regular intervals along the wall. Heavy wooden doors lined all four walls as far as Mark could see, each bearing a few glowing golden symbols in the center.

Reading the symbols to herself, Haatrin moved slowly now, speaking a language Mark didn't understand. Then she stopped in front of a door no different to his eyes than any other and stood aside. "The actual opening of this portal is not for me. You must grasp the handle and walk through. I give you my blessing, for whatever it may be worth in this venture. Perhaps we'll meet again—I can't predict. Some things are veiled even from such as me, because the results will be dictated by your choices and actions. I bid you a fair journey." Spinning on her heel, she walked away.

"We'd better not hesitate," Mark said. "Ready?"

Sandy shrugged. "We asked for this, so yes, no use in delaying." She drew him close for a kiss, sweet and warm in this cold stone chamber. "Whatever happens, if this works or if we fail, I'm glad we're together."

"Always," he said, hugging her. Then he studied the door. The curved handle was in the shape of a dagger, bent to form the arc, topped by a crown set with diamond stars. He wrapped his fingers around the metal, reaching to take Sandy by the hand, depressed the lever, and opened the door inward. Drawing her after him, he stepped across the threshold. His momentum carried him forward. Head spinning under an attack of ferocious vertigo, Mark closed his eyes and tried to retreat, but the solid weight of the now-closed door pressed against his spine. Knees buckling, he pitched forward, vision fading to black.

"Wake up, lazy outworlder!"

The voice was harsh, the motion accompanying the insult drastic. Mark and all his bedclothes were dragged from the narrow bunk and dumped on the hard tile floor. He struggled to his feet, half dazed and rubbing a numb elbow, as the whining voice continued ranting at him. Rude laughter came from the other cadets clustered at the door of his room.

"You're expected to be on duty in five minutes, Ensign Denaltieri, at the far west gate of the Obelisk Wing, and judging by your state of undress, you're going to be late. Demerits, Ensign, demerits in your first week aren't going to get you a high rating!"

Blinking, he saluted with one hand, clutching the sheet with his other. "Yes, Cadet Lieutenant Portuc."

Portuc aimed one last kick at Mark's jumbled pile of clothes and blankets as his companions laughed. "Uniform's gonna be nonregulation, hayseed, leaving it in a heap on the end of your bunk. You aren't going to last here. You'll wash out in a month at this rate. Easy to predict with an outworld hick like you. Barent assigned you Obelisk Wing duty as a favor. Take a word of advice from me and don't make him regret his choice!"

The door slammed shut behind his tormenters as Mark blinked, rubbing his forehead, confused. Portuc? But wasn't Portuc dead on Freemarket, murdered by Barent Kliin? "I'd better go easier on the cheap wine next time—that was some insane dream." Dazed, Mark staggered into the small bathroom adjoining his lowly ensign's quarters. He drew a glass of water and rinsed his mouth out. Leaning on the sink, he got a good look at himself in the mirror.

"What the seven hells?"

The face staring back at him was his own true enough, but smooth, unlined, a young man's visage framed by shoulder-length black hair. He shut his eyes until hot pinwheels threatened to blind him. He reopened them, leaning in toward the mirror.

The youthful vision stared back.

He gazed at himself in disbelief. Yes, he stood barefoot and naked in the spartan bathroom of his old barracks room in the least desirable cadet wing of the Imperial Palace on Throne.

Impossible. He hadn't been in this room for over twenty years.

"Which is the dream? This, or the other reality?" He splashed water on his face and rubbed his eyes. "Okay, *think*. Was I drunk last night at the cadet dinner and had a nightmare as a result? Or am I two decades older and dreaming in Nakhtiaar?" He ran more cold water and poured it over his head. As he shook the droplets away, he caught a glimpse of his eyes in the mirror and leaned in close again. "Did Barent or Portuc spike the wine last night at the banquet?"

The floor felt cold under his feet. His elbow tingled and ached where he had fallen on it a moment ago. He was undeniably somewhat hungover, a headache throbbing at his temples. Struck by an urgent thought, Mark straightened as he toweled his hair dry. If he *was* on Throne, reliving his early days as a cadet in a dream or hallucination, and if Portuc had been there so early to remind him of his duties, then this was the day he first met Sandy. The day her uncle had attempted to have her assassinated as part of his endless and obsessive plots.

An assassination Mark had prevented.

Thereby sending his life careening out of its previously well-defined path.

"Lords of Space, what time is it?" He ran into his bedroom, searching for the chrono. He still had the chance to intervene, because he now knew his way around Throne and its shortcuts, which the young Cadet Denaltieri had not. Grabbing a clean uniform from the storage space and shrugging into it took a few precious seconds. Buckling on his belt and ceremonial weapon, he noticed in passing the knife scar along his ribs had vanished. He fastened the tabs on the shirt, yanked on his boots, and shoved his way out the door before it had time to open fully. Other cadets gaped at him as he sprinted past them, pushing through the corridor and into the old-fashioned stairwell, hastening to the lower levels in leaps and bounds.

He'd been lost many times in his first weeks on Throne, much to the amusement of the other ensigns and more senior boys who'd grown up at court. There was no confusion in his mind where he was going now, though. To the far garden of Tsiolovad, Sandy's particular favorite. The sprawling arbors and flower beds were deserted most days and therefore free of the prying eyes and hordes of fawning courtiers infesting Throne. He made good time through the winding corridors and emerged from a doorway at the far end of the garden, out of breath but arriving before the assassins would make their appearance.

Sandy sat on a bench beneath a spreading shade tree, reading an ancient book, pages close to crumbling into dust under her delicate touch.

She was a young woman again, in her late teens like him.

He found that fact disturbing. Sandy's appearance today matched the vision he'd held in his heart for so many years in exile, but now he'd grown accustomed to the mature woman who was his partner and equal in their adventures on Nakhtiaar. This had to be some insane nightmare he was having. Pinching his arm, he closed his eyes for a heartbeat, trying to will himself to wake up in the bed on Nakhtiaar, but nothing happened. Taking a deep breath, opening his eyes to find himself still on Throne of the Past, he advanced across the lawn. He'd no choice but play this scene out.

Frowning, Alessandra marked her place in the book with a graceful hand. "Who are you? How dare you disturb my afternoon?" She stared at him as she spoke, her attitude and her voice showing no fear but much annoyance.

Feeling compelled to play along with the scenario Haatrin or someone had dropped him into, he said, "Forgive me, Your Highness, but you're in grave danger. Allow me to escort you to the main wing."

Her forehead wrinkled a bit as she considered his words. Then her expression lightened, and she nodded. "Oh, you're one of the new cadets, aren't you? Is this some game the others put you up to? The seniors relish teasing and embarrassing the boys from offworld. Such hazing shouldn't be allowed by the master of cadets." She waved a dismissive hand at him, already opening her book again. As her finger traced the page, searching for the spot where she'd stopped reading, she said, "You mustn't let them get you into trouble. You've no business here in the garden, and I'm not in any danger, I assure you. The boys are playing a prank." Glancing at him, she made a tiny shooing motion. "If you go out the way you came and keep going left at each corner, you'll end up in the central core of the palace and can navigate from there to wherever you're assigned to stand guard. I won't speak of this to anyone, don't worry." She flipped to the next page.

In his anxiety to get her to safety in case this was insane reality, not a dream, Mark lost his patience and forgot where they were in their personal history. Stepping forward, he took her elbow, trying to pull her to her feet. "Sandy—"

"*What* did you call me?" Clearly angry, as well as astounded at his easy familiarity, she straightened her spine. She grappled clumsily with the book, trying to avoid dropping it while she attempted to break his hold. "How dare you lay hands on me?" She was every inch the offended imperial princess.

Realizing his mistake, Mark tried to recoup with a respectful bow, releasing her elbow. "A thousand pardons, Your Highness. I'm new to court, as you've observed. I haven't learned the manners and speech yet."

"Manners can't be so different, even on the outer worlds. One doesn't clutch at a woman, known to you or not." Despite the acid tone of voice, she inclined her head graciously, a bit mollified by his apology. Stepping away from him as he released her elbow, she hurried behind the bench, closing the book and holding it to her chest as if for protection. "You may go, then. I won't mention this to your commander, but you must be more careful in the future, Cadet. Others at court aren't as forgiving as I choose to be today."

"I have to get you out of this garden, Your Highness. At once." Mark was insistent.

"I think you must be drunk, or mad." She backed away from him some more. As something at the far end of the flower beds behind him caught her attention, she pointed. "And who are these newcomers? Your friends? You'll all be in trouble, I warn you. This cadet joke has gone too far."

Mark didn't have to turn to know the three assassins had arrived. Now he'd lost the element of surprise, which had turned the odds in his favor in the original encounter. He hoped he'd gained the advantage of two decades as a trained killer. Would this young body respond to the older man's trained muscle memories? After all, he hadn't received that lethal instruction yet. Vaulting over the bench, he grabbed the outraged princess by the shoulder, shoving her behind him, saying as he did so, "They're here to kill you. Stay out of my way and don't interfere."

"Listen to him, girl," advised the man in the lead, laughing as he drew twin force daggers from his belt. His face was unaccountably pleasant, nondescript, with a smile inviting Sandy to share his amusement. "Once we've disposed of your young valiant defender, we'll slit your throat painlessly, I swear. We promised your uncle not to make you suffer. He has a soft spot for you in his heart somewhere, for all his hatred of your bloodline."

Mark heard Sandy take a deep, shuddering breath before she spoke. "This must be a mistake—my parents paid him a huge bribe to omit us from the feud."

The bearded, debonair assassin spat. "Your parents can argue with him later. My orders are to take you out of the equation."

"You're in the wrong place at the wrong time, Cadet." The thug behind the ringleader spoke to Mark with mock pity, saluting him with a dagger. "Convenient for us, though, eh, mates? We can frame him for the crime, and his family can pay reparations to the empress."

Mark launched himself over the bench at the first man, breaking the assassin's scrawny neck in one practiced, violent kick, a flash of relief adding to his adrenaline-fueled strength as he drew on his future training in this strange situation. The other two hired killers wasted no time in closing in on him, ignoring Sandy, who remained rooted to the spot where she stood. Her screams wouldn't bring immediate help. Bystanders on Throne stayed uninvolved in any incidents until the outcome made clear which side was safest to support.

He tried to counter the slashing attack from the second assailant, swearing and gritting his teeth as the force knife grazed his ribs, inflicting the wound whose scar he'd always bear. The deep gash wasn't enough to stop him from killing this opponent as well, stabbing his own dagger deep into the man's heart. Jacked up on adrenaline, Mark was immune to pain right now. The third conspirator bolted, dropping his force knives to the grass and sprinting for the far wall. Mark was having none of it, chasing him across the uneven ground, grabbing the assassin from behind as he fled, and wrestling him to the dirt. They struggled, Mark's blood drenching them both, before he succeeded in knocking his adversary out. At the last moment he used less-than-lethal force as he remembered this man had survived in the original version of the episode. The wretch died later under the tools of the empress's interrogators.

Shoving the unconscious man aside, Mark stood, staggering to lean on the bench, breathing hard. He stared at his last, surviving victim and then checked that the other two were indeed dead. His steps wavered, and dizziness assaulted him. He pressed a hand to his head and the other to his side in an attempt to staunch the blood loss. Disbelief that he was actually wounded contributed to his confusion. What the hells kind of dream was this? Sandy hastened to his side, her face white and anxious.

Blinking, he tried to focus on her. "Are you—are you all right, Your Highness?"

"I'm fine, thanks to you. Sit down before you fall." She guided him to the bench, his blood staining her fingers and her dress as she reinforced the pressure he applied to the gaping wound. "How did you happen to be here? Are you involved somehow?"

"No, I got lost," Mark lied. It had been true the first time, all those years ago. "I'm assigned to sentry duty at the west gate, with Barent Kliin, but I took the wrong corridor."

More men burst into the garden, but he could tell from a swift glance at the uniforms that these troops were loyal to the alliance encompassing Sandy's bloodline. The world was darkening, and he slumped from the bench to the grass. Weeping, Sandy cradled him in her arms, deflecting the attention of the guards away from him to the assassins. Horrified ladies-in-waiting pulled her away as the first of the medtechs arrived. He lost consciousness as his blood-soaked tunic was cut open by the medics.

"I forbid you to see this cadet again, Alessandra." Her mother's voice was cold, cutting. "You've thanked him sufficiently for saving your life, which was, after all, his duty as an imperial cadet officer. There's no need for you to be visiting him repeatedly in the hospital. Such condescension on the part of an imperial princess doesn't show you to your peers in a good light."

Surprised her usually remote mother was even aware she'd seen her rescuer, Alessandra shook off an odd sense that they'd had this conversation before and stepped away from the portal. "Are you afraid people will talk?" Pivoting to stare at her mother, she laughed. "No one cares what I do. I'm too far down the list of heirs to the throne to matter."

"I'm more concerned about what this cadet will think." Her mother shook a finger at her. "He's a Denaltieri, after all, a warrior, and you know how their clan is, always seeking advantage. His grandfather was Ekatereen's lover for a time, which is where the family got the bulk of their fortune and honors. This man may be seeking political or financial advantage from a liaison with you."

"But Mark—I mean, Cadet Denaltieri—killed two men and wounded the third to rescue me. I've never seen anything like the way he fought, except in the adventure trideos. He took a great risk for me."

"And for himself and his family. Surely the assassins would have pinned the blame for your death on him, and his family would've been in trouble. It's not a given that the empress would have interceded with Stastre to demand blood price for your death on our behalf either." Her mother frowned. "Although she probably does have a lingering affection for the Denaltieri clan, which might have outweighed your uncle's schemes. If you made more of an effort to please her, she'd pay more attention to you and we'd have a safer position in these delicate matters."

"This constant maneuvering and politics drives me mad," Alessandra said. "I'm sick of it. I refuse to simper and flatter and connive like the cousins you so admire."

"I know you prefer to think yourself above it all, but Ekatereen's blood runs in your veins, and that makes you part of the mix, unlikely though it may be that you'd ever sit on the throne." Her mother poured herself a cup of tea, no doubt liberally laced with strong feelgoods. "Getting back to the original subject, your father and I don't want to hear that you've seen this Denaltieri boy again. I'm sure he's quite handsome, but the time to take lovers is after your marriage, not before, Alessandra. There'll be others to choose from in the future, just as well favored as this cadet, I promise you. Although they do say the Denaltieris are unusually… blessed in their physical endowments." With a saucy wink, she sipped the hot beverage and sighed, relaxing into her chair. Words slurring a bit, she said, "You've a duty to the family to uphold."

Alessandra took a deep breath. Arguing with her mother, especially when she was under the influence of her favorite recreational drugs, was a futile and exasperating effort. "Not to upset you further, Mother, or deny the wisdom of your counsel, but I do need to see him today because I agreed to accompany Cadet Commander Barent Kliin to the hospital. Together we're to present Denaltieri with an award for his deeds. I funded the medal from my private stipend."

"Barent is highly regarded. It's an excellent stratagem to use this incident to move into his circle." Her mother's voice was approving. "Ekatereen is known to favor him above the others in this generation, although she'll keep playing them all against each other. Perhaps you're cleverer about the politics than you give yourself credit for. Very well, proceed with your plans for the day, after which we'll be done with the Denaltieri matter." Waving a languid hand, her mother leaned against the cushions and shut her eyes as the feelgoods hit her system.

Gritting her teeth in annoyance, Alessandra escaped into the corridor, working her way through the crowd of courtiers and minor nobility with practiced ease. Heading toward the courtyard where a family groundcar waited to whisk her to the hospital, she took perverse pleasure in her mother's assumption that this morning's ceremony was a scheme to attract the attention of the odious Barent Kliin. True, Alessandra chose to exert unusual energy in playing a courtier's game this one time, but the object of her planning was none other than Mark Denaltieri.

Biting back a sigh at the mental image of the gallant and handsome scion of a warrior clan, she hoped he was as good at intrigue as he was at hand-to-hand combat. Would he take the risk of getting to know her better? If they were both discreet, no one would ever suspect anything between them. After all, their stations in life on Throne were worlds apart. The intense attraction she felt for him didn't make sense, given that they'd just met, but the idea of never seeing him again was like a knife to the heart. She refused to deny herself a chance at learning more about Mark Denaltieri.

Now that he was out of the hospital, he was back on duty, with a schedule to uphold. Sandy knew that, knew he could get into trouble, so why was she late to this assignation?

Mark didn't remember her being tardy to their first clandestine meeting, away from prying eyes and wagging tongues, so why was she late in this dream? Leaning on the doorframe, he stretched side to side judiciously, hoping to ease the lingering pain from the knife wound. He'd forgotten how much it hurt to take a force knife in the ribs. He gazed into the golden haze of a Throne afternoon in midsummer, enjoying the quiet beauty of Sandy's most secret retreat, where he guessed she hid from the poisonous intrigues of her grandmother's court.

Any moment now, she'd hasten across the overgrown meadow to this long-abandoned library, so old it held crumbling books. The library was concealed deep in the oldest section of the palace, accessible through a series of corridors and winding garden paths that became overgrown the deeper one penetrated into the recesses of this quadrant of the grounds. She'd told him how she'd explored the abandoned areas of the complex as a child whenever she could escape her relatives and minders. The fact she was able to do so told him how little she mattered to them as a person or an imperial princess. It seemed no one much cared.

Well, he cared.

She'd shared the location of the hidden door with him on her final visit to his hospital room, the last she could make without arousing anyone's suspicions. With Barent Kliin looking on, no less. Mark grinned at the way she'd connived right under the bastard's nose. He stared at the overgrown, broken gate through which Sandy would pass. Her arrival was a certainty, he knew now, where his much-younger self had been nervous and skeptical. Maybe even a little scared about the step he was taking, becoming involved with an imperial princess, no matter how removed from inheriting the throne. When he'd left his home planet to accept the appointment to cadet school, his grandfather warned him against forming romantic alliances too early in his career, especially with the royals.

"The inheritance situation is too unstable right now," the old man said. "Guess wrong about which faction to become involved with, and your chances may turn to ash. You don't want to incur Ekatereen's wrath either, so stay away from anything and anyone likely to offend her. The empress is the center of the universe on Throne. Cross her at your peril."

Good advice. Too bad that in some ways he hadn't heeded it.

A small sound snapped his attention to the overgrown tangle of garden in front of him. Sandy walked into view, young and demure in her white dress. "I thought you weren't coming." Stepping over the threshold of the library, he went to meet her.

"I almost didn't." She stopped about two yards away. Wringing her hands, licking her lips, she avoided his gaze. He had the impression she teetered on the verge of fleeing.

This reality diverged from his memories of the events. He reached her in two steps, taking her into his arms, relieved she offered no resistance. He gazed into her eyes, realizing he was finally in the presence of Alessandra of the Future, the woman who'd journeyed with him to Nakhtiaar. She had the face of the beautiful girl, but her eyes were far too knowing.

"Thank the Lords of Space, you're back with me. When did you realize what was going on?" He hugged her, relief running through his body like a cool rain. He'd been afraid she might never catch up to him, dreaded the idea of going through this nightmare alone.

"Yesterday morning when I awoke. You called me Sandy last week, in the garden, which certainly seemed an odd form of address from someone I'd never met. Yesterday I realized why you called me by that nickname." Her lovely face was set in a troubled and sad expression, eyes hooded, lips turned down.

"What's the matter?" He kissed her on the cheek, nuzzled her neck playfully.

She studied their clasped hands. "You do realize if we stop now, right now, if we never let ourselves take this affair further, you can have your life back? Accomplish all the ambitions luring you to Throne in the first place?"

Her words surprised and shocked him, as if she'd slapped him. Astounded, never expecting this line of reasoning from Sandy, he released his hold on her. A flash of anger made his next words come out harsher than he'd intended. "Do *you* want your life as an untouched imperial princess back? Does knowing you'll become the heir mean so much to you?"

"Please, listen to me." She took another step away from him. "I'm consumed by guilt right now because of what's going to happen to you. All my fault! When I think about the hell my grandmother is going to put you through—"

Reaching out, he took her hand, tugging her into his arms. This was the Sandy he knew and cherished. He skimmed her forehead with his lips, a gentle kiss before tilting her face to his. "I love you. I can endure all the pain and hardships as long as I know we're going to be together at the end. I didn't have such comfort the first time I lived through torture and exile."

"You wouldn't change a thing? Not anything?" Toying with a fastening on his cadet tunic, she challenged him but made no attempt to escape his embrace.

"No. When I woke up in my cadet's quarters last week, all I could think about was getting to the damn garden before the assassins arrived. I had to save your life all over again."

She wasn't giving in yet. "What if we left right now? What if we escaped Throne together, today, and made a life somewhere else? Maybe even in the Sectors?"

He contemplated the intriguing idea for a moment. He had the skills to get them off Throne and safely to the Sectors. He hadn't forgotten a thing he'd learned—would learn—in the Special Forces. At the moment he was an unimportant cadet and she only a minor player in the imperial family's dynastic calculations. Not a Favorite of the Empress, Sandy wasn't spied upon to the same degree as other girls of her generation. At this point no one knew they loved each other, which could make an escape easier to pull off.

But even as he toyed with plans and contingencies, he shook his head. He led her into the library, joining her on the deep couch. "It's no good. Your grandmother would have us hunted down no matter where we fled for shelter. She'd stop at nothing because she never lets anyone or anything she considers to be hers escape her control. You know that. She'd have her own secret service after us, bounty hunters, every lowlife in the Sectors. The price on our heads would become astronomical until someone bagged us. A fugitive's life is cruel, hopeless."

"I know," she admitted. "I hate to think of what's coming, so soon. And all those sad desolate years until we find each other again."

He rubbed his hand over the velvet-soft skin of her arm.

"What are you doing? You're giving me goose bumps!" Laughing, she pulled away.

"I'm looking for the bite marks from Sherabti. Remember Nakhtiaar?"

"Of course I do. As clearly as I remember this life we've plummeted back into. I just don't know if we're trapped in a dream together, or if Haatrin's door really sent us through time to relive the turning point of our lives. What are you getting at?"

Waving his hand at the surroundings, he said, "I think this—all this—is some kind of a test."

Forehead furrowed as she pondered his guess, she said, "You mean we're being tempted with other possibilities to see what we choose?"

"I didn't have to go to the garden and save your life. When I arrived there the first time decades ago, it was by accident. I'd gotten lost, and I walked into the middle of a situation where I had to take immediate action to save you and myself." He rubbed a hand across his eyes. "When I woke the other day, the idea of abandoning you never even crossed my mind, but I think it must have been the first decision point in this—this test, if you want to think of the events in such terms. I think that's why I knew what was happening to us before you did. The initial choice—saving your life—was mine to make. And according to Babsuket, loathsome old crone that she is, I'm the weak link in your ability to use the mirror."

"You could have stayed away, let me die, and lived a totally different life," she said. "Followed the path you'd originally set out upon, as one of the empress's officers.

"No, I could *not*," he said, anger flaring that she could even suggest such a thing. "I love you, and I want to live my life with you, come what may. I'd give my life to save yours, here and now, or in the future, or on Nakhtiaar. If that isn't enough to satisfy whoever the powers are that control the mirror you desire so much, I don't know what else to do or say."

"I appreciate the effort you're making. If this test involves me choosing between the mirror and you, I'll always choose you." She kissed him. "How much of our history do we have to relive? What's expected of us if we're trying to repair the rupture Babsuket saw in our ability to wield magic?"

"I don't know and I don't much care, to be honest. I feel trapped." He stroked her back. "Not trapped by you. By the situation. But then, I think about Nakhtiaar, and I want to be *there*. It's become home to me—I belong. I never fit into the Sectors, and I certainly don't have a place in Outlier anymore. In Nakhtiaar I'm needed, part of something I believe in, somewhere I can make a difference."

"You mean working for Rothan, part of his rebellion against Farahna?"

He considered his answer. "I can help Rothan, not as one more spear carrier in the ranks but by teaching his army techniques, strategies, mentoring… There's more potential for me on Nakhtiaar. I can put my talents to use because we fit in there, both of us." He tapped his finger lightly on her chest. "You have a valued place whether you can use that damn mirror for anything or not."

"I know. But I could be so much more help to them if I could unlock the power in that mirror."

He frowned. "At first, life in Nakhtiaar was odd, primitive, compared to what we're used to, but the place grew on me. They're good people. We can help them. And we can be together freely there, you and I, and make a life, the way we never can here. Even if we did escape to the Sectors, we wouldn't have a happy life." He paused, trying to gather his thoughts to explain to her what he was beginning to realize himself. "In the beginning when we got to Nakhtiaar, you were angry with me because I wanted to stay on the move. I threw us into Rothan's quest to find the lost city and the Crown of Khunarum without hesitation, right?"

Her face was serious in the gathering shadows, her voice pitched low. "Yes, I was livid. And hurt. The oasis seemed so perfect, offered a wonderful opportunity to rekindle our love, a dream come true, for me at least. But I realized immediately you weren't comfortable, as if you were in a cage or a trap. Being with me wasn't enough for you."

"I never meant to hurt you." He kissed her to emphasize his regret. "I was confused by what I felt, seeing you again. Scared of reopening my heart to emotion after all the years of locking it inside. Keeping in motion, going into action represented an easy escape from having to deal with the feelings right away. But then, when you nearly died from the snakebite, when I thought I might lose you, I was ready. I wanted time out to be together and sort through our relationship, there in the Mikkonite village. But you were already caught up in the search for the mirror. Served me right for trying to hide from my emotions in the first place."

"I'm sorry."

"Don't apologize. You didn't ask the Moon Sisters to snatch you. I'll never take anything about us, or you, for granted ever again." He kissed her long and hard. "The mirror is part of who and what we're meant to be there, an integral piece of what we can do to help them. No one else has the ability but you. I accept that. Maybe our connection to the mirror is the reason Lajollae sent us there, which is fine by me. I love you. Lajollae's magic bubble took us to the one place where we could be happy and build a life."

Sandy left the couch, strolling along the walls, stopping here and there to pull a book off the shelf and leaf through it for a moment before setting each volume carefully in its place. "You know this room isn't here anymore."

"What are you talking about?"

"Grandmother had the entire wing burned and the gardens dug up."

He found the news distressing, like a punch to the gut. This library had been their one special place to be together, to be themselves. "Does it bother you to be here again?"

"No." She glanced at the crowded bookshelves, at the pillows and quilts she'd stacked on the old couch, then at him. "No," she repeated in a soft voice, a blush spreading over her cheeks. "It makes me happy to have a chance to revisit it with you."

Returning to the couch, she tugged at his scarlet uniform tunic and pulled him closer, kissing him with a hunger and a passion stoked by all their years apart. Sandy broke off the embrace, running her fingers through his hair. "I'm glad you want to return to Nakhtiaar, whatever happens. I felt at home the first moment we arrived in the Travelers' oasis, but I knew you were unhappy, restless—"

"Not anymore. I know what I want. I'm at a loss for how we get there, other than living through all the intervening years again."

"Thanks to you, at least I always knew what it was like to be loved, to be wanted for myself, not for my bloodline." She reached up and smoothed his hair off his face, feathered small kisses along his jaw. "I don't think any other imperial princess was ever so fortunate in that regard. Even though the time we had together was short, it gave me a foundation to make something of my life. I could never be like the rest of them, like her. The scheming and plotting, cruelty and treachery—" She took a shuddering breath and shook her head.

"No regrets?" he asked softly.

She stared into his eyes. "Not now, not ever. We took the chances together, same as we did—will do—on Nakhtiaar. If we don't stay true to ourselves and our history right now, none of the rest of it can happen. I won't relinquish our future. I won't give you up, not even to truly possess the powers embodied in the mirror. I believe in us."

Her words echoed strangely in the room. Assaulted by vertigo, Mark rose to his feet, keeping a tight grip on her hand. A door had materialized in the garden, surrounded by mist as the sky darkened and thunder rumbled. Keeping his balance with an effort, he tugged Sandy out of the room, stumbling toward the just-arrived portal. "Dreamtime is over, and we'd better not miss our return ticket."

The door opened easily when he put his hand on the handle, and they stepped across the threshold to find themselves in the middle of a desert on sparkling black sands. A smooth ebony road, darker than the glittering sand, began a few feet away from them, running toward the horizon as far as he could see. The sky glowed a midnight blue, although there was no moon or stars.

Far away, an eerie howl echoed and rose into an outright scream. A second and then a third answered. The sound pricked at the nerve endings and stirred ancient instincts of fear and flight. Releasing the door, which swung closed with a solid thunk, Mark said, "We'd better hurry." He realized the door had no handle on this side, no way to retreat if he and Sandy decided they'd made a mistake.

"But where are we?" Sandy glanced in all directions. "How does this place help us? It's a barren desert."

"No time to stop now. The road is our obvious next move. We have to have faith in the process, since Haatrin told us we'd been given permission to try our quest." Mark tugged her hand as the eerie howling echoed in the distance. "Come on, the road has to lead somewhere."

They walked through the featureless landscape for what his instincts told him was a long time, yet Mark didn't become tired or thirsty, and Sandy said she felt fine as well. Mark kept to the center of the road, which was about ten feet wide. Occasionally, he heard howling coming from quite a distance.

"I think I see something ahead," he said.

Moments later, he walked into a half circle of arching stones, Sandy right behind him. The stones were plain, uncarved, unadorned in any way, rooted deep in the black sand. A few had fallen and lay broken. Three causeways stretched away into the darkness as far as the eye could see. Each was lined on both sides by ancient, weathered statues, worn despite the utter lack of wind or moisture. Mark left Sandy standing in the middle of the paved crescent, while he walked the perimeter, staring out into each causeway, one after the other. The statues were different for each path. The one in the middle running straight toward the horizon featured vaguely feline beasts sitting on the plinths with plumed tails curled over their heavily clawed feet. The choice to the left featured only crumbling stones atop the plinths, representations of something or someone eons ago. Winged and bearded beasts guarded the third road, reminding Mark of deer, entwined antlers flashing some gilt here and there. Their dead, painted eyes stared at him in the gloom.

"Which one do we take? Any ideas?" Mark was stymied. "I doubt we have the luxury of making a mistake and then retracing our steps."

"I'm tiring of tests." Sandy joined him, staring at the dark ranks of statues lining the road. "Not the deer."

Pointing to the next road, he asked, "Cats?"

"I don't know." She took the mirror out of its pouch for a quick peek. "No help there. Blank as usual." She strode to the edge of the platform and took a step out onto the causeway of the feline beasts, then retreated to the neutral space of the crescent. "No. This road doesn't feel as wrong to me as the road with the horned creatures did, but it doesn't call to me either."

"But this other row is falling to pieces, crumbling under their own weight." He gestured at the remaining road. "We can't even tell what these statues used to represent."

"I know, but I think it's where we have to go." Sandy replaced the mirror in its embroidered bag. "I can't explain why, but I'm drawn to this road, repelled by the deer, and I got nothing at all when I stepped out toward the felines."

Much as it bothered him to rely on hunches in this uncanny situation, he realized he had nothing better to offer. "Well, then, let's move out."

Hand in hand, they hiked onward at a steady pace. Some of the statues or monuments were less dilapidated than others, but none was even close to being recognizable. Here and there a gap in the sequence appeared, as if the stones had gone to dust. Uneasy, Mark checked the roadway behind them often. "I think we're being followed."

"By what?" She glanced over her shoulder. "I don't see anything."

"It's like a flicker in my peripheral vision, as if whatever is on our trail ducks behind the statues or burrows into the sand when I check our six." He rolled his shoulders.

"And you wish for your blaster," she teased. "Even in a dream."

"Nightmare's more like it. Listen, we can't take chances here. When I fought for you back on Throne, the slash from the force knife was real."

"People don't die in dreams," she said.

"I'm not so sure about that anymore, especially in a dream like the one we're sharing. I think the stakes are high."

A few moments later, Sandy said, "Do you hear something? Like running water?"

He paused for a second. "Yeah, I do."

Mark broke into a run, tugging Sandy to force her to keep up, and in a moment more, they came to the broken end of their causeway. The road fell away, crumbled chunks of pavement and statues strewn down a gentle slope and into a sluggish river. The water eddied past the boulders with crystalline murmuring.

"Shallow, I hope, or we'll be swimming." He didn't relish the idea.

But when Mark descended the slope carefully, afraid of sliding in the loose black sand, he discovered the river was shallow, maybe six inches at the most. Beautiful golden fish darted here and there in the crystal clear water, weaving amongst water lilies and reeds.

Mark braced Sandy as she bent to remove her sandals and waded in, then followed her example, pushing against the slight tug of the current against his lower legs. The fish took no heed of them, other than to avoid direct contact.

"So refreshing." Sandy leaned over, cupping her hands, intending to drink.

"Watch out!" Mark tried to catch the mirror as it fell from the pouch at her belt, but he wasn't quick enough. The mirror plunged into the river, drifting until it became half buried in the sparkling sands. Little fish swarmed, drawn to the glint.

"How did that happen?" Sandy asked, bathing her face with the cool water.

"Maybe the latch broke—" Mark found it odd the pouch at her belt had opened so easily, the loop slipping from the ornate lapis bead securing the precious contents. He found he couldn't remove the mirror from the water, as if the sands had taken on the consistency of cement, holding the relic in place.

Sandy waded through the shallows to stand next to him. "Let me try." Reaching below the surface with both hands, she got a firm grasp on the three-dimensional handle and yanked. The sands released the mirror so willingly she fell backward and would have landed in the water herself if Mark hadn't caught her.

"Look!" Sandy held the artifact away from her as he set her securely on her feet.

Unearthly light poured from the mirror. As Mark watched, a golden shimmer started at the bottom of the handle, flowing up and over the tiny figures of the two goddesses and the warrior, then splaying onto the surface of the mirror itself. Water droplets rained from the mirror like beads of molten gold, pattering on the river's glassy surface. Sandy stared into the oval, which had never reflected anything before. Mark bent over her shoulder.

The gleaming surface reflected their faces, as a mirror should.

"We must be on the right path, then," he said. "Come on, let's get out of this water before we catch a cold. We need to get to the other side and figure out where we have to go next. I'm hoping the road continues."

"Do you think this is the end of the journey?" Sandy went with him, stumbling a bit on the pebbles at the river's edge since her attention was on the mirror, still gleaming but blank now. "What are we supposed to do next? Where are we supposed to go?"

"Don't give up on me now. We've come this far." He pulled her the last few feet onto the bank to stand next to him on the crest.

She bent to refasten her sandals. Gazing above her head, he checked the opposite bank.

Watching them from across the river, as silent and unmoving as the ancient statues, was a huge, reptilian creature easily twelve feet long, with half the body being a spiked tail. Its toes splayed over the sand in a way that suggested to Mark that the animal could cover the shifting surface rapidly. Raising its blunt-nosed head, the animal opened massive jaws, drooling blood-tinged saliva, flicking a long, vivid green forked tongue as if tasting the air. Rising on its stubby front legs, the creature took a deep breath and gave voice to a howling cry.

Sandy retreated a step. "*Tzerde*, how horrible. Is that what's been tracking us?"

"I think so."

The creature turned its head in their direction, hissing. As he watched, the beast flickered in his vision until he couldn't see it at all for a heart-stopping moment. "It must have some powers of camouflage, like a chameleon," he said. "A formidable foe."

Three more of the animals crested the hill, stopping where the first beast had been lingering. It came back into view, the camouflage fading from its body in ripples of color from head to the tail. The newcomers were slightly smaller, but Mark estimated each must weigh well over a hundred pounds. The leader snapped at one approaching too close, sinking its jagged teeth into the shoulder of the encroaching beast and ripping away a generous portion of flesh and muscle, which it spat out as the other beast cringed and screamed.

Hand to her mouth, Sandy retched. "Attracted by the power of the mirror maybe?"

"I'm not waiting around to find out." Mark grabbed her hand and fled. "This is our best chance, while the hunters are distracted."

Risking a glance over his shoulder, he saw the pack slinking down the slope to the river, growling. The original four had been reinforced by three more.

"They're coming. Once those beasts get onto the road, I've no idea how fast they can move, but if one manages to pull us down, we're done for."

He and Sandy sprinted, checking periodically over their shoulders to assess the animals' progress. He was dismayed to see how fast the predators moved on the road. Their camouflage flickered on and off, as if the creatures were challenged to match the deep blackness of the road. This was an advantage for Mark, allowing him to see where the pack moved. The leader gained on the humans, his followers close behind.

A few moments later, they passed a series of tall columns painted with colorful symbols, rising into the mists of the eternal night here. Interspersed with the columns were obelisks, also decorated with incised writing. Mark found it made him dizzy to try to peer too closely at any of the symbols. Gazing upward into the mists induced serious vertigo. "Maybe we're getting somewhere," Mark said. "Maybe we can get some help."

A few more rapid paces through the forest of columns and obelisks took them to the foot of a wall looming out of the dark. Light blazed to the skies on the other side of the obstacle. Mark estimated the wall was a good thirty feet high. The huge white limestone blocks resting on the black sands stretched in either direction as far as the eye could see. Spaced at fifty-foot intervals were gigantic statues of crowned figures seated on huge thrones.

"I don't see a gate—which way should we try first?" he asked.

Sandy held up the mirror, which emitted beams of diffuse light as she pointed it to the west. The illumination diminished as she moved it away from the original heading. "This way."

A few moments later, they came to a massive gate. A trio of huge snakes lay coiled in the sands in front of the portal. Their scales were a patchwork of gold, ruby, and emerald, and their eyes were like embers in the twilight. One reared on its coils, taller than a man stands, hood flared, hissing an unmistakable challenge as Mark ventured closer. The snake's weaving tongue was a needle of fire in the gloom.

"Now what?" Mark asked Sandy. "Any suggestions? We can't fight our way past those monsters."

Sandy took a step closer to the reptiles, avoiding Mark's outstretched hand. The largest serpent watched her, unblinking but swaying on its massive coils. Despite the vast difference in size, something about this creature's eyes reminded her of Sherabti.

"What the hell are you doing?" Clearly, Mark wasn't happy to see her move into the outsized reptile's strike zone.

She checked over her shoulder to find that their unearthly pursuers slowed and stopped, yellow tongues flickering. A smaller animal broke ranks, bloody saliva dripping from its triangular fangs. The stench of the creature's breath as it huffed a challenge was overpowering. One of the snakes lunged forward, biting off the animal's head. Thick red blood oozed like lava from the carcass.

A midsize pack member locked its jaw on the corpse's tail and dragged the body into the sands, where several of the lizards proceeded to fight over the prize. The alpha threw back its head, bellowing a challenge or a command to its disobedient minions. The pack ripped the carcass apart before slinking away into the desert, while the snakes watched with glittering eyes.

"This is costing us precious time. We have a right to be here, and we both carry Sherabti's venom in our veins, which should buy us something," Sandy said, returning her attention to the guardian in front of her. Impatience at the new obstacle pricked her nerves. She wondered if there was a time limit on this quest.

All three snakes became agitated when she mentioned the name of the ancestral goddess's serpent. The other two reared up, forked tongues hissing in and out of cruel fangs, hoods flaring wide. Sandy realized the snakes had retreated a few feet. Princess Sharesi's words about names having power came back to her. Moving carefully, she fumbled with the lapis bead holding the mirror's pouch shut and withdrew the artifact, startled for a moment by the intense golden radiance it gave off. Raising the mirror in her left hand, above her head, she said, "I bid you stand aside, in the name of Nuet." The syllables echoed against the walls, like muted thunder. Sandy took a step forward. The snakes retreated, hissing in jets of blue and yellow flame. She aimed the light from the mirror at first one and then another as she advanced, driving them into a slow, sinuous retreat. Hearing footfalls in the sand, she knew Mark walked at her back.

She'd gained maybe ten paces of progress when the largest serpent slithered forward, lowering its head to stare into her eyes, tongue flicking in and out.

Unblinking, the snake shifted an inch at a time, winding its heavy coils loosely around her body. She heard Mark shout her name as she staggered under the weight but waved him off when he tried to help. The snake's red tongue rasped against Sandy's cheek. She flinched, expecting pain. Relieved to feel nothing but a tickling sensation, she kept herself unmoving, not even breathing for the moment the caress lasted. Hissing, the snake rose high into the misty air of the place above her head before uncoiling and slithering into a crevice in the mighty wall. The other serpents followed suit, gone from view in the blink of an eye despite their massive girth.

Mark grabbed Sandy and gave her a big hug even as he chastised her in a gruff voice. "Magic or not, promise me you won't do anything so risky again."

Trembling from head to toe, she forced herself to speak as she tucked the mirror into its pouch. "We had to get past them somehow."

Shrieking filled the air, drowning out her voice before she could say more as the huge doors of the gate began to grind outward on their hinges. The sound reminded Sandy of men in agony as they're being tortured. She hoped Mark wouldn't have a flashback to his experience at the hands of Ekatereen's interrogators. Jaw set, he kept a viselike grip on her hand as if she was a lifeline. Sandy tugged him forward. The immense portal began to close before she'd cleared the opening. Sprinting, she led her companion away, moving deeper into wherever it was they'd arrived.

The doors clamped together with a solid thunk. Echoes vibrated as the screaming noise died away.

In the space of a breath, the air filled with the sound of a thousand wings and melodic bird calls. Then those too faded, replaced by the whisper of a soft breeze, sweet and perfumed. A light sprang up, golden, blinding, intensifying. Sandy kept her grip on Mark's hand, afraid she'd lose him in this incandescent display.

"Who arrives?" Coming from all sides, the booming voice was huge. "Who comes by this strange path? Who is to be announced to the gods?"

Better say something. "Seekers, come to ask for the right to use the Mirror of the Mother as was intended," Sandy said.

No answer from the voice, but the light intensified further. Sandy could see it now with her eyes closed. Mercifully, the glare dimmed to a more bearable level a moment later. Opening her eyes to check her location, she realized she was no longer beside the gate but standing with Mark in a vast room. Reminding her of Farahna's throne room, back in the capital city in the real world, this celestial chamber had been created on a much grander scale, reducing the queen's palace to nothing but a shabby imitation. A colorful tile floor was underfoot, and Sandy stood next to the first in a series of malachite columns entwined with painted, sculptured flowers, accented with gemstones and gold leaf. Impossible to see the ceiling clearly, details lost in shadows above. She thought she caught a glimpse of stars. "This place is beautiful."

"Welcome to the Palace of Irilkon, my king and ruler of the Exalted Ones." Haatrin walked toward them, toying with a musical instrument of some kind. She blinked, lush sable eye lashes sweeping to her cheeks. "You present a most unusual puzzle, Daughter of Queens. But we have watched, and it is now clear to us that this man is indeed your chosen and loyal consort, suitable for safeguarding the one who wields the Mirror of the Mother."

"I'd give my life for her," Mark said.

"In a sense, you did," Haatrin answered. "Sacrificing all those years as a result of your love, yet fearlessly stepping up to repeat the sacrifice, even in what you thought of as a dream. We understand now much about both of you that was unknown to us. As to the mirror," she said solemnly, "it sees above and below. It also remembers the totality of anything it has *ever* seen, Lady of the Star Wind, and can call upon those memories. But you must ask."

"Ask?" Sandy said.

Haatrin laughed merrily and said no more, shaking her head.

"Sometimes a thing may be granted." The disembodied, booming voice came for the last time.

A light shot from above, enveloping Sandy and spreading to Mark beside her. She felt as if she'd been hit by lightning, all the nerve endings in her body sparking and twitching uncontrollably. She fell to the sands, Mark falling across her as she shut her eyes against the burning glare.

All the bones in his body ached. Mark forced his eyes to open, finding himself facedown on the bed, Sandy curled next to him, moaning. Woozy, off-balance, he sat up. Smoothing her tousled hair off her face, he said her name, alarmed at how pale she looked. Shaking her by the shoulders, he called her name more insistently.

As if her eyelids had been glued shut, Sandy opened her eyes in slow motion. "We're back here?" Struggling to sit, she stared wildly around the room in the predawn light.

"So you—you had the same dream I did?" he asked, putting one arm around her shoulders and pulling her close. "Haatrin, Throne—"

"Giant snakes, black desert, yes, I was there with you. Where's the mirror?"

"Here." Getting a cramp where the handle dug into his leg, he pulled it out from beneath him, disappointed to find that while the artifact was in one piece, it was coated in dust, the surface dull. "Guess we wanted this crazy idea to work so much we dreamed the whole thing."

As he handed it to Sandy, the dust floated away in motes on the air until the flat surface gleamed in the flickering light from the oil lamp on the table next to the bed.

She studied it for a moment, turning the mirror over and over. "Haatrin said I had to ask the mirror, right?"

"As best I recall. My memories are a bit jumbled. But how it works here in the real world—"

"Her cryptic comment is all the guidance we're going to get, I think. At least she was friendlier about it than old Babsuket. I wonder…" Sandy rubbed her forehead as she contemplated the mirror.

"You wonder what?"

"Maybe I have to ask the right goddess."

"Or the warrior," he said, nudging her in the ribs.

She gave him a smile. "As a last resort. I never paid any attention to the alignment before when I was trying to make the mirror work for me."

He gazed into the mirror, catching a brief glimpse of their faces, and then the surface clouded over again. "Now what?" he said. "Was all of it real? Any of it? Did we succeed?"

"I think so."

"Do you feel any different?" he asked.

"Not really." She stretched. "Just sleepy. Not a restful night."

"It's not dawn yet. We can get a few more hours of sleep," he said, pulling her lower on the heaped pillows and drawing the sheets up. "I just hope we don't dream again. Being on Throne again as an untried young man was an unsettling experience, one I hope never to repeat."

He drifted off to sleep, only to be awakened a short time later by pounding on the bedroom door. Groggy, he reached for his blaster and swung out of the bed, pausing for a moment as his feet crunched on a dusting of glittering black sand sprinkled on the floor. Hoping there weren't going to be any more uncanny dreams in their future, he hastened to open the portal.

A disheveled Rothan stood in the hall, accompanied by a servant with a torch. Two guards stood at attention behind them.

Yawning, Mark set the safety on the weapon. "What's wrong? Is Tia okay?"

"Is she ill?" Sandy asked from behind Mark, leaning her chin on his shoulder as she circled his waist with one arm. "Should I get my medical bag?"

"She's gone into labor, and there's been so much blood," the king said. "The women are worried, and I would take it as a great personal favor if you would attend her, my lady."

"Of course. Let me get my robe and my bag." Sandy raced across the room to shrug into a more concealing garment and grab her supplies.

Mark joined her, hastily donning a shirt. He leaned close. "Isn't this too soon? She's hardly been showing at all – how many weeks along is she, do you think?"

Sandy frowned. "Not all women gain huge amounts of weight, you know, especially those who have nausea the entire pregnancy. Based on what Tia told me about when she believes she conceived, this would be somewhat early for her to give birth, but that's not necessarily an emergency. The bleeding could be worrisome, but let me see what the situation is."

"My mother felt we shouldn't bother you," Rothan said as the three of them hurried through the halls, the soldiers and servants trailing. "But she wasn't there when you saved my life when we first met at the oasis. I know of your magic firsthand. If anything happens to Tia—or to my unborn child—"

Sandy patted his shoulder. "Let's don't get too worked up yet. I'll do my best, I promise, if I'm even needed."

Rothan squeezed her hand and stood aside to let her enter the birthing chambers. He took Mark by the elbow and said, "We wait outside at these moments, drink beer, and pray."

"Happy to keep you company." Mark breathed a silent prayer to the Lords of Space to watch over Tia and her unborn child and set himself the task of trying to keep Rothan distracted from the worst of his thoughts. Not that he knew a thing about childbirth either, but he had confidence in Sandy.

A full day and a night passed, and Tia continued to labor in the birthing pavilion. Dawn was coming again. Walking through the billowing curtains, Sandy stretched and inhaled the cool morning air before walking to where Mark sat half drowsing next to Rothan on the bench right outside the pavilion entrance.

Tapping him on the shoulder, she said, "I need to talk to you. Now. In the garden."

He cleared the sleep from his eyes and staggered to his feet, peering past her. "Is the baby—?"

Glancing at the throng of courtiers, guards, and servants hovering a few feet removed from the king, she shook her head. "We can't talk in here."

She walked ahead of him to the edge of the gardens, checking left and right in the predawn gloom to be sure she and Mark were alone. Once they reached the small pond, Sandy paused, taking a deep breath, fighting tears, but she gave herself a mental shake. No time for sentiment if she was going to save Tia's life.

"The baby and Tia are both in danger of dying." She stopped, struggling for control.

Mark pulled her into his arms and held her shaking body. "I'm sorry, Sandy. I'm so sorry. What's happening?"

She drew back but kept her hands on his forearms, as if maintaining contact with him grounded her. "The labor isn't progressing, and Tia's losing strength. I'm thinking there was much more blood loss yesterday than what I was told when I got here. If only I'd—" She broke off again, tears of misery swimming her eyes.

"You had no way of knowing her distress was so serious."

Sandy allowed herself to relax into the hug Mark offered for a moment, resting her head on his shoulder. The backrub he gave her felt heavenly, but she couldn't stop the chorus of worries in her head.

"What exactly is happening? What can you do to help? You've got medical skills that physicians on this planet haven't even dreamed of."

Aware Mark sought to be reassuring, she hated to disillusion him. "The umbilical cord is wrapped around the baby's neck. I don't think it was that way during the whole time she's been in labor. It may have happened when we tried to shift him from the breech position last night. He can't be born the normal way."

"How do you know? I didn't think you brought any large scanners in your bag."

She gestured toward her belt. "I used the mirror, and I could see as clearly as if I did have a scanner. The cord is tight around his neck."

He frowned. "Used the mirror? How?"

"I don't know. I wished for a scanner, for a fetal monitor, for—oh, for a modern hospital! I was frustrated and helpless. The mirror started glowing, and when I took it out of the pouch, the reflection was clearly the baby in the womb. I only caught a glimpse, scarcely long enough to diagnose the problem."

"What can you do?"

"I have to operate. If we were on Throne, I could deliver her baby in two to four minutes, depending on whether there were complications. Minimal risk to mother and child." She sank onto the bench. "But we're not on Throne."

"Can you perform the surgery here?" Mark gestured at the empty sands.

"I know how to deliver a baby surgically. I've done it many times at home, where I specialized in obstetrics." She tried to give him a smile, which she knew was halfhearted. "But I need help. You're going to have to scrub in and assist me." She wasn't going to leave any room for argument. As a soldier, he should be able to handle the sight of blood.

"But how will you do it? You don't have what you need—how much did you bring in that medical kit of yours anyway?"

She raised her eyebrows. "Since I thought I was leaving Throne never to return, I packed a hell of a lot, including things I wouldn't normally carry. Why do you think the damn satchel is so big and so heavy? I can dilute one of the drugs to create a mild anesthesia that won't endanger the baby. I have a small traveling kit of laser scalpels, force clamps, cauterizers. I can do it, but I need at least one more pair of hands. We can get clean linens, boiling water…we'll make the operating field as sterile as we can. Technical issues don't concern me."

"What does?"

"How these people will handle the idea of surgery. Do you think we can talk Rothan into giving permission? And fast?"

Mark rubbed his chin, clearly considering her worries. "Maybe if we tell them it's a form of magic and we make sure he sees as little as possible of the actual procedure. Nakhtiaar medicine includes crude surgery, I know. I've heard Djed and the other soldiers talk about amputations for battle injuries and the like. But medicine for them is all tied up in their superstitions." He swallowed hard. "I've never done anything like this, but I'll try to help."

"I can tell you what to do. You've seen wounded men in the field, surely?"

He held out his hands, palms up, as if baffled. "Of course, but I never learned anything beyond the basics of first aid. Officers don't do battlefield medicine in the Sectors. The duty is left to the sergeants."

"Stay focused on the exact task I give you and listen to my voice. You'll do fine. I've talked many a new intern through their first surgery, and you're tougher than most of them were."

"All right." Mark swallowed hard, but his voice rang with resolve. "We need to brief Rothan, and probably his mother as well, since the women are in charge of anything to do with giving birth. They both have to give permission."

"I agree." Sandy was so impatient she could barely stand still. "Now."

She held out her hand. Mark folded his fingers over hers and walked across the garden and into the corridor leading to the birthing pavilion. Sandy drew strength from Mark's touch, the idea that she and her man were a team, working together in this medical emergency. She'd no doubt about her ability to perform what would be a routine procedure on Throne, but it was going to be much more tricky here in the primitive conditions of Nakhtiaar.

A small crowd of courtiers and priests hovered outside Tia's room. Rothan and his mother stood off to the side, conferring, but broke off their conversation as Mark and Sandy arrived.

"Tia and your son are going to die this morning unless I perform some of my own magic and save them." Sandy launched right into the heart of the matter. No more pussyfooting around the issues, which she'd done for far too long the day before, she now realized. Despite the cold knot in her gut, Sandy refused to stand by and lose Tia.

Rothan didn't seem surprised by her blunt pronouncement, although his face was a study in grief. He looked as if he'd aged ten years overnight. "We were just talking about how hard this labor goes for her and how she's losing strength." Passing his hand over his eyes, he said, "I fear for her. I think her difficulties must be because the cursed Maiskhan priest laid hands on her when we were taken before Farahna. I should have had a purification ritual performed for her once we reached home, but I never thought about it. Nor did she. So much happened."

"And I was unaware," Sharesi said, worrying the fringe of her blue-and-gold shawl. "We'd have performed the usual blessing at the Temple of Haatrin closer to the time the babe was due, but the Maiskhan curse brings the child disastrously early."

Impatient to initiate preparations for surgery, worried about her patient, Sandy opened her mouth to speak. Mark forestalled her with a subtle squeeze of her hand.

"That's what we believe as well," he said, apparently accepting for now the superstitious explanation. "My lady has a solution, a ritual she can perform. But it must be done at once, and without a large audience in order to work."

Princess Sharesi looked her age this morning, frail and hesitant. Even her voice sounded weak to Sandy's ears. "I fear there's more to this ritual than you want to share with us." She glanced at Rothan. "Yet what other choice is there? In all my years of experience, when a woman labors this long and hard with no result, the counters are cast and the loss of mother and child is recorded. We've nothing more *we* can do for her or for my grandchild except to pray, and I know the entire city is engaged in private and public supplication."

"I used the mirror," Sandy said, hoping that might give her listeners some reassurance. "The cord is wrapped around the baby's neck, and he's in distress. I have to get him out soon if I'm going to save either of them."

Rothan looked to his mother, but she tucked the loose ends of her cloak into her waistband and said nothing further. Taking Sandy's hand in his, the king said, "I give my permission for you to do this." He raised his voice, and the nearby courtiers and servants straightened to receive his commands. "Let all here be witness to my decree. There shall be no blame if this attempt fails and mother and child perish. Their lives are in the hands of the gods now."

Princess Sharesi inclined her head. "As His Majesty wills it, so shall it be done. I'll go clear the chamber of the midwives and the attendants."

"I need all clean linens on the bed and a fresh set to drape over Tia as well. Get me two pots of boiling water. I need Mark in there to assist." She laid her hand on Rothan's arm. Speaking for his ears alone, she said, "Let me prepare Tia, and then you can come and stand by her head, hold her hand. I think you should be there."

He raised his eyebrows, his expression one of confusion. "The husband isn't in the room during birth, according to our custom."

"Well, he is where I come from." Sandy was unyielding. "I think she'd want you there, don't you?"

He swallowed hard. "Your words carry force. Tia is a warrior in this battle, and I'll be her shieldmate, stand by her side for whatever comfort I can provide."

"Good." Sandy walked into the pavilion after the princess.

In a moment, all the many women who'd been gathered inside were streaming out, carrying damp and bloody linens, bowls, and other items. Several of the women were crying, and Sandy stared after them for a moment, glad to clear grief and defeatism from the room. Positive attitude was important in emergencies, which this situation had become.

"You can come in now," Sandy said to Mark, lingering on the threshold.

They both washed their hands in the hot water brought by the servants, using a cleansing solution from her supplies. She took Tia's pulse and then listened to her heart, shaking her head as she did so. "Come on, come on, where are the things I asked for? She's sinking fast. I wish I could give her some intravenous fluids, but there's no more time."

Clean linens were brought, and Rothan held his semiconscious wife while Sandy, Mark, and Sharesi remade the bed with fresh bedding. Tia's moans during each fresh contraction were heart-rending. "Lay her in the middle, right here." Sandy indicated the spot to Rothan. "Mark, help me rig the sheet to cover her and obscure the operating field." A bit clumsily, he followed her instructions, getting the desired arrangement in place a moment later.

The king laid his wife on the bed gently. "What next?" he asked Sandy.

"I want you to stand there, by her head, and hold her hand for me. I'm going to put her un—to sleep for a few moments."

Jaw clenched, Rothan seemed at a loss for words. He took one of Tia's slender hands and leaned over.

She opened her eyes at his touch and tried to smile at him. "I'm sorry, my love." Her voice was a whisper.

"Sorry for what, sweetling?" The king's tender voice nearly brought fresh tears to Sandy's eyes, but she gave herself a mental shake. No time for sentiment if she was going to save Tia's life.

"I can't give life to our child. I try and try, but I can't—"

"Hush, you're doing fine." He brushed her damp hair off her forehead. "I'm in awe of your strength. Sandy's going to help you now. The Mirror of the Mother showed her what to do."

"Tia, listen to me, okay?" Sandy hated to interrupt the tender scene, but time was of the essence. She kept her tone brisk, the way she handled medical situations. "In a moment, you're going to feel a tiny prick on your arm, and then you'll sleep for a short time. When you wake up, I'll be handing you a healthy son."

"Do whatever you can for the child." The queen closed her eyes, plainly a woman at the end of her endurance. Rothan took a damp cloth and wiped her face, kissing her cheek.

"I've never seen you quite like this," Mark whispered to Sandy.

"Well, I'm a doctor, what did you expect? Did you keep your hands sterile?"

"Yes." He held them out for her inspection, but she ran the tiny sterilizer from her bag over them anyway, then over the exposed portion of Tia's abdomen. She'd already redone her own hands, in the absence of surgical gloves. "You have to stand here." Sandy indicated where she wanted him to be. "When I've made the incision, you'll have to hold these force clamps here and here, pushing aside the uterine walls so I can get in for the baby. Anything gushes blood, you clamp it off with the cauterizing beam. Got it?"

"No, but once you've begun operating, I'll manage." He got a secure grip on the two tiny devices and rolled his shoulders. His expression was grim, as if he were going into battle.

Which he was, of a sort. "Good." Sandy met Rothan's gaze over the tented linen sheet. "I have to tell you, there'll be blood, lots of it, but she isn't going to die if I can help it. No matter what happens, I'll ensure she suffers no pain."

Rothan nodded, muscle in his jaw twitching. "We're in your hands, Lady, and grateful to have you here."

Taking a deep, cleansing breath, making sure her patient was unconscious, Sandy picked up the laser scalpel. "Here we go."

Her incision was straight, clean, fast, the way she'd done it a thousand times in the hospital environment. Mark moved in with the medical device to close off the bleeding as he'd been instructed, the need becoming obvious as soon as Sandy was done with her scalpel. Trusting him to carry out his assignment, Sandy lifted the small, unmoving baby free of his mother's womb, holding him in one hand and unlooping the umbilical cord with the other.

"Tie off the cord so I can cut it," she said.

"With what?" Somewhat wild-eyed, Mark stared at the items from her medical bag set out on a small table at the bedside.

Someone reached across the sheets to place a strand of catgut in his palm. With considerable annoyance, Sandy realized that despite her orders a young woman had entered the room while her attention was on the incision. Mark flicked off the cauterizer wand, set the instrument on the sheets, and tied a neat, fast knot in the cord. Sandy cut it then and took the baby boy a step or two away.

The child was blue, limp, silent.

"I can do this task, give me the child," the newcomer said, reaching for the baby. "You attend to the mother, else she dies."

Hoping the woman had an acceptable level of competence since she needed to concentrate on Tia right now, Sandy handed her the baby. Wrapping him in a blanket of soft cotton, the attendant held him by the heels and swatted him on the bottom. No reaction. She did it once again, and the baby startled, spread his tiny arms, hands in fists, and screamed, crying lustily.

Registering the strong cry with satisfaction, Sandy was hard at work, neatly closing the small incision in Tia's abdomen with another implement from her emergency kit, applying healing compounds from her Outlier medical bag. She'd removed the placenta and placed it in an urn by the table, having been made aware the day before that this was the local custom.

"She lies so still," Rothan said, voice despairing. "I can't rejoice for the birth of my son if I lose my wife this day."

"It's the anesthesia, the sleep drug I gave her. Not a problem," Sandy answered, summoning her best bedside manner to give reassurance. "She'll come out of it in a moment, which is why I have to work so fast. There, see? She moved."

Sandy finished her procedures as Tia stirred, attempting to sit. Rothan pressed her onto the pillows.

"My baby! Where's my baby?"

"Here, Your Majesties." The young woman, who'd silently been holding the crying infant, stepped forward and placed the screaming boy into Tia's arms. Rothan shifted to help support his wife as the baby stopped crying and began rooting for his mother's breast.

"Your son will be much blessed," said the nurse. She made a sign in the air over the baby and the queen, which glowed green for a heartbeat before winking out. "He will live long. His reign shall be one of peace and plenty. You did well, Lady of the Star Wind," she said with a sly grin and a wink over her shoulder as she walked to the doorway, passing Princess Sharesi.

"Who is that woman?" the princess demanded, turning to stare.

"One who takes an interest in these events," the nurse said with a merry laugh as the drapes fell shut behind her.

Sandy thought the laugh and the voice were familiar. Running into the hall, where knots of birthing women and courtiers waited, she glanced in both directions as the crowd stared open-mouthed at her. "Where is she?"

"Who, my lady?" asked an official.

"The nurse, the woman who just left us."

"There was no one." Several in the gathering exchanged puzzled glances. "All the birthing nurses and the maids are waiting over there, as ordered. No one has gone in or out of the room except for Princess Sharesi a few moments ago."

"Tell us, how fares it with the queen?" asked Sallea, standing with Khefer.

"She's fine, a healthy boy," Sandy answered a bit absently. Her nostrils were full of the scent of the purple river lily, which didn't grow within hundreds of miles of this mountain plateau.

She re-entered the birthing pavilion.

Mark tilted his head in a silent question.

"The courtiers and servants all claim no one came into the hall. Do you think she might have been Ha—"

"No names!" ordered Princess Sharesi, cutting Sandy's question off with an emphatic slice of her hand. "Speak no names of power! Always you're so reckless on this score. Leave it as She said—the boy will be blessed. He's blessed already indeed."

Mark walked over to take a peek at the baby, now drowsing in his mother's arms. "Wow, he has a lot of hair. What are you going to name him?"

"Hutenen Khunarum." Rothan checked with Tia for her agreement. Tired smile on her face, she played with the baby, admiring his chubby fingers, and repeated the name in a whisper as her son curled his hand around hers.

"Sounds good." Sandy approved of the choice. It felt right.

Mark wiped his forehead. "I need a drink of something strong."

"You did a great job," Sandy told him. "You could get work as an ops nurse any time."

"I can never thank you enough, either of you, for saving my wife and my son." Rothan's voice choked with emotion. "Always you're at hand in our moment of need."

"It was an honor," Sandy said. "As a doctor, I want to bring as many babies safely into the world as possible."

"No matter which world it may be," Mark couldn't resist teasing her.

"I'll have a large breakfast ordered," Princess Sharesi said. "And for you, my lord Mark, there will definitely be the plum wine you are so fond of."

Later, much later, after she and Mark had gone to their own quarters to try for a nap, and after making love, Mark raised himself on one elbow to stare at Sandy's face.

"What?" she asked with a laugh. "Have I broken out in spots or something?"

"You were magnificent today, operating on Tia under these conditions."

Mark was so damn competent at everything he did that his admiration made her heart beat faster, even as she realized with considerable annoyance she was blushing. "Thanks. I think you've said it about a hundred times this evening. Not that I get tired of hearing it! But except for the surroundings, it's a routine procedure." She gave him a quick kiss, then peered more closely at him, realizing he was trying to hide something behind his praise. "What's really on your mind?"

"What if the same thing happens to you? If we have children here someday and there are complications? What could we do about it? You can't operate on yourself, and I couldn't begin to even try. Could I? Could you talk me through it somehow? We can't count on the Goddess Haatrin to make an appearance again."

"I'll be all right, I promise you. What happened to Tia is a one-in-a-thousand occurrence. We Zhivanovs are hardy stock. Ordinarily, women in my family give birth with no problems. Consider how many descendants Ekatereen has, or had before the mystery virus hit, anyway."

Mark fell onto his pillow beside her, apparently not convinced. "Guilt is eating at me for dragging you into this low-tech world. The Nakhtiaar have proven to be good people, they do need our help, but the risks to you—"

She touched his lips with her fingertips. "Stop. We've had this conversation before, and I don't ever want to have it again." Kissing his cheek, she snuggled closer. "There are always risks in childbirth, no matter how civilized or high-tech a place is. I told you before, and I meant it, that since you came to Freemarket for me, I've been *living*, not simply existing. I'm content. I do think the mysterious nurse today was Haatrin, come today to help Tia and her baby but also to reassure *us*. She wanted to let us know we're protected. You haven't even considered one of the most exciting developments."

"Which was?"

"I used the mirror, remember? I wished to see something, and there it was! The experience was amazing, let me tell you. I wonder what else I'll be able to do once I figure out how to command the powers it holds."

"The concept scares me a bit too." Mark nipped at her ear. "I think we have to be careful with your tricky mirror."

"When did you become such a cautious soul?" Sandy laughed out loud at his expression. "I thought you were the adventurous one. Relax, go with the events, because you sure can't control them."

"I think you're right. I'm all about control, knowing what I have to do and getting it done. Since we got to this place, we've been carried along on the tide. Takes some adjustment. I also never, ever cared about anything or anyone in the Sectors, so I was free to take any risk. You know?"

"I know." She caressed his cheek. "And now?" she teased.

"And now, my beautiful princess, I care about every damn thing." He rolled his eyes.

"But some things are more important to you than others?"

"Allow me to demonstrate." His hand slid under the light sheet covering her naked body.

"Again?" she purred with a smile.

"There's no sword practice or battle planning today, so I have to practice something." Now it was his chance to tease her.

CHAPTER EIGHT

Two days later Mark and Sallea were drilling their cavalry recruits, putting the men and horses through maneuvers on a large field adjacent to the general's estate. Things were not going well, to put it mildly, Mark thought as they took a break to rest the horses. "The men are willing, but the training is too new to them."

"Riding itself is still a novelty," Sallea agreed. She handed him a waterskin. "I wish we had more instructors than just you and me. No offense, my lord, but you're much distracted with other matters."

"I know, but I rarely have a choice about what Rothan needs me to do." He surveyed his squad. "Right now, I wouldn't take them into battle, would you?"

Regretfully, she shook her head. "It would be a slaughter. Perhaps they could harry an enemy column, make attacks while the Maiskhan were on the march."

"Which is not how I told Rothan we'd use them."

Before she could answer, Khefer drove up the road that bordered the training field. Sallea sighed. "I suppose he's come to taunt us yet again." She ran a hand through her messy braid. "The man is besotted with chariots."

Since Khefer was gesturing to them, Mark said, "Guess we'd better see what he wants." He galloped to the road, Sallea close behind, followed by the flag bearer and the herald assigned to shadow them.

The captain had news. "We've been summoned to the province gate. Well, the two of you have, and I volunteered to drive you there. Rothan's already left, so we'd better hurry."

"What's going on? Has there been an attack?" Mark dismounted, handing his reins to the flag bearer. "Dismiss the troop," he said to the herald.

Khefer shook his head. "I don't believe so." He watched impatiently as Sallea and Mark climbed into his chariot, then he set his horses in motion the moment they were safely aboard.

The trip to the border was accomplished in record time with Khefer driving, and the three of them were soon climbing the ramparts to join Rothan, escorted by Nemiah, the efficient commander of the border who'd greeted them upon arrival, not so long ago.

The king was grinning, setting Mark's fears of an enemy incursion at rest. "We've got new allies," he said. "I've waited to greet them until you arrived, Lady Sallea, as they're well known to you."

She grinned. "As I told you two days ago, when Lakht observed the column in the mountain pass, my father's men have arrived at your gate, then?"

Rothan nodded, extending his arm to her. Mark wasn't happy that he hadn't been briefed but reminded himself Sallea didn't really answer to him. Her status as an ambassador put her in a unique category at Rothan's court. Khefer looked as surprised as Mark felt. The two of them trailed the king and Sallea as they strolled arm in arm through the fort and to the gate, where Nemiah waited to order the portal opened. Once Rothan gave permission, the doors were cranked apart, revealing a group of twenty Mikkonite standing at attention beside their graceful horses. One man who seemed familiar to Mark stood in front of the group.

As the troop saluted sharply, Mark remembered that the officer in charge had gone with them to the lost city of Amaraten. His name was Sethmre, and he'd stayed close to Sallea on the excursion across the desert. The lady walked through the gate to greet her people, returning their salutes before hugging Sethmre and becoming the center of an excited group of warriors, all talking at once while Lakht dive-bombed the area.

Mark gave Khefer a glance. The charioteer's jaw was clenched, his stance rigid.

"Have they come to escort her home, Your Majesty?" Khefer asked, brow furrowed.

"I hope they came to fight," Mark said. "I could use them in so many ways."

Rothan shrugged. "Once the initial excitement dies down, we'll find out. When Sallea told me a few days ago the men had been spotted by her hawk, she seemed to think her father had sent troops to fight under her command."

Sallea detached herself from her countrymen, returning to where the king waited, Sethmre striding beside her. "Good news, Your Majesty. As I hoped, my father renews his oath of support for you and has sent me one of our best squads to employ on your behalf, in whatever way I see fit. May I present Sethmre? He's my second-in-command."

"The extended conversation is best held out of the open," Rothan said. "We'll retire to the commandant's office. Mark, I'll need you. In the meantime, Captain Khefer, please escort the troops to the military compound at General Intef's estate and see to their accommodations."

Khefer saluted stiffly and moved to join the Mikkonite in the outer yard. Rothan caught his arm. "I'll expect you to join us at dinner."

Solemn expression lightening a bit, Khefer nodded. "It will be my pleasure, sir." He gave Sallea and Sethmre a sideways glance as they laughed over some joke, and then he marched away.

Efficient as always, Nemiah had wine waiting for them by the time Rothan brought them to the office. "A toast to your successful journey across Nakhtiaar," he said, raising the glass to Sethmre.

After the toast had been drunk, Sallea poured herself another and said, "Before I slipped off his ship the day you were taken to the tombs, Your Majesty, I made Demari promise to get word to my father about how events had turned out. I indicated I would make my way to your grandfather's estate, regardless of your fate, to carry news to him of how your excursion to the Empty Lands had gone."

"Thank you." Rothan nodded. "Had we not survived, that would have been a great comfort to my mother and grandfather."

"Our orders were to find Sallea here and report to her," Sethmre said, his voice gravelly and deep. "As we crossed Nakhtiaar, we heard much about how you'd gone to the afterlife, Your Majesty. I'm relieved to find the tales untrue."

"No whisper of him being alive? Being the true king?" Mark was curious.

"A few hints about the general setting up his own king, and we only began to hear those words as we drew close to this province."

"Interesting." Mark set his glass on the table with a thump. "I, for one, would like to request these men be assigned to my cavalry unit, under Lady Sallea's command, of course. We might be able to get my Nakhtiaar recruits whipped into shape by the time the war starts if we have Mikkonite tutors."

"That's my intention," Sallea assured him, grinning. She turned to Rothan. "I wish to fight for your cause, Your Majesty, and if I can do it surrounded by my own men, so much the better."

"My honor and good fortune to have such allies," Rothan said, raising his glass.

Days passed in preparation for the war to come. Mark and Sandy took refuge in the peaceful gardens as often as schedules allowed, making up for twenty years of separation. There were strict orders in the royal household that no one was to disturb them during these interludes unless the king himself declared an emergency. Therefore, Mark was surprised one afternoon to hear someone approaching their private pavilion.

"Excuse me, my lord?" Sallea stood on the crushed red rock border at the edge of the garden enclosure. Her face was drawn in lines of worry.

"What is it?" All sorts of dire things came rushing to Mark's mind, attack by the Maiskhan topping the list. The desert warrior princess had been unflappable in all the situations she'd faced, but at the moment she appeared quite agitated.

Sallea fidgeted for a moment, which wasn't her normal style at all, playing with her perpetually messy braid of blue hair. She sighed and met Mark's eyes. "It's Captain Khefer."

"What about him? Is he home?"

She shook her head. "He's in trouble, I'm sure of it."

Mark and Sandy exchanged surprised glances. "He left the day after the big ceremony and feast, the one in thanks for the bountiful harvest." Mark counted the days since the holiday. "So he's not due to return yet. No need to worry."

"Yes, my lord. He did leave then, you're right, but I have a bad feeling in my gut." She rubbed her stomach. "I—I am worried for him."

Realizing she was quite upset, Mark drew her into the pavilion and poured her a glass of his favorite plum wine. As he handed her the goblet, he said, "Khefer's a tough, smart soldier. He can take care of himself."

Sandy urged Sallea to join her on the couch, but as soon as she sat, the Mikkonite warrior unburdened herself about what more was bothering her. "We argued about this trip, about the necessity of him going to the city yet again. Our last words together were in hot anger. I think he's rash and takes too many chances. He almost got captured last time and very narrowly escaped. Did he tell you about it?"

"No. But even if he'd told us, we need the information he's gathering," Mark said. He shrugged. Khefer was doing what elite soldiers did in any society, acting as the tip of the spear. "Rothan would've sent him in anyway. Not because he's heartless, but because any mission you walk away from is successful. The whole invasion of Farahna's territory is on hold, waiting for Khefer to report whether his allies inside the city are ready to aid us and what they can do. He's the only person who knows the contacts in the resistance."

"I'm fully aware of the importance of what Khefer is doing—as my father's ambassador, I sit in the war councils along with you," Sallea said, impatience in her voice. "And give me credit for being a warrior myself." She rose and paced from one end of their small pavilion to the other. "But the premonition has grown stronger since yesterday, until I can't concentrate on anything else. I fear the misgivings are a sign from the gods he's in deep trouble. Even if my own emotions weren't involved, he's key to launching the invasion. We must do something." She flung the goblet at the far wall and covered her eyes with one hand for a moment. "If you won't help me, I'll go alone. No one here can overrule me on this."

Sandy spoke. "Let me try the mirror, see if we can get a glimpse of him maybe."

"You can use it thus?" Eyebrows raised, Sallea paused in her restless prowling.

Sandy grimaced. "Well, hit or miss. I've been practicing every spare moment I get. But I think it's worth a try in this case."

"Did you send Lakht out to search?" Mark asked the desert woman.

Hands on her hips, jaw clenched, Sallea stared at the sky as if the answers she sought were written in the clouds. "This morning. He flew along the mountain paths a great distance, two days' ride at least, but found no sign of Khefer, which only worries me more."

Lifting the mirror off her belt, Sandy adjusted the handle so the young goddess faced upward. Closing her eyes, she concentrated. Mark and Sallea moved closer, peering over her shoulder at the misty surface of the mirror.

Tendrils of fog rippled behind the glass face of the ancient device. Minuscule flashes of white light came and went in the mist. Sandy opened her eyes, pursed her lips, and whispered a soft breath onto the mirror. The surface cleared, showing only Sandy's worried face for a heartbeat.

Then Khefer appeared, shown from the shoulders up. Bruised and battered, his lip split, one eye purpled and swollen shut, the warrior was speaking to someone behind him. He and the unseen companion were apparently running, stumbling. Mark felt his own soldier's instincts rising and his adrenaline spiking in response to the overpowering sense of urgency and danger.

The vision evaporated.

Sandy blinked and sat down, Mark hastily moving to assist her.

"Any clue where he was?" Mark asked both women. "Did you recognize any landmark in his vicinity?"

Sallea shook her head. "The mirror shows my fears have a basis in fact. We must get to him."

Reaching out to take Sallea's hand, Sandy said, "Sometimes I get an inkling where the vision is located, but not this time. Sorry."

Mark squeezed her shoulder. "We got enough to confirm Sallea's hunch. He's in trouble but thankfully alive. Sallea, get Sethmre and four of our best men and meet me at the stables in fifteen minutes. We'll need trail supplies and extra arrows. A physician's kit."

"Yes, sir." She snapped the crisp Sectors salute instituted by Mark for his nascent cavalry troop. "Thank you, my lord." She hastened from the pavilion, long legs flashing as she took the shortcut across the gardens.

"She has it so bad for Khefer. The two of them grew so close on the long trek here from the tomb, but lately relations apparently have been strained between them." Leaning on the pillows as if her efforts had drained her, Sandy raised her eyebrows. "Do you have any idea how he feels about her?"

Uncomfortable with the topic, Mark got her more wine. "I think he deems her beyond his reach since she's her father's heir. He alluded to the problem once, after her men arrived and it became clear how extensive the Mikkonite kingdom is and how high her rank."

"But he's an officer, one of Rothan's inner circle—" Sandy broke off. "Well, the two of them will have to sort out the challenges. Are you going to go all the way into the city after him? Do you want me to come, since he might be injured?"

Mark shook his head. "I'm not risking you." He took her hand, raising it to his lips for a gentle kiss. "He'll have to survive until we bring him home to you for medical care. To your other question, I'm not venturing into the city without the army. Khefer was on the move in your mirror, so I'm hoping he's on his way back to us." Thinking about the officer and the information he might be bringing, Mark was unable to sit. Rising, fists clenched, he paced. "We need to know whatever he may have found out about Farahna's plans of course but, perhaps more important, he's a good man and soldier. I count on him when we do go to battle. He's forward thinking and creative on the fly, unlike some of these other contemporaries of General Intef's."

"I like Khefer. We owe him a lot. But I worry about you the most. I know, you're a soldier, you can take care of yourself, like you told Sallea about Khefer." Sandy rose from the couch, coming to slide her arms around him from behind, holding him close. "All right, I'll wait here. Go, time's wasting."

Pulling her to face him, Mark indulged in a kiss not nearly as long as he wanted and then left the pavilion, hurrying to the house to get his own gear. As he entered the cool, dim hallway, he paused before heading through a side corridor toward the large chamber recently repurposed to serve as a throne room. He stepped past the guards with a whispered word to the captain in charge, moving into the crowded room. Too late he remembered it was a general audience day, where Rothan had to listen to petitions and adjudicate disputes. Throngs of people came to these assemblies. Mark didn't want to attract attention, but he needed to give Rothan a quick briefing. Being taller than most Nakhtiaar, he caught the king's eye over the heads of the crowd.

Rothan finished delivering his judgment in the case before him and called a temporary halt to the proceedings, leaving the room while his audience bowed. Hastily, Mark exited the chamber before anyone could buttonhole him and hurried to the private antechamber to meet the king, arriving first.

"I don't know where you get the patience to listen to this stuff for a whole day," Mark said as Rothan walked in. "Some of these arguments are pretty petty for a king's attention. Doesn't anyone filter any of this before it gets to you?"

Crossing to the wine jugs on an ebony table along the far wall, Rothan laughed without much amusement. He poured himself a full goblet and offered one to Mark, who shook his head. "Goes with the crown, my friend. Yes, there are regional courts and judges, but right now all the residents of the province are curious about their new king. Time enough to change things after we win the war. But I'm glad of a moment's relief today. What brings you?"

"Khefer's in serious trouble."

"How do we know?" Brow furrowed, Rothan took a swallow of the wine.

"Sallea suspected something wasn't right, and Lakht couldn't find him within two days' ride of here, so Sandy checked up on him in the mirror just now. From the little we observed, he's been attacked and is on the run. I'm taking Sallea and four of my men. We'll ride the back trails, see if we can meet him."

"Don't you mean Sallea is taking you? She's so worried about Khefer she can't see straight." Setting the wine cup on the table, Rothan examined the tray of sweetmeats and breads, selecting a morsel. "Of course, go. I need you here in a ten day, though, for the conclave of provincial rulers. We'll be discussing the final strategies. I'll want your assessment of them."

"And of the rulers and their officers. I know. Wouldn't miss it."

Grabbing the goblet once more, Rothan drained it and set the flower-shaped alabaster cup on the table with unusual force. "Gods know I'd rather ride with you than return to the judgment chamber. I'm weary of the squabbles of merchants, farmers, and family members! Fair outcome to your journey, my friend. Tell the armorer if you have need of anything."

"Will do." Moving fast now that his duty to notify Rothan was accomplished, Mark left the private meeting room.

Sallea had the squad ready in the stable courtyard when he got there a few moments later. His own horse stamped and snorted, impatient to be in motion. Mark appraised the Mikkonite riders she'd selected. All good men, fierce fighters, seasoned and reliable. "Glad to have you each along on this mission." He swung into his saddle. "Let's ride."

Sallea led the column out of the confines of the estate at a gallop, past the edge of the city. At the point where Mark was on the verge of suggesting a more moderate pace, she reined in her mount, settling to a reasonable speed for traversing the mountain foothills.

The hidden trail wound across the range of peaks surrounding and protecting Intef's territory. The terrain was treacherous and unforgiving. It took three days of careful riding for Mark and his squad to make their way to the path descending into the great plain of Nakhtiaar. There'd been no sign of Khefer or anyone else, and the border patrol unit they encountered confirmed no one had penetrated the province.

At the farthest edge of Intef's domain, Mark and Sallea conferred, while their small troop waited, resting the horses.

"Worried as I am about Khefer, do we risk riding into Farahna's territory?" Sallea asked.

Mark shook his head. "We can't tip our hand. Not unless we're sure we know where to find him. Send Lakht out again. Tell him to fly no farther than a one-day ride could cover. We can't venture any closer to the city."

She bit her lip as if she wanted to argue, but she took her hawk to the edge of the plateau and sent Lakht off, riding the thermals to search.

Mark issued orders. "Cache the supplies. And then let's have a quick lunch while we wait for the bird to report. No cooking fire."

Several hours passed before the hawk returned, screaming a fierce greeting. Lakht swooped in for a landing on Sallea's reinforced, padded glove and took the tidbit she offered as a reward. Then woman and bird stared at each other for a long moment, sharing the memory of what Lakht had seen on his flight.

"A camp, about half a day's ride. Abandoned. A column of riders. Maiskhan. Going fast. Returning to the city," Sallea muttered as the images came to her from Lakht. "Two prisoners."

"Two prisoners?" Mark was surprised. Who could have been with the young officer?

"One of them is Khefer." Sallea broke eye contact with the hawk, wheeling to check Mark's reaction. She blushed. It had become a new habit of hers whenever the captain's name was mentioned in her presence. "I recognized him and Khefer is a person of interest to Lakht as well, because of what he means to me. Normally, Lakht doesn't bother to identify specific people when we're speaking mind to mind but he did name Khefer just now."

Mark decided to let that information pass without comment. "Good work. How many Maiskhan?"

"Ten." Sallea frowned. "Lakht showed me at least ten. There could be more. He wasn't interested in them."

"The enemy wanted to be sure of capturing Khefer. And whoever is with him." Mark gestured for the rest of the squad to gather around. "The odds are pretty good, ten of them to seven of us, if we can keep the element of surprise." He eyed the sun's position low in the sky. "I remember when we were rescued from the tomb someone told me the Maiskhan have superstitions about riding or fighting at night. I'm guessing they'll make camp in an hour or two. We'll ride straight through, have Lakht fly reconnaissance ahead for us so we don't overrun them. I intend for us to pull off a surprise attack before dawn. My highest priority after rescuing Khefer is not to leave any survivors to take tales of us back to the city."

"Neither I nor my men have the slightest reluctance about killing Maiskhan soldiers," Sallea said, hand on the hilt of her sword. "However many we slay here make fewer to face when we invade the lowlands."

The Mikkonite soldiers muttered agreement.

Glancing around the tight circle of warriors, he felt the chance of success was high. "All right, then, let's mount up and move out."

He worked his way down the last part of the mountain slopes before night fell, the Mikkonite following him effortlessly on their highly trained mounts. There was a full moon—Amrell yet again—which was an advantage on the early part of the ride. Mark kept the squad to an easy canter, with periodic breaks to walk the horses. He wanted to reach the Maiskhan before dawn, but he couldn't afford to have exhausted mounts when it came time to retreat. Lakht circled, a dark shadow in the night sky, crossing the moon as he patrolled. As the moon slipped behind the horizon, the hawk cried softly, and Mark halted the column with an upraised hand.

"The enemy is camped beyond the next rise," Sallea reported as Lakht made lazy eights in the sky and sent her images through their shared mental link. "One guard. The two prisoners are tied together in the center of the camp by the fire."

"All right, we ride in hard and fast." He pointed at Sethmre. "You're responsible for rescuing Khefer and the other prisoner. Pick a partner for the task and get our men out of harm's way as quickly as you can."

The warrior saluted in silent acknowledgment of the order.

"The rest of us will take care of the enemy soldiers." Mark drew his blaster, checked the charge, and replaced the weapon in the holster.

"You can't kill them all from a distance, my lord?" Sallea asked. "It would be so much easier to use your magic."

"I could, but my magic doesn't have infinite capacity. I'd rather keep it for emergencies. I'll use it fast enough if it's required to win, don't worry."

Mark led his cavalry crashing into the small Maiskhan encampment at full gallop. Sallea took out the single sentry with a well-thrown lethal knife, the blade choking off the man's yelled warning. Lakht dropped from the sky to attack a soldier rising from his bedroll, razor-sharp talons making short work of the foe. Riding to the center of the camp, Mark dismounted by the fire, standing over the helpless Khefer and the other man as a Maiskhan officer ran at him, sword in hand. Mark engaged the enemy in a slashing, no-holds-barred battle over and around the bound prisoners. The Maiskhan was a good enough fighter, but Mark was relentless. The skirmish ended with the enemy bleeding out on the ground from multiple wounds. Mark delivered the killing blow, pivoting to meet the next challenge as two more men rushed him. He shot one with the blaster to even the odds as he was raising his sword to blunt the second man's attack. Seeing his comrade die between one step and the next appeared to demoralize the oncoming warrior, who made a halfhearted show of force before trying to flee. Reluctant to shoot the man in the back but unwilling to let anyone escape, Mark gave chase, tackling the fleeing man to the ground. They rolled over, punching and wrestling, but the

Maiskhan was no match for Mark's hand-to-hand combat skills. He knocked the opponent out with a well-aimed blow to the throat.

Breathing hard, sword at the ready, Sallea ran up. "Is he dead?"

Mark shook his head. "Unconscious. We'll have to take him with us as a prisoner. I'm not leaving anyone behind to be questioned about us."

Turning, Sallea yelled to one of her men to bring rope.

"Situation report?" Mark cleaned his sword.

"All the others are dead or dying. Sethmre took Khefer and the other prisoner out of here, per your orders." She gave quick orders to the Mikkonite who ran to them holding a length of rope.

Leaving her to handle the task, Mark was free to assess the situation in the camp. "Leave the bodies here for the jackals," Mark said. "Take their horses. We can use more mounts, even if we do have to train them to the saddle. I'm going to check the tent, see if there's anything in there we need. Get going with the Maiskhan prisoner."

"Where do we meet?" asked Sallea as one of her companions ran to the horse line.

"Don't stop until you reach the camp where we ate lunch yesterday on the edge of the plateau. Now get out of here. I'll be right on your heels, I promise."

"You wish to ride so far before we halt?" Sallea followed Mark toward the small tent. "What if Khefer is badly wounded? What if he needs care?"

"He's tough, he'll make it. It's clear from the way they treated him that the Maiskhan wanted him alive, so I doubt if he's got any life-threatening wounds. Your men can bandage anything less serious. Now go, no time to talk." Not stopping to watch her ride out, Mark grabbed a torch and ducked under the tent flap. It took him only a few moments to search the small enclosure, seizing scrolls and maps, which he tucked into his saddlebag. He set the tent on fire before galloping away from the scene himself, hoping to cause a bit more confusion for whoever eventually came to investigate.

A few hours later, Mark rode past the sentry into his own small camp. With obvious pain and difficulty, Khefer rose from a bedroll by the fire. Leaning on Sallea, he came to greet Mark. She kept her grip on Khefer until he'd gotten his balance. Reaching around her, Khefer shook Mark's hand.

"Thank you for coming after me, my lord."

"Thank Sallea. She's the one who realized you were in difficulties." Mark took a waterskin from one of the Mikkonite soldiers and drank deeply before pouring water on his head and face. The long hours in the saddle, followed by a short but fierce battle and then more riding, had taken its toll.

"I have thanked her and will continue to do so." Khefer hugged the woman closer. She buried her face in his dusty, stained tunic. With a measure of astonishment, Mark realized she was weeping.

"I feared I'd never see you again," she said to Khefer, her voice muffled. "I so regretted the anger in our last moments together before you rode away."

"Shh, all forgotten now." Khefer tipped her chin so he could kiss her. "You were right, I ran a great risk. I had to go, though. There were things we needed to know. I won't be going to the city again, not until we return with the king and his army to wreak vengeance on Farahna."

Mark handed the waterskin to the soldier with a word of thanks and dried his face with his sleeve. He rested his hand on Khefer's shoulder. "You okay?"

"More or less. The Maiskhan beat me when they caught us, but their commander said he was saving the serious punishment for Farahna's pleasure later in the city."

"So who did we rescue with you? One of the good guys, I hope."

"Indeed." Khefer exuded triumph despite his bruised face and disheveled appearance. "My companion is Sapair."

"Name sounds familiar." Mark frowned, trying to make the connection.

"He served as Seroj's deputy at the royal palace. After Seroj died in the earthquake, the night you and our king were taken prisoner, Farahna elevated Sapair to chief official of the royal household."

Snapping his fingers, Mark said, "I remember Seroj. Fat little ass kisser. He deserved what he got—I shed no tears over him. Can't say I recall this Sapair, but if you vouch for him, that's good enough for me."

"Sapair's injuries are far more serious than mine," Khefer said.

"We'll camp here tonight," Mark told Sallea, who waited nearby in expectation of orders. "And leave at first light. We need to get to the general's compound as fast as possible. Will Sapair be able to sit a horse by morning?"

"Sethmre works on him even now, my lord," Sallea answered. "He has the healing touch and is trained as a physician's assistant, but this Sapair we rescued has been much tortured and hasn't regained consciousness."

"I want to see him for myself." Mark glanced at Khefer. "I'm going to need a debrief from you. Are you able to give details now, or do we need to wait?"

"Now is fine of course, my lord." Khefer saluted without his usual grace and fluidity, grimacing as the move apparently aggravated his injuries.

Mark frowned. "I'm no expert, but I think you have a broken rib or two. Let Sallea's trooper strap your chest before we ride out. Sandy's waiting to examine you when we get home."

Trailed by Khefer and Sallea, Mark walked to the fire, where the Mikkonite healer was on his knees in the flickering light, bandaging the stranger's hands.

Mark leaned over to study the unconscious man's face in the moonlight, augmented by the ruddy glare of the flames. This was the official who'd been so sympathetic to them in the holding cell the morning of Hutenen's burial. He was the one who'd brought them food, warm water to bathe in, and clothing.

"And now he's on the run from Farahna?" Mark asked Khefer. "What happened? And why should we trust him?"

"Sapair is a good man, loyal to the true gods. His partner is Ebnar, captain of the household guards. Ebnar is the one who helped me hide in the ranks after Hutenen's murder. He and Sapair have been my greatest sources of information about Farahna's plans all this time," Khefer answered. "She trusted them. Both men held key positions and overheard much of her planning with the Maiskhan. What one wasn't privy to, the other often supplied to me."

"What happened to Ebnar?"

"I'm not sure. Somehow he was betrayed. He played an even more dangerous game than I. When I entered the city this last trip, a trap had been laid for me at the inn where I was to meet Ebnar. After my narrow escape from the snare, I couldn't find out what happened to Ebnar, whether he was dead or imprisoned. I did learn Sapair had also been seized and was being held in a cell in the palace, awaiting execution. Even in these treacherous times, he has friends in the royal household who helped me rescue him and get out of the city. He was so badly injured we couldn't travel fast enough, and the Maiskhan managed to pursue and capture us on the trail. How did you know where to find us? Was it mere chance?"

Mark glanced at Sallea, uncertain how much of her private worry and premonition she wanted to discuss. The Mikkonite shook her head ever so slightly, and Mark said, "My Lady used the mirror to search for you. The vision she received made it obvious you were in danger. Then Sallea tracked you with Lakht's help." Hunkering down beside the fire, Mark studied the unconscious man as Sethmre finished bandaging his injuries. "What's wrong with his hands?"

"The queen's torturers broke them," Khefer said, face set in grim lines. "One bone at a time until all were shattered, I was told. In front of the whole court. She intended the torture as an object lesson in case anyone else thought of betraying her."

"Why ruin his hands?" Sallea asked, pale and swallowing hard.

Khefer grimaced as if he shared Sapair's pain. "His hands were the most important tools he had to practice his profession, keeping the records and the books."

"A man's mind is the most important thing," Mark countered. "If he can think and walk and talk, then there's hope. I don't know what Sandy might be able to do about this type of injury, but she'll try all her techniques."

"I've set the major bones in his hands as best I can, my lord." Rising to his feet, the Mikkonite healer stretched. "But I can tell the queen's torturers took extra care to smash the smaller finger bones to splinters. I'm glad he was unconscious while I worked. I marvel he survived."

Reminded too much of his own past, Mark didn't want to dwell on the details of the torture. "Can he ride tomorrow? Or be carried on a horse?"

"If he wishes to live, then he must, is that not true, my lord?" The soldier shrugged as he packed his kit. "We can't linger here. I've given him a distillation of the painkilling herbs we grow in Mikkon, which should give him relief for some hours."

"You speak the truth about not staying here. I'll sit with this man tonight. You need rest," Mark told Khefer. "We're going to be riding hard tomorrow. On second thought, I'll wait for your report—you can debrief the king and me together once we're safely home. Go, have something to eat and then sleep. That's an order."

Khefer saluted. Sallea helped him limp toward the meal being set out across the fire by the Mikkonites. Seating himself where the healer had been a moment before, Mark pulled the blanket over the unconscious man's shoulders before leaning against the tree sheltering his camp. A soldier brought him a plate of the simple trail food, which he ate before dozing off, having no doubt his men would guard the small camp well, especially with Sallea in their midst.

Some time in the middle of the night, a low moan from the patient woke him. Reaching for the waterskin, he propped the man up so he could drink, careful not to disturb Sapair's bandaged hands.

Wiping his lips on his sleeve, blinking, Sapair studied Mark in the scant light from the dying fire. "The Warrior of the Star Wind—how can this be? Have I gone to the afterlife?"

"Easy, you're not dead. You're with friends. We got you and Khefer away from the Maiskhan, and we've given you something for the pain. Tomorrow we're heading into the mountains, with General Intef's stronghold as our destination."

"There are rumors in the city about General Intef rallying the southern provinces and mounting a rebellion. There is speculation about the general setting up a king of his own or maybe trying for the throne himself." Sapair studied Mark's face. "Rumors abound of someone impersonating Rothan, as if he's miraculously returned from the afterlife."

"Rothan did survive, as I did, and he's king, the rightful king."

"He has royal blood, as his mother is Princess Sharesi, the last king's sister," the official mused. "In the absence of a full-blooded heir, he'd be next in line, if the gods so willed." Exhaling with a sound of relief, Sapair said, "These are glad tidings. Captain Khefer believed in a one-way flow of information, almost never discussing details of what transpired here in the south. Ebnar and I learned not to waste time asking him questions, which eventually proved to be a wise precaution on Khefer's part as I had nothing to tell the queen when she had me tortured." He shifted a bit on his pallet, trying to find a more comfortable position without jarring his bandaged hands. "I never became acquainted with Hutenen. He fell ill—or was poisoned, I should say—within a few days after he arrived at the city from the expedition to the far lands. My duties didn't take me into his presence more than twice. But Captain Rothan I dealt with. I judged him to be a good man, an honorable soldier."

"He is." Mark confirmed the assessment with no hesitation. "His grandfather General Intef is a tough, wily old campaigner too. I think the odds are in our favor to drive Farahna out."

Sapair lifted his bandaged hands as if to make a gesture, then winced. "I had no other choice but to serve her, you know. Ebnar and I kept our honor intact before the true gods by providing Khefer with as much information as we could gather. Farahna is a creature of the Maiskhan, for all she claims to be our queen. Their strange temple will be complete in a few months, and for the dedication, the enemy intend to demand ten firstborn sons from each province to be sacrificed. That atrocity is only the start of their harsh levy. Their leaders plan to sell Nakhtiaar citizens into slavery." Sapair gazed into the fire. "We're to be a subjugated territory of the Maiskhan king, stripped of all dignity, wealth, and freedom. I believed General Intef's rebellion might be our only chance to escape the fate she plans for our nation. Now I have increased hope, seeing you and hearing your news. It may be too late for me to serve as chief official in the palace any longer—"

Mark interrupted him before Sapair could pursue his defeatist thought. "Don't give up your position so fast. You can be useful to our king in other ways, even though your days as a spy are over."

"How so?" Sapair lifted his hands an inch or so off the blanket and winced. "I'll never hold writing instruments again, my lord. Farahna identified the most crushing revenge for my disloyalty, and her torturer excelled at the task. I live, but I'm useless for the occupation I trained my entire life to do."

"Rothan has been searching for the right person to organize his royal household and his court. The general's chief official tries, but he's old and set in his ways, so of course he and Rothan clash more often than they agree."

"I certainly know how to establish the household, run the inner workings of the court. It would be an honor. I always had many ideas about how things could be improved, done more efficiently." Sapair stopped, swallowing hard. "But having no use of my hands, I cannot—"

"She didn't empty your brain of knowledge. You can still talk, can't you? So dictate your orders to your own scribes," Mark answered with a soldier's practicality. "Now you need to get some rest. We're going to be moving out at dawn, and we'll be riding hard to get home."

With his bandaged hands, Sapair couldn't sit on a horse by himself, so he rode double with Khefer behind him as Mark's squad spent three days on the trail to the province. Sethmre kept the scribe well-dosed with painkiller but ran out on the last day. As they drew near to Intef's compound, Mark sent a man riding ahead to alert Rothan and Sandy what to expect.

When he rode into the courtyard of the palace at the head of his column, a crowd waited. Rothan, General Intef, and Sandy stood in a tight trio on the wide stairs leading to the palace entrance. Mark brought his cavalry unit trotting to the bottom of the stairs in perfect formation. Saluting Rothan, he dismounted.

"Got a badly injured man here," he said, going to help Sallea and her Mikkonite warriors in assisting Khefer and then Sapair to dismount from their shared horse. "And a prisoner. Not sure what information we can glean from him."

Khefer saluted Rothan as he accompanied Sandy down the stairs to them. Sapair attempted to sink to his knees before the new king, but Rothan forestalled him, catching him at the elbows, careful to avoid jarring the bandaged hands.

"You're welcome to my court, Chief Official. My queen and I owe you much for the courtesies you extended while we were prisoners." Raising his voice and speaking to the entire assembly, the king said, "Be it known to all men, I proclaim these broken hands are badges of valor, received in my service."

"You—you do me much honor, my lord," Sapair rasped out as the assembled crowd cheered. His knees failed him, and he collapsed in a heap at Rothan's feet, his fall eased by Mark, who stepped in as he sensed the injured man was about to collapse. The king withdrew a few steps to allow Sandy to move closer.

"Get him inside to my clinic," she said, gesturing to the waiting Mikkonites. "And you?" Hands on her hips, she assessed Khefer. "Broken ribs?"

"Sapair is the more desperate case, my lady," Khefer protested.

"I'll take your word for it, although I know you're stubborn. Come see me after you've talked to Rothan, then." She hurried after the men carrying her unconscious patient.

"Your Majesty," Mark said, "Khefer has a lot to tell you about current events in the city."

"Let's withdraw to my private chambers, and he can tell me his latest tale over some good wine. Lady Sallea, of course you're welcome to accompany us."

Mark looped Khefer's arm over his own shoulder and, being careful of the warrior's injured ribs, assisted him into the palace behind Rothan.

"My artisans finished the model you requested," Rothan said to Mark. "I think you'll be pleased."

"Can't wait to see it. "

"In the morning, after breakfast. Tomorrow we begin the planning for the battles to come. Finally."

"Waiting is the hardest part," Mark said, thinking over his many years of military service and countless deployments and missions.

"Well spoken, my friend. But the waiting is almost over now, thank the gods." Rothan ushered them into his private study.

The king and Mark had a four-hour session with Khefer. General Intef joined them. Dinner was brought at some point, consumed with no break in the conversation. Rothan, Mark, and the general grilled Khefer on the details of the Maiskhan plans, the new fortifications in the city, and countless other nuggets of intelligence he'd gleaned on his final trip undercover.

"Are we perhaps too hasty in accepting this Sapair into our inner circle?" General Intef asked as Khefer made reference to him yet again. "He was Farahna's chief official, after all. What if the information he and his partner provided is a deception? If we take action based on lies, the result will be disastrous."

Despite his broken ribs, Khefer straightened in his chair, face flushed and jaw clenched. "Sapair is loyal to the true rulers of our land. You don't trust me to double-check all information and verify conditions for myself?"

Eyes narrowed at the junior officer's tone, the general opened his mouth to retort, but Rothan forestalled him with a raised hand. "*I* trust Sapair. At great risk to himself on the morning of Hutenen's funeral, he provided comfort to my wife, an act for which there couldn't have been a double-sided motive at the time." A tired smile passed over his face. "Unless he hoped we'd tell the gods of his good deed when we reached the afterlife. Another factor here is that once I've taken the throne, there'll be no time to abolish the entire administrative structure of Nakhtiaar and rebuild it from scratch. Other vultures besides Maiskhan wait on our borders, ready to seize any moment of weakness. Having a man like Sapair to step in and take the reins, ensuring my orders and decrees are carried out, taxes properly collected, granaries filled, will be priceless." The king glanced around the table. "I appreciate the general raising a valid concern, in order for me to address the issue head on, but now that you've heard my answer, we need to move on to the next subject."

"Please, my lords, Khefer needs to seek the healer," Sallea said, the second or third time she'd brought his condition up, each time more insistently. "I can plainly see in this council how you rely on him, but if he doesn't receive the proper care, he'll be a broken spear, unfit for battles yet to come."

"Well said." Rothan rose from his chair, gesturing for Khefer to leave the audience. "We've heard enough tonight. Go, see the Lady of the Star Wind and then find your bed."

Khefer saluted. "Thank you, Your Majesty."

"You've done well. I'll expect you to attend the strategy session in the morning."

"We'll all be there," Mark said as he helped Sallea support Khefer.

Once they were making their way through the deserted halls, Khefer said to Sallea, "It was my duty to sit and answer the king's questions as long as he had a single one remaining."

"Stubborn as always," she replied, her tone calm. "It's your duty to remain fit for service. What kind of an ally would I be if I failed to remind you—and your king—of this?" She gave Mark a hostile glance, frowning. "No one else in the room appeared ready to make the case."

He stifled a smile. "Frankly, I was expecting Sandy to come and extract him from the meeting long before this. She knows how much he needs medical attention."

He shepherded the pair through the hallways to the suite of rooms where Sandy had established her clinic. He found her dozing on a couch jammed into the chamber next to Sapair's bed. One of her new assistants snored on a pallet off to the side. Sapair slept, but Sandy stirred as soon as Mark walked through the door with his companions.

Signaling for them to be quiet, she led the way into an adjoining room where many torches and oil lamps blazed.

"Took you long enough to come see me," she commented as she walked into the light.

"Rothan and General Intef needed to hear his whole story tonight so we can integrate the information into the planning tomorrow," Mark answered.

"Sit over there, Khefer, and let me check out your ribs," Sandy said.

"How's Sapair?" Mark asked as Sandy used the mirror to perform a slow scan on Khefer.

"Not too good. I gave him some heavy-duty pain meds from my dwindling supply."

"Can you help him with his hands?"

She frowned, rescanning part of Khefer's abdomen. "Okay, good, your spleen's not ruptured, just bruised. Lucky."

"Spleen?" Khefer stumbled over the unfamiliar term.

"Entrails," Mark translated. "Sandy? The guy's hands?"

"Well, Sethmre did a good job of setting the major bones in the field. He should have been a doctor, not a cavalryman." She gave Sallea a tired smile. "The smaller bones are smashed. As it is, Sapair will be able to use his hands to some extent but not with any fine motor skills."

"So, no writing?" Mark asked.

"No. The fingers won't heal with any great mobility or flexibility." She fastened the mirror on her belt and patted Khefer's shoulder. "Mostly bruises for you, Captain, some cuts and slashes. The ribs are broken, but all we can do is strap them. I'll give you something for the pain and medicine to keep the wounds from getting infected. Let me get the magic."

"He has to be conscious and coherent for the big meeting in the morning," Mark warned as she walked to the table where her medical bag sat. "Don't give him too much."

"He'll be better for a few hours of peaceful sleep. No worries."

"I know, you're the doctor." Teasing, he winked.

"Right, and don't you forget it!" Her fleeting grin was replaced with a frown. "I think I might do surgery tomorrow on Sapair's hands, though, clean up some of the internal debris and damage. It will help to a limited extent. I'm not an expert on that kind of delicate surgery, but I believe I can give him some hope." Sandy walked back with the inject and pumped the drugs into Khefer before the soldier could blink. "We need to get this stubborn soldier to bed before the meds take effect."

"I'll call a guard to help get him to his quarters," Mark offered.

"We'll be fine," Khefer demurred, sliding off the table. "Sallea can assist me."

"Okay, whatever you want. If you're sure—"

"I'm sure," Sallea answered for them both.

The couple left the room together.

"Remember how she once said she'd never fall for anyone but a desert warrior?" Mark asked Sandy as she straightened her medical supplies and closed her bag.

"Yes, before she met Khefer. How will her choice go over with her parents?"

"I've no idea, and I'm not capable of thinking about it tonight. Or this morning, whichever it actually is. Can we head for bed now too? Please?" Mark begged.

"Let me check on Sapair one more time, and then yes, to all your requests." Sandy was gone for a moment and then came back, took her bag from Mark, and strolled into the dim hallway, heading for their suite of rooms.

"You're unusually quiet," Mark murmured after the second turn.

"Hmm? Just reviewing the treatments I gave tonight and the next steps. It's funny, when I use the mirror to scan a patient, the act seems to augment the healing process. Sapair's hands look better now than they did when he arrived, although his condition is pretty bad. Farahna is such a barbaric bitch."

"Your grandmother the empress does the same sort of things."

Sandy sighed. "Yes, I know. What if I can use the mirror to heal?"

"Not just examine injuries, but fix them? Do you think you can?"

"Maybe. I wish I could have five minutes with Haatrin, ask her some specific questions."

Mark stopped in his tracks, swinging her to face him in the dim torchlight. "Not a good idea. The stakes are too high when any of those beings are brought into play. Tell me you're not thinking of contacting her somehow."

"No, I guess you're right." Sandy resumed walking, and Mark matched his stride to her shorter one. "I'm going to use Sapair as a trial subject, with his informed consent of course, since any improvement I achieve will be a blessing for him. I'm going to try visualizing how the bones in his hands should be when I check them with the mirror, see whether the magic can influence them to knit into proper shape."

Arriving at the door of their suite, Mark returned the salutes from the guards and ushered Sandy into their rooms. He took the medical bag from her, placing it on the floor before gathering her close. "You're pretty amazing, Lady of the Star Wind."

"Well, if I can put the mirror to such a use for Sapair, then I could do it for you. If you—if you're ever injured. You're what I care about the most. Am I awful to be so selfish?"

"I like it," he assured her. "And now I'm going to be selfish, and we're going to stop talking or thinking about anyone but ourselves. Come to bed, Your Highness, and let me practice *my* skills."

She laughed and let him lead her to the bedroom beyond the foyer.

Mark had requested the general's people to make a model of the territory in which the anticipated battles would be fought. Now the diorama filled one large room of the palace.

Rothan, Mark, General Intef, the other provincial rulers, and their senior officers crowded into the chamber the next morning. There was much exclamation as two servants rolled back the linen cover to reveal the intricate model, complete even to tiny soldiers, chariots, and fanged scaly monsters in the rivers.

Mark walked the length of the table, which took him from the capital city to the plains below the mountains. The artisans had done a good job. It was almost like studying one of the holographic maps used in the Sectors, which was why he'd insisted on it.

"So Khefer and Sapair tell us the main Maiskhan army is encamped here, on this side of the river," General Intef repeated for the benefit of the expanded audience. He gestured at the model soldiers in a formation beside the blue-painted river and drew his invisible path with the tip of his belt knife as he talked. "We'll sweep down from the heights and overwhelm them, drive them into the river where the beasts may eat them. Sapair says there are no more than six divisions."

Mark frowned. "Yes, but he also reported talk of another, larger Maiskhan army arriving, before the turning of the new year, right? To ensure successful occupation of the city and the surrounding area. What if the troops have disembarked by the time we get there? How long will it take us to march to the city?"

"One month," Rothan answered. "Conservative estimate."

"More than two months until the new year celebrations," General Intef said, tapping his belt knife against the side of the table. "Plenty of time to spare."

"A lot can happen in a month. We'd better have a backup plan," Mark persisted.

"We must keep the enemy forces from retreating into the city at all costs." Rothan touched the miniature of the main gate. "We don't have the ability to mount a successful siege."

"Not when the enemy can be resupplied from the sea. We've no naval forces to establish a blockade," Mark agreed.

Rothan chuckled. "I'll tell Chief Official Sapair to add a navy to the ever-growing list of priorities we must address after this war is over. Nakhtiaar needs a proper seagoing force, as you tell me at least once a day."

There was a small ripple of laughter around the room.

"Yes, you do," Mark said in all seriousness. "But creating a navy has to come later. So if the Maiskhan have six divisions by the river, how many men are we talking about?"

"Each division is one thousand men," someone answered from the crowd.

"And we have?"

"My Mountaintop province provides twenty-five hundred foot soldiers and a full division of five hundred chariots with drivers and archers," the general told him. "The West Plains and the Riverhold bring one thousand each, plus a smaller chariot force."

"The men of Riverhold are sloppy and lax, not well trained," Rothan said. "I hesitate to rely overmuch on them."

"You're right. We'll deploy them on the right flank, since the burden of the battle will be in the opposite direction," General Intef agreed. "Riverhold'll be in reserve. The Black Sands province, however, breeds fighters, you agree? And their ruler brings five hundred men."

Extending a hand, Rothan accepted the tablet bearing the current tallies of units and resources. Perusing the columns, the king scowled. "Even if each soldier fights like ten men, we remain outnumbered."

"Surprise is on our side, my lord," ventured one of the attending officers.

Rothan shook his head, staring at the plains where the battle would occur. "Have we heard anything from the other provinces? Will they send troops?"

Jaw set, General Intef balanced the knife on his fingertips. "I've heard from all but two. The cowards are afraid to march with us but prefer to sit and wait, guarding their own borders."

"See which way the winds blow, you mean," Rothan said. "It'll go hard with any who don't rally to my standard now and fight for the freedom of our land from the first trumpet call. There'll be no reward for latecomers to the battle."

If anyone in the room harbored doubt, the king's emphatic tone made it clear he wasn't going to forget who'd been his ally before victory was accomplished.

"I have hopes yet of receiving troops from West Canyons province. Her lord and I soldiered together as boys," the general said. "His capital lies a great distance from here. Perhaps their couriers are yet on the way."

"We can't wait any longer. We march in two days with what troops we have." Rothan turned away from the model to accept a goblet of wine from a servant.

Captain Khefer spoke. "My lord, if I may, I have a proposal."

Hearing a few whispers, Mark sensed some surprise in the gathering. Khefer was much too junior in rank to be consulted in this august assembly. On the other hand, he'd received golden honors from the king's hand as a reward for his work as a spy and was known to be high in Rothan's regard.

Gesturing with the goblet, Rothan said, "You may speak."

Khefer didn't hesitate to broach his idea. "What if we had a force of chariots and archers ready to hit the Maiskhan from behind, where their commanders don't expect any attack?"

"An excellent strategy, but we've no expectation of such a force." General Intef was dismissive. "The troops in the city may or may not rally to our cause. Your main contact was Ebnar, and he's been taken or killed. Without him or some other strong, loyal officer to command the units in the city and the palace, the troops won't fight or will be ineffective at best. Not much distraction for the Maiskhan. We've had no contact with the eastern provinces, so no allies will be coming to augment our forces. Neutrality from them is the best we can hope for."

"The city troops won't be able to respond in any organized manner," Rothan agreed. "Sapair and Ebnar also told you Farahna was dismantling the Nakhtiaar military structure piece by piece. I saw that myself in my brief time at the palace."

Khefer shook his head. "No, my lords, I don't speak of the troops left in the city. I propose taking one of our own companies of chariots and attacking from the rear."

"I'm listening." Rothan's calm voice silenced the discussion. "How would this be done?"

"We go through the mountains along this trail Sallea and I scouted when doing reconnaissance missions." Khefer traced the path with his hand, walking the length of the table. "The track comes out here, in a basin hidden from the view of those on the plains. The Maiskhan wouldn't see us coming, my lords."

"I like it." Mark appreciated the strategic possibilities. "Being attacked from the direction they believe is secure would cause chaos among the enemy forces."

General Intef smacked his fist on the table, making the miniature soldiers jump. "Impossible. The trail is much too narrow for chariots to traverse."

"I propose to carry the chariots, sir, and lead the horses," Khefer explained. "When we get out of the mountains, we mount up and attack."

Eyebrows raised, the general stared at Khefer as if the captain had grown a second head. "Carry the chariots? It can't be done."

"Wait." Rothan held up his hand. He paced the length of the table, studying the mountain trails. When he reached the area from which Khefer proposed to launch his surprise attack, he stopped, raising his head as he challenged the young captain. "You're positive you can do this?"

Voice rasping with annoyance, General Intef protested before Khefer could speak. "Your Majesty, we can't spare a company of precious chariots, horses, and archers to be lost in the mountains on a useless trek!"

Undaunted, Khefer didn't even glance at the irritated general but kept his focus on Rothan. "Give me leave, Your Majesty, and I'll get it done, bringing you victory, this I swear."

"I like your fire," Rothan said. "I give my permission for this bold maneuver. What do you need?"

"I want to take my own unit of chariots, my lord. I've been doing special training with the men in preparation for this mission. We won't fail you."

Rothan nodded. "Request anything you need for the effort."

"We'll leave tonight. I've kept my command stationed outside the barracks in order to come and go without much notice. There may be unfriendly eyes here, just as I was an enemy observer in the midst of Farahna's forces." Khefer bowed low and left the map room.

Mark caught him outside, offering the captain his hand. "All the best to you on this. It's a brilliant idea, even if General Intef didn't much like it."

Rubbing his chin as he grinned, Khefer said, "I think sometimes it's hard for the most senior officers to contemplate a new strategy."

"Well said. Quite diplomatic, in fact. We know damn well the old guard tried new things when they were fresh young lieutenants and captains in the field."

"Memory fades, my lord." Khefer winked.

Mark shook his hand, and Khefer took his leave.

Sandy hailed Mark from the other end of the hallway. He waited for her to reach him, kissing her quickly on the cheek. "I only have a moment—I have to get back to the planning session."

"I know. I just came to ask you to ensure Rothan includes my field hospital in his planning today. We have to be set up close enough to the combat zone to be effective. I'll need logistical support as well." She handed him a set of tablets. "I submitted this to Rothan myself yesterday, but then I thought you should have a copy. As his deputy for logistics, Sapair seemed to think my requests were reasonable."

Swallowing hard to keep his anger in check, Mark stared at Sandy. He shook his finger at her. "You are most emphatically not coming along on this campaign. This is going to be war of the most basic, savage kind. I can't protect you in the middle of a battlefield. Even if we surround you with Rothan's best guards, I can't guarantee your safety."

"Will you be safe?" she challenged him.

"Of course not—if I'd been born a man who wanted to be *safe*, I'd never have left my home planet. *Tzerde.*" He drew a long breath, striving for calm. "I've been in combat situations so hellish, seen and done things so appalling, I had to have them blocked from my memory or I couldn't function. In this war, I'll be fighting alongside Rothan. I've trained my cavalry to handle the duty. You don't belong anywhere near either type of combat."

"I have to be along on the campaign." Her tone was persuasive. "I can't ignore my duty as a doctor to take care of the wounded."

"You've never seen anything like the carnage of war."

"I'm a doctor," she repeated patiently. "I can't stay here and be useless when my skills and knowledge could save the lives of good men."

Livid, Mark glared at her. He couldn't accept her risking herself, no matter how noble her motives might be. "No."

Sandy tried another tack. "Sapair told us the rumors are all about how the Lady of the Star Wind has come again to Nakhtiaar, how she's an ally on the side of Rothan's claim as king. So I have to be there. I'm symbolic." She tried a small grin, but Mark remained unmoved. "Besides, we know the mirror is renowned as a powerful weapon, even if I haven't mastered that aspect of its powers."

Trying to divert the conversation, he pursued the topic of the mirror. "Are you making any progress?"

"I summoned a trio of dirt devils yesterday. And I made waves in the lotus pool." She laughed. "The gardeners weren't pleased."

"Sandy, if anything happens to you—"

She captured his hands. "Nothing is going to happen to me. This is what we're here for, our reason for ending up in Nakhtiaar. I'm sure of it. We each have to participate in our own way. You can't talk me out of this. You said yourself, more than once, that I was the most highly trained doctor on the planet, so how can I stay here in safety and abandon my duty to save lives? And it's not just me working one on one with patients. I can leverage my skills, direct other less-trained personnel, to save more of the injured. I *want* to do this."

He stared into her face and knew he was beaten. "At least promise me you'll stay at the field hospital during the fighting. No venturing onto the battlefield."

"I can't make that promise. If something happens to you, no force on this planet will keep me from coming to your aid, wherever you are." Her jaw was set, her eyes narrowed. "Let's be clear about that right now."

He knew when he was defeated.

The vast army's march from the mountainous province toward the flatlands was uneventful, although General Intef posted scouts in all directions, keeping watch for the enemy. Sandy treated a few minor injuries each night in her field hospital tent and conducted training for the army physicians and other men who'd volunteered to serve as field medics, as well as a surprising number of soldiers' wives and camp followers. Mark attended strategy sessions with Rothan and the provincial rulers and generals.

And then came the day the army arrived at its final encampment at the edge of the vast plains of central Nakhtiaar.

In the last hours of the night, ceremonies were held, favors begged of the gods. The combat units moved away from the camp and formed up as the strategists had designed so long ago in the war room at Intef's palace.

The army waited for dawn.

There wasn't much talk in the ranks. Here and there, a horse moved or a chariot rolled briefly out of position.

Mark sat on his restive horse, Sallea and the rest of his small cavalry unit behind him. He'd gone on uncountable missions, been in grave jeopardy many times, but never like this—in open, primitive battle with blunt-force weapons. Mentally, he reviewed the briefing he'd held with his cavalry, going over various scenarios and how they'd react to each. He and his unit were as prepared as anyone could be. Glancing at the moons for a moment, he wished Sandy was safe at the mountain stronghold, not nearby in their camp, ready to take care of the inevitable casualties. After holding him tight and giving him a protracted kiss, she'd told him to be careful, which amused him even under the dire circumstances. He didn't know how a man could be careful in the middle of a pitched battle and remain an effective fighter, but he assured her he'd try. He'd left her the civilian blaster as a precaution, even though the unit held no more than two or three shots at best.

Rothan stood in his large chariot, wearing a uniform much like any other officer's, but on his head sat a golden helmet with a blue horsehair crest and the symbol of the crown. He stared into the distance, where the unsuspecting enemy slumbered. A standard bearer waited at his side, holding the king's flag on a tall staff so Rohan's location would be known by all during the battle. Djed stood in a chariot on the other side of the king's, clutching his bow. Rothan's driver bent over, uttering soothing remarks to the nervous team of horses.

Mark checked his blaster again. It wouldn't be much use in this kind of close combat, but he wore it as a last resort should Rothan be caught in dire peril. He couldn't imagine going on a mission or into combat without it.

"His Majesty prepares to give the signal," Sallea whispered from behind him.

Turning his head ever so slightly, Mark asked, "Is Lakht in position?"

"Yes, he circles the enemy camp and reports no unusual activity."

Mark gathered the reins as Rothan signaled to the trumpeter. Defiant, golden notes pierced the morning silence, and the line of chariots took off, racing toward the unprepared enemy camp. Mark and his cavalry kept pace with the wheeled units. As they came closer to the walls of the camp, Rothan's archers loosed flights of arrows. Enemy soldiers fell from their posts as at least some of the arrows found targets. Horns blared now, calling the Maiskhan forces to action. The gates of the camp opened, and a few chariots raced to meet the oncoming wave.

One second, Mark was riding at full gallop, the Mikkonites and Nakhtiaar warriors riding at his back, launching arrows at the enemy ranks. The next moment, he was in combat, striking out left and right with his sword, cutting down enemy soldiers, his well-trained horse picking its way through the melee in response to his signals. Slinging their bows across their backs, Sallea and the troopers switched to swords or spears, using the advantage of height that being in the saddle provided. Many enemy soldiers attempted to engage with Mark and his cavalry unit as they plowed through the thick of the battle, staying in a tight formation, driving a wedge in the enemy forces. He had to work hard to stay abreast of Rothan's chariot in the crush of combat, slashing at anyone who came within range. He parried blows aimed at him. He dodged arrows or covered himself with his shield, continuing to move forward. An amazing number of ground troops boiled out of the enemy camp, but the element of surprise helped Rothan's forces to some extent. Many of the enemy soldiers hadn't had time to don body armor.

There was intense hand-to-hand combat, with Mark and his cavalry weaving through the packed battleground, wheeling at his command time and again to cut a swathe through another knot of fiercely struggling combatants.

Lakht swooped in and out of the fray, targeting anyone bold enough to threaten Sallea.

Then the battle ended all at once, the enemy soldiers breaking ranks and running away before the superior Nakhtiaar forces. Most didn't try to retreat to their camp but threw down their weapons and shields and fled past the camp, heading for the safety of the river and the city beyond.

Trumpets blared, ordering a recall of Rothan's troops.

General Intef shouted orders in a stentorian voice, trying to prevent their troops from giving chase to the enemy. Mark and Sallea, who had fought as hard as any of them and guarded his back well, led their unit close to the parked chariots to hear the orders.

"Send scouts to keep an eye on their retreat," General Intef ordered Mark, who nodded at Sallea. She launched Lakht into the air from her arm, selected five of her men, and galloped off in the direction taken by the fleeing Maiskhan.

"This victory came too easy, too fast," Rothan told his grandfather. Djed was binding a small wound in the king's left arm.

Jaw clenched, the general was grim. "Don't look askance at victory. We were fortunate to surprise them. The gods favored us in this. And we didn't need your Captain Khefer and his chariots, who I note haven't shown up as yet in any event. Perhaps he fell off the mountain." The general grinned at his own grim joke.

"I never expected the Maiskhan forces to crumble so easily," Mark agreed. "What are we going to do now?"

"Detail one company to take charge of the camp and the prisoners, and then we move on to attack the city," the general declared. "We need to take control of the city today. "

"The ragtag rabble we sent fleeing won't be much help to Farahna's Maiskhan forces in holding the capital against us," Rothan said. "Not if Nakhtiaar troops will declare for me."

"What's taking so long to form the columns for the rapid march?" the general demanded of no one in particular, striving to see through the dust and the haze of the warming day.

"Your Majesty!" A chariot swept up beside them in a cloud of dust. The passenger was a young officer whose name escaped Mark.

"What brings you?" demanded the general.

"The men of Riverhold have broken ranks to loot the Maiskhan camp, my lord."

"Their soldiers have no discipline at all." The general gestured to the officers waiting nearby. "Take ten squads and stop the looting. Get the Riverhold men into ranks at once. We've no time for this."

"We must not be in disarray," Rothan agreed. "I want to press on to the river now."

"We've got to get control of those rogue units first, my lord," the general said. "I'll go," Rothan said. "They won't persist in this greedy foolishness in my presence."

He set his chariot in motion toward the enemy camp. Mark rode after him, the other chariots following them. As he rode, he noted some disciplined columns of soldiers gathered around their standard bearers, heeding the orders of their officers, forming into companies to march again. But there were gaps on the right flank, where the Riverhold men should have been.

Wounded, an arrow protruding from her shoulder, Sallea galloped into the circle around Rothan. She struggled to stay in the saddle and Mark kept her from toppling to the ground as she came up next to him.

"A huge army comes across the river," she said through gritted teeth before collapsing onto her horse's neck.

"There's an army coming at us," Mark yelled, catching the unconscious woman before she could fall. He gestured for the nearest Mikkonite soldier to take Sallea. "Get her to our camp, make sure my Lady treats her wound. Go!"

"Gods preserve us, the Maiskhan have reinforcements," General Intef shouted. "Trumpeters, sound the call! The attack comes!"

Mark and his comrades were soon surrounded by shouting hordes of the enemy. Battle raged again on the plain. At some point, Mark's horse collapsed under him, and he fought his way free of the stirrups. Using his blaster indiscriminately now, he shot enemy soldiers getting close to Rothan. His small cadre of Mikkonite warriors stayed with him, most also on foot, fighting like demons. The general and the few remaining officers and troops surrounded the king, wielding their swords and spears desperately, but wave after wave of Maiskhan came at them. Mark was afraid their attempt to retake Nakhtiaar for its rightful ruler was failing when he heard the golden trumpets above the shouts and cries of battle. Swiping one hand across his eyes, he peered through the dust. A wave of chariots flying the king's standard swept across the plain behind the Maiskhan forces. Arrows cascaded from the sky like hail, pelting the enemy from behind, creating chaos in the Maiskhan ranks.

"It's Khefer and his chariots!" Mark yelled to Rothan. "We just have to hold on a few more moments, and they'll be here."

"Praise to the gods, he arrived in time!" The king beheaded an enemy soldier with his sword, pivoting and ducking under the blade of the next man, skewering him even as Djed shot two soldiers full of arrows in quick succession.

The conflict redoubled in intensity as the Maiskhan commanders apparently realized their chance at victory was slipping away under Khefer's attack from the rear. Mark struggled to stay in one piece and to do his part to keep Rothan alive. The individual enemy soldiers gave ground around him, terrified of his "magic" as man after man fell, burned as if by lightning. He knew the charge would soon be exhausted, but a blaster was no use if the rebellion lost the king.

And then no one else charged at him, no flights of arrows arced in. The battle was done.

His uniform dusty and bloodstained, Khefer rolled up to Rothan and Mark's position in his battered chariot, saluting as his driver reined the team to a halt. "My lords, I've come as promised!"

"In the gods' own time," Rothan answered.

"Let's drive these dogs across the river, toward the city, and kill them against the walls," Khefer shouted, shaking his fist at the retreating enemy.

"My chariot is done—the wheel is smashed, and the left horse is dead. Let me join you, and we'll chase these invaders together," said the king.

Khefer's driver stepped back as the captain took the reins while Rothan leaped into the chariot. Mark cut Rothan's surviving horse free from the traces so he could ride it bareback. He swung onto the horse as Khefer's chariot lurched into motion. The nearby trumpeter blew a summons to bring the remaining able-bodied men to their leader's side.

"I bring the reinforcements from West Canyon Keep with me as well," Khefer shouted. "We met them on the mountain trail, being of the same mind as I was, to create surprise."

CHAPTER NINE

"We can't attack the city gates and hope to get inside," General Intef repeated for the third time. "The Maiskhan hold the entrance and the nearby walls."

"My spies tell me more than half the Nakhtiaar units will fight under our banners." Captain Khefer clenched his jaw, tone barely civil, patience visibly threadbare. "When we attack, the loyal troops will move against the Maiskhan from inside the city."

The argument over strategy raged. Mark took the goblet of wine from the nearest servant and drained it in one gulp. War was thirsty work. The army had driven the fleeing Maiskhan forces toward the city and had indeed killed or captured most. A few had gotten inside the massive gates before the defenders slammed them shut. Rothan's forces established a makeshift camp outside of arrow range while the next moves were debated.

Rothan pointed his belt knife at Mark. "What do you think?"

He slammed the wine goblet on the table. "I say we go for it, throw the counters, as your people say. We need to take the city, get this war over with. Your army can't sustain a long campaign, and mounting a siege won't win this conflict for you. There's still the Maiskhan navy and the reinforcements they're supposed to be bringing. We've beaten this discussion to death."

"Capturing Farahna and cutting her treacherous throat will end the war." Sounding very sure, Rothan released his grip on the map of the city, allowing the scroll to curl away from him. "Prepare to attack within the hour."

There was a commotion at the entrance to the tent. The guards were pushing and shoving against someone attempting to come inside. The war council members jostled each other to see what was happening.

A bloodied, frantic soldier in the colors of the Mountaintop province fought with the guards. He caught Rothan's eye and shouted the catastrophic news. "The Lady of the Star Wind has been kidnapped!"

Conversation in the tent stopped.

"Bring him here," the king said.

Pain stabbed through Mark at the man's words, as if he'd been hit by a force knife in the gut. He went ice cold, clenching his hand on the edge of the table as he waited for the injured soldier to be helped closer so he could give details. "Is she alive?"

"Yes, my lord, as far as we know." The man talked in gasps, as if at the end of his strength.

Guards walked the messenger toward the council table, half carrying him the last few paces. Not caring about protocol, Mark shoved a stool closer and helped the man sit before he fell. The messenger addressed Rothan. "The Lady of the Star Wind was tending to the wounded on the battlefield across the river, Exalted One. A party of Maiskhan came through, capturing her and escaping in their chariots. It was as if they were searching for her, rather than fleeing the battleground."

The soldier swallowed hard. "The guards fought, but to no avail. There were ten or twelve Maiskhan, accompanied by the priests. After fighting off our troops and capturing her, the enemy rode in the direction of the new temple. Although injured, Lady Sallea took a horse to follow them. The rest of us gave chase on foot but were soon outdistanced. I myself heard the enemy say the Lady would be sacrificed to gain the victory for the Maiskhan." The man coughed up blood and sagged to the floor. "We did our best, my lords, I swear to you."

"Get this man to the surgeons," Rothan ordered.

"I have to go after her," Mark said. "We're wasting precious time!"

Rothan nodded once. "Take a squad of chariots. I pray the gods ride with you, my friend." The king extended his hand, and Mark clasped it.

He turned to go, finding Khefer at his side. The Nakhtiaar captain didn't hesitate for an instant. "My men and horses are ready, my lord."

As the two men left the tent on the run, Mark said, "We'd heard rumors from your spies that the Maiskhan might try to kidnap Sandy to overcome the prophecy about her and the mirror. That's why I ordered her to stay behind the lines in Rothan's fortified camp. What the seven hells was she doing on the battlefield?"

Khefer shouted orders to his men as he ran before answering Mark's furious question. "She takes her duty as a physician above all else, my lord, as I well know. I pray that Sallea and Lakht can delay the enemy as they attempt to carry the Lady to their temple." The captain launched himself into his own chariot next to Mark and a moment later made a sweeping turn out of camp and across the plains to the new road. Five chariots rolled in their wake.

"I hope Sallea doesn't make her own injuries worse in the process," Mark said, knowing Khefer had to be worried.

"Another hard-headed woman. I'm praying for her as well. Forgive me, my lord, but perhaps my prayers for Sallea are even more devout than the words I use to beseech help for your Lady." Cracking the whip above his team, the captain encouraged them to a new burst of speed. "Lucky the cursed Maiskhan priests wanted a road built from the city to their shrine," Khefer shouted above the clatter of hooves and the creaking of the wheels. "We can make much better time."

"Yeah, lucky." Mark's sweaty hands were clenched on the rim of the jolting chariot. His racing thoughts were chaotic, full of fear for Sandy. He swore. This was no way to go into the most critical combat of his life, trying to save the woman he loved. Taking a deep breath, he tried to center himself, concentrate, visualize the temple and its surroundings, plan scenarios.

"We'll get there, my friend." Khefer glanced away from the road for a second to reassure Mark. "Our gods must fight to keep the Lady from dying on a bloodstained Maiskhan altar."

Mark hoped Khefer was right. Sandy might have a chance if he and his hastily assembled force could get to the temple first and ambush the kidnappers. As the incomplete structure came into view, Mark could see how much progress had been made over the months since he and Sandy had traveled past it in their merchant disguise, fleeing with Rothan. The temple now stood two levels higher.

He got out his distance viewers from the small pack on his belt and trained them on the wide steps.

"What do you see?" Khefer shouted. "Are we in time?"

"No. The bastards are already there."

The chariot took a leap forward as Khefer cracked the lash over the heads of his team. "Any sign of Sallea?"

"Didn't see her. She might have been captured, one already injured warrior against overwhelming odds." Mark got out his blaster and checked the charge one-handed, bracing himself against the rail of the pitching chariot.

Lower than he'd ever gone without reloading, but there were no fresh charges on Nakhtiaar to be had.

He'd shot with reckless abandon in the last stand on the battlefield, saving Rothan's life time and again.

"Why don't you use your magic?" Khefer glanced sideways for a second.

"Too far. It's like an arrow. It has a certain range, magic or not."

Mark returned to watching the scene play itself out through the viewer. Raging inside, he felt nearly insane with frustration at being so close yet still too far away to help Sandy. "The priests are dragging her up the first flight of stairs." He watched, swearing terrible Outlier oaths, as Sandy was forced to climb farther up the pyramid to the rough, unfinished third level. Mark, Khefer, and their men were getting there but not fast enough, not nearly fast enough. The horses were gallant but tired.

Now the Maiskhan soldiers were gesturing in their direction.

"We've been spotted." He gave Khefer the grim update. A flash of blue in the crowd surrounding Sandy caught his eye, and he adjusted his focus. "More bad news—they've got Sallea too."

"Just a few more moments," Khefer promised. "The turnoff to the base of the knoll is close." He directed the team onto the road looping around to the half-finished temple. Clinging to the chariot rail as the right wheel came off the ground with the speed of the turn, Mark made no protest at the dangerous maneuver. Every second counted.

Mark watched in his viewer as two soldiers held Sandy, who he could tell was screaming her defiance at them. The soldiers and the priests appeared to be arguing among themselves now. The priests kept gesturing at the stairs to the uppermost level, where the first skeletal framework of the actual temple had been erected. The soldiers were paying more attention to Mark's oncoming force. The Maiskhan officer in command gestured at his men, who dragged a small flat rock over from a pile at the edge of the level. The three priests took Sandy, trying to force her onto her back over the makeshift altar. The Nakhtiaar slaves who'd been working on the construction crowded behind a line of Maiskhan guards.

Mark was convinced his grim fate was to watch his beloved Sandy sacrificed. He'd arrive in time only to extract a terrible vengeance. A sudden movement caught his eye. "Lords of Space!"

"What do you see?" Khefer demanded.

What Mark observed was nothing short of a miracle. Sallea had gotten her hands on a dagger, or had hidden one, and stabbed the Maiskhan officer holding Sandy in the back. As he fell, one of the imprisoned workers took his chains and whipped the legs out from under the guard standing in front of him. Grabbing the man's sword, the worker jumped forward to cut down the nearest priest. He yelled something Mark couldn't hear. Other slaves came to help their comrade and Sallea do battle. The Maiskhan guards in the immediate area were overwhelmed by the unexpected attack. The man who'd initiated the rebellion now had Sandy by one elbow, Sallea lending strength on the other side, and the trio withdrew toward the stairs up to the next level. Other workers formed a rough line around them, fighting the Maiskhan soldiers who came up the stairs in formation, swinging their swords to terrible effect against the lightly armed rebels.

Mark lost the angle in the final few nerve-shattering moments of the ride as the chariots came sweeping up to the base of the mound. Blaster at the ready, he jumped from the moving vehicle, taking the stairs at a dead run, heedless of whether his own men were behind him. Mark's grandfather, father, and uncles had often talked with pride of the blind red rage their warrior blood could summon in the heat of battle. Mark had never felt it, had assumed it was a story, a legend to embellish the family's reputation. The berserker rage flowed through his mind and body now, carrying him effortlessly on a wave of anger and adrenaline. He slashed at each Maiskhan who got in his way, cutting men down left and right with his sword, shoving past knots of struggling guards and workers.

He had to get to Sandy.

There was no other thought in his mind. Anger laced with a fine edge of fear for Sandy pushed the fatigue from his battle-weary muscles. He wasn't even aware of Khefer and the small squad of loyal soldiers struggling to ascend the stairs behind him, trying to defend his back.

Mark gained the third level. The desperate fight had moved to the next-highest platform. The slave who'd started the battle was still standing, fiercely in command of his ragtag force. He had Sandy at the farthest edge of the plateau, with his men between them and the Maiskhan. Sallea stood directly in front of the princess, one arm useless with the arrow wound she'd sustained in the earlier battle, but wielding a stolen sword in the other hand. Mark used a precious shot of dwindling blaster charge to kill a Maiskhan about to split Sallea's skull. The enemy soldier toppled off the edge of the terrace. As Khefer and his men toiled up the steps behind Mark, yelling their battle cry, the Maiskhan contingent realized the necessity to fight on two fronts. Mark broke through the last of the enemy soldiers, decapitating a warrior who dared to raise a sword against him. The Nakhtiaar prisoners parted to allow him to reach Sandy. She fell into his arms, white-faced, silent in shock, and he embraced her for a long moment, folding her as close to him as he could manage.

"She's taken no harm, my lord," Sallea said, "other than bruises and a few cuts perhaps."

"I owe you for defending her," he said over Sandy's head.

The man commanding the workers' rebellion saluted. "Ebnar, former captain of Farahna's household guards, at your service."

"You were the undercover spy for Rothan." The pieces fell into place for Mark.

The man bowed slightly. "I tried to send as much information to General Intef as I could about the Maiskhan troop strength and movements. After I was betrayed to Farahna, I would have been executed if the Maiskhan priests hadn't been desperate for strong slaves to finish this cursed temple in time for their rituals. Today I couldn't allow the Lady of the Star Wind to be sacrificed to their evil god in front of my eyes. I vowed to die first in the attempt to save her."

"You did well, all of you." Mark gazed at the former slaves clustered around him, wounded, gaunt, bearing the marks of their forced captivity and labor. "I owe you anything you want to ask of me. The king will also be grateful."

"First, the gods must grant our petition for the true king to take the city," Ebnar replied. He gave orders to his ragtag men. "We need the keys to these accursed chains. Get them from the bodies of the Maiskhan foremen."

Men saluted and moved to obey.

Mark realized why the officer's name was familiar. "You're Sapair's partner."

"You have word of Sapair?" Ebnar swung back eagerly.

"He escaped the city after you were taken, with the help of Captain Khefer here. We rescued the two of them from a Maiskhan patrol. He's now Rothan's chief official."

Ebnar's broad shoulders slumped in momentary relief. "I—I was so afraid Farahna had him killed. He never appeared in the slave quarters here, so I assumed he'd been executed. Nothing you could have told me today would have brought me more joy, my lord. Other than confirmation of the true king's total victory."

"Thank Khefer there. He broke Sapair out of the prison after Farahna's men tortured him."

"It was my honor." Although he had one arm around Sallea's waist, holding her close, Khefer shook hands with Ebnar. "You two did so much to assist my king, at great risks to yourselves. But how is the Lady?"

"A few minor scrapes and bruises," Sandy told them. "A bit shaky. I fought them at the battlefield, but I only had a few shots. They were pretty rough with me after they chased me down." She disentangled herself from Mark's embrace. "And is the city taken?"

"Not as of the moment when we left to come here. But Rothan and General Intef are confident our troops will prevail," Mark answered.

"There are loyal troops inside the city, I'm proud to say," Ebnar declared. "They'll fight under Rothan's banners. Khefer and I laid the foundation, spread the word of a true king coming to liberate us. We kept hope alive."

Mark said, "We'd better make plans for getting my Lady to safety at the camp."

Shuddering, Sandy rubbed her arms, gazing at the unfinished temple platform around them. "I approve of your suggestion. This place is evil."

Ebnar issued orders to his men, getting them organized for a march. Khefer conferred with his troops. Mark watched. Neither officer needed any interference from him, having matters well in hand.

"Mark." Sandy's voice was flat.

"What?" Alarm coursed along his nerve endings at her unusual tone.

"Look off there, out on the ocean." She pointed.

"*Tzerde.*" Mark unslung his viewer again to confirm the phenomenon. He hoped he was seeing wrong.

"What are those things?" Khefer squinted and held a hand over his eyes. "Ships?"

"The whole damn Maiskhan navy, I'd say. Loaded to the gunwales with fresh troops, is my guess." Mark lowered the viewer. His companions all had expressions of stunned dismay. He shook his head. "The enemy is technologically way ahead of our side on the water. Rothan doesn't have one ship to call his own, much less a navy to keep these sailors and the fresh Maiskhan reinforcements from landing anywhere their officers want, any time. We can't win this way."

"We must warn the king," Khefer and Ebnar said at the same moment.

"And what will he do?"

"What do you mean?" Eyebrows raised, Khefer appeared to believe there was only one possible answer to such a question. "He'll fight."

Mark hated to be the bearer of bad news, but the answer that was plain to him wasn't the one Khefer proposed. "If he's managed to batter down the gates, break into the city, and win the main battle, is he going to be able to keep this new Maiskhan army from coming in behind him and reclaiming the capital? Our side has no reinforcements arriving, as I understand it. Are Rothan's troops going to be strong enough to fight and win another huge battle later today? Or even tomorrow morning, against fresh men?"

Khefer exchanged glances with Ebnar. "If the gods will it—" the younger man started to say, his voice uncertain.

Ebnar shook his head. "No. Nor can he hold the city against an indefinite siege, which was to be your next question, I'm sure."

"The other provinces won't help?" Sandy asked.

Voice flat, Khefer gave his assessment. "Those who are loyal already stand with him today. The others will remain on the sidelines once the Maiskhan land such a massive army."

"And if Rothan flees to the Mountaintop province, even if we get there ahead of the Maiskhan on board those ships, even if we keep them out of the plateau, we'll never be able to break out and mount a successful campaign against them again. Not in this lifetime." Mark fingered his exhausted blaster, aware that he had nothing more to offer.

"What would you have us do?" Khefer exploded after a long moment. "Are you saying we should surrender? Give up, slink home to the mountains, and grow old under perpetual siege? This isn't like you. Where has your honor gone?"

Not offended, Mark said, "It isn't a question of honor, my friend. It's a question of whether we're reduced to our last chance."

"What chance?" Ebnar pointed at the ocean. "The Maiskhan sweep the gaming board with their armada. We've no more counters to play."

"We have one," Sandy answered him. "The other weapon we brought out of Khunarum."

"Weapon?" Ebnar stared at her, shaking his head in denial. "What can an ancient weapon do against thousands of fresh troops?"

Sandy unhooked the Mirror of the Mother from her belt. She appealed to Mark. "I've never been able to get the mirror to work for major things like this, but I have to try. I've got to do something, or this whole war is going to be lost. Today, in a few hours, as soon as those men out there hit the beach and get themselves organized, Rothan's triumph turns to ashes." She stared at the mirror in her hand and then at him.

Mark took two steps to stand in front of her, touching her lips with a gentle caress. "We have to believe it will work. We have to know deep in our hearts you'll be successful. See," he pointed out, "the farthest ships are raising sails to move on. Someone must have gotten away from the city, gotten word to them. The armada's going down the coast, probably to land and march to counterattack from the flank—that's what I'd do. Our window of opportunity is slipping away. We've got to do something now."

"What am I asking the mirror for—blaster cannons? My grandmother's star destroyers? What can I ask for here and now to help us?" She bit her lip and checked the horizon. "The only thing I can think of seems crazy, but it might work. Haatrin told us the mirror remembers everything it's ever seen, right?"

Eyebrows raised, Mark waited for her to clarify what she was getting at.

"The mirror saw the tidal waves drowning the City of Khunarum. A giant, rogue wave right about now would swamp those ships out there and save the day." She laughed, a little edge of hysteria in the tone. "What if I could conjure a tsunami?"

"You can do it. I know you can. You have to ask, like the goddess told you. " Mark took her by the hand, leading her a step or two away from the others, closer to the edge of the temple terrace. "This is what we're here for. This is what you needed the mirror for. It has to be. Nothing else we've done so far matters, other than keeping Rothan alive in the first place, maybe."

The first ships could be seen moving off into the hazy horizon, going south. She took a deep breath and then squared her shoulders. "All right." As usual, the mirror's shining surface reflected nothing but mist. "But what to ask?" She rotated the handle, clicking past the young goddess figure and the older woman of wisdom, bringing the warrior to the top.

Raising the mirror in her left hand, reflective surface facing out to the ocean, she extended her right hand to Mark without looking at him. He took it, placing it on his heart and holding it there, his fingers wrapped around hers.

"You can do this. We can do it."

Sandy nodded, grip tightening on his hand as if she was trying to crush his bones.

"I call upon the Mirror of the Mother—remember what was seen on the final day in the Land of Khunarum, call it forth for me—the earth must quake, the wind must blow, the ocean must rise—now!" Sandy's voice wasn't loud, but it was steady and determined.

A buzzing, hot, electric shock ran from Sandy to him, through his body to his feet, rooting him to the spot. His heart started pounding in an uneven rhythm. A definite quiver ran through the massive granite blocks of the terrace under his sandals. He heard shouting behind him but didn't dare divert his attention from what Sandy was attempting. Anyone other than his beloved was on their own now, as far as he was concerned. Stones at the edge of the terrace heaved and collapsed away from the construction site like it was a crumbling cookie as the ground shook with increasing tremors. He wrapped his free arm around Sandy's waist, bracing her against his body, keeping her upright with difficulty.

"I demand waves. I demand nothing less than the giant, earth-killing waves which swallowed Khunarum." Sandy spoke louder and faster now. Her hand clenched around the handle of the mirror. "I command you to bring me those same waves, here and now, today!"

"The water's pulling back!" The sight was so wrong, so abnormal, it made Mark dizzy. The ocean receded, yard by slow yard, leaving behind fish by the thousands to flop on the wet sands. "Lords of Space, you're doing it!"

He heard voices behind him, cursing, praying, exclaiming, but he remained focused on supporting Sandy with whatever she might ask of him.

Far out to sea, a shape reared itself sluggishly upward, filling the entire horizon. In the blink of an eye, it raced toward them, a monster wave, growing ever taller as it came, foaming at the crest.

Sandy stayed locked in her stance. Winds howled around them. Sea foam blew. Mark couldn't see the beach any longer, for all the sand and the mist and foam. A belated concern as to whether their group was safe crossed his mind, but it was far too late to take any other action or relocate now. The forces she'd unloosed through the mirror were awe-inspiring. He retreated, one step at a time, drawing her with him. There was no escape as the wave came inexorably onward.

"Link arms, link arms!" Ebnar yelled, getting his meager forces to form a human chain, holding on to the heavy ropes attached to the massive building blocks, and to each other. The Nakhtiaar soldiers grabbed Mark and Sandy and pulled them closer, trying to offer some protection from what was coming.

The Maiskhan ships were swallowed, struggling to climb the face of the impossible wave, or else turning broadside to it and disappearing under the millions of tons of force, broken to splinters and kindling in the blink of an eye. He felt sorry for the enemy soldiers and sailors, but no one would have suffered for more than a second.

The wave filled his entire field of vision, coming at them. Mark knew they were going to drown, swept away. He fought the wind to gather Sandy into his arms, so she wouldn't see their doom, but she shoved him to the side.

"I command you to stop!" she screamed, her words ripped away in the howling gale. She flipped the mirror over, pressing it to her chest, facedown. "The task I set you is done. Enough! Enough, be still!"

The wave broke against the sides of the half-finished temple but didn't crest it, to Mark's utter amazement. The impact of millions of gallons of water sent shudders through the tons of stone, but the mound and terraces had been well built, and only a corner of one lower tier shattered, floating away in the current. Then the water receded, washing the entire area around the base of the pyramid clean to bedrock.

Moments later, the ocean was peaceful, gleaming in the sun, back in its proper place. Small sets of normal waves formed and came in to break against the sloping beach in the distance. Of the Maiskhan armada, there was no sign, not even debris.

Drawing apart, Mark stared at Sandy, wide-eyed, afraid to even touch her.

She laughed, shaking her head. "You asked me to call on the mirror, remember? The gods told us it was a fearsome weapon."

"Holy Lords of Space, I had no idea what we were unleashing. Are you all right?"

"Yes, I'm fine." Sandy gave him a serene smile. She ran her hand through her disheveled blond hair to restore a semblance of order, and blushed. "I'm better than fine. I'm pregnant."

"What?" His brain refused to process the message for a moment.

"I ran the test this morning. I thought I was. I *hoped* I was, and the test results confirmed my intuition. We're having twins."

He caught her in his arms again and swung her around while the soldiers cheered.

Descending from the half-finished pyramid, Mark and Sandy took their time. Captain Khefer and Ebnar shouted orders to the newly freed slaves and soldiers. At the base, the two officers formed the motley crowd into ragged columns and then began marching along the pitted and broken remnants of the muddy road toward the city.

"Nothing will ever grow here again, will it?" Sandy gazed around as she walked. "The salt water will have killed even the roots."

"Perhaps such an outcome is best," Captain Khefer answered. "The ocean waters wiped away all the evil the enemy sought to plant here, on the soil of our country."

"True enough." She sighed, leaning heavily on Mark's arm. "I'm so tired."

"We'll take it slow, I promise," Mark said. "And I'm sure Rothan will send us help."

"Or come himself," Khefer answered. "Reinforcements arrive!" He pointed at the far-distant city. Mark counted a substantial number of chariots on the way to meet them.

"Do I hear trumpets?" Sandy asked.

"The sweet sound of victory," Mark answered.

A few moments later, he had confirmation when the chariots swept up to them, under the command of Nemiah.

"What's news?" Mark yelled.

"The city is taken!"

A great cheer rose from the former slaves and the soldiers.

"When the king moved to attack the walls, the gates were thrown open and soldiers loyal to him came forth." Nemiah provided more details as the noise of the cheers quieted. "As soon as we were sure we weren't walking into a Maiskhan trap, our king and his troops marched triumphantly into the city and occupied the palace. We are to take you to him there," Nemiah said. "My orders are to accomplish the trip with no delay. The king is impatient to have the Lady of the Star Wind and her consort at his side."

"What happened to Farahna?" Mark asked.

"She wasn't found, my lord." Nemiah seemed to take it as a personal failing on his part.

"She escaped?" Mark was somehow not surprised. The one time he'd been a prisoner in front of her, he'd gotten the distinct impression of a clever, consummate survivor. He would have been more amazed if Farahna had allowed herself to be captured.

"Not good," Sandy said.

"No, not at all," Khefer agreed. "One piece of bad news mixed with the good. Let us make haste to the palace."

As many as could crowded into the chariots Nemiah had brought, leaving the rest to continue their march under the command of one of Ebnar's former officers. The procession entered the wide-open gates of the city to the sound of cheers from crowds on the walls and lining the streets. As the chariots swept along the central avenue toward the palace in the distance, people threw flowers at them, cheered for Rothan, and wept. An unbroken line of soldiers from the allied provinces formed a barrier between the street and the crowds.

"So different today than when we were marched out with Hutenen's casket, remember?" Mark said to Sandy.

Tossing her head, Sandy laughed. "This is much better."

Rothan stood on the steps of the palace, waiting for them. He was still garbed in his dusty, stained uniform, but wore the golden Crown of Khunarum on his head. Surrounding him at a respectful distance were General Intef, the other leaders, a gaggle of priests, Sapair, and others. Mark recognized most of them, but a few faces were new to him.

Guards from the allied forces were positioned at each entrance and along the walls.

"I hope Rothan plans to be cautious about accepting allegiance from anyone who worked for Farahna," Mark said to Sandy. "We're all going to have to be careful and watch ourselves in this place. Inevitably, there'll be traitors and turncoats left in the crowd, hoping to stay under the scanners."

"Yes, but Sapair and Ebnar will know most of them, which helps," she answered. "Rothan's never going to be a trusting soul again—he's made that amply clear."

"No. Anyone who hasn't ridden with him to this point will have a hard time being accepted into the inner circles of power."

"My most loyal courtiers, I welcome you to our palace, now and forever under the sway of the true gods of Nakhtiaar. Victory is ours!" Another cheer went up from the assembled nobles and soldiers as the king greeted Sandy and Mark and their companions.

Rothan led the way to the throne room. Today there were no musicians and no dogs. A crowd of officers, nobles, priests, and others prostrated themselves as the royal party walked by. Rothan showed no hesitation as he ascended the towering throne before giving permission for the assembly to rise.

The king conducted a ceremony of thanks, including blessings by various high priests but cut the assembly short, to the visible surprise of many in the room.

"General Intef, commander of my armies, has his orders concerning the search of the city for Maiskhan stragglers and other fugitives," Rothan announced. "Tomorrow we'll begin the work of installing my court and designating officials. I'll publicly recognize those in my army who distinguished themselves in the battle, and rich rewards shall be theirs. I'll take the oath of fealty from nobles, priests, scribes, and judges. Proper sacrifices will be made at the major temples. Tonight, however, I wish to consult with my inner court. All others are dismissed."

The crowd bowed, buzzing with muted conversation. People filed out of the throne room under the implacable gaze of the soldiers. In this inner sanctum, the guards were all from the Mountaintop or Mikkonite forces. Rothan descended from the throne as the soldiers closed the huge gold-leaf-encrusted doors behind the last stragglers.

"Congratulations." Mark clasped his friend's outstretched hand and was drawn into an exuberant hug. Rothan pounded him on the back.

"It wouldn't have happened without you and your Lady. The city yielded itself to me with no great effort on my part, thankfully. There was no need to fight house to house or burn large swathes of the buildings, as I'd earlier feared might be required. And the wave summoned by the Lady to crush the Maiskhan navy more than fulfilled the prophecies." He grinned at Sandy. "But the victory isn't secure while Farahna remains alive. There's no sign of her, her son, or her closest

Maiskhan advisers and guards. Come, Sapair has prepared a more private room so we can strategize. We must talk about what to do next in our hunt for my enemy."

Rothan led them through a series of corridors and antechambers, arriving eventually at a good-sized dining room where a lavish dinner awaited. There were no servants in the room, and the guards saluted and left as soon as the group entered. The doors closed behind them.

"The food?" Mark paused as he reached for a plate. It smelled delicious, and he was starving, as his rumbling stomach would attest, but he was wary, remembering what had happened to the original Hutenen in this very palace.

"Every morsel of this mouthwatering meal came from our supplies, brought from home. The food was prepared and watched over by General Intef's servants," Sapair answered. "I'm well aware of how careful we must be with the king's safety, my lord. And yours."

"Sorry, no offense meant." Selecting a roll, Mark took a bite.

"None taken," Sapair assured him. "I'm relieved you perceive the potential dangers. Merely because the city declared itself for Rothan doesn't mean all the traitors have been removed. We must remain vigilant."

"As long as I live," Rothan agreed. "And my son too will have to exercise caution when he sits the throne. There'll always be those who seek to get ahead by doing evil."

Sitting at the head of the table, the king removed the heavy golden crown, setting it beside him with an audible thunk. He sighed and rubbed his forehead. "Thing weighs on me as if I wore the very sun. My head aches."

"I can do something to help," Sandy offered. She checked with Sapair. "Have my medical supplies been brought from the camp on the other side of the river?"

Ebnar and Sapair had been having quiet words off to the side of the room, but the chief official snapped to attention as he heard Sandy's question.

"I'll have them brought to you now." Sapair issued an order to one of his administrative minions standing by, and the man left at a run.

"Please, you're my dearest friends and closest advisers. We don't stand on ceremony in private. There are no eyes to see us abandon protocol tonight." Rothan waved his hand. "Sit, eat while we figure out how to find Farahna. Sapair, Ebnar, I command you to join us at the table as well."

As he held Sandy's chair for her, Mark asked, "Can you use the mirror to show us where Farahna is? Or did you burn out the magic for now by delivering the tidal wave?"

"Good question. I can try asking for information." Sandy removed the mirror from her belt and stared into it. She left her chair and walked over to show the mirror's face to Rothan. "I think you need to see this."

The others moved to cluster around and peer over her shoulder.

"It's Farahna, all right," Khefer said.

"But where is she?" Rothan asked, his voice puzzled. "In a tunnel or a cave of some type?"

"And where she is, she's in a good mood, laughing, not worried about getting captured." Mark tried to get a closer view over Sandy's shoulder.

"Indeed, her jovial mood is a bad omen for us." Rothan drummed the fingers of one hand on the table.

"There are no such caves or tunnels in the city or at the harbor," Khefer stated with confidence. "I'd have found them and used them for my own purposes a long time ago if there were. I explored some strange and remote places while I was spying."

The images faded into the perpetually churning gray mists of the mirror.

Resuming their seats, the gathering returned to dining.

"This palace was originally built by survivors from Khunarum, right?" Mark took a serving of roast fowl, giving Sandy the most succulent portion and ladling sauce over it.

"Yes. What does the history of this place have to do with finding Farahna?" Rothan asked, pouring wine.

"Remember the palace in the Lost City? Riddled with tunnels. Why wouldn't the people from Amaraten build the same kind of thing after relocating here?" Mark explained the logic behind his theory. "Sapair, have you ever heard of such tunnels?"

"Nothing more than rumors, my lords. What ancient building is not rumored to harbor a secret passageway or two?"

"We were building them into the cursed Maiskhan temple, I can assure you," Ebnar added, spearing a piece of fruit and adding it to his plate.

Fists clenched on the table, Rothan was the picture of frustration. "She can't be allowed to flee. If she's alive, the Maiskhan will continue to use her as a claimant to my throne. She'll be their centerpiece for fomenting rebellion."

"She could be anywhere," Mark said. "The mirror never gives much hint as to the surroundings."

"No, even if I ask it again, we'll get much the same picture," Sandy agreed. "Sorry."

"We could search for weeks and not find her, Your Majesty," Ebnar ventured. "She and her companions will stay on the move if she's smart."

"He's right, there's no time for searching," Sandy thought out loud. "But what if I ask the mirror to show me specifically where she *will* be? Maybe tomorrow at sunset?"

"The mirror hasn't seen the event yet, Sandy," Mark said. "How can you ask for a future view?"

"There's a theory about time circling around on itself, like a giant snake."

"Like our old nemesis Sherabti?" he asked, rubbing his wrist.

"But if the theory is true, then the mirror has seen the future and the past," she said.

"Do you believe it?"

"It's worth a try." She gave a small laugh. "I'm beginning to think the mirror's only limits may be what I think it can and can't do."

"After today's tidal wave, I'm inclined to agree." He was still in awe of the miracle his beloved had wrought with the mirror's help. "I'm glad you're on my side."

"Let me try this for you?" Sandy checked with Rothan for his assent.

"Of course. Far be it from a king to refuse the Lady of the Star Wind, who wields such power," he said with a wide smile. "After what you did today, destroying the Maiskhan armada, Nakhtiaar owes you anything you might request, and I'll gladly grant it."

Sandy raised the mirror, the crone facing her from the handle. "I ask to see the future," she said in a conversational tone, as if talking to the goddess. "I ask to see where the evil one will walk tomorrow evening as the sun sets."

There was a flash of red light from the mirror. A life-size image projected into the center of the room. Sandy came close to dropping the mirror. "Well, seems I've learned a new trick."

"Does anyone recognize the place?" Mark remembered that brevity was the most inconvenient aspect of visualizations from the mirror.

He watched Farahna walk onto a beach in the ruddy sunset. A fat sun rode the sky inches above the horizon, its much smaller binary a dot close by. Maiskhan soldiers surrounded the deposed queen. A small boat could be seen rowing toward the beach, while a larger ship rolled in the troughs of waves offshore.

"I know where it is! I recognize it," Khefer yelled.

The vision winked out.

"Sorry." Khefer apologized as everyone turned to glare at him. "But I do know the cove," the captain assured his listeners. "I recognize the rock formations. It's to the west of the harbor."

"She'll be there at sunset tomorrow." Sandy put the mirror in its soft, padded pouch at her belt.

"And we'll be there to greet her," Rothan vowed. "We must post guards there now, tonight, in case she should emerge from hiding earlier than the mirror foretells."

Khefer left his seat and saluted. "I'll see to it at once, Exalted One. I'll go myself and take my own charioteers, men whose absolute loyalty we can trust."

Sallea left her chair to join him. "I'll send Lakht aloft to search out the place and keep watch with you as well."

By late afternoon the next day, the king and his inner court, along with a detachment of soldiers from the Mountaintop province, arrived at the beach and hid from view, joining Khefer and Sallea. The mouth of the cave was well camouflaged by brush and a large flat rock, but Mark had no trouble recognizing the location shown to Sandy by the mirror.

He was relieved they didn't have to wait long before a Maiskhan ship sailed over the horizon and prepared to drop anchor. Djed was first to see the vessel with his keen archer's eyes. He pointed it out to the rest of them. Mark checked it out through his distance viewer. "Maiskhan, all right. Damn! We have to get them out of the picture. I don't want anyone else coming to this beach party tonight. And the mirror showed us a small boat coming ashore, remember?"

"What do you propose?" Rothan asked. "As you remind me constantly, I have no navy."

"Sandy, do you think you could get the mirror to conjure a strong wind?" Mark asked. "Not a gale force, but close to it, to push them out to sea and keep them there?"

She kissed him on the lips. "We'll soon find out. I did do dust devils while we were staying at Rothan's home in the mountains. This would be similar." She picked up the mirror, lined up the younger goddess with the reflective faceplate, and made her request.

"I don't think it's working," Khefer said hesitantly as a moment or two passed and the air remained dead calm.

No sooner had he spoken than the sails of the ship puffed out with such force the vessel came close to heeling over, picking up speed as it rode the waves. The captain tried to maneuver, tacking in various directions, but the wind in the sails pushed him inexorably toward deep water. The wind adjusted to match each new trick the Maiskhan tried, and in a few moments, the vessel had sailed from view.

"Wow, I'm exhausted." Sandy sat on a handy log with a thump, rubbing her temples and nearly dropping the mirror.

"Worse than the tidal wave?" Mark came and massaged her shoulders as she leaned against him with a grateful sigh.

"Kind of, because I had to sustain the request for wind myself. The tidal wave took on a life of its own yesterday. All I did was ask for it. Then I think some force beyond my abilities gave the mirror a power surge."

"The gods," Rothan said. "It must have been the true gods, working through the mirror and you."

"Shh, I think I heard something." Khefer made a violent hand gesture. He pointed at the rock and brush concealing the mouth of the tunnel. "Movement."

"This is the moment we've been waiting for," Rothan said with immense pleasure. "Now Hutenen will be avenged. We must greet her and her Maiskhan soldiers properly."

"Hang back here, Sandy, please." Mark unsheathed his sword.

"No problem. I'm a doctor, not a fighter." She held him for a heartbeat as he brushed past her with Rothan and the others, taking positions in concealment, just shy of the beach. "Not unless I have to be."

Calm as he always was in a combat situation, Mark crouched low in the brush with the others. The flat rock shifted sideways. A Maiskhan soldier stuck his head out of the tunnel, peering around, sword and shield at the ready. The man ducked inside for a second and then walked out, followed by six more Maiskhan. An officer strolled onto the sands next, brushing his shoulders as if to remove cobwebs or dust.

"Gaddaf, their commander," Mark hissed at Rothan.

Brow furrowed, Rothan swore. "I remember him."

The officer scanned the horizon with narrowed eyes. "It appears the ship is late, Great One," he announced in a loud voice. "But it is safe for you to come out here to wait."

Farahna strolled out of the tunnel, carrying one of the fat dogs, another yapping at her heels. She seemed as calm and collected as ever. Her dress was impeccably draped, gleaming white, her jewels lavish. She had her customary makeup on. "Build a fire while we wait. And make me a place to sit. Cook something. I'm hungry." Her petulant tone carried easily to the watchers.

"At once, my queen." Gaddaf took his cloak and swirled it around her shoulders. "This will warm you."

Preening, smile self-satisfied, she leaned into his arms.

Rothan lifted his sword and stepped out of hiding. "No need to go to such effort. You'll not live long enough to suffer from the cold or satisfy your hunger, Farahna."

Eyes wide, mouth open as words failed her, Farahna sank onto the nearest boulder, one hand fisted over her heart. As the dog in her lap yapped and the other circled in the sand next to her, she looked around frantically, seeking an escape route.

The Maiskhan formed a defensive circle, the commander eyeing Rothan and the forces he'd brought. The enemy were outnumbered by the king's men, some of whom had slipped behind the Maiskhan to block any attempt at retreating into the cave.

"Don't hope for rescue or reinforcements," Rothan warned, seeing Gaddaf glance out to sea again. "The Lady of the Star Wind commands the winds as well as the waves. You underestimated her to your peril and the defeat of all your plans. She's banished your ship far out to sea. There's to be no escape tonight."

"No escape perhaps. What say you to a trade?" Gaddaf asked as calmly as if he and Rothan were discussing horses or grain.

"What do you have to bargain with, Maiskhan?" Rothan was contemptuous. "I think the counters are stacked on my side of the table."

Gaddaf grabbed Farahna by the wrist and dragged her from her seated position to hold her tightly against him, clenching his other fist on the hilt of his sword. She resisted him, kicking at his shins, cursing, but the Maiskhan ignored her. "I'll give you this bitch alive. I'm sure you want your vengeance. She's worthless to us now, having brought us to ruin. Give your word to allow my men and me free passage from this beach, and I'll hand her over. We won't resist you or protect her. Do what you wish with her, but let us go."

"Bold words for a man surrounded and outnumbered, with the ocean at his back," Rothan answered. "You can choose to die or you can choose to surrender to my mercy. No other choices."

Farahna cursed and threw the squirming lapdog in the Maiskhan's face. As he fended off the yelping pet, Farahna drew a dagger from her elaborate overskirt and slashed his throat. He fell at her feet, bleeding out, eyes wide and stark. She kicked him in the stomach, cursing.

"Enough of this—take them!" Rothan commanded. His soldiers surged forward and tackled the remaining Maiskhan. One man chose to fight and was cut down in short order. Disheartened, his comrades fell to their knees in the sand, begging for mercy as the soldiers locked them in chains.

Farahna remained standing off to the side, eyes wild, expression feral. She kept her grip on the bloody dagger.

"No one is to lay a hand on her," Rothan said as his troops looked to him for orders. "I'll not have her death on anyone's conscience. No one is to account for her death at the final evaluation of their soul."

"And what is your plan for me, upstart?" Farahna asked. The words were rushed, tension threaded through her tone. She was breathing hard. "Are you going to cut my head off with your sword? Put *me* in chains? I am queen and cannot be touched."

"You were never the rightful ruler, you bitch." Rothan pushed past his guards in his anger. "At best, you were the regent before you stole the throne from Hutenen."

Mark took three steps to be in position to shoot the woman with one of his last remaining blaster charges if she attacked Rothan or even got too close to him.

Sapair walked forward to stand at Rothan's side. He carried a golden tray with a single humble red clay cup sitting on it, the sort of mug a peasant would drink from.

"The penalty for treason against the throne is death," Rothan said, his voice somber as he passed judgment.

"I'm queen, the rightful ruler of Nakhtiaar. You're the thief, not me. You've no right to sentence me." She tossed her head in a proud, contemptuous gesture.

"Your judgment won't be in this life, but will come at the hands of the gods when you stand before them in a few moments. No peaceful afterlife for you, no rebirth, no redemption."

Mark observed that Rothan's vehement words shook her for a moment, but she raised her chin and beckoned to Sapair.

"Bring me the sour wine selected by this pretender for my pleasure."

Mark was concerned Farahna would try something against Sapair. He noticed Ebnar shifting his stance in the sand next to him, apparently in response to the same fear for his partner.

Farahna dropped the bloody knife in the sand and kicked it away. She made no threatening gestures but reached to take the crude clay vessel. Sapair stepped back a little too hastily after she had the drink in her hand, losing his balance in the sand. Although he recovered, Mark knew his dignity suffered.

She laughed. "You've healed to an amazing degree, Sapair. But you'll never forget my vengeance. It shows in your actions—you still fear me." Farahna held the humble cup with both hands, lifting it to the heavens. "I dedicate this sacrifice of my life to Mithtravar, great god of the Maiskhan, who is the only true god."

"Blasphemy, Farahna?" Rothan said. "A poor choice for your last words on this earth."

She laughed. "I became a bride of the god many years ago, as a child. My family dedicated my life to Mithtravar and to the success of our Maiskhan blood. I don't blaspheme against him. I sing his praises." Raising the potion to her reddened lips, she took the poison in a single gulp before hurling the drinking vessel against the rocks, shattering the mug into countless pieces. She clutched her throat, staggering as the swift-acting poison swirled through her body. "Your gods have no power over me, Rothan." She fell onto the sand, convulsing. "No power." Her voice was barely loud enough to be heard over the sound of the waves. "Mithtravar, answer me now in my moment of need."

Mark caught a flicker of motion behind them from the corner of his eye. He wondered if the Maiskhan boat had managed to come ashore after all. But the newcomer was no human. A man, eight feet tall, strode toward ashore in the waves. He was naked save for an intricately woven headdress of plumes knotted into his thick black hair. His eyes were yellow, the pupils slitted, giving off a faint glow. He was built like a wrestler or a weight lifter, Mark thought, all bulging muscles and sinew. He could break any of them in half without breathing hard. Twenty or thirty of the purple flowers floated in the sea foam around his ankles as he continued to pace forward through the water, perfume filling the air, overriding the salty scent of the sea itself.

"Rothan." Mark touched the king's shoulder.

The man walked onto the beach and stopped.

"Obektirr, god of the sea." Rothan named the newcomer with no hesitation.

Mark heard the soldiers behind him repeating the name with awe and shocked voices, withdrawing to the side of the beach, leaving Rothan and Mark alone. He risked a quick glance. The other men were prostrated on the sand. Sandy stood by, mirror in hand, watching the drama.

Rothan cleared his throat and bowed his head a fraction. "I greet you, Exalted One."

"And I greet you, brother." The man's voice was deep, gravelly. When he spoke, he revealed sharp, pointed teeth. "I'm here to finish undoing the evil wrought by she who lies before you. I take her to the judges and her fate."

Rothan pulled Mark toward the prostrate soldiers, away from the god.

Obektirr fastened his eerie gaze on Farahna's limp form as she drew breath intermittently in harsh gasps, far gone in her journey toward death. Walking forward, he picked her up, cradling her in his mighty arms. He walked to the water, ignoring the humans on the beach. As he strode into the waves, scattering the floating flower blossoms, a blinding flash of light strobed. When Mark's vision returned, the only thing in sight was a giant white predatory fish swimming out to sea, twin dorsal fins cutting the waves. There was no sign of Farahna. A moment later, the creature ascended the face of an incoming wave and vanished right before the water curled over and broke.

"Who, or what, was that?" Sandy asked, coming to him and putting her arms around his waist.

"Obektirr," Rothan answered. "Rise, my people, and rejoice. The Exalted One has taken Farahna away, even as he said. She'll be judged, and she won't go into the afterlife. Her twisted soul will be snuffed out like a spent candle. Our work is done, our task complete. The land of Nakhtiaar is free from the evil she nurtured."

"Gods be praised!" Djed called out, dusting the sand off his knees and chest.

A few busy weeks later, the Festival at Dendke arrived, the first at which King Rothan and his queen would preside.

The sun rose over the peak of the temple with excruciating slowness. Then, all of the sudden, the long rays reached to illuminate the king, bathing him in morning's fire. Rothan was tall, handsome, his face calm. The towering golden Crown of Khunarum was the final element in the tableau of the personification of power. Tia stood by his side, regal, composed, and beautiful. His nobles and officers were positioned off to the side in order of rank. Her ladies-in-waiting clustered behind them. Princess Sharesi held the baby, Prince Hutenen, who was quiet today, staring around at the people.

There was a cluster of white-robed priests and priestesses. The celebrants who served the ruler of the gods, Irilkon and those dedicated to Haatrin were prominently positioned.

Mark and Sandy were to the left of the royal couple, a few paces back.

The waiting throngs gasped at the spectacle. Sapair, garbed in fine robes and with golden and ruby beads woven into the braids in his hair, stepped forward and thumped his staff of office on the rock platform. The sound echoed off the surrounding cliffs.

"The gods proclaim king Rothan as one of their company. Show respect and allegiance to our rightful ruler!" His trained baritone carried to the farthest reaches of the crowd.

Slowly at first, in ones and twos here and there, people knelt. Then, in a rush, the entire assembly bowed. Sapair made his obeisance to the monarch with a grand gesture and moved aside. Rothan strode to the edge of the platform to address his people.

"Citizens of Nakhtiaar, hear my words and know we are done with false rulers and foreign gods! I, Rothan, of the House of Intef, wearer of the Crown of Khunarum, have been chosen by the ancient and true gods of our land for this task. I've been to the underworld and risen again. I defeated the armies of the enemy on our lands and in our city. My allies of the Star Wind have raised the ocean itself to swallow the Maiskhan ships at sea. As we have triumphed in war and cast out the enemy, now shall we prosper and rebuild our nation. Never again shall we bow our heads to any outside rulers or their false gods. I charge you now to rejoice with me, to thank our gods and then to carry the word to others. I charge you to repeat the news that the rightful king is come, bringing peace to our land."

Hand in hand with Sandy, Mark watched the cheering crowd. She squeezed his fingers, and he glanced at her with a smile.

As soon as this ceremony concluded, he and Sandy had fast Mikkonite horses waiting to carry them on a trip to their private mountain aerie. *We earned a vacation.* He'd have Sandy safely in the city again well before the twins were due, of course, but Mark wanted their honeymoon, and Sandy concurred enthusiastically. Rothan had married them earlier in the morning by the light of smoking torches on this very spot, using words Mark had given him from the Outlier marriage ceremony. The Nakhtiaar had no formal wedding ritual, but Mark and Sandy wanted to have the words of their homeland said, to make their vows to each other as they never could have done in Outlier itself. Having the ceremony witnessed by their friends added to the joy. Khefer had stood as best man, Sallea as maid of honor with Lakht perched on her well-padded arm, and Tia had acted as Sandy's matron of honor.

His wife—and how he enjoyed using the term—wore her wedding dress, a finely pleated white linen gown, with a rich golden and jeweled collar Rothan had given her. She was stunning to his eyes, with the slight signs of pregnancy enhancing her beauty. He wore what passed for a Nakhtiaar dress uniform, including a pair of golden wrist guards and several large, jeweled badges on his chest, signs of his rank and rewards in recognition of his valor in battle and service to the king. Those meant more to him than any of the honors and awards he'd received in the Sectors. He'd commissioned Sapair to have a ring made for Sandy, with the warrior crest of his clan incised in enamel on top. He himself wore a plain gold band on his left hand and the ring of the Star Wind on his right.

He and Sandy had given solemn promises to stay on in Nakhtiaar, acting as Rothan's advisers for as long as he sat on the throne. There were remaining challenges in store, with Farahna's son unaccounted for and the Maiskhan empire looming as a threat. All of it could wait, as far as Mark was concerned.

He and his princess had found a place and a home for themselves.

Rothan's ceremony was coming to an end, the dancers making their graceful final movements. "Just a few more moments," Mark said into Sandy's ear as he clapped for the dancers.

Her smile took his breath away. "I've waited all these years for you. I can wait five more moments."

And life was good…

***

Thank you for reading *Lady of the Star Wind*! I hope you enjoyed it. If you did, please help other readers find this book:

1. This book is lendable, so send it to a friend who you think might like it so he or she can discover me, too.

2. Help other people find this book by writing a review.

3. Sign up for my new releases e-mail http://wordpress.us7.list-manage1.com/subscribe?u=2a337b96e2ee1ee1250004b9d&id=7462393c9es0 you can find out about the next book as soon as it's available.

4. Follow me on twitter @vscottheauthor

5. Come like my Facebook page: https://www.facebook.com/pages/Veronica-Scott/177217415659637?ref=hl

ABOUT THE AUTHOR

Best Selling Science Fiction & Paranormal Romance author and "SciFi Encounters" columnist for the USA Today Happily Ever After blog, Veronica Scott grew up in a house with a library as its heart. Dad loved science fiction, Mom loved ancient history and Veronica thought there needed to be more romance in everything. When she ran out of books to read, she started writing her own stories.

Married young to her high school sweetheart then widowed, Veronica has two grown daughters, one grandson and cats Keanu and Jake.

Veronica's life has taken many twists and turns, but she always makes time to keep reading and writing. Everything is good source material for the next novel or the one after that, right? She's been through earthquakes, tornadoes and near death experiences…Always more stories to tell, new adventures to experience—Veronica's personal motto is, "Never boring."

Veronica is a three time winner of the SFR Galaxy Award and a National Excellence in Romance Fiction Award.

She's the proud recipient of a NASA Exceptional Service Medal but must hasten to add the honor was not for her romantic fiction!

Blog: http://veronicascott.wordpress.com/
Email: veronica.scott.author@gmail.com

VERONICA'S OTHER TITLES:

Wreck of the Nebula Dream

Escape from Zulaire

Mission to Mahjundar

Star Cruise: Marooned

Star Cruise: Outbreak

Priestess of the Nile

Warrior of the Nile

Dancer of the Nile

Magic of the Nile

Ghost of the Nile

Healer of the Nile